Mitakuyasin Yakima Valley
(We all are related)

Wicahpi Win
(Star Woman)

Bonnie J Hunt

Lawrence J Hunt

CAYUSE COUNTRY

A FLOOD OF EMIGRANTS CROSS THE 'BIG OPEN' THREATENING TO OVERWHELM THE CAYUSE HOMELAND

by

Bonnie Jo Hunt

and

Lawrence J. Hunt

Will you ever begin to understand the meaning of the very soil beneath your feet? From a grain of sand to a great mountain, all is sacred . . . .
Peter Blue Cloud, Mohawk

A LONE WOLF CLAN BOOK, VOL. IV

Library of Congress Catalog Number: 99-093177
International Standard Book Number: 1-928800-03-3 (Vol. IV)

A special thank you to our fine editorial staff for their detailed
and tireless efforts to make this book right. We are especially
indebted to Donna and Keith Clark (TERRIBLE TRAIL) for
their gracious help in reviewing historical facts relating to the
Meek Cutoff, the disastrous crossing of the
Oregon desert, 1845

Published by Mad Bear Press
6636 Mossman Place NE
Albuquerque, NM 87110

The authors wish to express their deepest appreciation to all who
support ARTISTS OF INDIAN AMERICA, INC. (A.I.A.) in its
work with Indian youth. All proceeds from the sale of CAYUSE
COUNTRY go to further the work of A.I.A. For information con-
cerning A.I.A. contact Mad Bear Press. Contributions to A.I.A. are
tax deductible and most gratefully received.

Cover designed by ORO ENTERPRISES w/an original painting by
Ricardo Chavez-Mendez. Visit his Online Gallery at
http://www.oroenterprizes.com

Back cover photo courtesy Norma Ashby, "Tse Tse Kum Kee"
Princess Thunder Woman, Blackfeet

Published in the United States of America by
First Impression, Inc., Albuquerque, NM

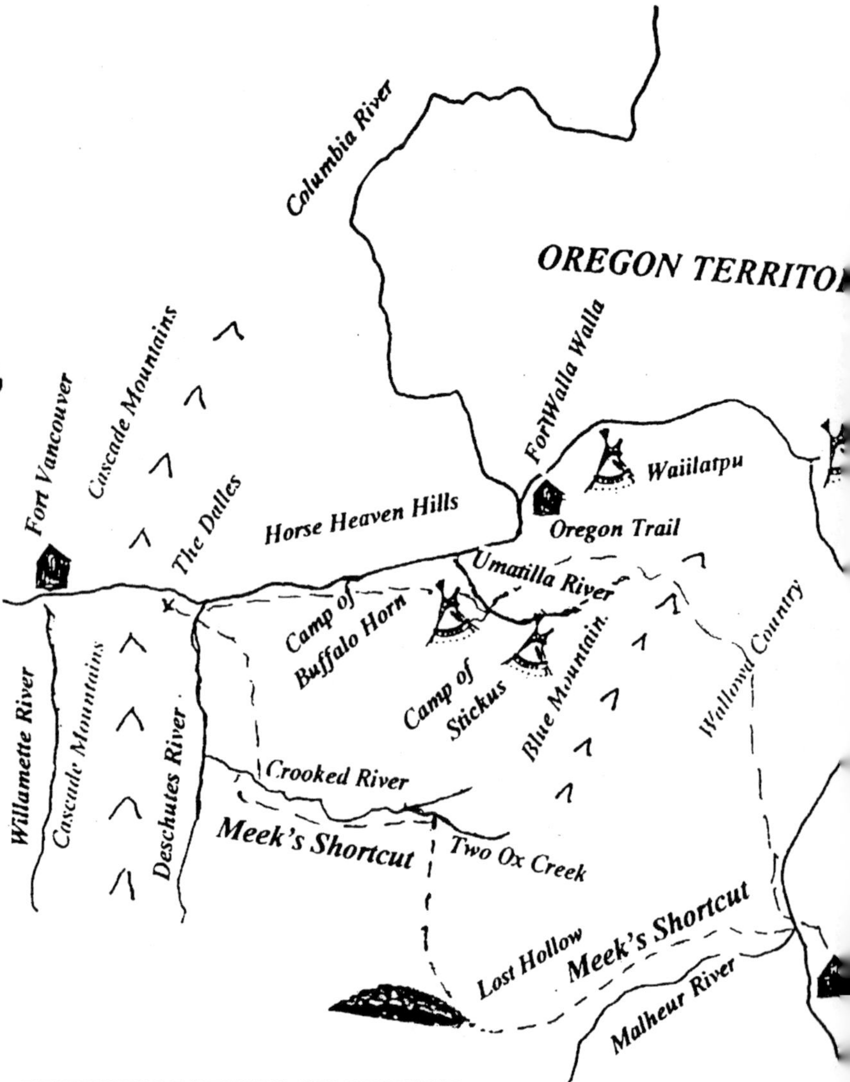
Columbia River
OREGON TERRITO
Fort Walla Walla
Waiilatpu
Cascade Mountains
Fort Vancouver
The Dalles
Horse Heaven Hills
Oregon Trail
Umatilla River
Camp of Buffalo Horn
Camp of Stickus
Blue Mountain
Wallowa Country
Willamette River
Cascade Mountains
Deschutes River
Crooked River
Meek's Shortcut
Two Ox Creek
Lost Hollow
Meek's Shortcut
Malheur River

STEPHEN MEEK'S SHORTCUT ACROSS THE OREGAN DESERT

"We go along finely until we come to Fort Boisien . . . when along came a man by the name of Meiks, who said he could take us a new route . . . Two thirds of the imigrants ran out of provisions . . . But worse than all this, sickness and death attended us the rest of the way . . . Upwards of fifty died on the new route."

Letter of Anna Maria King to her mother, brothers and sisters, April 1, 1846

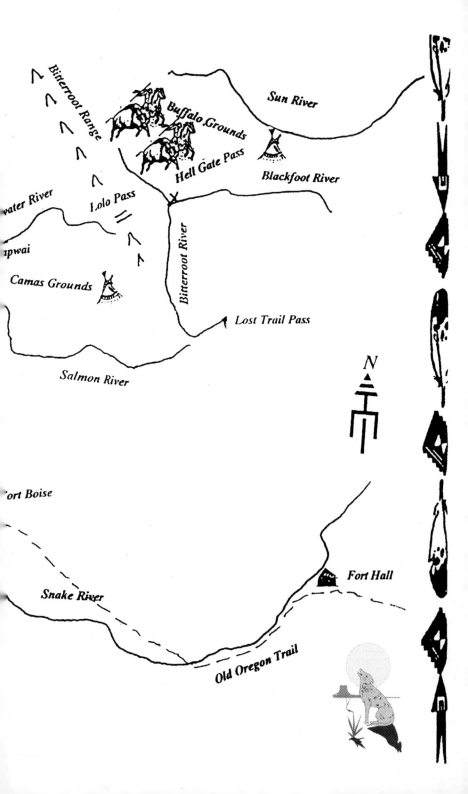

This book is dedicated to Lydia French Johnson (Cayuse/ Yakama) and Isadore Johnson (Yankton/Sisseton/ Wapeton Sioux) -- two people of integrity who devoted their lives to the preservation of our traditions, spirituality, generosity and creative skills.

CAYUSE COUNTRY

Foreword

I was not brought from a foreign country and did not come here. I was put here by the Creator.

On a hill overlooking Waiilatpu, Washington, the site the Cayuse called "Place of Rye Grass," stands a stark granite obelisk commemorating the Whitman Mission Massacre. Like a giant sword, it shouts defiance. Does it speak for the martyrs who died here or the despoilers? Perhaps the coyotes that crouch on the hill at night and howl at the ghostly moon know the answer, or perhaps the sighing of the lonely wind in the trees whispers what happened here.

The spark that ignited the disaster may have occurred October 3, 1842. On that day mission leader, Dr. Marcus Whitman, left Waiilatpu. The decision was made abruptly; only members of the mission family knew why he went. He could not have chosen a worse time to leave. The Cayuse served by the mission were in turmoil.

A mysterious sickness was killing their people. Rumors that threatened their very existence ran rampant: a representative of the Great White Father in Washington was only a few days ride away with orders to enforce a dreadful code of laws that would shatter their way of life; if the Cayuse people did not remove the missionaries from their land they would be destroyed (this warning was spread by brother Indians from the east); it was Missionary Whitman's plan to return with an army and take over the Cayuse homeland. These frightening rumors were carried from one encampment to another. At night people huddled in their lodges not knowing what the next day might bring.

Finally, instead of an army, Whitman returned with a caravan of homesteaders, the first major wave of Americans to pour down the Blue Mountain slopes into Cayuse country. The natives watched in astonishment that gradually turned to horror as the "land canoes" cut erratic trails through grassy hillsides, leaving behind deep ruts in virgin tribal soil. Following the wagons came herds of livestock that denuded pastures.

The intruders were armed with fire sticks that they fired care-lessly, killing unneeded game, allowing the meat go to waste. They startled Cayuse herds, scattering horses and ruthlessly taking animals they fancied without payment. They camped wherever they desired, need-lessly chopping down trees, leaving campsites cluttered with debris and human waste. The Cayuse were horrified. These people had no regard for Mother Earth.

Tension ballooned until it had to explode. Time seemed to stand still, waiting for that explosion to occur.

CAYUSE COUNTRY

I

One can never be sure of what a day may bring to pass.

Ohiyesa, Santee Sioux

It was the Season of Falling Leaves. Poplars, oaks, willows and locust trees had already turned yellow and gold. Cool breezes swept up the valley from the distant Great River Gorge. The air brought with it the smell of snow. Honking sounds of geese flying south drifted down from the gray sky above. Wrapped in a blanket, Tiloukaikt, leader of the Waiilatpu Cayuse, thoughtfully smoked in his tipi lodge. Worries plagued him. Had his people stored sufficient foodstuffs to carry them through the winter ahead? Did the vast horse herds, the wealth of the Cayuse, have sufficient fodder and pasture to survive? Then there was the mysterious sickness. His people always had been hardy and healthy but lately, when falling ill, they often died, sometimes overnight.

Tiloukaikt's two sons burst into the lodge. "They say the missionary man leaves. He goes to big village called Washington," Shumahici, who had taken the Christian name, Edward, excitedly reported.

"The missionary man is foolish," Tiloukaikt said, surprised by the news. "No one journeys across the Big Open in the Season of Falling Snow." He puffed on his pipe and watched the tendrils of smoke spiral up to disappear into the smoke hole overhead. This mission man was another worry. Why should he leave so abruptly? Was the man crazy in the head? Tiloukaikt scowled. He took pride in the fact he could read the character of a person like tracks in fresh snow. Medicine Man Whitman was not crazy. He did nothing without good reason. Something extremely important moved him to make the dangerous journey. What could it be? The thought made Tiloukaikt uneasy. He had the foreboding feeling that whatever the missionary had in mind did not bode well for his people. As usual, the arrogant missionaries, who lived on Cayuse land and used their pastures, forests and streams, did not bother to consult with them. Somehow, he had to find out what caused the missionary man to leave at the very worst time of year.

Tiloukaikt hurriedly knocked the coals from his pipe. "Send word to the elders. We hold council," he instructed his two sons.

\#

Marcus Whitman faced the most crucial challenge of the Waiilatpu mission's short life. Everything he had worked for and every plan he had for the future were on the verge of collapse. The mail bag's arrival, always looked forward to with great anticipation, brought bad news. The Mission Board members directed him to sell the mission or shut it down. The arbitrary decision was a slap in the face. He and his wife, Narcissa, had sweat blood and shed tears in establishing the mission. They could not bear to have all their efforts turn to dust. "We'll fight!" Marcus vowed. Although it was against Mission Board rules and against the wishes of his fellow missionaries for him to make the journey, he decided the only way to reason with the Mission Board was to travel east and plead his case.

It was a stupendous undertaking. As Tiloukaikt reasoned, no man crossed the Big Open during the Season of Falling Snow. The first snows already had fallen in the Blue and Rocky Mountains. Both ranges had to be crossed. Old timers predicted the worst winter in years -- even beasts of the forest and plains would be lucky to survive. To add to the perils, beyond Fort Hall the Sioux and Cheyenne were on the warpath. It could be fatal to venture there.

Without its leader, the mission at Waiilatpu was also at risk. The Cayuse had become embittered with the presence of the mission on their land. Several angry clashes between Cayuse and mission folk already had occurred. However, before leaving, Marcus Whitman met with Tiloukaikt and Tamsucky, the two leading troublemakers. Already forewarned, they did not express surprise. They would watch over the mission in his absence and wished him a peaceful, trouble-free journey. Marcus Whitman failed to notice the crafty glance the two Indians exchanged -- what a foolish man, leaving all of his possessions and his woman unguarded for who knew how long.

Whitman's fellow missionaries urged him to wait until someone from the Willamette Valley could be recruited to take his place. Whitman firmly brushed their protests aside and began to pack. Every hour that passed placed the mission in greater jeopardy, he insisted. He asked fellow missionary, William Gray, to recruit a man to manage the mission. Gray, who did not approve of the Oregon Territory missionary effort and had made up his mind to leave Waiilatpu, grudgingly agreed. He packed his possessions in a two-wheeled cart and left straightway for the Willamette Valley.

With one companion, A. J. Lovejoy, an Indian guide, two hardy Cayuse ponies, three mules and a small dog called Trapper, Marcus Whitman took the trail east. One mule and Trapper would not get beyond the Rockies; starvation would force the travelers to butcher them for food.

Narcissa Whitman stood at the mission gate to watch her husband leave. She was desolate. Already her heart ached with loneliness. She was not well. It was all she could do to take care of three half-blood children left in her care. What would happen to them if she should not be able to carry on? To add to her fears, she had doubts about her husband's traveling companion. The missionary couple had not known him long. In a hasty letter written to her parents, she described Mr. Lovejoy as, "... a respectable, intelligent man and lawyer, but not a Christian."

Narcissa had the strongest urge to call her husband back -- insist she go along. She would endure any hardship to visit for even a day with her parents, her four sisters and four brothers. She inwardly groaned. Did any of them realize the lonely, demanding life a missionary led? For a moment tears blinded her. She had made the decision to dedicate herself to mission work never realizing how hard it was to be separated from loved ones and the comforts of her Plattsburg, New York home.

The travelers disappeared into the haze that often appeared at this time of year. As Narcissa turned away her eyes fell upon the Cayuse village. Smoke from lodge fires spiraled skyward to add to the gloomy haze. She shivered. The village was like a fire breathing dragon, silent now, but when would it come alive? To block out the menacing sight, she hurried inside the mission house only to see her husband's comb, pencil, journal and compass that she had neglected to pack, lying on a shelf. "Oh!" she moaned. But for the sake of the three adopted half-bloods, she would have taken to her bed.

Narcissa's nerves had no rest. Two nights later stealthy sounds came up the steps leading to her bedroom. She knew at once it was an outsider. The footfalls came nearer, then stopped before her door. The latch lifted. The door cracked open. She sprang out of bed and pushed it shut. The intruder was stronger. He pushed in, a figure wrapped in a blanket that fell away revealing a nearly naked body. Narcissa screamed as loudly as she could. The intruder snatched up the blanket and fled.

The bold attack upset everyone at the mission. "I ain't stayin' here," a man with a black beard and protruding belly announced. "These Cayuses are blood thirsty killers. Who knows when they'll be back an' cut our throats whilst we sleep."

A half-blood Nez Perce, a lad of fourteen who worked around the mission, watched the panic spread. He would have attempted to calm the distraught people's fears but who would listen to a half-breed? He had seen the attacker leave the mission house. He saw him stop outside the compound fence where his companions who had stood guard waited. They trotted away gleeful at the disturbance they had created. It was an exciting game. The turmoil they wrought would encourage them to make more forays. The danger to Narcissa Whitman and her household was more acute than ever. The half-blood lad swung upon the back of his black and white pony and galloped toward Fort Walla Walla.

Archibald McKinlay, the fort factor, quickly responded. The Scottish factor had seen the tension build between the Cayuse and the missionary establishment. He was not at all surprised it surfaced while Doctor Marcus Whitman was absent. He arrived at Waiilatpu mission to find Narcissa too shaken and ill to travel. Ignoring her protestations, he padded a wagon bed, carried the sick woman downstairs and transported her and her three adopted half-blood children to Fort Walla Walla where Mrs. McKinlay fussed over Narcissa, making her as comfortable as the rough accommodations of the trading post would allow.

#

The terrible winter had finally passed but the warm weather of spring was late. In a tipi on the mission grounds, the Nez Perce mission boy thrust his toes outside the warm buffalo robes and quickly jerked them back. How he wished he could remain snuggled in the furry co-

coon. Even if the weather turned favorable, he hated to face the day and chores forced upon him. William Geiger, the missionary man who replaced Marcus Whitman, was a kind person but helpless as an old woman. He was afraid of Tiloukaikt and the Cayuse villagers. He insisted the mission half-blood boy be at his side from early morning until late at night to act as interpreter. On this day he wanted him to ride to Fort Walla Walla to post a letter and collect mail that arrived by river boat from the Willamette Valley.

The Nez Perce lad groaned. The tipi lodge was like a block of ice. He built a low fire and warmed his hands, then carefully braided two feathers in his shoulder length hair. One feather was all white, the other white tipped with a splash of red. They had been worn by his uncle who, fifteen years before, had frozen to death while searching for horses in the Season of Deep Snow. The feathers were talismans representing *Wyakin*, the sacred spirit that would accompany and safeguard him through life. In spite of the missionaries' objections that the wearing of feathers smacked of paganism, he felt naked without them.

The slender youth opened the tipi flaps, stepped into the cutting wind and started toward the blurs of yellow -- the lighted candles that shone through windows of the mission house. In the semidarkness, he stumbled and nearly fell. A frozen rut in the roadway had tripped him. He hopped on one foot and clutched the other, grimacing with pain. He stiffled a groan and hobbled on.

#

The mission boy did not suffer alone. Throughout the uplands elders said it was the harshest period of their lives. Never in memory had such strange events occurred. Beginning with the Season of Falling Snow nothing had gone right. Dire rumors of war kept the people unnerved. Flocks of ravens, normally wintering elsewhere, filled leafless trees and picked at barren fields of corn and wheat. Jack rabbits, unafraid of man, dog, coyote or wolf, raced along sagebrush trails. Grazing horses whinnied and galloped away as herders approached. More deaths than usual occurred in the villages and camps of the Cayuse.

The Hudson's Bay calendar on the wall of Fort Walla Walla's trading room announced the year of our Lord, 1843. Every sundown

Chief Trader McKinlay chalked an X on the date. Cayuse who observed the strange behavior murmured among themselves. Those who had taken lessons at the mission school in Waiilatpu understood the white man's calendar. They wondered what coming event required such careful watch on the passage of time. Superstitious elders reckoned the chief trader placed a mark of evil on that day. They spoke softly. The spirits of their ancestors were restless. They could sense something terrible was about to take place.

The elements seemed to support the elders' superstitions. It was time for spring grass to appear. Instead, the rolling plains remained bleak and bare. Blustery winds whipped through the Great River Gorge, blowing down lodges, uprooting trees and swamping river craft. Damp, heavy mists hung over streams and lowlands. Even those who remained inside were chilled to the bone. Hunters, herders, but especially fishermen, fared badly. They were forced to labor in weather that turned rawhide shirts and pantaloons into coverings as stiff and cold as sheets of ice.

When the chinook winds of spring finally came, they did so with vengeance. The snow smothered mountain peaks, slopes, passes and valleys released their moisture in torrents. River bank residents anxiously watched water levels rise to flood village streets and pour into living quarters. Debris and mud-laden gullies and creeks, strengthened by the flood waters, went on rampage, tearing out willow groves, displacing boulders and sweeping aside key landmarks that had survived through the ages.

Islands in the rivers disappeared; sand bars were sheared away as though carved by gigantic knife blades. The natives, with roots imbedded in myths and legends, quaked with fear. Why did Mother Earth do these terrible things? Was she angry with those who cut her surface with hoe and plow? Many members of the upland tribes believed this was so. They abandoned cultivated plots wished on them by the missionaries and returned to their former way of life, depending on the hunting grounds, camas fields and fishing streams for their livelihood.

No Cayuse watched the weather and the devastation it caused with greater concern than Buffalo Horn, a powerful man of medium years who took pride in everything he possessed. His vast horse herds pastured on fertile grasslands bordering the lower Umatilla. Every day he inspected his four-legged friends, his heart filled with sorrow. Livestock that had survived the winter were mere hides and bones. With their usual feeding grounds befouled, the animals were forced to forage on willow bark and pungent, distasteful sage and greasebrush. Buffalo Horn debated what to do. Should he keep the herd in place and hope the weather would turn, allowing the gazing grounds to be renewed? Or should he take his horses into the highlands where perhaps they would fare better?

Buffalo Horn never made important moves without scouting ahead. Were the trails safe? Were the rumors true that a great column of Blue Coats would soon enter Cayuse land through Blue Mountain passes? If that were so the high pasture lands would be directly in their path. He could lose the entire herd. Riders from the west brought an equally ominous rumor. An army led by the Indian Agent White was marching up river. He was coming to enforce a dreaded code of laws. If the horses remained in home pasture they would be in this army's path. What to do? What to do? Buffalo Horn slapped his quirt against the leg of his buckskin leggings and shouted for Eldest Son.

"Ride to Redcoat fort," he instructed. "Listen to people speak. Do Blue Coats come from east? Does the man called White move up river? We must know these things. They will tell us to stay or go. If we act unwisely our horse herds will fade away like winter snow."

Cloud Bird, named for the hawk that circles high in the sky, reluctantly mounted up. He hated the journey to the Redcoat fort. It was a half-day's ride through sagebrush, rocky outcroppings and little else. He faced a chilling wind that blew through the gorge that channeled the Great River on its course to the sea. Worst of all, Cloud Bird feared the news would not satisfy his father who would ask who he saw, what they said and how they said their words. Every detail he would have to know.

The ride was just as grueling as Cloud Bird feared. He wearily dismounted at the fort gates. Nevertheless, he took time to water his horse and tether it near a patch of grass. He had no idea how long it would take to learn news his father could use. With the air of a person of importance learned from observing his father, he folded his arms across his chest, held his head high and strode into the trading room. He had nothing to trade so leaned against the wall to watch and listen. There was little business and few words to hear until Chief Trader McKinlay chalked off another day on the white man's calendar. A crowd gathered to observe the ritual, speculating on what it foretold.

Near dusk Cloud Bird departed to follow the trail on the south bank of the Great River. He had learned little news of value. Besides speculation on why Trader McKinlay kept such close track of time, talk at the fort centered on the absence of Missionary Whitman. The Boston medicine man had lived among the Cayuse for six snows; then, without warning, he deserted them. Did he go to bring back an army of Blue Coats as rumored?

"Very bad things are coming. Messenger bring talking paper. Missionary man Geiger much troubled. Be watchful," a villager from Waiilatpu had warned.

Cloud Bird grimaced. Fear was the enemy. The Cayuse had dealt with unseasonable weather and the lack of pasture before. People would shiver and freeze and horses would turn lean but both people and horses would survive. Hard times followed by good were Mother Earth's way of keeping everything in balance. Yet a cloud of uneasiness hung over the land. The Cayuse were not the same. The teachings of the Boston missionaries had turned the tribe into a collection of strangers. Even elders quarreled and fought among themselves. Some, like Stickus and Five Crows of the Umatilla Cayuse, believed in the hairy faces' Christ. They said the missionaries' teachings were good. They taught the proper way to live. Tiloukaikt, whose people lived in Waiilatpu near Whitman's mission, opposed the religion that condemned sinners to everlasting fire. He said missionaries were evil, their intention was to blind Cayuse people with words from the Great Spirit Book and take all they possessed.

"Aaah!" Cloud Bird muttered. Life was so confusing. Every path one chose led to trouble. As if to support the dour prediction, his horse, weary from the day's long ride, came up lame. Cloud Bird dismounted. He lifted the injured hoof and groaned. There was still a long way to go; daylight was nearly gone. He glanced down river toward the setting sun resting like an orange ball of fire on the water. Slowly it slid from sight as if swallowed by the jaws of an endless snake, leaving a chilly gloom of twilight in its wake.

II

Rise up! Look sharp! Go see to the horses,
maybe the wolves have killed one.

Morning Song, Nez Perce

The ride to and from Fort Walla Walla seemed to take forever. The biting cold wind cut through the mission boy's buckskins as if his skin was bare. He delivered the mail that had arrived that morning by river boat and went to put away his black and white pony. Before he removed the saddle, William Geiger, the temporary mission manager, ran from the mission house. "You have to return to Fort Walla Walla," he shouted. "I must get a letter off post haste."

Instead of one letter, Geiger wrote two. One he wanted Archibald McKinlay, the fort factor, to send down river by courier. The other he asked his half-blood helper to hand deliver to Stickus, the leader of the Cayuse on the upper Umatilla.

"These are important -- the one to Stickus crucial," Geiger said. "The fate of the mission may depend on its safe arrival." Knowing Stickus did not read or speak English well, Geiger explained the letter's contents in detail so the boy could translate the message.

Again, the mission boy entered the gates of Fort Walla Walla. He handed the letter to be sent down river by courier to Factor McKinlay who stuffed it in the mail pouch and shook his head. "Poor laddie. Old Woman Geiger keeps you on the run it seems. You look as tuckered as a broken boot string. Come in and have a cuppa."

The mission boy hesitated. He was on an errand of urgency and should not dally. McKinlay noticed his reluctance. "Look, son, Rome wasn't built in a day and I expect it took Nero a couple of days to burn it down. A sip of tea is not going to change history of the world one way or the other, certainly not here in Cayuse country."

The Nez Perce followed the redheaded Scots into the back room. He didn't like the strong tea he served but he was cold and tired. Any respite was welcome. He often did not understand the

Hudson's Bay man but enjoyed listening to his brusque speech. The factor clipped off every word as though glad to get rid of it, much like a chipmunk eating seeds and spitting husks. McKinlay's back room, where he entertained visitors, also fascinated the Nez Perce lad. Almost every inch of the walls and floor were covered with objects of interest. From ceiling rafters hung skins of coyotes, deer, elk, bear, buffalo and the hide, head and horns of a shaggy mountain goat. Along the walls protruded antlers of elk, deer, moose and the spikes of antelope. Draped from them were rawhide lines, coils of rope, bridles, saddles, rifles and an assortment of rattlesnake skins with rattles attached. At the base of the walls lay bundles of furs, bags of meal, drums of molasses, stacks of pots, pans and buckets, crates of small trade goods and many items the mission boy could not identify. In the only open area sat a flimsy wooden table and four rickety chairs that were also covered with a variety of articles. The thick air smelled of decay, must and rodents. A potbellied stove gave off little puffs of smoke, giving the room's interior a gloomy cast. The stifling closeness and disorder in which the hairy faces chose to live, baffled the Nez Perce youth. They cluttered their abodes with everything imaginable whether it was of any use or not. How different from the way he lived in his tipi. His possessions were sparse; everything had its place. The lodge was bright with sunlight and filled with fresh clear air. When he moved he could do so at once. After a day no one could tell he had been there.

McKinlay unloaded a chair, cleared a space free of clutter on the table top and motioned for his guest to sit. He rinsed a couple of tin cups, filled them from a pot on the stove and handed one to the mission boy, the contents as heavy and dark as molasses. The boy took a tentative sip and nibbled on a hard, tasteless chip the fort factor called biscuit.

"What is your man, Geiger, up to anyhow?" McKinlay asked, settling himself in a chair. "Tiloukaikt have him fussed?"

"A man named White is on the way up river. Mr. Geiger wants to make him welcome." The Nez Perce lad fell silent. He was chattering like a flock of crows. Geiger would disapprove. He distrusted anyone connected with Hudson's Bay.

"Hmm!" McKinlay grunted. "So there is a fox in the henhouse. "No wonder the natives are restless. That White fellow's as cunning as

Trickster Coyote. He'll force his laws on the Cayuse while Missionary Whitman is gone. Ah! The pompous ass -- thinks he's Moses carrying the tablets of stone." He cocked a questioning eye.

The Nez Perce youth did not know what McKinlay meant by tablets of stone and did not want to reveal his ignorance. He set the mug down, hoping the factor would not notice he barely had tasted the contents. "I must go to upper Umatilla."

"Ah, yes, duty calls. God's speed!" McKinlay followed the quiet mission lad outside to watch him mount and ride through the fort gates. He had a liking for this solemn youth who guarded the interests of the mission so faithfully. He was an Indian person one could depend upon. How pleasant it would be if they were all like him.

#

Cloud Bird tethered his lame horse in a clump of trees. Uneasily, he looked around. Tribal storytellers said spirits of three Cayuse maidens haunted this section of the river. In ancient times when animals ruled the land, Trickster Coyote tormented three young women who came here to fish. He raided and destroyed their fish traps but the maidens were not intimidated. They rebuilt the traps and guarded them so diligently Coyote fell in love with the fisherwomen and married all three. For a while they lived happily together but Coyote became jealous. In a fit of anger he turned two wives into stone pillars. The third wife he made into a cave. Then he turned himself into a boulder so he could stay and guard all three.

Above Cloud Bird towered the two stone pillars. The sinking sun splashed a patch of pinkish orange on their tips. Gradually the color faded into a foreboding gray. Behind the pillars the largest coyote he ever had seen appeared. Raising its muzzle skyward, it uttered a mournful howl. The sound reverberated as though an answering howl came from the opposite canyon wall. Cloud Bird shivered. How he wished his horse were whole. He would gallop away as fast as it could go.

Muffled hoofbeats drifted up the trail. The coyote vanished. Cloud Bird hid behind the trees, cocking his Hudson's Bay musket. A horseman came into view riding a black and white pony and leading a black pack mare. Cloud Bird watched the rider approach with envy. Either of these horses could easily take him on home. "Oh-hah!" It was the half-breed mission boy. What brought him here? He was seldom seen away from the mission compound. Cloud Bird stepped out from the trees and held up a hand. The mission youth pulled up. "You have trouble?" he politely asked.

"Horse lame." Cloud Bird studied the young rider who had the demeanor and carriage of someone much older. "Why do you come on Buffalo Horn land?" he tersely asked. "Mission people not welcome." Cloud Bird was annoyed with himself. Why did he make talk with this mission boy? All he had to do was unhorse him, take his mount and be on his way home. His father would approve. Buffalo Horn disliked missionaries and hated what they were doing to Cayuse country. These hairy faced ones put up lodges of brick and wood on the best land. They fenced and cultivated good pasture grounds. Look at the mission boy's horses, sleek and frisky. They were kept that way on fodder and grain raised on Cayuse soil. Look at his own lame animal, thin and gaunt; every bone standing out like the leafless limbs of a dead tree. It was only right that he take the mission boy's horses. He had to be up to mischief. Outsiders knew better than to pass through Buffalo Horn land at night.

Unaware of Cloud Bird's thoughts, the young Nez Perce dismounted. In the mission school he had been taught to help travelers in distress, even though they be unfriendly. He quickly took in the lame horse and the absence of camping equipment. "Your horse let you down and you are not provisioned to spend the night?"

Cloud Bird grunted, surprised by the youth's concern.

The Nez Perce youth glanced at the pillars on the escarpment. This was not a campsite he would have chosen. The superstitious believed the fisherwomen's spirits guarded the bend in the river. Travelers told of seeing ghostly figures on the river bank busily repairing fish traps. Others reported sighting a white coyote as large as a wolf bounding through the hillside rocks and brush, snapping and snarling at the ghostly fish trap builders, trying to keep them from completing their work.

"I will make camp with you," the mission youth finally said. "I have dried meat and meal, plenty for both of us."

Cloud Bird grunted an unintelligible answer and busied himself with the lame horse. Out of the corner of his eye he studied the mission lad. He was half afraid of him. The boy appeared innocent but had a horrendous history. He even made the missionary woman Whitman uneasy. She did not adopt him as she had her three other half-bloods. His name was Michael Two Feathers. His father was a mountain man, his mother Nez Perce. While Two Feathers was still a child his mother took up with a passing stranger, a former Hudson's Bay trapper. The man was a cold-blooded killer. The mission boy's mother was not much better. It was said she persuaded the stranger to kill her mountain man mate. After her mate was dead the two of them lived together. Then the man she had taken up with also met a violent death. Rumor had it the mission boy was involved and was forced to leave home. For two years he had taken refuge at Whitman's mission, working as a member of the mission staff.

Cloud Bird scowled. The mission youth made camp as placidly as an old woman. Did he not know this place harbored spirits? Was he unaware of their presence? And where was he going? Besides a buffalo robe and two blankets to shut out the chilling river wind, he had a sack of meal, a pouch of pemmican and dried strips of the missionary's spotted buffalo called cattle. In this starved land, where in the depth of the past winter wolves were reduced to eating each other, the bountiful supply of eatables the mission boy possessed was beyond belief.

Michael Two Feathers divided the food into equal portions and politely handed Cloud Bird his share. Cloud Bird pushed it away. His mouth watered but in the lodges of Tiloukaikt's village it was rumored poisoning had been done. Medicine Man Whitman, who tended Tiloukaikt's people, gave the villagers a medicine that brought death while Bostons with the same sickness and given the same medicine lived. Was mission food like the mission medicine, good for hairy faces but deadly for the Cayuse? Cloud Bird's hunger pains were more powerful than the threat of death. He reached for the food, wolfing it down. No mission boy would dare poison a son of Buffalo Horn.

Michael sensed his companion's distrust. He knew little about him but much about his father, an outspoken foe of the mission. When the missionaries first appeared Buffalo Horn warned his tribesmen the Bostons' presence augured no good. The hairy faces spoke words as sweet as honey but in the end they would cause ill fortune to befall the tribe.

Buffalo Horn's opposition was a vital reason the mission had not done well. The Cayuse people respected Buffalo Horn. He was rich in horses. His herds dotted the pasture lands of the lower Umatilla. The animals he raised were magnificent specimens, many standing more than fifteen hands high. Tribes from all over the Northwest came to bargain for Buffalo Horn's breeding mares and stallions. So highly were they regarded, one stallion often brought thirty or forty ordinary horses in trade.

Even the way Buffalo Horn had earned his name gave him fame far beyond the boundaries of the Cayuse homeland. While on a buffalo hunt he downed a cow and plunged a spear into a bull. The wounded animal turned on him, goring the youthful hunter's mount. Unhorsed, the young hunter seized the bull by the horns and swung up on the animal's back. Unable to shake his tormentor, the enraged bull blindly charged into a rock embankment, knocking animal and hunter senseless. When the hunting party found the youth his hand clutched a broken buffalo horn.

Michael pulled a blanket around himself and closed his eyes. It had been a mistake to stop. He should have traveled through the night and completed his mission. Barely did he fall asleep before Cloud Bird shook him awake. The fire lay smoldering, partially doused by what remained of camp water. The light of a half moon cast eerie shadows on the rocky cliffs. Then Michael heard it -- the sound of galloping hoofbeats. A rider was fast approaching from the west. Cloud Bird crouched behind a boulder, his flintlock cocked and aimed at the bend in the trail where the horseman would first appear. He curtly motioned for Michael to take cover. It was probably only a frightened late Fort Walla Walla visitor in a hurry to put the spirits of this ghostly place behind him, Michael thought, but did as Cloud Bird ordered.

The horseman thundered up and would have raced past but Cloud Bird jumped from behind the boulder to hail him. "Ho! Ho"! he shouted. The rider pulled to a stop, then cantered up and slid off the sweaty mount to clasp Cloud Bird by the shoulders.

"Brother! This is not a good place to spend the night." Red Calf stopped speaking to stare at Michael as he stepped out of the shadows.

"Two Feathers," Cloud Bird explained.

"Mission Boy! Why camp with him?"

Michael went back to the warmth of his blanket. He was accustomed to such slights. People did not know how to deal with him. He was half Boston and half Nez Perce. The Bostons considered him Indian. The Cayuse thought him mongrel. He made them uneasy. His startling blue eyes beneath dark eyebrows and shock of black hair aroused expressions like that of his Grandfather Lone Wolf when he discovered his prized mare had given birth to a three-legged colt.

Michael closed his eyes but could not shut out the sound of the river, the wind, the coyotes or the excited talk of Buffalo Horn's two sons, Cloud Bird and Red Calf.

"Many hairy faces come from down river," Red Calf reported. "Leader called White bring troublesome laws . . . ."

Michael was surprised. Red Calf's report was true, the same as received by Geiger at the mission. Elijah White, the man appointed Indian Agent by the US government, was coming to Waiilatpu with a party, but not in the numbers Red Calf predicted. Perhaps no more than two canoes of men would travel up river as far as The Dalles. From there they would transfer to horses. If all went according to plan, Geiger had explained, White and his law enforcers would arrive within a week. This was the message Geiger sent to Stickus with an invitation to meet with the Indian agent at the Waiilatpu mission. Geiger reasoned that Tiloukaikt and his people would be less likely to make trouble if Stickus and his peaceful Cayuse were close at hand.

Michael attempted to sleep but the brothers' voices could not be ignored. "The Season of Turning Leaves will bring our people more danger," Red Calf said. "Missionary Whitman soon leads many hairy faces in land canoes into Cayuse country."

"Land canoes! It is not possible! Mountains will stop them."

"Missionary man has special magic. No one travels over mountains in Season of Deep Snow. Shoshoni man say Missionary Whitman pay no attention -- ride through snowy mountains on mule."

"Land canoes are different -- cannot cross mountains."

"Missionary man will do so. Nothing stops him." Red Calf insisted. "Buffalo Horn is much worried. Land canoes carry women, children -- many things. When hairy faces see places they desire, they stop to build stone and wood lodges. They feed their horses and spotted buffalo they call cattle in fields with best pasture. They do not leave. They stay and more follow. They build more lodges, bring more horses and cattle to graze on Cayuse pasture. Buffalo Horn says we must stop them or soon hairy faces with their land canoes will pour down mountain passes like floods after spring winds turn winter snow to water."

Michael listened, amazed to hear Buffalo Horn's foreboding predictions. How many other Cayuse believed as he did, that their homeland would soon be overrun by caravans of wagons from the east? When Michael set out with the message for Stickus he thought it foolish, the mission manager was acting like a frightened old woman. After listening to Red Calf it seemed a very wise move. Stickus had accepted the Christian religion and was a supporter of the mission. His presence was necessary if unbelievers like Tiloukaikt and Buffalo Horn decided to create confusion among the people.

Michael's troubled thoughts kept him awake until the morning star appeared, then he slept the sleep of the dead. When he awakened the sun was high. The Buffalo Horn brothers were gone, so were their horses. Michael jumped to his feet and ran to where he had tethered his pony and pack mare. They were not there. He searched the area to see if they had strayed. There was not a sign of them anywhere. He understood clearly what had occurred. Cloud Bird and his brother could not resist the temptation. They had stolen the sleek, well fed horses. His four-legged friend he affectionately called Magpie was in the hands of Buffalo Horn, the man who hated anything connected with Whitman and his mission.

Heartsick, Michael rolled up the sleeping robe and one blanket, hiding them in a thicket of brush. How could he have been so stupid? He had slept through the morning hours like a hibernating bear. The loss of his beloved black and white pony was more than he could endure. Nearly blinded by tears, he put one rolled blanket under his arm and started on the long, painful journey to the upper Umatilla.

III

"Sir, if you knew how sweet freedom was, you would defend it with axes!" That is what the Indian says to us.
Wendell Phillips

"Hiya!" The curt sound cut through the darkness. A night bird flew from a patch of locust trees, its fluttering wings creaked as it swept close overhead.

"Who goes?" The voice was sharp. "Stranger, make yourself known."

Michael Two Feathers stopped dead still. Startled guards were known to be quick on the trigger. He was almost too weary to answer. The trail had been much worse than he remembered. He had followed a cul de sac that ended in a sheer cliff and had to retrace his steps. He ran into a swamp that took an hour or more to circumvent. Late in the day his moccasins had worn through. Frequently, he stopped to stuff sagebrush bark into them in futile attempts to plug the holes. Then darkness fell. The going became harder still. More than once he stumbled and fell, cutting his face and hands. Every muscle ached. He felt as though he had been run through the grinding stones of the mission gristmill.

The nervous guard walked steadily forward, the long barrel of the trade musket gleaming in the dim moonlight. The upper Umatilla Cayuse had also heard rumors of invaders penetrating their homeland. Strangers were regarded with suspicion. The guard, a youth not much older than Michael, studied the stranger's disheveled appearance. "He's only a boy. What is he doing stumbling through the brush at this hour of night?" he thought to himself. But boys could be on errands of mischief. "Why do you come in black of night?" he demanded. "Why are you not home in your lodge?"

"How I wish I were," Michael thought. But he could not rest until he completed his errand. "It is important I see your chief, Stickus. Missionary man Geiger sends message."

Once satisfied Michael was not an enemy, the guard ushered him into an empty brush hut. "Wait here," the guard ordered. The place smelled of dry sage and rodents. Michael was too tired to care. To sit down and be off his tortured feet was a relief but he had to deliver Geiger's letter.

"Take me to Stickus," Michael insisted.

The man with the rifle uttered a cluck of impatience. "No one wants news in the darkness of night. Whatever message you bring can wait until dawn."

Michael was too tired to argue. He pulled off what remained of his moccasins. He should do something about all the cuts and bruises but it was too much trouble. He unrolled his one blanket. The guard did not leave but shifted from one foot to another. Michael knew he was dying to ask what message he carried.

"What news is it you bring?" the guard finally asked.

Michael held out the white envelope that gave off a ghostly sheen in the dark.

The guard uttered a sound of impatience. "Black marks on talking paper! No one in the camp of Stickus understands that."

"Yes, I know," Michael replied. It had been wise of Geiger to explain the message he was sent to deliver. Michael laid down and rolled up in the dusty blanket. He was too exhausted to sleep. He groaned. "Why did I stop and make camp with the sons of Buffalo Horn?" he muttered to himself.

The first rays of dawn had yet to penetrate the brush hut when Stickus, the leader of the upper Umatilla Cayuse, accompanied by the guard, appeared. A half-dressed, sleepy-eyed boy carried a torch to light their way. Michael, still sleepless, held out Geiger's letter. Stickus, a tall shadowy figure, glanced at the letter and gave a cluck of dismay.

"Does mission man try to make me look foolish? He knows I do not know the mysteries of talking paper. Come to my lodge. Tell me in words from your tongue what message say."

Michael struggled to get up, then sat back unable to stifle a moan. His bruised feet were bundles of pain. Under the torchlight the blackened and swollen flesh had the look of dead game left too long exposed to the sun. Stickus uttered a sympathetic cluck. "Fetch the medicine woman," he ordered the guard.

For more than an hour the old woman bathed Michael's feet, picking slivers, thorns and barbs of various burrs from the flesh. She covered the cuts with salve and then wrapped a pungent smelling poultice around each foot. Stickus stood by, his straight figure motionless. Occasionally he uttered soothing sounds like a protective sitting hen watching over a wounded chick. He liked this young Nez Perce. He was polite, quiet and possessed good common sense, except why did he walk across the rocky, brush-filled terrain in moccasined feet to deliver a message for that foolish man who sat in the place of Missionary Whitman?

"Next time travel by horse," he instructed.

"I began the journey on my pony but while I slept Buffalo Horn's two sons stole it and a pack mare."

Stickus grunted. "Very bad."

Michael understood what he meant. Once an animal entered Buffalo Horn's herd it did not leave unless traded, sold or stolen. If he were to get his animals back he would have to steal them.

Only after Michael's feet were properly cared for would Stickus listen to the words of the talking paper. While Michael read Geiger's call for help Stickus sat motionless. He did not like what he heard. The time had come when hard decisions had to be made. Taking his people to Waiilatpu was a serious matter. They had not recovered from the Season of Deep Snow. Many were ill and others too feeble to travel. The horses were thin and weak. Neither people nor animals were in condition to make a journey. Besides, he had no liking for the man called Elijah White. He was a pompous creature filled with self-importance. To ask his people to show support for him was distasteful. He wished his friend Missionary Whitman would return. Without him the Waiilatpu mission was nothing.

The long silence made Michael uneasy. He glanced at the weathered face of the Cayuse leader. Did he understand the message? He started to speak but Stickus held up a hand to silence him.

He thanked Michael for delivering the message, ordered food to be brought and left the brush covered shelter. He needed time to think. He wanted to do what was right but there was a time to act and a time to do nothing. He knew how much the missionary establishment needed his help. There were not many in the tribe who the missionaries could count on as friends. Stickus, himself, did not know how many of his own followers believed the missionaries' teachings. It was hard to visualize the Christ God dying on a cross. The missionaries said one had to have something called faith to make this belief real.

His people believed in spirits and legends but these beliefs had been handed down from generation to generation. The people accepted them because they knew the hearts of the people who spoke of these things were good and true. His people did not know what lay in the hearts of the hairy faced missionaries. They had a way of speaking one thing and doing another. They said you must be kind to everyone and not take the name of God in vain but then went out and cursed at their dogs, beat their oxen and shouted at their children for no reason at all. They said it was against God's law to steal even a farthing but they thought nothing of fencing and plowing good Cayuse land, turning their horses and spotted buffalo called cattle on Cayuse pasture or chopping down trees that had given Cayuse people protective shade for a lifetime.

The guard who had encountered Michael during the night, gave Stickus an anxious look as the Cayuse leader, frowning with concern, left the brush shelter. He could tell the news the youth brought was not good. The guard went to his lodge and sat beside the fire. He stared into the flames and scowled. "What is the matter? Are you ill?" his concerned mate asked. "Soon all of us will be ill," he snapped. "The mission boy brings bad news." His mate placed food before him and stood waiting patiently for her mate to say more.

"Missionary people, false people. They say they give us a new, more beautiful way of life. All they give us is trouble." He tossed the food basket aside. Would this woman of his never learn to prepare a proper meal?

As in most villages, news of a stranger's presence quickly

passed from lodge to lodge. The new arrival was soon identified as the Nez Perce boy who worked for Medicine Man Whitman. His arrival was seen as an ill omen. No messenger brought good news late at night. Certainly not one who struggled on foot through the brushy, rocky, rattlesnake infested terrain that separated the Umatilla Valley from the mission grounds at Waiilatpu.

In his own tipi lodge Stickus was just as troubled as his followers. He had to make a choice; he had to stand by the missionary establishment or turn his back. It placed him in an agonizing situation. He considered himself a good Christian. Christians went to the aid of those in need. He vividly remembered Missionary Whitman quoting the words of the god, Jesus. "The good shepherd giveth his life for the sheep." Stickus knew little of sheep or shepherds but he understood what these words meant. Sheep were like Cayuse horses, shepherds like Cayuse herders. Many a Cayuse herder would give his life to keep his horses from harm.

The thought of horses brought to mind another worry. Stickus left the lodge and strode toward the pasture where his colorful Cayuse ponies grazed. Usually, the sight of horses dotting the rolling plains pleased Stickus and cleared his mind. On this day the ploy failed. His eyes betrayed him. In the distance Buffalo Horn's vast herd reminded Stickus of the old warrior's opposition to the Waiilatpu mission. To show support for Indian Agent Elijah White would go against the wishes of this powerful neighbor. If Buffalo Horn had his way all hairy faced people would be gone, swept from the face of Mother Earth.

Stickus caught and mounted a horse to ride north. It was said Buffalo Horn intended to take his prize animals to early summer pasture. Perhaps he already had gone. If that were true it would make the decision whether or not to travel to Waiilatpu easier. He would not have to deal with Buffalo Horn's displeasure. From a hilltop Stickus surveyed Buffalo Horn's pasture lands. They spread over miles of river bottom land and extended into rolling hills covered with sage. Here and there groups of horses meandered in the high brush searching for any edible tidbit that would help ease the hunger pangs that racked their bodies. The large number of animals made it clear Buffalo Horn had not yet made his move to new pastures.

Two horses, more sleek than the rest, picked away at bark in a stand of willow trees, one a black and white splotched pony, the other a plain black. Stickus frowned. These were the mission boy's ponies. Here was something else that would raise Buffalo Horn's ire. The Nez Perce youth would not rest until he retrieved his horses, an impossible task. Buffalo Horn would not consider giving them up, especially not to a member of the detested Waiilatpu mission. The wealthy horseman was certain to claim he acquired them by trade or they strayed on his land and therefore were his. Who was to stand up to him and say he lied?

Stickus left the hilltop to inspect his own herd. What animals could he give Michael Two Feathers that would satisfy him? He feared there were none. Stickus muttered to himself. It was not a good day. One should never make decisions when the head was muddled with troublesome things.

Stickus put away his horse and gave it an affectionate slap. He sat in his lodge and filled his pipe. He motioned to his woman, Kio-noo, to sit beside him. He wanted to talk. "It is the wish of missionary man Geiger we travel to Waiilatpu. The man called White comes with his laws."

Kio-noo studied her mate's careworn face. Her heart went out to him. He tried so hard to do what was right. Only when he was terribly troubled did he ask for her advice. She thought over the matter carefully. There was more to it than just making the journey. When they arrived in Waiilatpu they would be expected to meet with Indian Agent White. He would want them to accept his laws. To make these laws work among their neighbors, the Nez Perce, the Indian agent insisted one man be made chief of the tribe. This chief was then expected to enforce the laws. There was no reason to believe Indian Agent White would treat the Cayuse differently. Who would be chosen as chief of all Cayuse? Buffalo Horn? Tiloukaikt? Five Crows? Stickus? There was not a man among them who would please every band in the tribe.

"These laws will cause much trouble," she finally said. "We

have always followed the ways of our fathers. Why should we now need laws to tell us how to live?"

Stickus nodded. He marveled at the way Kio-noo's mind worked. She always seemed to understand the difficulties he faced. She could foresee the turmoil White's code of laws could cause. Few people even understood what the Indian agent meant by code of laws. Five Crows, who still attended the mission school in Nez Perce country, had seen these laws on talking paper. He even brought some of the papers back to his village on the Umatilla. What good did that do? Hardly anyone understood the mysteries of talking paper. The few who could did not like the things it said.

Stickus put away his pipe and left the tipi lodge. He walked to the brush hut where Michael rested. Stickus was no further in finding an answer to Missionary Geiger's request than when he first received the message. For courtesy sake he could not keep the mission lad waiting forever but he could insist he remain until his feet were healed.

Michael had finally drifted off into fitful sleep. The soft sound of Stickus' footsteps jerked him awake. He struggled to lift himself upright. The Cayuse leader pushed him back. "Stay off your poor feet," he ordered, not unkindly.

"I must return. The missionary man will think I have had trouble or ran away. If you will loan me a horse . . ."

Stickus put up a hand to silence Michael. "I wish to answer Missionary Geiger but words do not come easily. I must think of my people. I cannot order them to go here or go there because a missionary wishes it. Men are hunting elk in the Blue Mountains. Others are sick and too weak to travel. Many fear this man White sets a trap. He will lure us into it like a hare into a snare." Stickus fell silent.

Michael understood. He knew all about the fear of being trapped. The very blood that coursed his veins had him trapped. He was caught between the white world and the Indian world; neither one accepted him. His lighter skin, blue eyes and desire to learn the ways of his Boston father, even caused his mother to turn against him. She did everything she could to change him; took him out of the mission school; sent him on a vision quest; taught him the old traditions and myths when animals ruled Mother Earth; and forced him to do all the things her forefathers had done when they were youths.

"Missionary Geiger is a much worried man," Michael finally said. "When I do not return . . ." The expressionless look on the Cayuse leader's face silenced Michael. Stickus had spoken. One did not question what he said. Michael leaned back on the bulrush padded pallet. "I shall wait," he said simply, hiding his disappointment. He had things to do -- rescue Magpie and the black mare from Buffalo Horn, then hurry back to the mission. His heart told him his Boston brother, Joe, would be among the men who would arrive with Indian Agent Elijah White. Joe promised on his return they would take the trail east to visit New England country where their father had been reared and where their grandparents lived. The dream of accompanying his brother on this wondrous journey was the one thing that had kept his spirits up during the long distressful winter.

IV

Both fear and faith sail into the harbor of your mind,
but only faith should be allowed to anchor.

Anonymous

Joe Jennings, along with his two trapping partners, rode up the south bank of the lower Columbia River. It was a clear but crisp morning. In the lowlands heavy dew hung on the evergreens, falling like rain when the riders brushed against them. High runoff from the heavy mountain snows made the river turgid. Below the thundering rapids at the Cascades of the Columbia, the force of the current churned the white-crested water into foam. Around and around in a circle the waves swept, sending up clouds of spray. Above the roar of the river came the piercing cry of sea gulls. The white/gray birds hung in the air above the swirling water like a flotilla of kites. In the backwaters brown heads of bulrushes made a weird dance as the current swirled out of the whirlpools to attack their spindly ranks.

The riders paid no attention to these acts of Mother Nature. They rode silently, heads bowed against the droplets of dew and the cool chill of the wind. All three men were in a bitter mood. They'd had their fill of trapping but what else could they do? Since coming west they had done nothing but trap for beaver. They had few other skills. Without employment and with no prospects, man is a lonely and dispirited animal -- nothing looks bright, especially while passing through a sodden, gloomy forest. Of the three men, Joe Jennings' thoughts were the most dour. He had made the promise to take his Nez Perce half brother east. He had counted on a profitable trapping season that would have made the journey possible. Instead, the winter trap lines barely produced enough beaver pelts to cover expenses. The western mountains were trapped out. The era when a mountain man could make his livelihood taking beaver pelts was over.

Near dusk a ferret dashed from a bush and across the riders' path. A gray mule on which a squat man of middle age was mounted, uttered a startled hee-haw and jumped sideways, pitching the rider into the trail side brush.

"Yuh, dirty, low-down, sneaky varmint. When I catch yuh I'll skin yuh alive." Still muttering, the squat man picked himself up and gave chase. The mule ran into a thicket of thorny brambles and came to a dead stop. The errant animal was meekly led back to the trail accompanied by hoots of laughter from the two watching riders.

"Next time take a horse. I told yuh, mules don't ride worth a damn," a thin, tall man with a face shaped like a hatchet, scolded.

"Shut up!" the squat man retorted. "I ain't goin' no farther. What's the hurry anyways? We ain't got nowheres ta go. Ever since leavin' the Siskiyous we been runnin' like the devil was on our tail."

The trappers made camp in a gloomy glen in full view of the rushing waters. A disturbed night bird uttered a squawk and flitted out of the shadows. From across the river came the eerie call of a loon. Youthful Joe Jennings shivered. He did not like the place. It was filled with spirits of the ancients. According to traditions of local Indian tribes, near this spot their Great Spirit created a land bridge across the river, The Bridge of the Gods. The benevolent Deity wanted the people to be friendly, to pass freely from one side of the river to the other. All went well for a while. Then, two Indian chiefs from opposite sides of the river fell in love with the same maiden. Competition for her hand was intense. The two chiefs had a jealous quarrel. The quarrel turned into a fight. The people joined in. Many warriors were slain. The needless violence infuriated the Great Spirit. He destroyed the bridge. The stones fell into the river forming the rapids which became known as Cascades of the Columbia.

The roar of the river, the dark brooding evergreens, the steep cliffs that blocked out the sky, waterfalls that fell from heights obscured by clouds and the mournful whistle of the wind, gave Joe Jennings the same uncanny feeling he'd had as a child walking by the church cemetery on a dark night. He almost could sense the mysterious power that destroyed the bridge and hear the frantic cries of the people who plunged to their deaths. Legends predicted a new bridge would one day again join the two banks together. Joe could not imagine that happening. When the gods destroyed something it was gone forever.

The next morning the trappers awakened to find the river mist so thick they barely could find the animals. The tall thin man with the hatchet face was irked. "Why did we stop in this place, anyhow. It gives me the spooks. I feel like they's witches an' goblins hidin' behind every rock, tree an' bush."

Near mid-morning the sun broke through the mist and the way became brighter. The following day the riders rounded a rocky bend to see the entire horizon open up, sunlight everywhere. "Hey! Ain't thet The Dalles yonder?" the squat man exclaimed. "Maybeso, we kin scrounge up some decent vittles. Me poor stomach needs a rest. We been livin' on wild game so long I cain't look at another carcass of deer, rabbit, duck or grouse."

Near the Methodist mission of Wascopum the ragtag trapper trio ran into the party Indian Agent Elijah White had recruited to accompany him to the homeland of the Cayuse. Despite the ominous rumor of a large force marching up river, White's party -- a few farmers taking off from spring plowing and young lads out for adventure-- was weak and ill-equipped. The total number consisted of twelve volunteers and a few Indians employed to paddle canoes. White and his entourage had just put ashore and were beginning to set up camp when Joe Jennings and his companions rode in.

Elijah White, equally as nervous as the Cayuse who awaited his arrival, guardedly watched the mountain men approach. They were a rough lot, dirty, bewhiskered, their clothes tattered and shapeless. Even their mounts and pack animals looked hard and mean. When they came near the leader, a slender youth in his early twenties, held up a hand in the traditional greeting of the plains.

"May we camp with you?" he politely asked. A slight New England accent tinged the words. The youth gave no sign of impatience as Indian Agent White made an arrogant inspection of the travel weary animals and dusty, weather-worn outfits.

"Name's Doctor Elijah White," the Indian agent finally answered. "Washington has seen fit to appoint me agent of all Indians in Oregon Territory. I'm on a mission of some importance. I cannot condone anything that may cause trouble."

"I can assure you we have neither the inclination nor the means to liquor up, shoot up the camp or hurrah the natives," the young man said. "We've come off a hard winter in the Siskiyous. We're on our way to Waiilatpu. If you're going that far perhaps we should travel together. Rumor has it the plateau tribes are somewhat unhappy. If things are as bad as we hear, we may need to stand together."

"Yeah! Strength in numbers," the Indian agent grunted. "Join us if you like. What did you say your name is?"

"I didn't say, but it's Joe Jennings. This here is Hawk Beak Tom," he pointed to the tall bean pole man with the hatchet face. "The man on the gray mule is Deacon Walton. He took orders for the ministry. Unfortunately, they didn't stick." The squat rider grinned, doffing his fur cap to reveal a head as smooth as polished leather.

The trio of mountain men methodically went about making camp on a patch of ground above the mission. From there they had a view of the river trail that disappeared in the folds of the forested hills to the west and to where it faded into the barren rocky bluffs that bordered the river to the east. Above them rose a tree-fringed escarpment that overlooked the mission buildings. After hobbling the stock, the trappers set up a lean-to shelter, then inspected the shacks and cabins that made up the site called The Dalles.

"Don't 'peer promisin'," the hatchet faced man observed. "Howsoever, some kind soul might take pity on us an' give a handout. I feel 'bout as empty as a fresh dug post hole."

"Nobody's goin' ta give a scruffy bunch like us a thing. Yuh seen how thet Injun agent eyed us. A cornered badger'd hev a more invitin' look. Poor cuss, probably takin' his job a mite too serious."

"Yeah," Hawk Beak agreed. "He don't 'peer perzactly friendly, do he? I'd best take me shootin' stick. There was a couple of cottontails a ways back. If nuthin' better comes up we'll have somethin' fer the pot. Come along, Joe, let Mule Skinner Deacon guard camp. Maybeso, there's somebody down here who'll offer a drop of firewater," Hawk Beak said hopefully, as the two trappers walked down the slope. "I'm 'bout as dry as burnt toast."

Joe remained silent. After a winter closeted with the beanpole trapper, he would have rather been alone. Even so, he strode along, keeping his irritations to himself. Oddly, they did run into someone they knew, a trapper named Peg Leg Smith.

"By gum! Fancy meetin' a one-legged rascal in this part of the territory," Hawk Beak greeted. "This calls fer liftin' a jug."

The meeting left Hawk Beak frustrated. Peg Leg had no jug and was in a big hurry. He barely said hello. "What the hell's the rush? Too stuck up to chew the fat with a couple of galoots fallin' on hard times, are yuh?" Hawk Beak demanded.

"I ain't tryin' ta high hat yuh. Sourdough Sam's waitin'. Wouldn't advise touchin' him fer a snort. He's in high lather ta git on the trail." Peg Leg hoisted a sack of provisions on a shoulder. He lowered his voice to a hoarse whisper. "I cain't tell yuh where, but we's off prospectin'. Gold nuggets big as hen's eggs' ve been reported in the Oregon desert. We aim ta git our share." He thumped away on his wooden leg before the two trappers had a chance to learn anything more.

Hawk Beak shook his head. "Cain't believe a word he says, wouldn't recognize truth if it hit him 'tween the eyes. The polecat's jest tryin' to get out of givin' us a snort."

Perusal of the scattered town buildings was also a disappointment. "Ain't a kind soul in sight," Hawk Beak complained. "Might as well go huntin'."

From a scum laden pond a flight of ducks took off heading for the escarpment, then swung directly overhead. Hawk Beak threw up the rifle and shot. The lead mallard fluttered frantically and then dropped. While Joe retrieved the duck, Hawk Beak reloaded. They strolled a little farther. Hawk Beak shot again; this time he caught a jack rabbit at the top of its leap. On the way back to camp a bushy-tailed squirrel scrambled across their path and ran up a yellow barked pine. Another shot rang out. The squirrel flopped on the ground, then righted itself and disappeared into the rocky escarpment.

"Hmm! Getting a bit rusty, aren't you?" Joe asked.

"Yuh reckon Peg Leg was talkin' straight, nuggets big as hen's

eggs?" Hawk Beak mused as the three trappers munched an unappetizing stew of duck and rabbit. "Sounds awfully good. Prospectin's
somethin' we ain't tried. Might be the answer."

"Not me," Deacon said. "I'm done wanderin' 'round like a
headless chicken. We ain't made enuff in the last two years ta feed a
hummin' bird an' I daresay our luck ain't gonna change. I'm headin'
straight fer the Sweetwater an' live off the ol' woman fer a spell.
What're yuh plannin', Joe?"

"I'll probably stay in Waiilatpu for a while, visit with Michael
and the Whitmans. Don't take offense; but I feel the need to spend
time with civilized folks."

Hawk Beak and Deacon fell silent. The mention of Joe's half
brother's name brought memories flooding back of when times were
good. Michael Two Feathers was the son of their dead partner. They
had affectionately called the big mountain man Little Ned. They were
present when Little Ned first met Michael's mother, Raven Wing. Then,
in the lean-to where Buck Stone's band of trappers spent the winter,
they had watched Raven Wing's belly swell as Michael took shape in
her womb. Shortly after the birth they carefully inspected the baby,
making certain he had all his fingers, toes and male parts. It was Little
Ned's eastern family that was a puzzle. They never knew it existed
until Joe suddenly appeared at Gimpy's Horse Emporium in St. Louis.
Even then it was two years later, long after Little Ned was buried in
the Bighorns, that they learned Joe was their dead partner's son and
half brother to Michael Two Feathers.

"Hmm!" Deacon cleared his throat. "Maybeso, yuh'll not
find Waiilatpu ta yer likin'. A couple of Agent White's crew say Doc
Whitman ain't at Waiilatpu. He sashayed east last fall, left family an'
flock. In his absence things hev plumb gone ta hell. Mrs. Whitman
was attacked and had to leave. Right now she's right here in The
Dalles, stayin' at Wascopum Mission. A man named Geiger's taken
over at Waiilatpu but I guess he ain't up ta the job. Feather Head's
son set fire ta the gristmill an' granary. Tiloukaikt, Buffalo Horn, Gray
Eagle an' others been talkin' warpath. They been palaverin' with the
Walla Walla, Nez Perce, Yakama, Spokan an' whomsoever else'll

lissen. They got the idea if'n they jine together they kin wipe out all white folks in the region."

"Ah!" Hawk Beak snorted. "Yuh cain't put stock in gossip talk like thet."

"I'm tellin' yuh jest what I heerd," Deacon snapped.

The news stunned Joe. If the Whitmans had left Waiilatpu, what happened to his Nez Perce brother? For over two years the mission had been his home. The poor fellow must be at his wits' end. He mentally kicked himself. He should have taken him along to the Siskiyous. Joe jumped to his feet. Perhaps it was mere gossip. He had to learn the truth. A member of White's party was happy to talk.

"'Bout the ruckus up river, can't say I know much more than what's floatin' aroun' camp. It ain't lookin' good. I been tellin' Elijah we should've waited, scouted the lay of the land afore bustin' up there layin' down the law. Now thet he's Injun Agent, he don't lissen ta nobody -- funny how a little power goes ta a man's head. Guess I'm as damn fool as him. I should be home at Tualitan Plains plowin'' an' sech 'stead of wanderin' off on a goose chase. Guess I was tired of hearin' the old woman goin' on 'bout the drownin' at the Falls. Yuh'd of thought they was kin. Guess she was heated 'cause I didn't warn thet tenderfoot, Cornelius Rogers, 'bout the river. Yuh could tell right off he didn't know shucks 'bout river boatin'.'"

"Cornelius Rogers! What happened? I knew him when he taught school at Whitman's Mission in Waiilatpu."

The Tualitan Plains farmer shook his head. "Poor fella's gone. Fresh married, yuh know. He an' wife an' friends went canoein'. Got caught in the current an' went over the falls of the Willamette -- no one could save 'em from those swirlin' waters, thet's fer certain."

Joe gazed blankly at the evening bank of clouds that had formed above the barren bluffs on the far side of the river. Two high flying hawks hung like black crosses against the billows of white. Why did people come to this wild land and suffer tragedy when they could have remained comfortable in New England homes? For that matter, what kept him here? After nearly four years in the mountains and western plains he possessed nothing more than the tattered, weather-worn clothing he wore. He was a disgrace to the human race. He had left his twin sister, Tildy, to cope with their aged grandparents while he roamed around with no responsibilities at all. Then, after discovering he had an Indian brother, he ran away again. He left his half brother at Whitman's mission because he didn't want to acknowledge they were kin. Disgusted with himself, Joe turned on his heel, leaving the Willamette Valley homesteader rambling on about the tragedy that occurred at Willamette River falls.

It was well after dark before activity in the camp began to wind down. White's party had traveled up river by canoe but from here on they planned to travel overland. Preparations for the change in mode of transport kept all hands occupied. From late afternoon and well into the night, White and his men worked breaking horses acquired from a band of Wascos. The wild mustangs crow-hopped, bit and kicked, throwing off riders and busting saddle girths. The pack animals were equally hard to tame, skittering in circles, spilling loads, lashing out with teeth and hooves, keeping the entire remuda ready to bolt. Blasphemous shouts and yells of rage echoed down from the escarpment walls, bringing shouts of rebuke from within the Wascopum mission compound.

The next morning, sleepy-eyed, the campers awakened to the thunder of galloping hoofbeats. A group of Indian horsemen, yelling and waving weapons, stormed into camp. The riders, on shaggy unshod ponies, milled around until the leader identified Indian Agent White's tent. The horsemen, looking as unkempt as their mounts, formed a circle around Agent White's shelter and began to chant. "Hiya! Hiya! Hiya!"

"What the devil's going on?" White blustered, appearing with hair disheveled and clothes awry. The leader of the Indian party, carrying an ancient Hudson's Bay musket, swung down from his horse. His companions also dismounted. They advanced on the Indian agent, surrounding him until he had no way of escape. Standing nearly nose to nose with White, the leader delivered a long, animated speech.

"What's goin' on here?" Hawk Beak asked. "These people're 'bout as happy as a batch of hungry hogs at an empty trough."

"Any fool kin see thet," Deacon said in disgust.

As abruptly as they appeared, the Indian party mounted up and galloped away.

"What's makin' these people so fussed?" Hawk Beak asked White.

"Nothing! Nothing!" the Indian agent growled. "Just a little misunderstanding."

The cause of the trouble soon emerged. On his last trip through Wascopum White had imposed his code of eleven laws on the local Wascos, the same code he insisted the Nez Perce and Cayuse adopt. Upon learning White was encamped at Wascopum, the Wascos organized a delegation to complain the laws were not good and could not be enforced.

Deacon pulled at his tangled beard and shook his head "If these laws upset the patient, peace-lovin' Wascos, I'm wonderin' what's goin' ta happen when this White galoot tries ta ram 'em down the throats of the feisty Cayuse."

V

Worry is a morbid anticipation of events which never happen.
Russell Green

Although a young man, William Geiger took his responsibilities as temporary manager of the Waiilatpu mission seriously. He had known Narcissa Whitman before she married, sang with her in the Plattsburgh, New York Presbyterian church choir. He was dedicated to the Whitmans and their missionary work. To the best of his ability he maintained the mission buildings and grounds. Except for the burned gristmill and granary, the mission compound had changed little from the day Marcus Whitman departed. The sight of these ruins pained Geiger but he did not have the means or time to rebuild them. Spring tilling and planting absorbed his time and energy.

Although the physical appearance of the mission remained much the same, Geiger could see that the mission's spiritual influence had waned. The natives did not take to him. The Cayuse regarded him as an interloper, a stranger. They had their quarrels with the Whitmans but they grudgingly respected and felt comfortable with the missionary couple. They had given them land, helped build their mission, tended to their fields, listened to their stories of the Great Spirit Book called Bible, and grieved with them when the missionaries' baby child, Alice Clarissa, fell in the river and drowned. The missionaries in turn taught the Cayuse the mysteries of talking paper, tended to their sick, ground their corn and instructed them in the mysteries of tilling and planting. Yet the ties that bound them together were now a source of resentment. To have the missionaries suddenly depart, almost without saying good-bye, hurt. It was not the way people who cared and shared lives treated one another. It took no great wisdom for Geiger to realize the resentment would not fade away until the Whitmans returned.

The deadly sickness that had descended upon the Cayuse village was Geiger's greatest concern. For a while there was hardly a lodge that did not have one or more members stricken. Noises from the Cayuse village kept Geiger awake at night. Oftentimes they were angry shouts directed at the mission house and the room where he slept. The constant chant of medicine men and eerie keening of women shattered him most. The sounds of their frantic attempts to heal and cries of grief were made more chilling by the lonely whistle of the wind as it swept across the fields and whipped around the mission house eves. Then came the unearthly lamentations announcing death. In one week alone Geiger recorded one or more deaths a night.

As winter deepened the sickness worsened. Week after week of near sleepless nights had the youthful missionary near the end of his tether. Those faithful to the mission kept begging him for help. "Medicine! Medicine!" a distraught mother beseeched. "Babies much, much sick. No get better." The usually stolid face was twisted with grief. Geiger went through Doctor Whitman's medical supplies, doling out what he guessed might do good. His ministrations did not slow the sickness nor end the deaths. Resentment against the mission establishment began to smolder and finally rose to fever pitch. Where was Medicine Man Whitman? Why did he desert them when they needed him most? A group led by Tiloukaikt virtually dragged Geiger to the Indian village to witness the distress. The writhing, feverish victims, pitiful moans of children; the pleading looks of mothers, the helpless expression of fathers and the close, stifling smell that accompanied sickness, left him so weak and distraught Geiger could barely totter home.

Before Geiger recovered from the village visit, he was accosted again by a delegation led by Tiloukaikt. The man named Feathercap pounded on the mission house door, calling for him to come out. Edward, Tiloukaikt's son who had attended the mission school and spoke passable English, acted as spokesman.

"Hunters from buffalo country come," he said. "They tell of Medicine Man Whitman. He travels with Blue Coats from land beyond River of Many Canoes. It is said more hairy face warriors come up river from valley."

"Your hunters are mistaken. No soldiers are crossing the

plains and no warriors march up river." Geiger's answer only made matters worse.

"How you know?" Edward retorted. "You no see over mountains. You not been down river. Why speak things of what you know nothing?" After venting their feelings, the Cayuse turned to stride back to the village, talking vehemently among themselves.

Trembling from the ordeal, Geiger went inside the mission house and barred the door. He sat down at the kitchen table and attempted to collect himself. The days were ticking away. Soon Elijah White would appear. "Damnation!" Geiger swore. "What am I to do?" The messages he sent Stickus and down river went unanswered. The latter message had been to Narcissa Whitman who, with her three adopted children, was staying at Wascopum mission. He had written Narcissa of the building resentment, urging her to return. "You and the children must come by yourselves," he warned. "Sickness and fear of invasion have the people in panic. There is no telling what might happen if Indian Agent White blunders in and attempts to force his code of laws on the Cayuse."

#

Narcissa Whitman had received the message. The news did not surprise her, but the thought of returning to Waiilatpu left her feeling weak. She was not well. Her eyes bothered her. She had constant headaches. She could not write or sew without spectacles. Even then these chores were most painful.

"What a heavy cross missionaries are forced to bear," she uttered after struggling through Geiger's letter. She spoke in such despair her three adopted children threw their arms around her. They clung to each other for comfort, but not for long. Narcissa pushed the children away and told them to collect their things. Her friend, William Geiger, was right. She must return to Waiilatpu. Her husband, Marcus, expected her to be there. Without either of the Whitmans present the Cayuse faithful to the missionary effort felt abandoned. She also agreed with Geiger; Elijah White should not be allowed to blunder into the Cayuse homeland with his code of laws before she arrived. His coming could spark the explosion that would destroy the mission. The thought sent a cold chill racing up her spine. All she and her husband had worked for could be lost in the blink of an eye.

Narcissa's fears were reinforced when the band of disenchanted Wascos surrounded Indian Agent White's tent. The short, fierce powwow with the usually placid Wascos made her cringe. It was obvious Elijah White had little patience or empathy for Indian people. He had always been somewhat pompous and overbearing. Now he seemed worse. After the Wascos departed Narcissa put aside her dislike of White and invited him to visit. She politely asked him to postpone his trip to Waiilatpu. "I should go to Waiilatpu first," she said. "The people must know we have not forgotten them." Shaken by the confrontation with the Wascos, the Indian agent agreed.

White's decision left the trio of trappers in a quandary. They could wait for the Indian agent and enter Cayuse country with the strength of numbers, or journey on by themselves and hope for a friendly reception. They could also accompany Narcissa Whitman and her small party but that was immediately ruled out. She was traveling by water and they had horses and pack animals to consider.

"I say mosey on," Deacon suggested. "Things cain't be as bad as they say. Besides, I ain't sure but what it's best ta stay clear of this galoot, White. Those Cayuse ain't goin' ta take ta him at all." Deacon had obtained a copy of White's code of laws. Taking metal-rimmed, begrimed spectacles from a jacket pocket. He perched them on his nose and laboriously read the paper and uttered an oath.

"Lissen ta this. 'If anyone takes a horse an' rides it without permission, or takes any article an' uses it without liberty, he shall pay fer the use of it an' receive thirty ta fifty lashes, as the chief shall direct.' Didja ever hear anythin' so stupid? What right-minded Injun's goin' ta whip one of his own people fer somethin' as simple as thet?"

The trappers set off on the rocky trail that led to the escarpment and on to the plateau. It was a hard day's ride to Cayuse country but as soon as they were on the treeless plain the trappers felt as though they were in hostile territory. The elements did little to ease the feeling. A cutting wind blew down river chilling them to the bone. Weeds, large and small, skipped across the sage lined trail like live creatures racing to escape a storm. A lone coyote skittered out of the way, its tail between its legs. Hawk Beak swung the barrel of his Hawken around to track it but didn't shoot. "The poor critter looks as miserable as we feel," he said.

On the second morning the green willow and locust trees that bordered the Umatilla River came into view. The sight did little to reassure the trio of travelers. Except for the wind that whistled through the dry weeds, the land was quiet. In the swales and on the hillsides a scattering of horses grazed listlessly. They looked poor and unkempt, something unusual for Cayuse stock. As the riders approached the Umatilla, herders appeared on the hilltops. More horsemen arrived until the ridge that overlooked the trail was lined with silent watchers. Boys on ponies and on foot circled the grazing livestock, driving the animals toward faint tendrils of smoke that drifted above lodges on the banks of the Umatilla.

Hawk Beak, riding in the lead, pulled up. "What's the matter? Do these folk think we're gonna steal their nags?" He put a spyglass to his eye and adjusted it to study the horsemen on the ridge. "Don't 'pear perzactly hostile, an' don't 'pear perzactly peaceful. What do yuh make of it, Joe? Yuh know these Cayuses; maybeso yuh kin figure what's goin' on."

Joe scanned the horsemen, searching for someone he recognized. This was Buffalo Horn's range. He always rode a stallion as dappled and gray as the sagebrush that blanketed the Cayuse highlands. But Joe saw nothing familiar. He swung the spyglass back along the ridge. A small body of shaggy ponies trotted out of a gully and on to high ground. There was a horse with a better coat than the rest -- no two horses . . . What was it about them that made them different? He put the glass down to rest his eyes, then studied the animals again. The black and white patched horse had the exact markings of Magpie, the pony his brother loved. Nearby was a black that looked familiar, too.

"Don't jest gawk." Hawk Beak scolded. "Tell what yuh see?"

"I thought I recognized a couple of horses." Joe thoughtfully put the spyglass away. He must be mistaken. Michael's horses wouldn't be running with Buffalo Horn's herd, not unless . . . A frightening thought flashed into his mind. Buffalo Horn had long opposed Whitman and his mission. Could he have raided the mission? Were the rumors true? Was the situation worse than reported? Had the Cayuse launched the campaign to wipe out all white people on the plateau?

"Let's get moving," Joe urged.

"Yeah! I don't see anybody rollin' out the red carpet," Hawk Beak agreed. "Fort Walla Walla ain't fer ahead. Maybeso, Factor Mac'll tell us what's goin' on. He usually has his ear close to the ground."

Gingerly, the travelers advanced. The horsemen on the ridge silently watched them pass, then, in a body, turned to follow. Joe felt the hair on the back of his neck stiffen. Any moment war whoops could ring out. Perhaps a war party waited ahead in ambush. On the near bank of the Umatilla they stopped to water the horses and size up the crossing. Not a soul did they see on the opposite bank. Joe glanced back. The Cayuse continued to trail them but made no attempt to catch up.

"I cain't figure 'em," Hawk Beak said. "Yuh don't know whether to git yer Hawken out or ride like hell."

The reception at Fort Walla Walla was equally as cool as that of the Umatilla Cayuse. At first Archibald McKinlay thought they were the advance riders of Indian Agent White's party. "Don't palaver about your laws on these premises. This is Hudson's Bay property. If you're going to make these Cayuses law abiding citizens, do it someplace else." McKinlay clipped the words out in his usual brusque speech.

Rather than being offended by the Scots' gruffness, Joe respected him. Here was a man who brooked no nonsense. The Cayuse were his customers. He had no desire to do anything that would make them unhappy with Hudson's Bay. Of course he had orders from Fort Vancouver not to acknowledge Elijah White's appointment as Indian agent. To do so would infer the US government had jurisdiction in Oregon Territory.

"I guess Doctor McLoughlin doesn't especially like White, is that it?" Joe asked. He referred to John McLoughlin, Hudson's Bay's head mogul who, from his base in Fort Vancouver, ruled the company's Northwest chain of trading posts. Although McLoughlin treated Americans kindly and fairly, he was under great pressure by his London superiors to do everything possible to discourage American settlement in Oregon Territory. The Pacific Northwest was a potentially rich and strategic region the British hoped to add to their empire.

"No, I don't suppose he does," McKinlay agreed. "But that's beside the point. The White Eagle wants peace. He doesn't want this agent of yours upsetting the Cayuse. It's already touch and go. Things haven't been right since Whitman left. If the good doctor marches back with soldiers, like they say, there'll be hell to pay." McKinlay stopped to fill his pipe. He puffed a bit and shook his head. "I get up every morning wondering what the day will bring. People ride in with rumors this disaster's going to strike or that calamity will happen. Last week it was this White fellow on the way up river with a party armed to the teeth. This morning a bloke from the west brings word Narcissa Whitman and her brood are coming by themselves."

"We kin vouch fer thet," Hawk Beak said. "Missus Whitman an' party was loadin' up when we was leavin' The Dalles."

"I'm glad something good is happening, although I don't know what the poor woman can do by herself. It's her husband these people want. Until they find out what he's up to they'll be out of sorts."

"What about the mission workers? Are they all right?" Joe asked.

"Far as I know, they're fine. The man Geiger's a bit rattled -- sending messages right and left, keeping the mission boy on the go."

"What about the mission boy?" Joe asked. "When did you see him last?" The sight of his brother's two horses in Buffalo Horn's herd had haunted him all the way from the Umatilla grazing grounds.

"Oh, I don't know, must've been about a fortnight back."

Joe would have questioned McKinlay further but the Scotsman brushed them off. "I can't natter with you blokes all day, I have work to do," he said and disappeared into the back room.

The trappers left Fort Walla Walla little wiser than when they arrived. A short distance from the fort gates Indians began to appear on both sides of the trail. They had reined their colorful ponies about to follow. They did not ride near but kept their distance. They were silent, gliding through the brushy, rocky terrain like ghosts.

"It's as plain as the nose on yer face, these buggers hev been waitin' fer us. I don't like the feel of this, at all," Deacon said. "I'm not sure but what we should've put up at the fort."

All the way to Waiilatpu the Cayuse horsemen kept pace. When the trappers arrived at the mission compound another group of Indians impassively watched them ride in. The horsemen who had followed the trappers pulled up to block the trail back to the fort.

"I ain't sure I like this," Hawk Beak said, his voice hushed. "Half the Cayuse Nation must be here an' we're right smack dab in the middle of the lot. Hey! What's this?"

From the mission house stepped a bearded figure. The crowd parted to make way for him. He walked up to the three horsemen. "I'm William Geiger," he said. "In Doctor Whitman's absence, I'm in charge of the mission. What news do you bring?" He spoke in a low voice as though he did not want the crowd of natives to overhear.

"News! What news we supposed to bring?" Hawk Beak squawked.

"You came from down river, didn't you? Well, what's going on down there? Is help on the way? I'm trying to hold things together with spit an' string and it isn't working." Geiger's voice rose a decibel. It was obvious he was under great strain.

"Narcissa Whitman and children are on the way, should be here soon," Joe said encouragingly.

"Thank God. Maybe she can talk sense into this bunch." The temporary mission manager turned and quickly walked back into the mission house, firmly shutting the door behind him.

"Hospitable chap, ain't he?" Deacon observed.

"Maybe somebody here can tell us what's going on," Joe said, glancing over the gathering that silently looked on. He searched for his brother Michael but there was no sign of him.

"Why do these people keep starin' at us?" Hawk Beak muttered. "Act like we'd been raised on sour milk."

Feathercap, the man Deacon called Feather Head, stepped out of the crowd. The trappers knew him from previous trips to Waiilatpu. The Cayuse man sidled close. "Plenty riders come?" he queried.

Joe shook his head. "No, just us three. Missionary lady and children come by river." To make certain Feathercap understood, he supplemented the spoken word with sign language.

Feathercap frowned. He held up three fingers. "Three riders? No more?"

Joe nodded.

Feathercap reported the news to the watchers. A rumble of mutterings filtered through the gathering, then, slowly, the people began to disperse, children scampering toward the Indian village, smiling and skipping as they went. The horsemen blocking the trail to Fort Walla Walla reined about and rode away.

"Kin yuh beat thet?" Hawk Beak exclaimed. "We sashay in here thinkin' we'd lose our hair. All the while these folks're skeered to death, thinkin' we was lead scouts fer an army marchin' up river to do them in."

VI

Hear my voice, O God, in my prayer:
preserve my life from fear of the enemy.

Book of psalms, LXIV

For the first time in weeks William Geiger slept soundly through the night. The thought that Narcissa Whitman would soon arrive put his mind at rest. Refreshed, he went to work on the many tasks he had let slide. The announcement of the missionary woman's return also seemed to affect the Cayuse. There was less commotion in the village. The people remained away from the mission grounds. Women and children began to work the fields for planting. The men inspected their herds, cared for the new colts and anxiously watched over mares about to foal. The trio of trappers appeared to be the only group without purpose. They could not make up their minds as to what they should do. Deacon Walton was anxious to continue on to join his Cheyenne family on the Sweetwater. Hawk Beak argued that while it was still peaceful they should try prospecting the Oregon desert.

Joe Jennings did not want to leave. The absence of Michael Two Feathers and the sighting of his horses among the herd of Buffalo Horn, worried him. He already felt guilty about the manner in which he had treated his Indian brother. It was not Michael's fault he had been sired by a white father and had an Indian mother. He had promised to take him home to meet their New England relatives. He made the promise with tongue in cheek. Deep in his heart he knew he didn't intend to go through with it. He was afraid to take his half-blood brother home. The shock could be the death of staid Granny, so proud of her lineage dating back to the Mayflower. Then there were the gossipy neighbors. The Abernathy family was more effective than a newspaper. They would launch a maliciously embellished whispering campaign that would be the talk of the community for weeks.

Joe groaned. How could he stand himself? He was as weak and narrow-minded as any of his relatives. He was a traitor to his own flesh and blood. During the long winter months he had tortured himself with this guilt until he finally came to grips with the situation. He vowed to accept Michael as his true blood brother, treat him with respect and love him as he should. He would not rest until he found Michael and made peace with him and with himself.

Joe questioned mission workers. No one knew anything about Michael's disappearance. Most of them were leery of the lad who made his home in an Indian tipi. He was so silent. The steady, startling blue eyes appeared out of place beneath the dark eyebrows and shock of black hair. When he looked at a person the penetrating gaze seemed to search one's very soul. They had no idea where he went, only were glad he was gone.

The older trappers also found Michael's absence disturbing. They had looked forward to seeing the son of their former partner again. He was an important part of their past. The trappers put aside their plans to leave. Together they rummaged through Michael's tipi lodge. Sharp pins made from willow sticks held the tipi flaps sealed, as was the Indian custom when occupants planned to be away for any length of time. The interior held little more than a bulrush stuffed sleeping pallet, two cooking utensils and a few reed mats. The smoke hole flap was drawn tight to keep out rain and birds. The inspection revealed nothing of Michael's whereabouts.

The search increased Joe's anxiety. The place where Michael had lived was as forsaken as an abandoned bird's nest. Although he had been in the tipi before, it had been summer. Everything had been bright and green with chipmunks and squirrels chattering and skittering about. He remembered a scolding robin that flitted back and forth guarding its nest in a nearby tree. The grass had been a thick carpet in front of the tipi where Michael and he sat watching the busy bird. Now the grass was just beginning to appear, the locust tree nearly bare of foliage, the robin's nest gone. The squirrels and chipmunks were still loggy from the long winter's sleep. Overhead dark clouds blotted out the sun. A cool breeze whistled through the tipi entrance sending a shiver up Joe's spine. Why hadn't he taken Michael with him instead of leaving him to live alone in this cold, lonely lodge?

"Ain't proper fer us to be nosin' aroun' someun's diggin's like this," Hawk Beak complained. "Any half-witted person kin see Michael vamoosed, maybeso gone fer good, leastwise didn't leave much behind."

They stepped outside to be greeted by the cawing of two huge crows perched in the bare locust tree. "By gum! I hope somethin' hasn't happened ta Michael," Deacon exclaimed. "These damned crows. Me Cheyenne missus'd say a pair of 'em cawin' like thet is a message of doom."

"Quit gabblin'," Hawk Beak scolded. He gave his partner a sharp, frowning glance, motioning his chin toward Joe, who had his back turned. "Michael's near grow'd. He kin handle hisself."

Belatedly, Joe went to the mission house to question William Geiger. "Two Feathers! Ah, yes, the rascal left some time back. I sent him with messages, one to Narcissa Whitman to be sent down river and another to Stickus on the upper Umatilla. If Narcissa is on the way her message must have been delivered. No word from Stickus. But that's Indians for you. They never do anything in a hurry."

Geiger's indifference infuriated Joe. "You mean you haven't tried to find out what happened to him?" he demanded. "What kind of missionary are you, don't even look after your own people? Michael could be in trouble and you don't even give a damn."

"Now, now, collect yourself. There'll be no cursing on mission grounds. You should know better than that."

"There'll be plenty of cursing if Michael has come to grief. I saw his horses on the lower Umatilla. If he fell into Buffalo Horn's hands . . . That Cayuse hates the mission and everything connected with it. Who knows what he might have done to Michael."

"The boy is probably visiting," Geiger said soothingly. "You know how Indians regard time. A day, an hour, a week, it's all the same to them. Do you suppose if we lived that way life out here would be easier?"

"Ah!" Joe snorted in disgust. With this cipher in charge no wonder there was talk of shutting the mission down.

#

Stickus made it a habit to ride to a distant hilltop every morning where he had a view of Buffalo Horn's southern pasture lands. He was waiting for the wealthy horseman to make a move. If he rounded up his horses to drive them to Blue Mountain pastures, that was the time to rescue Michael's ponies. The dust and commotion of rounding up the scattered animals would give a perfect cover. Horses were always going astray. In the dust and confusion riders could easily cut out the Appaloosa pony and black pack mare and keep them hidden until Buffalo Horn's riders were well out of the way.

After completing his inspection Stickus returned to visit Michael in his brush hut. The poor lad's feet had taken longer than expected to heal. When it appeared they were on the road to recovery, a poisoned thorn puncture turned purple. When it was nearly healed the other foot turned bad and began to secrete pus. Now, a fortnight after he arrived, Michael was up and around, anxious to return to the mission at Waiilatpu. Stickus frowned. He could wait no longer. He had to prepare a message to send to Mission Man Geiger.

Stickus was almost upon Michael's brush hut before spotting the strange horse that stood in front. It was not a Cayuse pony and not a Cayuse saddle. Stickus wheeled around. If the rider had been sent by Missionary Geiger or Indian Agent White, he did not want to see him. Then he heard a peal of laughter. Whoever it was could not be a threat. It had to be someone Michael knew and liked. He heard the stranger speak. He knew the voice. While he tried to put a name to it, out of the hut came a young man with white face followed by Michael. The Boston brother! He had met this young man called Joe before. It was good. He came in search of his half-blood brother. Stickus held up his hand in greeting. In sign language, he invited the brothers to his lodge for a friendship smoke. When he reached for the pipe, he remembered that Missionary Whitman did not approve of tobacco. Instead of offering the pipe, Stickus had Kio-noo fetch a basket of honey flavored meal cakes.

While the young men silently munched on the tasty cakes, Stickus covertly studied the newcomer. He was different than most hairy faced ones. His eyes were clear and honest. His tongue was straight. He said what he meant. He was respectful and polite. He did not look down on Indian people as many hairy faces did. These two boys would bring joy to any lodge. Now that they found each other, what would they do? Would they remain in Cayuse country or would they journey to lands beyond the River of Many Canoes, to the village called Boston where their father had his roots?

Stickus jerked his mind out of its reverie. There were more pressing problems to worry about. He had to answer Geiger's message. Michael's horses had to be rescued. If he were to take his band to Waiilatpu there were many preparations to make. "What happens at mission?" Stickus asked in the sketchy English learned from his dealings with mission people.

"Mission Woman Whitman comes up river," Joe answered, employing sign language with the spoken word. "Indian Agent White will also soon arrive. He wishes to council with your people."

Stickus stroked his chin. He had put off sending a reply to Geiger's message hoping something would keep the Indian agent and his code of laws away. Now that hope was shattered. He inwardly groaned. Why did the hairy faces force things like this on his people? After the hard winter it was all they could do to recover and live normal lives again.

Stickus poked at the fire. Thoughts of Indian Agent White gave him a chill. He glanced at his two guests, who happily chattered like magpies. If these brothers, who had grown up in different cultures, could get along so well, why should not the Cayuse with the same way of life be able to do the same? There was no reason for them to quarrel among themselves. When confronted with crises like the coming of Indian Agent White they should act as one people, speak with one voice. The coming of Agent White and his code of laws should bring them together instead of splitting them apart.

A startling idea suddenly occurred to Stickus. Buffalo Horn's stealing of Michael's horses could give White's laws their first test. He had a scanty knowledge of the laws. Five Crows, who attended the mission school in Nez Perce country, had returned home with them written on talking paper. He translated the laws in a council meeting, urging the elders to adopt them. Stickus did not remember them all but one stuck in his mind. "If anyone steals he shall pay back twofold. If it is over the value of a beaver skin, he shall pay twofold and receive fifty lashes." Stickus thought of Buffalo Horn's two sons and smiled to himself. "That would bring those arrogant youths down out of the clouds." The thought delighted Stickus so much he took a bite of cake so large it almost made him choke.

#

In early April Narcissa Whitman and her party arrived at Fort Walla Walla. Always hospitable, Archibald McKinlay invited the missionary lady and her adopted children into his home. They stayed overnight but Narcissa was anxious to trek on to Waiilatpu. The sight of the burned gristmill and granary hurt sorely, but Geiger's tilled fields and his obvious efforts to keep up the mission grounds pleased her. A stream of Cayuse from the village came to welcome her home. They asked about her mate; when was Medicine Man Whitman to return? Narcissa pretended not to understand. To distract the well-wishers she handed out little presents of sweet meats that sent the children squealing with delight. When the treats were gone the gathering drifted away. The return of the missionary woman pleased them but the absence of her man was as troubling as ever. The disturbing thought he would return with an army of Blue Coats would not go away. Then, lurking overhead like a hungry turkey buzzard, was that hairy faced Indian agent with his code of laws.

Narcissa Whitman also awaited White's arrival with dread. When he did arrive her fears and those of the Cayuse appeared to be unfounded. Narcissa had barely greeted the Indian agent before the wealthy horseman, Buffalo Horn, who she feared would give the most trouble, galloped up the trail from Fort Walla Walla and into the mission house yard. White, anxious to please, treated Buffalo Horn with special care. He invited him to a ceremonial smoke, gave a few gifts and assured the leader of the lower Umatilla his herds were safe; there was no army coming from either the west or east. Most of the Cayuse present took the agent at his word. Buffalo Horn said nothing. He noted White's uneasy appearance and the effusive manner in which the Indian agent spoke. He had the look of a man not telling the truth.

Elijah White was indeed uneasy. He had failed to get the Cayuse to accept his code of laws the previous winter. He did not intend to fail again. Shortly after his meeting with Buffalo Horn, he sent messages to all tribal leaders to gather in council: Stickus on the upper Umatilla; Tiloukaikt at Waiilatpu village; Five Crows on the middle Umatilla; and Buffalo Horn were all invited to talk and feast on barbecued beef.

Elijah White waited impatiently for answers. One day, two days, three days, finally on the fourth day responses to his invitation dribbled in. All four Cayuse leaders replied they were too busy to meet with him. Spring work kept them in their villages. The rejections infuriated Elijah White. He stomped around the mission house kicking at chairs and at one point took the Lord's name in vain.

"What is the matter with you?" Narcissa scolded, "throwing a tantrum and speaking like that in front of the children?"

"Yes, but these dad-ratted Cayuse are stubborn as mules. I know what they did. They got together and agreed among themselves not to come. Too busy! Bah! Whoever saw an Indian too busy to feast on barbecued beef?"

White was not far wrong. The Cayuse savored their independence. Even Five Crows who understood the laws and favored them, ignored White's summons. "Why should a hairy faced outsider tell us what to do?" he was heard to say.

The Cayuse knew that if they came to Waiilatpu, White would use every ploy possible to force them into accepting his code of laws. They were well aware of the consequences. Indian Agent White with the help of the local missionary, Henry Spalding, had persuaded their neighbors, the Nez Perce, to adopt the laws. Missionary Spalding then used them to his advantage. He assigned tasks fit only for women and children to warriors and hunters. Those who refused to work or obey the laws were whipped. Even Ellis, the appointed chief of all Nez Perce, had revolted. The situation became so tense Missionary Spalding sent messengers to the Willamette Valley for help. Spalding's frantic requests were what gave credence to the rumor that an army marched up river.

On the upper Umatilla Stickus observed the impasse that existed between Indian Agent White and the Cayuse leaders with unease. Sooner or later White's invitation would split the Cayuse people apart. Some had already voiced readiness to meet with the Indian agent and accept the laws. They were afraid if they did not, the army that was on the march from the east would take their lands and destroy their possessions. Others adamantly opposed Agent White and his code of laws. They were ready to take to the warpath, remove all whites from their lands. Tribal elders who desired peace, longed for Marcus Whitman's counsel. They needed advice. They wanted to hear from Yellow Serpent, leader of the Walla Wallas. They insisted Chief Ellis and other important tribal members of the Nez Perce be present at the Waiilatpu meeting with Agent White.

"Blast them all!" White exploded. "Next they'll ask for the Great White Father from Washington to come to Waiilatpu." Nevertheless, he agreed to invite the Walla Wallas and Nez Perce but chaffed at the delay. He inspected the plots the Cayuse had under cultivation, had afternoon teas with Narcissa Whitman and made an inspection trip of the Blue Mountain timberlands. Still he found the wait insufferable. Early one morning he informed Narcissa he was leaving for a visit to Henry Spalding's Lapwai mission on the Clearwater River. He insisted Hawk Beak Tom and Deacon Walton accompany him. Both trappers knew mountain men who had taken Nez Perce wives and settled in Lapwai.

From the front stoop of the mission house Narcissa Whitman watched White's small caravan depart. In a way she wished she were leaving, too. Each winter that passed seemed harder to manage than the last. The winter of 1842-43 was the most difficult of them all. Without Marcus she felt only half of herself was present. The other half journeyed the mountains and plains with her husband. He had left in October. Here it was mid-May. During all this time she did not know if he lived or lay in a lonely trail side grave.

During the long, harsh days of winter Narcissa's thoughts

often dwelt on happenstances that had been crucial turning points in her life. There was the night she attended church and heard Reverend Parker speak of the four Indian men who had trekked half way across the continent in search of missionaries who would come to their homeland to teach them the ways of the white man's path to heaven. The ardent desire of these "heathens" to seek Christianity moved her to volunteer for mission work. In a nearby village Marcus Whitman also was so moved. Their mutual commitment to serve Indian people led to marriage and the arduous trip to Cayuse country.

Then there were less happy events that turned one's life around. The most heartbreaking was the day two year old baby daughter, Alice Clarissa, drowned. Marcus was studying the Scriptures for the Sunday service. It was dinner time. The table was set. The food was cooked, ready to eat. Alice Clarissa was hungry. "Mamma," she said. "Supper ready -- Alice get water." No one paid any attention. The child suddenly disappeared and was never seen alive again. Only afterwards did they realize what had happened. The little girl took two cups to the river to fill them. What she did next, no one knew. Whatever it was, baby Alice Clarissa went to her death in the swollen waters of the Walla Walla River.

Inside the mission house Narcissa reached for quill, ink pot and paper. She had written Marcus so many letters she had lost count. Hardly was he out of sight before she started the first. Then, one after another they poured from her quill pen. Whether or not he received the letters she did not know, but now was no time to stop writing. Perhaps some traveler going east would deliver this message. Marcus should be aware of what to expect on his return. At present calm existed but the temper of the proud Cayuse rose and fell like mercury in the thermometer. What it would be like after Indian Agent White's council took place was hard to predict.

Narcissa glanced out the window to see Feathercap, the troublemaker, crossing the mission compound, walking toward the Indian village. Involuntarily, she shivered. He strode through the mission compound as though he personally owned every stick and stone. His savage countenance, high-handed manner and cruel streak had long irked her. She had done her best to overcome her revulsion. Her efforts were in vain. No amount of Christian training would change this uncivilized man. She was certain it was he who attempted to break into her room soon after Marcus had gone. Feathercap blamed his son for the destruction of the gristmill and granary. She had the feeling he lied. The senseless destruction had the mark of his cruel mind.

Narcissa turned back to the blank page. What she really wanted to tell Marcus, she couldn't. For all she cared the British were welcome to the entire Oregon Territory, or better yet, let the Indians keep it. This part of the world was not meant for civilized folk. It only brought them pain and grief.

Narcissa laid down the quill and sighed. Was she not a good Christian? Unlike Eliza Spalding at the Lapwai mission, she was unable to view Indians as equals. True, they were God's creation, but so were the untamable grizzly, the smelly skunk and the prickly porcupine. Perhaps the Nez Perce were different than the Cayuse. Tackensuatis, known as Rotten Belly, said they were. He had warned Marcus the day the Waiilatpu mission site was chosen that the Cayuse would give trouble. Rotten Belly had insisted the Whitmans come and live among the Nez Perce. How she wished her husband had listened.

VII

*Formerly we enjoyed the privilege we expect is now called
freedom and liberty; but since the acquaintance with our
brother white people, that which we called freedom
and liberty becomes a stranger to us.*

Teholagwanegen, Mohawk

As the day for Agent Elijah White's council meeting approached, the weather turned pleasant. The sun warmed valley floor brought out the coarse grass which gave the site its Cayuse name, Waiilatpu, Place of Rye Grass. Shiny new leaves on fruit trees Marcus Whitman had planted rippled softly in the spring breezes that fitfully sprang from the river. Grasses and bulrushes had grown high enough to partially cover the ugliness of the blackened remains of the burnt granary and gristmill. A myriad of wild flowers opened their petals to add color to the deceptively peaceful scene. Bees, capturing the sweet pollen nectar, hummed their busy tune. A flock of chirping redwing black birds, swarmed around searching for insects and seeds.

Into this scene of pastoral beauty rode Buffalo Horn and his people from the lower Umatilla. As was his custom, Buffalo Horn, with the shaman, Gray Eagle, and his two sons at his side, were well in front of the column. The spirited dappled gray stallion Buffalo Horn rode jerked its head up and down like a mount new to bit and bridle. The stallion's passing sent mares in Tiloukaikt's pastures kicking and squealing. Horses tethered near village lodges stomped and reared, breaking the rawhide lines that held them. A mule in the mission corral bolted, ramming against the railing with such force the rails split, making an opening large enough for the crazed animal to bolt through. A blacksmith, working a nearby forge, dropped his heavy hammer to give chase. Two of the smithy's dogs awakened to run pell-mell after their master.

The mission area had an air of a county fair. Each arriving delegation put on a display of color and excitement as if vying for a prize. The men rode handsome animals covered with painted stripes, circles and designs of every kind. From the horses' manes, tails and riding equipment fluttered plumes, glittering trinkets and little tinkling bells. The riders were just as brilliantly adorned, with exposed flesh streaked with every color of paint. Headdresses, thick with plumes of colorful feathers, adorned their heads, some chains of feathers so lengthy they trailed down to end at the heels of bead and quill orna- mented moccasins. Many wore bone, bead and porcupine quill deco- rated rawhide breast coverings, giving the bearers the regal look of kings. Arm bands and braid ties glittered with shiny metals, dentalium and ribbons of bright colored cloth. Everything possible was done to impress Indian Agent White.

Five Crows, who had a reputation as a dandy, led his group in wearing a vivid shirt made of scarlet cloth and rawhide. The scarlet front of the shirt was joined to the back with rows of porcupine quills held in place by webbings of horse hair. From his neck hung a looking glass pendant enclosed in a tiny wooden frame. His pleated hair was kept in place by sparkling ties. The bleached buckskin that formed the back of his shirt glittered with polished elk teeth and intricate beadwork. His collar was a black otter tail. Taking advantage of the opportunity to display his elegance, Five Crows, waving a shield and a lance with bright ribbons attached to the shaft, guided his prancing mount from one arriving delegation to another.

Immediately following Five Crows' group came Peu-peu- mox-mox (Yellow Serpent) of the Walla Walla. He led his delegation into the council grounds to make camp next to Buffalo Horn's people from the lower Umatilla. The arrival of so many horsemen at once created confusion. For a while arguments among the different del- egations threatened to halt the council meeting before it ever started. Geiger, attempting to bring order to the situation, ran back and forth issuing orders that no one could understand or paid any attention to. Narcissa Whitman watched from the mission house windows. She knew she should be welcoming the delegations but her feet refused to take her outside to do so. Michael and Joe also stood by and watched the confusion develop without making an effort to lend a hand.

It had not been a good morning for the brothers. Upon leaving the camp of Stickus, they had planned to raid Buffalo Horn's herd and retrieve Michael's ponies but Stickus would not hear of it. "Make big trouble," he warned. "Wait, better time will come."

The brothers did not argue. They respected the Cayuse leader and would not go against his wishes, but Michael remained determined to rescue Magpie and the black mare. He insisted Joe ride with him to the hilltop overlooking Buffalo Horn's pasture land. Again he was frustrated. There was no sign of his black and white pony or the black mare. He and Joe rode in silence all the way to Waiilatpu. Soon after the brothers' arrival the colorful delegations began to appear. They had just put their mounts in the mission corral when Buffalo Horn on his prancing dappled gray stallion rode in, sending the milling horses wildly in circles and the mule bursting through the rails.

"This man makes trouble wherever he goes," Michael stated. "I wonder what mischief he will cause this day."

Joe watched Buffalo Horn and his band make camp. "Hmm!" he grunted. "He's left his herd lightly guarded. Maybe this is our opportunity. Let's fix this corral fence and decide what to do."

Barely did they begin work on the damaged corral when a large party of Nez Perce arrived. Michael immediately spotted his relatives. "I must welcome them," he said, darting away.

Joe stopped work to stare. Curiosity consumed him. These were his relatives, too! The tall, dark people dressed entirely in buckskin with quills, animal teeth, bones and beads and shoulder-length hair, sitting down to a meal in Granny's dining room with all of its highly polished and lacquered bric-a-brac was incongruous. How could he take Michael to meet them? What if the entire Lone Wolf clan should decide to visit? The thought unnerved him so the hammer he swung hit his thumb. The pain was so agonizing he howled.

Nursing his throbbing thumb, Joe studied the Indian family. The two uncles laughed, chatted and playfully poked Michael in the ribs much as male members of any reunited New England family would do. While the men sat on buffalo robes to visit, Quiet Woman went to work unpacking and setting up camp. Joe was pleased to see Michael jump up and help his grandmother raise the tipi poles and draw the lodge coverings into place. He was especially interested in the tall, slender uncle, Vision Seeker. Michael said he had the uncanny power to predict the future. He experienced visions and dreams that foretold many events; good or bad hunts; successful or failed missions; the arrival of storms; and the deaths of people. These mysterious abilities set him apart. Tribal members were half afraid of him. Many believed the Great Spirit walked and talked through him. As he sat chatting with Michael, Vision Seeker appeared much the same as did any young Indian man.

The younger uncle, Running Turtle, was quite different. He was as squat and round as Vision Seeker was slender and tall. As he got astride his pony to take the horses to pasture, he reminded Joe of Mother Goose's Humpty Dumpty. His roundness teetered on the horse's bare back as if any moment he would fall. Michael said Running Turtle was so overshadowed by serious-minded Vision Seeker his parents treated him as though he were still a child.

As Running Turtle led the horses away, a brilliantly dressed horseman stopped him. They exchanged words. The rider then made straight for the Lone Wolf camp. The scarlet shirt front identified him as Five Crows, the flamboyant Cayuse leader from the middle Umatilla. He reined his mount to a stop, let the bridle reins drop and slid down to squat by Vision Seeker. Lone Wolf, Michael's grandfather, reached for his pipe bag. Five Crows raised his hand. He did not have time to smoke. Joe studied the man with interest. Five Crows had a checkered background. Even the Cayuse had mixed feelings about him. He was a man determined to have the best of everything. At present he attended the Nez Perce mission school at Lapwai. His hope was to become a member of the Christian church. It was said his herds equaled those of Buffalo Horn. Much of his wealth came from choosing the right mates; he had five wives. Because of his multiple wives Missionary Spalding had been censured by the Mission Board in the east. The board claimed he turned a blind eye to polygyny.

Whatever brought Five Crows to the Nez Perce camp, it had to be important. He did much of his talking with his hands. He pointed to himself, then to the village of Tiloukaikt and at the camp of Buffalo Horn and finally to where Stickus and his band from the upper Umatilla had set up their lodges. Apparently, Vision Seeker's response was unsatisfactory. Five Crows made a motion of displeasure, picked up the trailing bridle reins, swung up on his colorfully decorated mount, kicked it in the ribs and galloped away. Vision Seeker did not appear disturbed. He visited with Michael, joking and chatting as if nothing unusual had occurred.

Joe turned away. The family picture with its love and companionship suddenly gave him an acute feeling of homesickness. He was reminded of pleasant evenings spent by the New England hearth -- Christmas and Thanksgiving gatherings -- Halloween and church festive occasions. He thought of his father. It saddened him that he had enjoyed so little time with him, actually never got to know him. He knew nothing of his father's life with the Nez Perce. For ten years Little Ned lived with these people -- loved them -- cared for them -- took one for a wife. What a strange man, leading a double life. Which family did he care for most, the one in the east or the one in the wilds of the west?

He was no better than his father. He meandered from place to place with as little regard for time as any Indian. It was summer again and he had not sent home a cent, not even a letter. He turned and walked dejectedly to the blacksmith shop where he found Hawk Beak who had ridden in from Lapwai with Indian Agent White. The hatchet faced trapper was accompanied by an equally scraggly mountain man called Hare Lip Bruce. One glance was sufficient to realize how the man got his name. From somewhere the roguish twosome had acquired a jug of liquor. Both were slightly, but garrulously drunk. They loudly talked of finding gold in the Oregon desert.

"If a one-legged man an' a rump-sprung creature like Sourdough kin find the yeller stuff, able-bodied galoots like us should make a fortune," Hawk Beak said with exaggerated confidence.

"Yeah! Yeah! Cain't yuh jest see us pickin' up gold nuggets like buffalo chips off the plains," Hare Lip Bruce enthused. He took a long swig from the jug and offered it to Joe. Joe turned away. He didn't need firewater and he didn't want to converse with a couple of half-drunk trappers. He wished Michael would finish visiting with his folks. He wanted to find out what had excited Five Crows. Would it ruin their plan to rescue Michael's horses from Buffalo Horn's herd?

#

Gradually, more Indians came to enlarge the gathering. Clusters of tipis, like conical mushrooms, sprang up to surround the mission compound. A small band of Palouse appeared, swaying so gracefully with the movement of their mounts they gave the appearance of being extensions of their colorful ponies. They kept to themselves, raising a few lodges near the base of the steep hill that rose up to overlook the mission compound. A band of Umatillas appeared to quietly make camp near the orchard that was in fragrant bloom.

Indian Agent White made the rounds of the camps. He promised a speedy meeting followed by a bountiful feast. He still glowed from the success of his trip to the Nez Perce. While at the Lapwai mission he assisted Reverend Spalding and other churchmen in selecting nine candidates for membership in the First Presbyterian Church in Oregon Territory. In nearly seven years of mission work this brought the church's Indian membership to a sum total of eleven.

The council meeting finally got underway with pomp and ceremony. Dressed in elegant robes, the Indian leaders sat in a circle for the ceremonial smoke. They saluted the four directions, Father Sky and Mother Earth. When protocol was satisfied, Indian Agent White stood to read aloud each law and explain it at length.

"The first law states that 'Whoever willfully takes a life shall be hung,'" he began. A member of the gathering who understood English gasped.

When the translation was made and everyone understood the method of punishment, a hush fell over the crowd. Killing a man by putting a rope around his neck and strangling him to death was beyond their comprehension. Such a death was only fit for fowls whose necks were wrung before preparing them for the cooking pot.

The second article of the code met with equal dismay. "Whoever burns a dwelling shall be hung." The reading, explanation and translation went on and on. After the initial outburst the crowd remained quiet. From time to time individuals shifted uneasily; others sat stock still, their expressions changing from disbelief to dismay. When the last law was read and explained, Yellow Serpent of the Walla Wallas slowly rose to his feet to speak.

"Are these laws made by God or made by man? Are these laws made for Indian people or do they rule Boston people as well?" A murmur swept throughout the crowd. Yellow Serpent's words were wise. It was one thing if the laws came from the spirit world, quite another if made by ordinary humans who walked the paths of Mother Earth. If they came from the Great Spirit all people, including the hairy faces, should obey them.

"These laws are indeed handed down from God," White replied. "In ancient times a holy man descended from a high mountain carrying blocks of stone upon which God, Himself, inscribed words such as these. The laws were meant for all peoples whether they be white, red, yellow or black."

The translation made the crowd murmur again. Laws imprinted on stone by the Great Spirit were good. Ancients of their own tribes recorded great hunts, victorious battles and legends on rocks and walls of stone. However, they knew little about yellow or black people. A few had seen trappers at rendezvous with black skin. Old timers like Lone Wolf remembered a black man who traveled with the explorers, Lewis and Clark. Others had heard it said the hairy faces kept black people as slaves. To rule slaves by the same laws as those observed by their masters was odd. Yet, there was something noble about it. Fearless beings could do such things. Tribes of the plateau were that kind of humans.

Yellow Serpent, watching his people, understood their thoughts. If they were satisfied, it was best the laws be adopted. He stood again to speak. "The laws of God will be the laws of our people," he announced.

Other tribal leaders, mainly those of the Cayuse, doubted the wisdom of adopting the laws. There was a pause in the proceedings while they argued among themselves. When asked if they had made up their minds, Buffalo Horn and Tiloukaikt said no. They needed time to think. It was too important a decision to make in haste. Five Crows said yes. He was prepared to adopt the laws. Then it was the turn of Stickus to speak. Rather than face Indian Agent White, Stickus turned away from him and spoke to the people. "Our Nez Perce brethren live by these laws. Is it not wise to seek their knowledge? Are we too proud to listen to their words?"

"Let our neighbors speak," came a reply from the crowd.

Vision Seeker's skill with the Boston's language and knowledge of their talking paper, made him a natural spokesman for the Nez Perce. He stood, adjusted his blanket and silently surveyed the gathering. His dark, emotionless features gave no hint of his thoughts or the position he would take. The strong resonant voice carried to onlookers at the very edge of the meeting grounds.

"Many of you have seen the mountain we call *Yamastas* where all our people went when all things on Mother Earth were swallowed by the great flood. Our people survived this peril and went on to become the great tribe we are today. These honored, trusted ancestors traveled this path without a written language; they had no laws marked on talking paper. The language they spoke and the laws which governed them were rooted in their hearts. By looking into their hearts they knew what was bad and what was good."

Vision Seeker paused to let his words sink in. "I ask you to look into your hearts. Do you see this code of laws written there? If you do that is good. The laws will be followed and all will be well. If your heart does not hold these laws, and I fear that many hearts do not, there is great trouble ahead. If you are wise you will read what your hearts hold. Only your heart can tell you if these laws are good or bad."

Again Vision Seeker silently surveyed the gathering. Then, just as impassively as when he had stood to speak, he sat down. He pulled the blanket tightly around his shoulders, his eyes fixed on the distant horizon. Not a muscle quivered as Indian Agent White gave him a furious glare and jumped to his feet.

"It is well and good to listen to words written in one's heart,"

White said, his voice so strident a flock of magpies in a locust tree near the foot of the hill flew up and away. "When it comes to establishing and enforcing laws it does not work. One heart may say one thing, another person's heart may say something entirely different. To work properly laws must be the same for everyone. To make this so we put our laws on talking paper. In this way all people see the same laws and therefore know when they do right and when they do wrong.

"We thank our good Nez Perce friend for his eloquent and well meant words. But is it right for the Nez Perce to say how the Walla Walla, Cayuse or other tribes shall conduct themselves? No! It is not right. Each tribe must decide for itself what is right and what is wrong. They must chose a chief who, like Yellow Serpent, knows what is best for his tribe. The chief is the one who accepts the laws. He is the one responsible for seeing that they are observed. Since the Cayuse have no tribal chief, it is time they have one who is not afraid of making important decisions like this."

Buffalo Horn, always alert to opportunity, leaped to his feet to tell the people why he should be Chief of all Cayuse. Before Buffalo Horn finished his harangue, Five Crows stood up to argue his cause. Educated at the hairy faces' Nez Perce mission school, he knew the hairy faces' language and mysteries of the talking paper. These abilities alone were sufficient reasons for the people to choose him to guide the Cayuse through the stormy times that would surely come. "I know the ways of the Great Spirit Book," Five Crows argued. "Since these are God's laws, a man who walks and talks with God should see they are enforced."

"Ah!" uttered Joe who sat beside Michael on the top rail of the mission corral. Now he knew why Five Crows made his visit to the Lone Wolf camp and left so agitated. The ambitious Cayuse leader wanted to be chief so badly he implored Vision Seeker to speak on his behalf and Vision Seeker refused.

The debate went on until White, who favored Five Crows, arbitrarily stated Five Crows would be Chief of all Cayuse. The announcement created chaos. Buffalo Horn jumped to his feet. Furiously he shook his fist at the Indian agent.

"You act in haste," he shouted. He then turned to address the crowd. "A chief must be a leader, a man who knows our ways and customs."

Buffalo Horn gave Five Crows a scathing glance. "This man has a lodge on the Umatilla. Does he live there? No! He sits in Lapwai mission school, learning things of the white man's world. Will this knowledge make him do good for our people? Is this man to tell us what is right and what is wrong? Our Nez Perce friend spoke wisely; laws should be in one's heart. This man, Five Crows, has nothing in his heart. It is as empty as a squirrel's nest at the end of the Season of Melting Snow."

"Hiya-ho!" someone shouted. One did not slander a fellow tribesman, especially in front of outsiders. The crowd began to rumble. Everyone was on his feet. White shouted for order. No one paid him the least bit of attention. Joe nudged Michael. They both jumped down from their perch on the rail fence. Now was the time they had been waiting for -- the perfect opportunity to cut free Buffalo Horn's dappled gray stallion.

VIII

There is a time coming . . . when many things will change.
Strangers called earth men will appear among you.

Sweet Medicine, Cheyenne

Michael uttered an exultant yell. Frisky as two colts the brothers darted away from the turbulent crowd. No one paid them the least attention. Into the higgledy-piggledy collection of tents and tipis they raced, dodging through narrow passageways and hopping over tether ropes and lodge ties. Startled by their sudden appearance, people who had remained in camp popped out of their shelters like startled prairie dogs.

"Hurry! Run to the council grounds. A Cayuse chief is chosen," Michael shouted. The people, mostly women and children, began chattering -- should they go or stay? The vindictive clamor from the council meeting had risen to fever pitch. Something serious was indeed underway. A mother snatched up her child and raced for the grounds. Everyone quickly followed. The brothers grinned. The pathway ahead was clear. There was no one to witness the deed.

Buffalo Horn's prized mount was tethered close to the horseman's lodge. The large dark eyes grew round; the dappled gray pulled on the halter line, jerking its head and pawing the ground. The brothers had approached the high-spirited animal too quickly. Michael put out a hand and spoke soft, soothing words.

"Easy! Easy! We will not hurt you. We come to set you free." The big horse reared up as though to charge, the front hooves thrust out as weapons. Michael stood his ground. The front hooves dropped to the ground; the horse backed away, its eyes flashing. Then, with its powerful hind legs, it kicked Buffalo Horn's lodge down.

"Whoa!" Michael reached for the rawhide tether line. The horse swerved away, the big hooves tearing up huge chunks of turf.

Joe could see the frightened animal would never let them near. The only way to free him was to cut the tether line. Joe unsheathed his knife. The sight of the shiny bare blade terrorized the stallion even more. The big horse arched its neck and viciously jerked its head. The sharp hooves pounded the collapsed tipi lodge to bits. With a mighty heave, the halter bands burst.

Freed from halter and tether, the stallion wheeled about, knocking a second lodge down. With a snort, it galloped for the open fields. The big animal raced by other tethered mounts, sending them skittering, rearing and snorting. One horse after another broke free. With tether stakes and lines trailing, the excited animals bolted in all directions. More lodges collapsed. Bedding, robes, packs of possessions, anything left in the way, was trampled and scattered by the flurry of flying hooves. A cyclone could not have created greater damage. Clothing laid out to dry was snapped up by trailing ropes and stakes. The fluttering garments bounced along raising clouds of dust. Dogs, aroused by the commotion, barked and gave chase. Horses still tethered whinnied and ran in circles. The thunder of hoofbeats drifted across camp to the council grounds. "Horses! Horses!" an excited youth shouted, "the animals are running free!"

A council member turned to look and began to shout and run. "The boy is right! The horses are getting away. It's a raid! Hurry, or all will be lost." Arguments were forgotten. The election of a chief ignored. Nothing was more important than saving their precious horses. Men whose mounts had not broken free snatched up their weapons, swung on the backs of their mounts and rode wildly after the fast disappearing horses. Joe and Michael, who had kept their mounts securely tied nearby, mounted up and galloped away, too. Men left afoot ran frantically to the pasture to catch a horse from Tiloukaikt's herd. The animals, already spooked, scattered like frightened quail. Buffalo Horn stared at his broken lodge and the space where his stallion had stood. His mounted son, Red Calf, raced up to give him his hand. He pulled his father up behind him. With a shout and a slap of the reins, they sped off riding double. From the campsite came shouts of alarm followed by shrieks of horror as women and children spied their ruined lodges and trampled possessions. Running hither and thither, they attempted to retrieve what items they could. A frightened youngster, a mother who had lost her child, and frustrated Indian Agent White were the only ones left on the council grounds.

With its neck arched and mane streaming in the wind, Buffalo Horn's dappled gray galloped directly through Tiloukaikt's herd. Stallions snorted and turned to give chase. Mares squealed and scattered in all directions. A drove of geldings whinnied and wheeled in a circle, then took off after the fast disappearing stallions. Breaking through fences and trampling seedlings, the frenzied animals raced through outlying fields, leaping streams and irrigation ditches. Tiloukaikt's herders hurried from the Indian village to turn the stampeding animals. Their efforts were fruitless. It was like trying to stop the flow of the Great River at flood stage.

Joe and Michael rode alongside the exasperated pursuers. At the edge of Tiloukaikt's pasture lands, where they were hidden by a thick bank of trees, they reined to a stop. After the last group of horsemen swept by, they turned to gallop west to take the trail to the lower Umatilla. When sounds of the frantic chase receded, the brothers pulled their mounts to a trot. They grinned at each other, then laughed so hard they nearly fell from their saddles.

They passed through the rugged rocky bluffs that channeled the Great River on its way to the ocean. Below the basalt wives of Coyote they stopped to rest. From here on they had to be watchful. They were on the fringes of Buffalo Horn's pasture lands. After spring flood waters receded, the horseman liked to graze his animals in grassy glens along the south bank of the river. Herders often remained with the horses to keep them from straying. Stumbling onto one of Buffalo Horn's men could spell disaster. Joe glanced at the skyline. The sun had dipped below the escarpment.

Michael searched for the camping gear he had left on the trip to deliver Geiger's message to Stickus. It was where he'd left it. "Why not make use of it," Joe suggested. "Camp here for the night and start early in the morning. There's no point in pushing our luck."

At sunup the brothers again were on their way. They had spent most of the night shivering around a small campfire. They were stiff, sore and hungry but in high spirits. So far, there was no sign of

Buffalo Horn or any of his riders.

They crossed miles of sagebrush and rocky terrain before coming to the open grasslands that stretched to the Umatilla River. The brothers dismounted near a spring, watered their horses and drank their fill. They were starving. Michael's hidden cache had contained little food. They tethered their mounts in a thick cluster of sagebrush and hiked up a rocky slope. From a hilltop they gazed across a landscape dotted with the many horses Buffalo Horn and his people possessed. Only in the far distance did they see signs of human presence, tendrils of smoke drifting skyward from village lodge fires.

The brothers hunkered down to search among the grazing animals for Michael's two horses. Bays, browns, blacks, buckskins, duns, grays, roans, piebalds, pintos -- every color and marking met their eyes but none resembled Michael's two lost horses.

"We have to move nearer," Joe said. "We'll never spot them from here. It's getting so I can't tell one horse from another."

Keeping behind a protective screen of sagebrush, they made a wide circle to the south, frequently forced to hide. Herders came to rope a horse or chase a few animals into pole corrals. None of the riders appeared to act anything but normal. News of the council meeting disaster apparently had not reached the lower Umatilla. Late in the morning the brothers heard voices coming straight for them. Before they could hide two boys came into view. They stopped to stare. Michael gave them a friendly wave. "Hunting cottontails," he explained.

"Rabbit trails there." The boys pointed to the east, the direction the brothers had traveled.

"Thank you." Michael gave the boys another friendly wave. "They will not say anything until tonight," Michael said with assurance he did not feel.

Another tense moment came when two riders from the east galloped through the sagebrush and onto the grassy plain, scattering the grazing horses as they passed. They rode so near the brothers could hear the horses snort and see sweat marks on their sides.

Michael motioned toward the riders. One was Cloud Bird,

Buffalo Horn's eldest son. "They bring word of trouble in Waiilatpu. Every rider in the village now will be on guard," Michael warned.

The brothers retreated into a protected ravine, one that still provided a view of the pasture fields. The two riders barely disappeared into the village before a group of horsemen rode out to circle the herd, combing through outlying bushes and tree groves for strays. They drove the horses toward the village on the river. In a short while another group of horsemen appeared, headed by Cloud Bird and leading spare horses east on the trail toward Fort Walla Walla.

Joe grinned. "We're safe. They have no thought for us. Buffalo Horn sent Cloud Bird for fresh mounts. He is having trouble rounding up the runaways. Now we can start searching for your pony and mare in earnest. The home village is practically left unguarded."

Late in the day they found the two horses grazing in a patch of grass near the Umatilla, close to the river bank village. Michael breathed a sigh of relief. He almost had given up. He started for the black and white pony he had named Magpie, but Joe pulled him back.

"Wait until dark. Someone may be watching. No need to raise an alarm."

"I will not go to them. They will come to me. Then we'll see if someone watches." Michael dropped to his knees and crawled through the brush to the edge of the grassy plot. He put two fingers to his lips and whistled. The black and white pony raised its head, lifted its ears and whinnied. Slowly it cantered toward Michael. As Magpie entered the fringe of brush Michael wrapped his arms around the pony's neck and buried his head in its mane. He was so choked he barely could speak. Never before had he realized how much he loved his four-legged companion. "Come, boy, we're going home," he said, patting his precious pony on the soft black muzzle.

The black mare soon followed. The brothers tethered the horses in a clump of thick sage and sat down to wait. After dark they mounted up and wended their way south, leaving Buffalo Horn's pasture grounds behind. The next afternoon they ran into the leader of the upper Umatilla Cayuse and his party returning from Waiilatpu. Stickus held up a hand in greeting.

"You did not stay to eat the meat of the cow that pulls the plow?" he said to Michael, referring to the ox Agent White had killed and barbecued. The Cayuse leader's sharp eyes examined the black and white pony and mare. The reason for the young men's absence from the council grounds was quite clear. They had probably caused the commotion that turned the council meeting upside down. That was the trouble with youth, it was impatient. He should have told them of his plan to test White's code of laws. It was too late now. These two young men had to face the wrath of Buffalo Horn on their own. He lifted his hand to motion the column forward.

Stickus had enough worries to trouble him without getting involved in anything more. He had taken part in every council deliberation. The discussions usually ended up in wrangling. Hardly a Cayuse in the crowd believed in the laws, yet they had been adopted. No one gave the consequences serious thought. Many of the people voted for acceptance only to get the meeting over. They were tired; they were hungry. They wanted business matters settled so they could feast on Agent White's delicious smelling barbecued ox.

The Indian agent was as shortsighted as the Cayuse, Stickus thought. White chose Five Crows as chief, not because he was a leader but because he had attended the Nez Perce mission school at Lapwai and knew the ways of the hairy faces' talking paper. The Indian agent would soon find the new Cayuse leader was hard to manage and changeable as the weather. When things were good, he was there to take credit. When times became difficult, he was not to be found.

Stickus muttered to himself. Why couldn't he have stood up like Buffalo Horn and said what he thought? It was bad enough to have Five Crows chosen as chief of the Cayuse but soon he also would be named a member of the missionaries' church. If anyone deserved membership in the Church it was himself. No Cayuse lived by the teachings of the God, Jesus Christ, more faithfully than he. The injustice was like a knife thrust in the heart. In many ways the Christian religion was cruel, Stickus thought. One had to wait until after death to receive its rewards.

Stickus urged his mount into a lope. He wanted to be by himself, away from the eyes of his followers. They knew the disappointment he suffered and wondered what he would do. He could not face the prospect of living under Five Crows' rule. He had a good notion to leave the upper Umatilla, take his people away. That was the answer. He would take his people over the mountains to buffalo country and hunt the shaggy beasts, erase thoughts of the Waiilatpu council meeting from his mind. He would forget Five Crows and Indian Agent White and his miserable code of laws.

After Stickus and his band disappeared from view, Joe reined his horse in. "The cat's out of the bag. Stickus and his band know what we've done and where we are. If any of his people are friendly with Buffalo Horn, they may very well tell him of meeting us -- that we have taken back the horses from his herd. Who knows what Buffalo Horn will do." Joe shook his head. "From here on we'd better travel with caution, maybe after dark. We've gone to too much trouble to fail now."

They came to a gully and followed it until they were well away from the trail. After a mile or so a cottontail dashed out of the brush. Joe quickly lifted his rifle and shot. The rabbit gave a few hops and dropped. "It's about time we had something to eat," Joe said. "The thought of missing Agent White's barbecued meat has my empty stomach growling."

They stopped near a little spring. While the horses grazed they made a fire, cleaned the rabbit and put it on a spit. They couldn't wait for the meat to cook and nearly ate it raw. Michael never felt happier. He had his beloved black and white pony back and was in the company of his Boston brother. "What more can I desire?" he thought. Riding and camping with his brother gave him a thrill unlike he'd had since his father took him on an overnight trip down the Kooskooskie. He wanted to tell Joe about it but did not know if he should. He knew so little about his Boston half brother. He was as difficult to understand as the Great Spirit Book called Bible. Joe never asked questions, never talked of himself, never spoke of his Boston home and eastern family and never expressed any desire to learn about their father's life in Nez Perce country. Boston Joe was as much of a mystery now as he was two summers ago when they first met.

Joe was having his own troublesome thoughts. He had made a quick review of his life and did not like what it revealed. He kept going in circles, from one failure to another. He drifted around like a shiftless no-good. He trapped in the winter and lazed about in the summer. He did not have a cent to his name. He was no good to anyone. What would Tildy and the grandparents think if they knew just how worthless he had become?

"You know we have a sister in Boston country," Joe suddenly blurted. "She's the same age as me. We are twins."

Michael stared at his brother. "Sister!" To learn he had a sister was beyond his comprehension. That she was a twin to Joe made the shock that much greater. Among his people multiple births were looked on with horror, as unnatural. They were caused by the "Evil One." Oft as not one and sometimes both newly born were put to death. Michael covertly studied his half brother. He looked all right but what about the sister? Was she deformed? He was afraid to ask.

"Was it hard for your mother to care for two babies?" That was a safe question.

"She never had to. Mother died when we were born."

Michael looked away. So the "Evil One" took the life of the mother and allowed the newborns to live. He studied the horizon in silence. He wanted to learn more about this Boston sister but felt it unwise to question his brother further.

IX

He stood amid halls of State,
In tattered garments fringed by storms,
And told how he had ridden with fate.

Whitman's Ride for Oregon, H. Butterworth

At the edge of the sandy coastal lands of Massachusetts Bay, where the terrain slopes up to meet rocky hills left by ancient ice sheets, lay the Jennings farmhouse that had been the family home since Puritan days. Here was where the mountain man known in the western wilderness as Little Ned was born and reared. Here was where the twins, Joe and Tildy, entered the world and where their mother left it at their birth. Neither the historic ancestral land nor these events held any interest for Tildy Jennings that spring of 1843. Every day she awakened at the first light of dawn dreading what the day would hold. Granny, the only mother she and Joe had ever known, lay downstairs dying.

Every morning the awakening ritual was the same. With unseeing eyes Tildy stared at the ceiling attempting to force her mind to accept the trials of another eighteen hours after which she could fall back into bed and enjoy a short period of forgetfulness again. The effort to compose her thoughts did little good. In desperation she seized a pillow and pressed it over her ears to stop the terrible sound of the elderly lady's painful breathing echoing up the stairwell. There was no escape. The tortured rasps permeated every room, grating like a dull saw on already frayed nerves.

Over the weeks Tildy asked herself time and time again, why did God with all of his mercy, torture this good woman? Granny had lived a life of hard work and self-sacrifice. Without straying one whit, for a lifetime she had observed the Ten Commandments and heeded the exhortations mouthed by Pastor Barclay and his predecessors who occupied the local Presbyterian Church pulpit. When it came to observing the laws of God and man, Granny was as hard and unyielding as the rocky soil on which the farmhouse stood. Yet, for days Granny lay suffering, her eyes bleak with the great pain that racked her thin wasted frame. Now she had lapsed into a blessed coma but the terrible, rasping breathing became more and more distressful hour by hour.

Tildy took a deep breath, got out of bed, wearily dressed and stumbled down the steep stairs. Besides sick room duties, barnyard and household chores awaited her and she had to keep a watchful eye on Granddad. With his mate bedridden, the old man was lost. His aimless wandering about the farm was almost as disconcerting as watching over her grandmother who lay dying.

Tildy built up the fire and put the teakettle on. Her thoughts turned to her brother, Joe. What was he doing? Why didn't he come home? Why should she shoulder all the drudgery and heartbreak alone? She had encouraged Joe to leave, to travel west and find their father. That didn't mean he was free of all family ties and obligations. He had been gone nearly four years. In that time he had written once, a letter from a place called Green River, a terse note, little more than an announcement of their father's death.

Tildy made a pot of tea. When it had properly steeped, she poured a cup for the overnight nurse and took it into the sick room. The nurse looked up from her knitting to give a tired smile and a perceptible shake of her head. There was no change, it said. Only Granny's harsh breathing made it known she lived.

Tildy poured a second cup of tea. She placed it on a platter with a bowl of sugar and small milk pitcher and carried it down the hall to her grandfather's room. She knocked on the door. "Granddad," she called. A trembly voice answered.

Tildy placed the platter on the night table. The melted candle stubs told her Granddad had slept badly, if at all. The spasmodic quiver in her stomach worsened. If he should also take to the sickbed . . . The thought was too horrible to pursue. She returned to the kitchen and poured herself a cup of tea. Absently, she stirred the contents until they were cold. If both grandparents died what would happen to her? Where would she go? What would happen to the farm? It already had fallen into disrepair and she could not afford hired help. Again, her thoughts turned to her absent brother. Until these last crushing weeks she had not realized how much she needed him. Someday soon she would need him even more. The decision that had to be made should come from him, the male heir to the Jennings' fortune, even as miserable as the inheritance now appeared.

Tildy glanced at the ticking clock and quickly jumped up and emptied the cold tea in the slops. What was she doing sitting like a lady of leisure? From the hen house came cackling of unfed chickens; from the barn came bellows of unmilked cows; from outside pens came bleats and snorts of hungry lambs and pigs. Every living creature on the farm seemed to demand attention at once. Then there was Pastor Barclay. He would arrive for his daily visit. He always managed to appear while Granddad was having a late morning snack. He said it was the right hour to meditate and pray with Granny. Granddad claimed he timed it so he could tie into Tildy's hot muffins.

Pastor Barclay arrived on schedule. The thin bay mare stopped dead still in the drive, her head hung low in relief as the heavy, rotund figure rolled from the hack. The shaggy tufts that grew down to cover the pastor's ears, the green unblinking eyes with deep, dark lines below them; and the huge gray coat with its pockets bulging and flapping with pamphlets, church bulletins and prayer booklets, gave him a nonhuman appearance. He reminded Tildy of the fluffy, watchful barn owl that kept the barnyard free of snakes and mice.

Unaware of the impression he presented, Pastor Barclay proceeded to perform his ministerial duty. He asked after Tildy's and Granddad's health, saw the nurse who was leaving to her carriage, and disappeared into the sick room to pray over Granny. The Jennings family, especially Granny, were faithful members of his flock. At one time Pastor Barclay had high hopes for youthful Joe. The pastor saw in him the makings of a man of the cloth but Joe was a disappointment. When it came time for him to attend the theological seminary he disappeared. Some said he went west to live the life of a mountain man like his father. Probably just as well, Pastor Barclay had long since decided. If Joe had taken after his father, he was off on some goose chase that wouldn't amount to a hill of beans.

Pastor Barclay came out of the sick room with his usual grave expression. He accepted the cup of tea Tildy offered. His thick, hairy-backed fingers wrapped themselves around a hot muffin. He took a large bite. His unblinking eyes solemnly studied Tildy as his huge jaws rhythmically moved.

"My dear girl, all this work and worry are turning you into skin and bones. Take yourself from the farm for a while. I say, there's a box supper tonight at the church. It's a social to raise money for Dr. Marcus Whitman, the missionary who works among the pagan Cayuse Indians. The new schoolmaster, Sandy Sanders, is adrift. I'm sure he'd welcome the opportunity to rescue a lovely damsel in distress. Please say you'll come."

Tildy shook her head. "What if Granny should wake up and need me? I would never forgive myself if I weren't here."

Barclay sucked the sweetness from each blunt finger and reached for another muffin. "My dear, your grandmother is no longer here in spirit. Angels are her companions now. If not already in heaven, she is halfway up the golden stairs. Our earthly presence no longer matters to her. I urge you to give yourself a break. Come to the box supper. You'll enjoy hearing Brother Whitman tell of his hazardous journey across the continent and arduous work among the redskin savages. Who knows? In his travels he may have run into your brother, Joe."

Tildy's eyes brightened. "Why, of course. If church services were around Joe surely would be there. Perhaps Missionary Whitman also knew Father."

For the first time in days a burst of energy coursed through Tildy's veins. She jumped to her feet and began to put away the tea things. Before he knew it, Pastor Barclay was hustled out the door. He gladly would have eaten another muffin but they had been whisked away. Tildy finished cleaning the kitchen and quickly swept through the rest of the house. At last there was a chance to learn what had really happened to her father and find out the whereabouts of Joe.

After the hurried house cleaning, Tildy spent the afternoon

preparing for the evening outing. She had a neighbor boy, Saul Abernathy, kill and pluck a chicken which she fried for the box supper. She sponged and ironed wrinkles from her good dress, the one she kept for special company and Sunday services. She ignored her grandfather's inquisitive glances. She did the chores and prepared the evening meal early. She dressed carefully and slowly. All of a sudden she had serious qualms about going unchaperoned with a man she had not formally met. If Granny were capable of passing judgment Tildy was certain she would disapprove. At the last minute Tildy set aside the food she had boxed and tied with a red ribbon. She did not feel right about the evening's outing. When the carriage rolled up and her escort came to the door, her resolve to remain home was shaken.

Sandy Sanders was unlike the man she envisioned, the stern teacher who caned students for the slightest misdemeanor. His freckled face had the shiny look of a fresh-washed schoolboy hoping to make a good impression on the first day of school. Tildy opened her mouth to make excuses. From the anxious look on the boyish face she sensed the poor man had suffered many previous rejections. She did not have the courage to add to them. She handed him the box supper and took his arm. He assisted her into the carriage and sat beside her, carefully keeping his distance. The carriage moved forward. Except for clucking at the horse, Sandy said nothing and Tildy was suddenly too exhausted to encourage conversation. Other than the plod of horse hooves, creak of harness and grating sounds made by turning wheels, the ride to church was made in silence.

The festive air of the church gave Tildy a feeling of guilt. Here she was having a good time while Granny lay dying. She glanced around for Sandy. She should not have come. She must ask Sandy to take her home. Before she could catch the youthful schoolmaster's eye, Pastor Barclay claimed her and introduced the guest of honor, Doctor Marcus Whitman.

Again, the mental image of the man she expected to see failed her. Instead of a tall, robust giant who strode across the continent in seven league boots, before her stood a person of medium age and medium height. He gave a stiff bow, looking awkward and out of place. Tildy felt a surge of sympathy. Here was a man accustomed to dealing with "savages," who conquered the wilderness and lived under the constant threat of death, now forced to beg for handouts from a group of mousy churchy people who had never ventured west of Springfield, Massachusetts. He was neither neat nor handsome. It appeared he had dressed in haste. His tie was awry -- shirt wrinkled and cuffs worn. Above a compact torso rose a large head covered with iron gray hair. He had a rather prominent nose with wide nostrils. A short clipped beard and mustache gave him a stern expression, yet the penetrating, sunken eyes examined her kindly and with interest.

In spite of the missionary's ordinary appearance, Tildy felt awed by his presence. The exploits of this man had already made history. For weeks Boston papers were filled with his accomplishments. He had crossed the high Rockies and rugged western plains in the dead of winter to plead with congress to save Oregon. The ride was so important to the future of the United States, professors at nearby Harvard College compared its historical significance to the midnight ride of Paul Revere. Still in the smelly buckskins he wore on the cross-continental journey, he wrangled audiences with Secretary of State Daniel Webster and President Tyler to warn them that if the US government did not act promptly Oregon Territory would fall to the British. He demanded troops be sent to lay claim to the land and protect US citizens. After leaving Washington Whitman traveled from one city and village to another seeking funds and promoting Oregon. He wanted the people's help in relieving the lot of the Indian. But most of all he wanted to have this vast western wilderness settled by US citizens. In the spring he hoped to lead the largest caravan yet to make the trek across the continent.

After the introductions, Marcus Whitman gave his beard a quick brush. He glanced at Tildy, the deep set eyes twinkling with amusement. Tildy suddenly realized she had been staring. She cleared her throat to speak but what could she say to this man who gave advice to the President and Secretary of State? Then she remembered this was her chance to learn about her father and brother. She quickly asked if he had known Nathaniel Jennings and Joe Jennings, father and son who worked trap lines in the Rocky Mountains.

The missionary looked away, seemingly absorbed in the activities at the end of the hall. A crowd had gathered around the table on which were stacked the box suppers. The people were waiting for the auctioneer to appear. Each box supper was to be bid on. The highest bidder then had the pleasure of sharing the box supper with the lady who prepared it. The money raised would go into Missionary Whitman's fund. "Did this young lady know about her father's life out west?" Whitman wondered. She certainly knew little, probably nothing, about her father's Nez Perce family.

"Yes," he carefully answered. "On my first trip west I met your father at the trappers' yearly rendezvous. The time sticks in my mind because on that occasion I removed an arrowhead from the well known mountain man, Jim Bridger, and another from some fellow whose name I don't recall. Your brother, Joe Jennings? Of course I know him. On several occasions he has visited our mission at Waiilatpu. If I remember correctly, last fall he and two trapper companions left to go trapping in the Oregon mountains they call Siskiyous. I must say you resemble each other. Quite a remarkable likeness."

"There should be. They're twins," Pastor Barclay interjected.

"Ah, so that explains his good looks and winning ways," the missionary said graciously. He moved away to greet others but his mind lingered on the handsome young woman. Her eager, expectant look left him with a feeling of guilt. Had he done right by omitting to tell her about her Indian relations? He fervently hoped not. When he next saw young Joe Jennings he must sit down with him and have a heart to heart talk. The young man should realize that matters like this surface, usually at a most inconvenient time.

There was no reason for Marcus Whitman to concern himself over Tildy. All evening she savored the news. Joe was alive and apparently well. And now she knew how to get in touch with him. She would send a letter with Missionary Whitman asking Joe to come home, or at least help with advice.

The evening ended as pleasantly for Tildy as it began. Sandy

Sanders bid an exorbitant price for Tildy's box supper. She daintily nibbled at the fried chicken while he wolfed his down. It was obvious the freckled-faced young man did not eat well. A protective feeling welled up inside her. He needed someone to take care of him. On the ride home Sandy's apparent shyness disappeared. He talked a blue streak. Tildy was pleased to find he was well read and surprisingly knowledgeable about national affairs.

"Dr. Whitman has done this country a great favor," Sandy declared. "He says Mr. Webster was on the verge of trading US claims on Oregon Territory to the British for New Foundland and the cod fisheries there." Sandy shook his head. "Brother Whitman rescued us from disaster but there's plenty still to be done. George McDuffie, the senator from South Carolina, claims Oregon is too far away and too difficult to reach to be of any worth. He said it would take the wealth of the Indies to run a railroad across country to the mouth of the Columbia.

"I hope this doesn't bore you, but I get upset with the narrow-minded thinking that goes on in Washington. McDuffie is an example. When asked if Oregon had agricultural prospects, he replied, 'I would not, for that purpose, give a pinch of snuff for the whole territory.' Isn't that stupid? Brother Whitman says the soil out there is so rich almost anything grows. He believes people like McDuffie will soon change their thinking. I dare say they will if Brother Whitman goes to Washington very often."

Sandy glanced at Tildy sitting quietly at his side. "I'm sorry. I don't know why I'm blabbing like this. I really don't care a fig about Oregon. I'm happy to teach school in civilized New England." The remainder of the trip to the Jennings home was made in silence.

Sandy Sanders handed Tildy down and walked her to the porch. For a moment their eyes met. Sandy's demeanor had changed from that of a fresh-faced schoolboy to that of a male on the trail of a prospective mate. Shaken by her perception of his intention, Tildy hastily said good night and stepped inside. Granddad Jennings sat at the kitchen table, his face a picture of misery. Tildy knew at once. During her absence Granny had died.

X

*On the arrival of Dr. Whitman in Washington he found
he had not started one day too soon to save the
northwest coast for the United States.*

Wm. Barrows, OREGON; THE STRUGGLE FOR POSSESSION

Granny Jennings' burial was less distressful than Tildy anticipated. It was wonderful to know her long suffering grandmother had
been finally released from her agony. Pastor Barclay and the neighbors, especially the Abernathys, pitched in to help lay Granny to rest
in the family plot. But Tildy's troubles were far from over. She faced
the funeral expenses and the terrible mound of bills that had collected
during the long illness. They all seemed to come due at once.

Granddad Jennings was no help. For days he did little but sit
in the rocker and stare into space. He did not seem to care what was
taking place. When Tildy asked about the family savings he gave her
a blank look. Whenever money came into the house from Granddad's
pension or the sale of farm produce, it was Granny's habit to set aside
a portion of the amount received for the church and an equal amount
for the cracked sugar bowl that sat on the top kitchen shelf. "Who
will not keep a penny never shall have many," was a favorite saying of
hers. But when Tildy went to look the sugar bowl was empty. The
savings set aside in the bank were gone, too. The money went to
satisfy Boston specialists who Granddad had called in to prolong
Granny's life, the bank clerk said, sadly shaking his head.

The farm did realize a small income from the sale of milk and
eggs and Granddad received a monthly pittance from the academy
where he had served as headmaster. These amounts barely kept
food in the larder. Tildy gradually came to realize the Jennings family
was one step from the poorhouse.

During Granny's illness and immediately after her death, helpful neighbors brought gifts of food: slabs of bacon and joints of hams
from smokehouses; vegetables and fruit from cellars; and dishes of

various kinds from kitchens of generous housewives. A few days after the funeral this flow of free foodstuffs ceased. Now, it seemed, nearly every mouthful came from the shelves of the village store.

Tildy awakened every morning dreading the day ahead. Bill collectors arrived with smiles and left with scowls. She didn't even have words of hope to give. In the past annual drafts arrived from her father and finally one from Joe. These Granny had hoarded, parceling the dollars out over the months until the next bounty arrived. During the past two summers there had been no such windfalls. There was no reason to believe this year should be any different than the last two.

Next door neighbors, especially the Abernathys, pitched in to do what they could to help keep the farm from foundering. Melody Abernathy, who once had been sweet on Joe, worked the fields, plowing, harrowing, seeding and harvesting. Teenager Saul Abernathy, watched over the horses and cows. He pitched hay down from the loft and mucked out the cow barn and stable, keeping them reasonably clean. Bithiah Abernathy, the youngest of the Abernathy tribe, searched the orchard and windbreaks for stray chicken nests and collected the eggs. At times Bithiah milked the cows and slopped the pigs. Even with this help, every day was filled with work and worry for Tildy, partly because Granddad remained in a trance. He did no work. He gave no advice. He barely uttered a word from morning until night. She was afraid to leave him by himself for fear he might take his own life.

"I see no way out of it," Pastor Barclay said one afternoon on a visit to the farm. "You must sell the place. You cannot continue like this. The church can give some help but our resources are limited. If you decide to sell, I'll pass the news around."

Sandy Sanders, who, since the church box supper, had become a regular caller, also bashfully hinted she should sell out and move in with him; as his lawful wedded wife, he hastened to add.

Tildy tactfully sidestepped Sandy's proposal. She had no intention of tying herself to a schoolteacher whose future was no brighter than her grandfather's had been. Working and living in one place all her life only to end up church mouse poor had no appeal.

As the days passed into weeks and Granddad did not improve, Tildy began to think more and more about Pastor Barclay's advice and Sandy Sanders' offer of marriage. Neighbor Abernathy also took her problem to heart. Next year Melody was getting wed, he said. The young man who would become his son-in-law would take over his farm. He and Mrs. Abernathy had decided to homestead in the west. Brother Whitman's talk of Oregon had given them itchy feet. If she wished to sell the Jennings' acreage he'd speak to the prospective son-in-law. He was a man of means, Abernathy hinted, and could easily pay generously. That would solve her financial problems and give her the opportunity to move into town where she could give Granddad better care.

Tildy thanked Abernathy for his concern, but could not bring herself to make such a drastic decision. The home had been in the family since before the Revolutionary War. Old timers claimed a decisive battle had been waged between the rock fences that separated the Jennings' pasture from that of the Abernathy farm. It was the only place Granddad had ever lived. It was unthinkable to ask him to leave, especially so soon after Granny's death.

Later Sandy Sanders came to call. Again, in his bashful manner, he suggested she sell and move into town. He was enlarging and fixing up his house so she and Granddad could live there in comfort. To keep neighborhood gossips quiet, she could stay at his sister's place until a proper mourning period had passed, then they would wed. That night Tildy sat down and wrote her twin a letter. She would never forgive herself if Joe unknowingly returned to find the old home place occupied by strangers. She addressed the envelope in care of Marcus Whitman and put it out for the postman. Tildy was not aware that oftentimes it took nearly a year for post to reach an addressee in far off Oregon.

#

Buffalo Horn was beside himself. He had spent the better part of two days running down and rounding up his animals that had scattered from Waiilatpu to beyond Fort Walla Walla where the Snake drained into the Great River. To his painful distress, Buffalo

Horn found his favorite mount disabled. The frog, the soft cushioning of the front left hoof of the dappled gray stallion, was so badly gashed, the big horse could barely hobble. Buffalo Horn was unable to bring the injured animal home, leaving it in Waiilatpu. He borrowed a mount from Tiloukaikt's herd, a lean, mouse colored animal with a wall-eye, an animal he normally would have disdained to ride.

Everything about the Waiilatpu council meeting had conspired to humble him, Buffalo Horn thought glumly as he jogged along on the jarring journey home. He had lost the coveted post as Chief of all Cayuse to his neighbor, Five Crows. The knowledge stuck in his craw like a cocklebur. The obnoxious man possessed some of the best grazing land on the middle Umatilla. He did not tend to it himself but left it in the hands of his wives. That was another thing about the disgusting creature. Five Crows collected wives like most men collected battlefield trophies -- four of them or was it five? The thought was so disturbing Buffalo Horn dug his heels into the poor wall-eyed mount's sides, making it jump, nearly pitching him into the brush.

Arriving at his home village did little to soothe Buffalo Horn's ruffled nerves. His sons, tired from chasing after stray horses, lay asleep. He roughly prodded each of them awake. "Get up, lazy ones," Buffalo Horn scolded. "There is work to do. Roundup our horses. Bring them close to camp. After two sleeps we take them to pasture in high country where grass will soon appear."

Grumbling to themselves, Cloud Bird and Red Calf went to do their father's bidding. They rousted out their fellow herders and rode away from the village toward the far corners of Buffalo Horn's grazing lands. Throughout the day the horsemen rode to and fro, flushing horses from ravines and out of pockets of high brush. The air grew thick with dust and pungent with the smell of greasewood and sage. From meadows along the Great River to the sand dunes and rock-ridged escarpment that marked the southern border of Buffalo Horn's pasture fields, the riders scoured the countryside until every animal: gelding, mare, colt and stallion had been brought in. When the task was finished Buffalo Horn mounted the borrowed mouse colored horse and circled the herd, his sharp eyes intent on every milling animal. He prided himself on knowing the markings of every horse he possessed. His sons rode with him, weary and sore from the day's work but pleased in the knowledge of a job well done.

After they circled the herd, Buffalo Horn, rode back and inspected the animals more closely. He scowled. "Two are missing," he said.

"Father, you are mistaken," Cloud Bird protested. "We rounded up every horse in our pasture grounds."

Buffalo Horn glared at his oldest son. "Do not tell me what horses I see and what horses I do not see. An Appaloosa and a black mare are not here."

The brothers glanced uneasily at each other. When they brought the mission boy's horses in they told their father they found them grazing on the north range. He did not question his sons but took them at their word. As he always did when horses strayed onto his pasture fields, Buffalo Horn immediately claimed them as his own. He was particularly pleased with the black and white pony. It had the appearance of racing stock and was certain to bring a good price. He was also pleased with the mare. It was in good shape and had the look of stamina. He would use it on the trek to the Blue Mountains.

Red Calf, who read his father's mind better than did his brother, quickly answered. "Father, these animals were so special we held them in a pasture near the village."

"Good! Good!" Buffalo Horn gave his sons a glance of approval. "Your actions are wise. Bring them here."

Feeling pleased with themselves, Red Calf and Cloud Bird rode to the meadow bordering the river. The pasture field was empty! The black and white pony and black mare had disappeared.

#

Forty miles away as the crow flies, the two horses also gave Michael Two Feathers and Joe Jennings reason for concern. Now that they had rescued the animals, how could they keep them safe? Stickus had warned them that when Buffalo Horn found the horses missing he would make big trouble. That was why he wanted them left in place until after the council meeting. Joe glanced at Michael and shook his head.

"Stickus is right. When Buffalo Horn finds these horses gone he'll be madder than a wet hen," Joe said.

"Let him be angry." Now that he had Magpie back Michael was going to keep his four-footed friend, no matter the cost. He patted the silken neck and smiled.

Joe could tell Michael had not seriously considered the consequences that were certain to result from their rescue of the horses. They rode along silently for a while, but the thought of an irate Buffalo Horn and the actions he might take would not go away. It would be just like him to gallop into the mission compound and take a quirt to anyone who crossed his path.

"I think we'd better not show up in Waiilatpu with your pony and mare. Your black and white Appaloosa stands out like a bonfire on a dark night."

"We could paint the white spots black," Michael suggested.

The idea was so ridiculous Joe glanced at his brother in surprise. "That won't fool an expert horseman like Buffalo Horn. He'll see through it in a minute. Then, what'll you do with the black mare, paint her white?"

"Perhaps Lone Wolf and Vision Seeker will take them to Lapwai for a while," Michael said hopefully. "There they will be safe."

Joe nodded. "Good thinking. Let's wait until after dusk before we approach the mission and hope no one is waiting."

#

Indian Agent White was busy packing, preparing to leave for the Willamette Valley. He was anxious to get away. "Dad burn it!" White muttered to himself. The meeting had ended in complete chaos. What had gone wrong? In spite of the Nez Perce man's idiotic warning that laws must lie in one's heart and the wrangling between Buffalo Horn and Five Crows, he had kept the meeting reasonably well under control. Then that damned dappled gray stallion of Buffalo Horn's got loose and all hell broke out. In his pique at not getting named chief did Buffalo Horn have his men cut the stallion free to disrupt the meeting? What better way to embarrass the new Cayuse chief than to create pandemonium just as everyone was hoping to sit down to a barbecue feast?

White finished packing his bags. He wanted to be far away from the plateau before the Cayuse returned to their villages and began to think seriously about the code of laws they had adopted. He was in no mood for another hassle. Anyway, his presence was not needed. The tribe had a chief. It was up to Five Crows to enforce the laws. Yet, he had doubts about the new chief. Perhaps he should not have been so hasty and waited for the people to select their own chief. Five Crows was an educated man but arrogant. Would this new honor go to his head? From his actions, it already had done so. After the announcement that he was selected chief, Five Crows stalked around the council grounds, lifting his feet high like a tom cat wading through sticky mud. The disgust of the other candidates did not bode well either. Would they cause trouble, especially that Buffalo Horn? He was not the type of man to take something like this lying down.

White carried his bags out, strapped them on the pack mule and walked toward the mission house to say good-bye to Narcissa Whitman. The Indian agent saw Lone Wolf's band of Nez Perce still encamped and altered his course to avoid them. He did not want to hear another word from that seer into the future, Vision Seeker. Halfway to the mission house the sound of hoofbeats thundering down the Fort Walla Walla trail stopped White in his tracks. A pair of dogs ran under the compound fence rails and down the dusty roadway to bark. Through the open gates galloped Buffalo Horn trailed by his two sons. The three riders pulled their mounts to a skidding stop, throwing a cloud of dust in the Indian agent's face. Buffalo Horn leaped off his foam covered, mouse colored, wall-eyed mount and strode up to White, his blunt nose level with the Indian agent's face. In his right hand he held a riding crop which he swished menacingly back and forth. In a voice that rang above the heavy breathing horses, Buffalo Horn began a scolding tirade. White backed away, followed step by step by the angry horseman who finally thrust the riding crop into the retreating Indian agent's shirt front.

"How dare you threaten me! How dare you touch me!

What does this man want? I don't understand a word he says." White wiggled and dodged until his back was against the corral fence.

Buffalo Horn's two sons dismounted and came forward to stand shoulder to shoulder with their father. Frantically, White turned to the Lone Wolf camp for help. "Why do you stand there? Help me! What's the matter with these crazy people?"

Vision Seeker strolled forward. He said a few words to Buffalo Horn. The horseman turned to face him. A rapid flow of words came from the horseman's lips, accented with wild swings of his whip.

The Indian agent adjusted his clothes. "Well, what does he say?" he demanded.

"Buffalo Horn says two horses were taken from his herd," Vision Seeker translated. "He wants them back. He says it is your duty to see they are returned."

"It is out of my hands. If a crime has been committed he should take his complaint to Chief Five Crows. He knows good and well the chief of the tribe is responsible for enforcing the laws."

Vision Seeker translated this to Buffalo Horn. The enraged Cayuse leader took a menacing step toward White, causing the Indian agent to flinch. Vision Seeker held up his hand. "Agent White is right," he said to Buffalo Horn. "Your people adopted the laws. It is up to the chief of the Cayuse to see they are obeyed."

"These laws are like toothless wolves," Buffalo Horn snarled. "All howl and no bite. Who will enforce them? Five Crows!" He spit on the ground. He turned his back on White and motioned for his sons to mount up. All three horsemen galloped away as fast as they had appeared.

White pounced on Vision Seeker. "See what your talk did. Already the Cayuse doubt their laws." He strode away, his boots sending up angry puffs of dust with every step he took. At the mission house door he turned and shook a fist at Vision Seeker.

"I knew these laws would cause trouble," Vision Seeker said more to himself than anyone else. "The Cayuse people are not ready for them and this man White is too blind to see it."

In the mission house kitchen Narcissa Whitman ordered her

two helpers, Helen Mar Meek and Mary Ann Bridger, to set the table and went about preparing the evening meal. She had witnessed White's quarrel with Buffalo Horn. She, too, saw trouble ahead and feared for the Indian agent's life. She induced him to remain at Waiilatpu overnight and invited him to take part in the evening meal. The Indian agent agreed. It would be good to give Buffalo Horn a chance to cool his heels, he decided. He washed his hands in the river and when called to dinner sat down at the end of the table usually reserved for Marcus Whitman. He folded his hands and, without being invited, said a long prayer of blessing. His thoughts were anything but spiritual. While he prayed he silently patted himself on the back for the astute manner in which he got the Cayuse to accept the code of laws. Then he cleverly had avoided a ticklish situation with Buffalo Horn. He also warned himself to get out of the country before Five Crows found out what a mess he was in.

Lone Wolf and his family also prepared to partake of their evening meal. Joe and Michael, who had appeared as dusk fell, were invited to join them. The circle of men waited patiently as Quiet Woman deftly placed baskets and bowls of food before them. Joe eyed the preparations uncertainly. There were no plates, forks, spoons or knives. He would have to wait and see how to proceed. Lone Wolf looked skyward and then at the ground. He thanked Father Sky and Mother Earth for the bounty they had provided. On the far side of the circle Michael put his hands together and bowed his head to repeat the mission learned Christian blessing. The ceremonies completed, Lone Wolf put his hand in the nearest bowl and lifted a fistful of food to his mouth. Everyone but Quiet Woman, who remained watchful in the background, began to eat.

The food and the partakers of it were different at the two tables but conversation was much the same in the mission house as it was on the buffalo robes laid out in front of Lone Wolf's tipi lodge. White advised Narcissa Whitman to take herself away from Waiilatpu, if possible to the Willamette Valley. Until the people became accustomed to living under the code of laws, the Cayuse tribal lands would be unsettled, he said. At Lone Wolf's table, Vision Seeker, who was aware of the brothers' daring rescue of the horses, gave Michael much the same advice. It was best Michael leave Waiilatpu. If he remained at the mission Buffalo Horn was certain to search out the horses. It was foolish to think he could keep them hidden from the horseman. And he should not place any faith in the Indian agent's code of laws. They would not protect him. When Michael suggested the two horses be taken to Lapwai his grandfather, Lone Wolf, agreed but Vision Seeker frowned.

"The Nez Perce have enough problems without making enemies of Buffalo Horn," Vision Seeker said. "Right now he is like a dog that sniffs a porcupine and gets a nose full of quills. He will not forget the hurt until he has turned prickly porcupine upside down and given the unprotected belly a good nip."

Joe, who felt responsible for Michael's predicament, suggested Michael and he trade horses. He would take the pony and mare out of the country. He already had made up his mind to travel with Hawk Beak Tom and Hare Lip Bruce to search for gold in the Oregon desert. It was doubtful if Buffalo Horn would trail the horses there. Vision Seeker approved of the plan but Michael was reluctant. Now that he had Magpie back he did not want to let him out of his sight, but he saw no other way to keep his four-legged friend safe.

Vision Seeker's insight was correct. Buffalo Horn was like the sore-nosed dog. He could not forget the hurt of losing two horses. He vowed he would not let them go without a fight. Already he had lost face. He did not intend to have his reputation sullied any further. After leaving the mission he and his sons rode directly to Tiloukaikt's village. Savagely, Buffalo Horn told Tiloukaikt how Agent White had brushed him aside.

"He tells me Five Crows will enforce the laws. Foolish man! It makes me sick to think of what he has done to the Cayuse."

From Tiloukaikt's village Buffalo Horn and his sons rode on to Fort Walla Walla where the Cayuse leader complained to Trader McKinlay of his treatment and the way the code of laws would be managed. Buffalo Horn imparted the news in the belief it would turn Hudson's Bay against the Indian agent and the mission at Waiilatpu.

He argued that if the Redcoats acted promptly they could shut the mission down for good.

Fort Factor McKinlay said little but listened intently. He had no intention of taking part in the quarrel but it was important to remain friends with the Cayuse. He nodded agreeably, his mind busily sorting through the information. If what this Cayuse man said was true, pompous Indian Agent White had badly overstepped himself.

"Hmm!" McKinlay grunted thoughtfully, encouraging the leader of the lower Umatilla to keep talking. Perhaps this was his opportunity to make his mark on history. John McLoughlin, his superior at Fort Vancouver, did not recognize Elijah White's authority and did not want the obnoxious American meddling in Indian affairs. If sufficient rancor was aroused among the Cayuse perhaps they would send the Indian agent packing. That would please those in charge of Hudson's Bay and their politician friends in London. Every American that arrived in the Pacific Northwest was a threat to the British empire. As soon as Buffalo Horn and his sons left the fort, McKinlay sent a courier down river with a message apprising John McLoughlin of the temper of the Cayuse and Agent White's actions.

#

The authorities at Hudson's Bay and politicians in Great Britain had good reason to keep a close eye on happenings in the land of the Cayuse. At the time McKinlay's messenger left Fort Walla Walla, a large number of homesteaders had gathered on the west bank of the Mississippi ready to make the long trek across the plains. The recruiting work of Missionary Whitman had paid off. A newspaper reporter claimed a thousand people and one hundred twenty wagons were prepared to move west along with large herds of horses, cattle and mules. It was the largest immigration yet to set off on the long, torturous journey to Oregon Territory.

XI

If you are going to Oregon by all means go this spring . . . every man's neighbor and friends will move in that direction.

Jessie Applegate, 1843

The open space where the Waiilatpu council meeting took place was quiet and bare but the rancor it caused lingered on. The rumor that Marcus Whitman would return with an army to enforce the code of laws hung over Cayuse country like a menacing cloud. So worrisome was the threat, Tiloukaikt ordered scouts to watch the trails and report the comings and goings of every person entering or leaving the mission grounds. Suspicious activity of any kind could mean trouble. Watchers reported the departure of the three mountain men. One rode the mission boy's black and white pony and led away his black pack mare.

Tiloukaikt knew Buffalo Horn was anxious to retrieve the mission boy's horses but it was not his affair. He sent no word to Buffalo Horn. Instead, he gave orders for the watchers to keep the news to themselves. He did not want to get involved in anything that could cause trouble. The council meeting and its aftermath already had his people in turmoil.

Shortly after the trio of mountain men departed so did the last of the Nez Perce. They took the trail east to Lapwai. Michael Two Feathers, the mission boy, rode a ways with them and then returned. In a few days he, too, was gone. A watcher followed him to the camp of Stickus. He was last seen riding with Stickus' band en route to buffalo country. This report sent Tiloukaikt into a quandary. What was the matter with Stickus? It was no time to go buffalo hunting. Tiloukaikt thoughtfully puffed on his pipe. Was he the only Cayuse leader acting responsibly? Buffalo Horn was on a rampage. Five Crows, now Chief of all Cayuse, rode around flaunting his fancy clothes. Normally steady Stickus had fled across the mountains. Was there something happening that he was missing?

Tiloukaikt's unease increased when scouts noticed unusual activity in the mission compound. The missionary woman, Narcissa Whitman, also was preparing to leave. On the day of her departure she was trailed to Fort Walla Walla. There she joined a Hudson's Bay brigade that boarded river boats bound for Fort Vancouver. Tiloukaikt sat in his lodge mulling over the latest news. Why was everyone deserting the mission? Had Missionary Whitman left for good and sent word for his woman to follow? If true, the hated mission would soon fall into ruin and their troubles would be gone.

Tiloukaikt scowled. His thinking was false. Once hairy faces built wood and stone homes and put fences around land, they burrowed in and multiplied like prairie dogs.

#

"Blast it! Another day an' nothin' to show fer it," Hawk Beak complained as the former fur trappers turned gold prospectors made camp for the night. All three were disgusted. Gold was even more elusive than the wily beaver. For three weeks they had searched for the yellow stuff. Every ravine and stream was certainly hiding a bonanza but for all the searching and digging they had done, the only rewards they received were blisters and sore muscles. "We're gittin' nowhere," Hawk Beak continued to complain. "It's all the fault of thet miserable Peg Leg. If we find him I'll shake the gold whereabouts outta him. Yuh kin betcha yer life on thet."

Hawk Beak's attempt to pick up his friend's trail also ended in disappointment. Only a bearded man guiding a pack train across country remembered seeing Peg Leg and his companion. "Yep," the bearded man said, scratching his head. "If I remember correctly, t'was two of 'em. Mean lookin', tight-lipped fellas -- didn't say where they'd been or where they was goin'."

Undaunted, Hawk Beak still insisted they go deeper into the desert. They were certain to stumble onto gold. Joe had nothing better to do so went along. They traveled beyond Crooked River, stopping along the way to scout every gully, canyon and ravine. Scrub juniper and short-needled pine covered the terrain. From one horizon to the other everything looked much the same. Nowhere did they see the slightest hint of human life.

Unlike when they went into the mountains to trap, where each man worked a trap line by himself, Hawk Beak and Hare Lip Bruce remained close to Joe as if afraid he would find gold and not let them know. The constant togetherness quickly got on Joe's nerves. Hawk Beak grumbled and Hare Lip scratched, chawed and spat. Neither one said anything helpful or cheerful all day long. Right away Joe sensed the search was doomed. Not one of the three knew what gold looked like in the raw. Nevertheless, they proceeded to patrol the desert from the Deschutes to the Snake. Not the least speck of gold did they discover.

For the most part the gold seekers lived off the land. Antelope, deer and rabbits shot in the hills and on the plains and fish taken from the streams, were the viands served up when they were lucky. At other times they fell back on the small store of dried corn and beans they brought from Waiilatpu. With each passing day Joe became more and more disenchanted. He was wasting good time, time he should apply in doing something worthwhile. More and more he caught himself thinking of Tildy, Granddad and Granny. How disappointed they would be to see him now -- dirty, ragged and poor as the worst vagrant that called for handouts at their kitchen door. He wished he had one of those generous Granny handouts now. He hadn't tasted anything as good as Granny's cooking since he'd left his former New England home.

#

At the time Joe Jennings had these thoughts he would not have recognized the Jennings' farm. Tildy did not wait for an answer to the letter she sent Joe in care of Marcus Whitman. Reluctantly she agreed to do as Pastor Barclay, Sandy Sanders and Abernathy advised; she sold the farm and moved into town. The place where Joe had lived the first seventeen years of his life quickly experienced a drastic change. The old red barn where he spent many hours milking cows, was gone. The new owner immediately had it torn down. In its place he built a hen house as long as the driveway into the farm. From it came the busy sounds of clucking, cackling hens, the shrill chirp of chicks and the crowing of roosters. Abernathy's prospective son-in-law had his heart set on becoming New England's poultry baron.

Feeling guilty over selling the farm without Joe's approval, Tildy often returned to visit their old home. Every time the place came in view and she saw the changes that had occurred, she was perturbed. But what could she have done differently? As it was the price of the farm barely covered the debts that had piled up while Granny had been ill. To make ends meet Tildy worked several days a week as cook and housekeeper. The move to town did produce one good result; Granddad took a turn for the better. He found the next door neighbors were former students he had taught and counseled through a half-dozen years. Now they had children of their own and kept asking his advice about their studies. That was all Granddad needed to bring him back to life.

One problem did not go away. It hung over Tildy's head like Damocles' sword. Each week Sandy Sanders became more and more persistent. He wanted to set the wedding date and make plans for after they were married. Tildy put him off but he was not discouraged. He made a habit of calling several times a week bringing flowers and gifts for her and news of school happenings to Granddad. Sandy's visits left Tildy exhausted and feeling helpless. She wanted and needed his friendship but not at the price of marriage. At heart Sandy was a good person. The children at school loved him. He went to church, did not smoke or drink and hardly ever said a cross word. Pastor Barclay, the Abernathys, and everyone else for that matter, said how well matched they were. Mrs. Abernathy suggested she and Sandy have a double wedding. Melody and her intended would join them in the nuptial event. Wedding expenses would be cut in half that way, she shrewdly advised.

"I'll do nothing of the kind," Tildy informed her. "I won't make any more important decisions until we hear from Joe. He may expect Granddad and me to move out west. If that happens I don't want anything to stand in the way. I should hear something soon. I sent a letter to him in care of Brother Whitman. He will surely pass it on to Joe."

#

Tildy's letter was the last thing on Marcus Whitman's mind. He had more than enough concerns of his own. He did not captain the wagon train of homesteaders he recruited but felt responsible for every person who answered his call to populate Oregon Territory. He was fully aware of the challenges the wagon train members faced. People and livestock would traverse trails where wagons had never passed before. The difficulties were not unlike those Hannibal encountered in crossing the Alps. Families whose previous experience of hard travel had been over well worn roads between towns and villages of New England and the Ohio Valley now faced making a track through virgin land. Every day was filled with unexpected hazards: swollen river crossings, Indian war parties, insect hordes, high winds, dry camps and gully washing rains.

The vagaries of nature and hostile Indians were not the only perils. People witlessly endangered themselves. They used poor judgment, taking chances when they should have played it safe. They did not take care of equipment. It broke down and often they had no spares. They treated livestock carelessly. Mules, horses and cattle sickened. Oxen developed harness sores and went lame. The travelers were equally careless about their own health. They became needlessly sick from drinking bad water or eating strange berries or toadstools. They even fell beneath the iron-tired wagon wheels, lacerating flesh, mangling limbs and crushing bones. This tragedy happened to a child over whom Marcus Whitman sorrowfully read the last rites.

Riding a long-eared mule, the missionary was everywhere. Not only was he looked to for guidance in breaking trail, he was the wagon train's spiritual leader and doctor as well. He held services on the Sabbath, tended to the sick, set bones, delivered babies and provided counsel for people with problems they could not solve themselves. When no one else volunteered for hazardous duty, Marcus Whitman was there. At the Fort Laramie River crossing, high water from the runoff of melting snows blocked the trail. There was no other way but to turn wagon boxes into flat bottomed boats and pull the awkward craft from the eastern river bank to the one on the west. To do so someone had to swim across and anchor a line to the far river bank. Few in the party could swim. Those who could did not have the courage. Marcus Whitman had to swim across himself.

West of Fort Laramie Whitman received the first letter from his wife since he left Waiilatpu. The letter told of the troubles with the Cayuse; the attempt to break into Narcissa's room; the burned granary and gristmill; the fears the Indians had of soldiers coming up river; and their reluctance to adopt Elijah White's code of laws.

Whitman thrust the letter in a shirt pocket and did not look at it again. His first duty was to get these pilgrims to the promised land, he told himself. The mission would have to solve its problems the best way it could. At Fort Hall, Whitman had a more pleasant surprise. Riders with a pack train of supplies sent by Narcissa and the Spaldings of Lapwai, awaited him. Also on hand was his old Cayuse friend, Stickus. The leader of the upper Umatilla Cayuse had summered in buffalo country. A scout brought the Indian leader the news that Missionary Whitman, followed by a wagon train, had crossed South Pass and was approaching Fort Hall. Rejoicing at the thought of being reunited with his missionary friend, Stickus immediately set out for Fort Hall. With the missionary man back again all would be well in the Cayuse homeland, Stickus kept repeating to himself. His band could return to their home on the upper Umatilla and live in peace.

Whitman was pleased to receive the supplies from Waiilatpu and Lapwai and greet his Cayuse friends, but all did not go well at Fort Hall. At this point travelers had to decide whether to continue by wagon or transfer their belongings to pack animals as previous wagon trains had done. Captain Grant, the Hudson's Bay factor at the fort, argued it was impossible to proceed to Fort Walla Walla by wagon - - the terrain was too rugged and the Blue Mountains impassable except by pack animals. Whether Grant spoke truthfully or had instructions to stop the emigrants before they went farther, Whitman could not determine. In his own mind the wagons would get through. Three years previously the mountain men, Joe Meek and Doc Newell, had driven teams and wagons from Fort Hall all the way to the banks of the Umatilla.

The travelers, sick and weary from months on the trail, did not know who to believe. A man who should know the rugged trail ahead said it was impossible to accommodate wagons. Marcus Whitman, who they respected and depended upon, said they could get through if they only tried. The abandoned wagons parked higgledy-piggledy around the fort did little to inspire confidence in Whitman's argument. It appeared as though most of those who had previously traveled the track thought it best to discard wagons in favor of horses and pack animals. Despite the overwhelming evidence for making the change, many heeded Whitman. Under his guidance they had made it safely this far. They would not lose faith in him now.

However, lack of agreement on how to proceed split the wagon train apart. Discipline was abandoned. Groups went ahead as they pleased. Exasperated by the dissension, Whitman rode with the lead wagons, urging laggards to follow close behind. "The worst of the trip is still ahead," he warned. "The Blue Mountains have yet to be crossed. Early snows often block the passes. If that happens wagons mire down. Weary animals flounder. All you possess may be lost."

Beyond Fort Boise the column was forced to ford the Snake River. Here, a tragedy occurred that would haunt Marcus Whitman for the short years he had left to live. Myles Eyres, a man he had persuaded to take the trip to Oregon, fell into the river and was swept away. His body was never found. His wife and three children were distraught and penniless; the family wealth was carried in the money belt fastened around the husband's waist.

Whitman piloted the train across Powder River and into the Grande Ronde Valley. There a messenger brought word Reverend Spalding and his wife were deathly ill. Spalding thought his wife so near death he requested friends to hurry to Lapwai to take part in her burial. The news stunned Whitman. Eliza Spalding was the stalwart member of the Nez Perce mission. Immediately, he saddled up his mule and hurried ahead. Before leaving he asked Stickus, who knew the country well, to guide the wagon column through the Blue Mountains. Without hesitation, the devoted Christian Cayuse agreed.

#

Herders who guarded Buffalo Horn's horses in the foothills of the Blue Mountains, were the first in the Cayuse homeland to see the column of wagons. They left their herd unattended and galloped away at top speed. On lathered mounts, they rode into Buffalo Horn's village shouting the news. "Many-many, white mens come."

Buffalo Horn didn't believe the report. He scolded the herders and ordered his horse brought up. His people were too upset to even see straight. Accompanied by his sons, he made the long ride into the high country to see for himself. From a long distance away he stopped to stare. Like a chain of white ants, a line of covered wagons wended its way down the slopes. Buffalo Horn urged the gray stallion, recovered from its injuries, into a gallop. At the pasture lands he ordered his sons to round up the herd. He had no intention of allowing a single animal to fall into the hands of this hairy faced horde.

Back and forth Buffalo Horn and his sons charged, flushing animals out of thickets of trees and brush and hidden pockets among the hills. All the while Buffalo Horn ranted at the herders who had sheepishly returned. He called them idiots with no more sense than brainless children. How could they have let so many hairy faces take them by surprise?

The sight of Stickus, his Umatilla River neighbor, leading the wagon train added fuel to the horseman's ire. He jerked on the stallion's reins so viciously the dappled gray nearly pitched over backwards. He rode up to Stickus, seething. "Why do you bring these peoples to our land?" he demanded.

Buffalo Horn was not the only one stunned to see one of their own people lead the column of hairy faced ones and their land canoes into the Cayuse homeland. Entire families rode out to silently watch the hairy faces guide their wagons down the foothills and through the grasslands. The land canoes cut deep tracks like heavy, sharp-bellied snakes might make in the soil. The animals which pulled the land canoes had the look of smooth-skinned, light-colored buffalo cows with large ears and long horns. They were bony and thin. They walked with heads low, swinging them slowly from side to side as tired dogs did when searching for places to lie down.

The people driving the beasts did not look much better. They wearily plodded, paying little attention to where they were going. The men wore headgear heavy with grease and dust. Their coats hung on them like shapeless sacks, the kind one used to store grain in through the Season of Deep Snow. The legs of their pantaloons stopped short of shoe tops to expose thin shanks coated with dirt, sores and bruises.

The women rode in wagons or walked alongside the weary smooth-skinned animals, wearing dresses that had seen many washings. Although the sun was not out, great hoods of bonnets covered their hair and faces. They barely looked up. Only the youngsters appeared to have any life. The girls and boys skipped along, kicking up dust. One boy waved a knife at the Indian watchers. "Come near me an' I'll take yer scalp." His shrill voice ended in a squeak.

Michael, who had summered with Stickus in buffalo country and traveled with the Cayuse leader to Fort Hall, rode along with the wagon train. He found the journey unpleasant. The travelers eyed him with distrust. His buckskin dress and the two feathers fastened in his long hair made him appear completely Indian. Mothers whispered to their daughters and herded them away. Male youths gave him looks that seemed to dare him to make one false move. They discussed him as though he were deaf and dumb -- a creature much like the polecat or porcupine that they would put up with as long as he kept his distance. More than once he heard the words "Dirty Injun." He maintained his normal impassive expression, but at times he wished he had not gone to school. If he did not know what these people said he would not have the overwhelming urge to ride them down.

After Missionary Whitman left the column in care of Stickus, the words were increasingly hateful. There were loud and lengthy arguments about whether or not the Indian guide piloted the wagon train over the best route. When wagon wheels neared the edge of cliffs, or when climbs were extra steep and the teams flagged and had to double up, the teamsters shouted abuse at Stickus. This infuriated Michael, yet he maintained his calm and rode alongside the wagons as if everything were all right. Stickus, riding ahead of the column, remained oblivious to the complaints. He had promised his friend, Marcus Whitman, he would guide the wagon train through the mountains. Nothing was going to prevent him from doing as his Christian brother asked.

After a particularly hard day with breakdowns and only a few miles traveled, there was much talk among the teamsters of ignoring the Indian guide and continuing on their own. "Whitman says this man knows the country better than anyone," one voice said. "We'd be fools not to follow him."

"Yeah, but this Injun has never driven a team and wagon. How does he know where they can go and what they can do?" an angry voice answered.

"That's right! I say we git rid of the Injuns. Injuns don't count fer nothin' anyways. I'm surprised Whitman puts stock in 'em."

"How do yuh git rid of 'em? Yuh cain't talk to 'em, tell 'em ta go away."

"Why shoot 'em, of course. Ain't yuh heered, only good Injun is a dead Injun?"

"What about the kid? He ain't done no harm."

"Shoot him anyway. No need ta leave witnesses."

Michael rode up to the speaker, so close his horse brushed against the sleeve of the man's coat. "If you want to go to your graves in these mountains, shoot us. Before you find your way out you and your people will freeze and make food for the wolves."

The teamster's mouth dropped open, his eyes large as saucers. "I'll be switched. He speaks American bettern' we'uns."

From that day until they broke out of the Blue Mountains, the travelers treated Michael with respect and meekly followed Stickus. When the open vistas of rolling plains that extended as far as the eye could see appeared, the travelers uttered whoops of joy. Yet, neither emigrants nor their Cayuse guides realized the historic roles they played. They had just opened the Oregon Trail.

XII

How can the spirit of the earth like the white man?
. . . Everywhere the white man touches it, it is sore.

Anonymous, Wintu

The herd was safely back on home pasture, but Buffalo Horn was apprehensive. He paced back and forth in front of his lodge, lashing the leg of his leggings with a quirt. How did one protect his land and possessions from these hairy faces? They had just arrived and already they were everywhere.

The more Buffalo Horn thought about it, the more furious he became. He thought he had been wise to move his herd down from the mountains. What good had it done? His precious animals were now in as much peril as before. One column of land canoes led by Stickus had cut across country toward the mission grounds at Waiilatpu but another party made straight for his pastures on the Umatilla River. The plodding smooth-skinned creatures that pulled the wheeled vehicles appeared intent on running him down. He'd put a stop to that. He mounted up and ordered his sons and a group of waiting armed men to follow. They galloped away from the village, heading straight for the trail that descended from the Blue Mountains. When scouts sighted the column of white covered wagons, Buffalo Horn held up a hand to halt his followers. "Let us watch these crawly things," he said. "Before engaging an enemy one must understand him."

The line of wagons inched slowly down the slopes, slithering and undulating like a snake feeling its way through a cactus patch. Relentlessly, the smooth-skinned creatures that pulled the wheeled vehicles plodded forward. Rocks, brush, ravines -- nothing deterred them. In spite of himself, Buffalo Horn was impressed.

"These people are like determined turtles," he said to his sons. "They crawl slowly, bringing their lodges with them on round things called wheels. These people are weary and weak but are dangerous. They carry long-barreled fire sticks that outshoot our arrows by a great distance." Buffalo Horn fell quiet. The column of wagons approached the Umatilla. With a great amount of shouting, order giving and bustling to and fro, the invaders made camp in a locust grove alongside the river bank.

"Even when camped they are strong," Buffalo Horn said to his sons. "See, they place these land canoes in a circle and build their campfires inside where people are protected by these wheeled things called wagons. They are not troubled with lodge poles and tipi coverings. Their lodges are already prepared. When they break camp there is no trouble -- no packing -- no delay."

Buffalo Horn silently watched the camp activity. The people scuttled back and forth like honey bees feeding on blooms of a thistle. The campsite was well chosen. Trees gave the people shade and firewood. The river provided them with water for the animals, washing, cooking -- for all their needs; and there was ample pasture. The camp had a permanent look Buffalo Horn did not like. Was this the end of their journey? Did they plan to settle on his rich Umatilla pasture lands? The thought made his blood run cold.

Buffalo Horn had reason to be concerned. The travelers, weary from the torturous journey through the Blue Mountains, decided the camp on the Umatilla was a good place to pause and rest. Some families lingered a few days; others remained a week. When the hairy faces did move on, they forded the Umatilla and turned north into Buffalo Horn's best pasture land. The relentless iron-tired wheels crushed fields of grass, smashed waist high sagebrush flat and muddied creeks and watering holes. The ground where the intruders camped was left trampled bare and littered with human waste. Outriders gave chase to grazing Indian ponies, spooking them so they were wild for days, leaving them scattered to the four winds. Buffalo Horn watched the trespassers' irresponsible actions with anger and bitterness. He had Agent White's laws read to him. There was not a single law that covered such outrageous behavior. He strode to Shaman Gray Eagle's lodge to vent his wrath.

"What kind of people are these hairy faces? They abuse all things on Mother Earth. They take what pleases them and, like wolverine, destroy what they leave. Missionary Whitman is to blame. I warned our people about allowing him in our midst. No one would listen. Now, see the mess we have; hairy faces on Cayuse land as thick as gnats in the Season of First Grass." In his agitation Buffalo Horn walked back and forth snapping his ever-present quirt against his leggings. Receiving little satisfaction from Gray Eagle, he mounted the dappled gray stallion and rode toward Waiilatpu.

Buffalo Horn found Tiloukaikt more sympathetic. "It would have been better if Missionary Whitman returned with an army of Blue Coats," the Waiilatpu Indian leader commiserated.

Tiloukaikt had even more reason to feel threatened than Buffalo Horn. The nearby mission grounds, and the land surrounding the mission, were crowded with the intruders' wagons, horses and cattle. Where the grass wasn't beaten into the ground by passing hooves and wagon wheels, it was consumed by the voracious trail-lean livestock. The mission buildings overflowed with people. Watchers reported every room was filled. The space that had been set aside as a classroom for Cayuse students housed more than a dozen people. It was said children of the hairy faces even slept behind the mission house kitchen stove.

Michael Two Feathers was as appalled by the turn of events as any Cayuse. He had hoped when Marcus Whitman returned life at the mission would be the same as before the missionary left. When the wagons came to a stop and people poured into the mission buildings he saw that would never be. No longer was this a mission serving Indian people. It had turned into a stopover place for the travel weary, sick and impoverished newcomers. Finding sufficient food to eat became a problem. Like a scourge of locusts, the invaders cleaned the mission of provisions. Sadly, Michael packed his belongings, sealed his tipi lodge and rode away. Until things returned to normal, again he would seek refuge with Stickus on the upper Umatilla.

Indians were not the only ones disturbed by the influx of settlers pouring through the Blue Mountain passes. Hudson's Bay couriers made haste to report the flood of homesteaders to Fort Vancouver. The news was passed on to company headquarters in Fort William and then transmitted to London. Executives responsible for Hudson's Bay northwest operations sent a stern warning to Fort Vancouver's Chief Factor, John McLoughlin. Under no circumstances was he to do anything to encourage settlement by Americans. Fort Vancouver was becoming little more than a service post for American settlers, the authorities claimed.

For Marcus Whitman, the man who had caused all the furor, the influx of settlers was a delight. His hazardous winter crossing had paid off. Events were falling into place as he hoped. The homesteaders were certain to save Oregon for the United States. In high spirits, Whitman inspected the mission compound, making plans to expand the amount of cultivated ground. He also saw a need to increase the number of cattle, pigs and sheep. The 1843 wagon train was just the first of many caravans of wagons that would bring homesteaders to the west. Each fall when the newcomers arrived the mission had to be prepared to provide them with supplies.

Watchers and workers from the Cayuse village observed Whitman's expansion efforts with apprehension. Tiloukaikt and a group of elders met with the missionary. "No more Cayuse land for Whitman mission," Tiloukaikt declared. "You have much more than you people need. The mission is like a disease that makes red sores. A sore starts here, another comes there. Soon everywhere is one big red sore. So it is with the mission. You take one piece of ground; you take a second; soon you have all ground in Waiilatpu. No ground left for Cayuse."

Tiloukaikt's fears were certainly warranted but he also had an ulterior motive for keeping the mission from expanding its cultivated land. Like a wise old owl, he saw the handwriting on the wall. These hairy faces were as numerous as drops of rain. The trickle of homesteaders who passed through the Blue Mountains had carved a channel for the deluge that was certain to follow. There was no way of stopping this floodtide. Like Whitman, he foresaw the trade that would result. He wanted his villagers to receive the benefits of providing provisions for the horde of people that was sure to come.

As the Cayuse busied themselves with their cultivated plots, their anxiety lessened. Many of the emigrant families who crossed the continent and wintered in Waiilatpu, packed up and left for the Willamette Valley. Mission workers began to have more time for the natives. For a while calm descended on Waiilatpu. Taking advantage of the peaceful situation, Marcus Whitman journeyed to Lapwai to visit the Spaldings. While he was there the missionaries selected new native members for the church. They agreed on nine inductees, bringing the Indian membership to twenty-one. One of the new members chosen was Five Crows, the only Cayuse admitted.

On the upper Umatilla Stickus received the news in silence. He could not understand his friend, Whitman. He observed the missionary's teachings and did his bidding. He had taken over the wagon train and guided it safely through the Blue Mountains. In doing so he had earned the enmity of his Umatilla neighbor, Buffalo Horn. What had he received in return for his Christian efforts? Nothing. For all the consideration Whitman had given him he might as well be a heathen.

Michael Two Feathers watched his Cayuse host with concern. Stickus so badly wanted to be acknowledged as a good Christian and accepted as a member of the mission church. In the evenings Stickus and Michael often discussed the Book of Heaven and the God, Jesus Christ. The immaculate conception of Jesus bothered Stickus. How could Mary give birth if she had never been with man?

"It is not the way of things," Stickus said. "All living things are brought forth from seed. Every living thing has its beginning this way."

Michael, himself, was perplexed by this incredible miracle. "God planted the seed in some mysterious way we cannot see," he said finally.

"Ah, yes. God can do anything." Stickus puffed on his pipe and stared into the embers of the lodge fire. There were so many strange things about the white man's religion one had to learn, it was a wonder anyone got to the place called heaven.

Although Michael badly missed the privacy of his tipi home in Waiilatpu, life on the Umatilla was pleasant. He kept busy with the horses, snared rabbits and grouse for the cooking pots and weeded the rows of corn, squash and potato plants. He helped with the harvest and dug pits in which the Cayuse stored their winter's food. Stickus had a special pit in the floor of his tipi sufficiently deep to keep a supply of squash, potatoes and root crops safe from winter freezes. He carefully covered the pit with poles, a bed of bulrushes and on top placed layers of buffalo robes. From all appearances it was merely a comfortable place to sit or sleep.

"It is wise to have a hidden store of foodstuffs close at hand," Stickus explained. He said no more. "Did Stickus foresee some catastrophe?" The words were on the tip of Michael's tongue but he remained silent. It was not polite to pry into people's affairs.

Although Stickus treated him as a family member, Michael longed for Waiilatpu. He missed the classroom, most of all the books. Reading was such a pleasant and rewarding experience. Michael's greatest love was tales of ancient times and faraway places. They lifted him up and carried him into a wonderland. His troubled thoughts vanished; he was at peace with himself. Every story was filled with new discoveries. To relive these moments of rapture, Michael began to relate the tales he especially enjoyed to Stickus and neighbors who gathered around to smoke and talk after the evening meal. He told how the turtle out raced the hare, about the boy who called wolf and of the lazy grasshopper who enjoyed himself all summer and had nothing put by for winter and had to beg of the always busy ant.

A good storyteller attracted many followers, especially when the tales were so novel and different as those Michael told. The story that gave his audiences the greatest pleasure was of David and Goliath. The people loved to hear how youthful David slew the giant Goliath with a slingshot and a single pebble. The story especially thrilled the youth whose daydreams were filled with heroic deeds and countless coups. After the storytelling session where David slew Goliath, a body of youth lingered behind to question Michael at length about this strange weapon that hurled a stone so swift and true it penetrated the skull of a giant.

Michael knew little about biblical slingshots but was loath to reveal his ignorance. As best as he could, he described the legendary weapon. The following day there was a scramble to find rawhide to fashion slingshot pockets and hurling thongs. All afternoon rocks thudded against tipi sides, skidded into campfires, thumped against horses, making them shy, and sent dogs yipping. Flying rocks even ricocheted into the bushes where villagers went to relieve themselves. At first Stickus and the elders were amused. When their favorite mounts broke their tether lines and ran pell-mell through the village, they became annoyed.

"If you want to slay giants, do it somewhere else, not in camp," Stickus ordered.

The slingshot shooters were not deterred. They went to the pasture fields, hillsides, and creek bottoms to perfect their skills. Michael observed the determined efforts to master the slingshot with a sinking heart. He had created a monster. Sooner or later the slingshooters would challenge him. If he did badly his standing among the people would suffer. He had to get busy and learn how to use this weapon that felled giants.

Michael constructed a sling and rode some distance to a rocky ravine where he could practice without being seen. Always a close observer, he noted the ways of the good marksmen and those of the bad. He used these details to perfect his skills. In a few days his pebbles struck the boulder target three times out of four. The last time he managed this feat a group of boys, who had secretly watched the performance, scampered out of the bushes and ran for the village to spread the news. Michael was never challenged to a single duel.

As winter passed and spring approached, worries beset Michael. His Boston brother might return to Waiilatpu and not know where to find him. It was not only Joe he was concerned about but also Magpie, his black and white pony. All winter he longed for his four-footed friend. Without Magpie he felt lonely and lost. The pony was the last link he had to his former Lapwai Valley home. Sometimes, at night when the howls of coyotes drifted down from the hills, he longed for his people. Would his mother welcome him back? Probably not. Every time she looked at him she would see the big mountain man who had fathered him. Now, after hearing about his

Boston relatives, Tildy, Granddad and Granny, he secretly hoped in some way they would eventually come together and include him in their family. It was a foolish dream. No Boston wanted an Indian relative. The way the wagon train people derisively said the only good Indian was a dead Indian was proof of that. His own father had never mentioned eastern relatives. Was he ashamed of them or of his Nez Perce family or merely disgusted with himself for living among Indian people? People were so hard to understand. Horses and dogs were usually much better friends.

Michael rolled his belongings into a neat pack and brought in the horse Joe had exchanged for Magpie and the black mare. He had already informed Stickus and Kio-noo he was leaving but still he thanked them again and asked if he could do anything for them in Waiilatpu -- perhaps Stickus would like to send a message to Missionary Whitman. Stickus declined. He had no desire to see or hear from Whitman again. He watched Michael ride away, his heart heavy. He feared for this Nez Perce lad who worked so hard and took life so seriously. He would like to counsel him but how did one give advice to a half-blood with a foot in two worlds, yet not welcome in either one?

XIII

*Far more crucial than what we know or do not know
is what we do not <u>want</u> to know.*
Eric Hoffer, THE PASSIONATE STATE OF MIND

Marcus Whitman had not slighted his Cayuse friend, Stickus. He knew the depth of the man's loyalty and his devotion to Christianity. The second year they were in Waiilatpu Stickus came to the mission ill and weak, asking for help. The Whitmans took him in, personally cared for him and eventually healed him. From then on Stickus was a dedicated Christian and loyal friend of the missionary couple. Narcissa Whitman, called Stickus "an excellent Indian" which was indeed high praise coming from her. When her husband returned from Lapwai and reported Five Crows had been given membership in the Church and Stickus had not, she looked at him with disbelief.

"Why that's . . . it's scandalous. Five Crows is nothing but a self-promoting showoff. Look at him, riding around the country on that fancy stepping horse in all his finery. How can Henry Spalding have sanctioned him? The man has five wives. You know what people are saying? 'Here comes Five Crows with five wives. Now that he is chief he seeks five more.' He's a downright polygamist."

Marcus Whitman shook his head. "I know. I argued for Stickus but Henry already had made up his mind and wouldn't change it for the world. Five Crows attended the Lapwai mission school. He is Spalding's convert and is Chief of the Cayuse. By bringing him into the Church Spalding believes Five Crows will persuade many of his tribesmen to accept the Christian faith. It's a shame how politics rears its ugly head in almost everything mankind does. How in the world can I explain to Stickus why Five Crows was chosen and he was turned down?"

The people themselves also were stunned by the choice. Stickus had a reputation for fair dealing, for abiding by the Ten Commandments and for having concern for every member of his band. He was known as a man with "good heart." Five Crows had an opposite reputation. He thought only of himself. He reveled in living frivolously. Soon after becoming Chief of the Cayuse he ordered his wives from his lodge in hopes of replacing them with a winsome Fort Walla Walla officer's daughter. When he went to the fort to ask for the daughter's hand, he was rebuffed. Outraged, Five Crows returned to his village and in spite took a slave girl for a wife, creating a scandal that for days had tongues wagging across the Cayuse homeland.

Marcus Whitman was too busy preparing the Waiilatpu mission for the anticipated influx of emigrants to allow the dispute with Spalding to trouble him for long. He envisioned the Waiilatpu mission as a major supplier of provisions for needy arrivals. He saw to it the gristmill was rebuilt. He expected to grind grain into flour that would bring five dollars a hundredweight. The travelers would want meat. He carefully supervised the feeding and care of the livestock. Fattened choice beef would bring six cents a pound, he calculated. He ordered additional ewes from the Sandwich Islands. Wool would be a salable product, one that should be in great demand, he thought. He planned a sawmill in the forests of the Blue Mountains and made a special trip to select a building site. His plans were so ambitious that when presented to the Mission Board they received skeptical reviews.

"We are not quite sure you ought to devote so much time and thought to provisioning the settlers, thus making your station a great restaurant for the weary pilgrim on the way to the promised land," a Mission Board member wrote.

In spite of the spurt of activity, neither Narcissa nor her husband were well. Doctor Whitman diagnosed his wife as having a tumor near the navel. Her condition, along with a house bulging all winter long with emigrant boarders, strained her endurance and temper. It was all she could do to get through each day without breaking into a fit of weeping or screaming.

Marcus Whitman was also not his normal self. The overland journey had taken its toll. A growth developed on his foot which made him rely on a cane, sometimes a crutch. All winter and spring the doctor and his wife had difficulty managing the daily mission affairs. Upkeep and chores were let slide or turned over to emigrant lodgers who did only what had to be done.

Upon his return from the camp of Stickus, Michael was greeted warmly. "You are just the man we need," Marcus Whitman enthused. "Fall will soon be upon us. Before we know it the next wagon train will arrive. An experienced hand like you will save our lives."

Michael was pleased with the warm welcome but disappointed to find his brother Joe had not been seen or heard from since he and his two companions departed for the Oregon desert. Narcissa Whitman did say she expected Joe any time. She had a letter addressed to him from New England. She was obsessed by the letter. Often she picked it up to examine it, wondering what message it contained. Each time she did she wished Joe Jennings would come and take the letter away before she broke down and opened it. She so desperately wanted news from home.

Michael quickly fell into a work routine. He took care of the livestock, helped clean up the mission compound and worked alongside Phil Littlejohn who had been hired to manage the planting and cultivation of the fields. Frequently Michael was asked to accompany Marcus Whitman on medical calls. While the doctor tended the patients Michael visited with the people and listened to their troubles. In this way he learned that the apparent calm was only skin deep. Natives who lived near the mission were still troubled by the threatening rumor that they were in danger of losing their land and possessions. An Iroquois half-breed named Tom Hill, kept visiting Tiloukaikt's village spreading words of doom. Hill hated the entire white race.

"These intruders will take everything you own. They will leave you homeless and without possessions as they did my people in the east," he warned. Michael attempted to ally the villagers' fears but few listened. He was the mission boy. He repeated the words of Missionary Whitman.

Michael often saw the envelope addressed to Joe that was kept on a shelf above younger children's reach. When no one was watching, he inspected it, carefully turning it over in his hands. Like Narcissa, he wondered what message it contained. Was it news from

Boston relatives? It must carry words of importance. As far as he knew, it was the first and only piece of mail Joe had ever received.

#

All winter and spring Michael was not far from the thoughts of Joe Jennings. Every time he saddled and mounted the black and white Nez Perce pony he was reminded of his half brother. He had soon tired of prospecting for gold and was sick of the Oregon desert. Worst of all, the prospecting venture left him more destitute than ever. The last straw came when they finally caught up with Peg Leg Smith and Sourdough Sam.

"Yuh ol' codgers, where's all these gold nuggets big as hens eggs? Give us a peek at 'em," Hawk Beak demanded.

"Cain't show yuh a thing. Gold! It's here all right but slippery as a wet snake. Jest when yuh think yuh got ahold of it, it's slips outta sight. Fool's gold, some calls it. Looks like the real stuff but it ain't."

"Yuh mean yuh galoots been traipsin' all over this here desert an' ain't come up with a single nugget?" Hare Lip Bruce exclaimed.

"Well, yuh been doin' the same, ain't yuh," Peg Leg retorted.

The next morning all four gold seekers gave up the search. Peg Leg and Sourdough traveled east. "Maybeso we'll run inta ol' Jim Bridger," Peg Leg said. "The cuss's the only smart one of the bunch. We hear tell he opened a tradin' post, fixin' on makin' his fortune on sellin' supplies ta homesteaders sashayin' 'cross the plains."

Hare Lip Bruce went south to California. An old prospector had told him in confidence sandy creek banks there were strewn with gold nuggets. One could pick up a fortune in no time at all. He urged Hawk Beak to go along. The lanky mountain man declined.

"Prospectin' ain't my idea of fittin' work, grubbin' in the dirt like a Mexican badger. Look at us, we been diggin' an' messin' all over the Oregon desert an' ain't got a bean to show fer it. I aim to do somethin' worthwhile fer a change."

As soon as snow cleared from the mountain passes, Hawk Beak and Joe made their way into the Willamette Valley. Hawk Beak insisted they visit Doc Newell, Joe Meek and other mountain men who had settled there. Reluctantly, Joe went along. During all the months spent with Hare Lip Bruce and Hawk Beak he'd had his fill of mountain men. But they continued to cling to each other, stopping at each settlement they came to inquiring for work, anything with pay. They settled for cutting posts and splitting rails. The wage was miserable. Hawk Beak figured it came to a penny a post and found.

From dawn until dark they swung ax and maul until they barely could straighten their backs or open and close their fists. Only on the Sabbath did they rest and, like good Christians, attended church. On one occasion they went to a camp meeting where Reverend Jason Lee conducted revival services. On the edge of the crowd where he could chew and spit, Hawk Beak almost swallowed his cud. Among the pious present was Hawk's old friend, Joe Meek.

"I swear," he exclaimed so loudly the preacher gave him an reproving glance. "Thet ol' hoss committed every sin in the book. Now, look at him. He's gived hisself to God an' thinks he's bright an' spotless as a newborn lamb."

Later, with supplies replenished and equipment refurbished, Joe and Hawk Beak left the Willamette Valley. They followed the Columbia River to Wascopum. After a stopover, they continued on to Fort Walla Walla where they visited with Chief Factor McKinlay.

"You ask about the mission at Waiilatpu. Not much to tell. As usual, the Cayuse are uneasy. Just when it looked like things were settling down, a half-breed troublemaker named Hill came and stirred the pot. He says the Cayuse are heading down the trail to ruin, likened their fate to his people back east, Iroquois, I think he said he is. It's these damned pilgrims that keep the pot boiling. Whitman brought in a batch last year. An even larger wagon train is expected this fall. These people pouring into Cayuse country have the natives nervous as old maids. They're ready to jump at the drop of a hat or squeak of a mouse. I just hope they don't take a notion to jump this way. Fort Walla Walla isn't exactly prepared for a native uprising."

With these depressing words ringing in their ears, the two riders continued on trail to Waiilatpu. Michael was the first to see them arrive. He threw down his hoe and ran across a field of waist high corn. From the mission house poured Narcissa's brood of half-blood children. Narcissa, herself, stood at the kitchen door wiping her hands on a gingham apron. Joe felt a tightening in his throat. It was almost like coming home. Hawk Beak was also moved.

"I swan," he exclaimed. "Ain't it a sight fer sore eyes?"

Michael ran straight to Magpie, wrapping his arms around the neck of his black and white four-legged friend. The children hopped up and down with excitement. They asked where the visitors had been and what they brought with them. Hawk Beak and Joe looked at each other in dismay.

"Consarn it!" Hawk Beak said in exasperation, "we're comin' as barren as a pair of skinned beaver."

Gifts were not needed. The youngsters pulled them into the mission house kitchen and sat them down at the table. A hurried but delicious meal was prepared and set before them. After they finished eating Narcissa clapped a hand to her head. "Oh! I nearly forgot. There's a letter for you, Joe. Marcus brought it with him last fall."

Joe took the envelope. A sinking feeling gripped him. It was addressed in Tildy's carefully written script. Even though she wrote a fine hand, she hardly ever put pen to paper. Whatever she had to say had to be urgent and more than a year and a half had passed since she had written. Everyone at the table quietly watched and waited. News from the east was so precious it was an expected ritual to share messages from home. Ignoring the expectant faces, Joe slid the envelope unopened into his pocket.

Later, at the foot of the hill, in front of Michael's tipi lodge, Joe took his skinning knife and carefully slit the envelope open. As expected, the letter was brief. Tildy was not one to write two words when one would do.

"My dear brother,

Granny passed away. Granddad is not well.
Doctor bills and expenses have kept us deep in debt.
I see no way out but to sell the farm. It is important
you make the decision. The farm is the only inheritance
you will ever receive. Please come home or send
word what I should do.

The Abernathys ask about you. They are
thinking of selling and moving to Oregon. If your
cap is set for Melody, you had better hurry. She
and a man are walking out.

Otherwise all is well. I envy you your freedom
in Oregon Territory.

Your loving sister, Tildy."

Joe folded the letter and stared vacantly at the smoky haze
that colored the rolling hills a dark shade of purple. A feeling of deso-
lation gripped him. It was so acute he felt sick to his stomach. He had
planned to go home but had waited too long. "Aagh" He couldn't
stand himself. Even if he were near he had nothing to give. He glanced
at the date. By this time Granddad also may have died. He rubbed
the film from his eyes. He was suddenly aware of Michael who sat
quietly at his side. Absently, he handed him the letter.

Michael hesitated. He did not know the person who wrote
the message. It was not right for him to read the news the letter
contained. Besides, whatever the talking paper said, it was not good.
It made his brother sad. However, Michael read it through. It was a
laborious process. He was accustomed to the printed word, not these
fancy flourishes. When he finished he, too, stared at the distant horizon. Joe's grandmother had died. For a moment he did not realize
she was his grandmother, too. It was hard to picture a Boston lady
for a grandmother. Had she been like Quiet Woman? He did not
think so. He could not imagine a Boston woman packing and unpacking camp gear, setting up and taking down tipis or pounding kouse
root into flour. He did understand the vacant feeling death in the
family left behind, he thought, remembering his father's death, for one.
And, although she was still alive, in his heart his mother also had died.
She would never welcome him inside her lodge again.

From the mission house window Narcissa Whitman watched
the brothers. She knew from their postures the letter contained dis-
heartening news. The youth sat motionless until evening darkness hid
them from view.

XIV

I am willing to go to any field of usefulness . . . as physician,
teacher or agriculturist, so far as I am able.

Dr. Marcus Whitman

Buffalo Horn had long prided himself on his memory. He never forgot a slight, an enemy face or a horse that had been part of his vast herd. The morning after Joe Jennings and Hawk Beak Tom arrived at Waiilatpu Buffalo Horn called his sons, Red Calf and Cloud Bird, to his lodge. He had seen the black and white pony and black mare pass on the trail to Fort Walla Walla. The horses were in the possession of two dirty, ragged hairy faced ones. He knew these riders. They were friends of Missionary Whitman and the Nez Perce mission boy.

"I want those two horses. Seek them out and bring them to me," Buffalo Horn ordered.

"Steal them?" Cloud Bird queried.

"Do I have to tell you everything to do? You have raided for horses before. Use your head. Do what needs to be done."

Although Buffalo Horn took quick action, like a chess player, he had given careful thought to his move. On the morrow Yellow Serpent of the Walla Walla and he planned a trip to the land called California. They intended to take a herd of horses there to trade for cattle. The black and white pony would make good trading stock. A Nez Perce pony was prized for its endurance, unusual markings and ability to traverse the most difficult trails. The pony would be the showpiece of the herd. Buffalo Horn liked his plan. He rubbed his hands together in glee. By taking the two horses out of Cayuse country they would cease to be a source of trouble and he would have his revenge against that mission boy and his Boston brother who he knew were responsible for the council meeting disaster.

Cloud Bird and Red Calf were not nearly as gleeful. They bridled their mounts and set off for Fort Walla Walla, grumbling to themselves. Cloud Bird even ventured to question their father's wisdom. "Perhaps he has too many years. He does foolish things. He has become a child again," he said to his brother.

Red Calf gave Cloud Bird a sharp glance. "Do not make fun. We must do as Father wishes. He has a hurt to heal. These horses will help make it well."

The brothers followed the trail to Fort Walla Walla. They asked the fort factor about the two hairy faces. McKinlay astutely deduced they were up to no good. However, he told them what they wanted to know. The horsemen were last seen on the trail to Waiilatpu, he said. He watched the brothers leave with satisfaction. The more friction he caused between the mission and the Cayuse the better for Hudson's Bay and the British. He had half a notion to send a messenger to Fort Vancouver to inform his superior, John McLoughlin, of the events he was certain would take place.

Red Calf and Cloud Bird stopped at Tiloukaikt's village. When entering the territory of another it was politic to make one's presence known. They also wanted to question Tiloukaikt's sentries who noted the comings and goings at Whitman's mission. Yes, the two hairy faces, one with the head shaped like a tomahawk and the mission boy's Boston brother, were at the mission, they were told. The two mountain men had taken the evening meal at the big house and had laid out their blankets near the Nez Perce half-blood's tipi at the foot of the hill outside the mission grounds. The black and white pony and black mare were staked in a close by pasture.

Late in the day Cloud Bird and Red Calf mounted up and rode toward the mission. There was no hurry now. The task that faced them was far easier than they had anticipated. Secretly, they wished it was more challenging. It would be a doubtful coup. There would be more danger in stealing washing from defenseless females.

Tiloukaikt knew what Buffalo Horn's sons intended. He wasn't certain he approved. If things went awry, or even if things went right, his people were certain to receive blame. If the plot was foiled and something happened to Buffalo Horn's sons, that also would be bad. Buffalo Horn would be furious. It would be just like him to raid the mission and burn it to the ground. Tiloukaikt sent for his scouts and ordered them to follow the two horsemen. If trouble broke out they were to rescue the brothers and send them on their way home.

The whitewashed mission house loomed into view. Cloud Bird and Red Calf reined to a stop. They dismounted and pulled their mounts into a patch of rye grass that was as tall as their heads. The horses started tearing and champing on the thick foliage.

"This is no good," Cloud Bird declared. "These animals make more noise than a flock of magpies." The brothers decided to circle behind the hill and remain there until dark. As twilight deepened, they tethered their mounts and reconnoitered. They rounded the hill and crept forward. The black and white pony and black mare were not where Tiloukaikt's watchers had reported. They crawled through a thicket of trees. They came to an open space and looked up to see the mission boy's tipi nearly overhead. They scuttled back into the brush. For a long moment they lay listening, their ears close to Mother Earth.

"Brother!" Cloud Bird whispered. "These people are wise. They keep the animals tethered near the lodge. Hear them - - they feed on the nearby grass."

Red Calf grunted a reply. The task was more difficult than they first thought. How were they to capture these animals and return to collect their own mounts? Buffalo Horn would skin them alive if, while stealing two horses of the enemy, they lost two of their own. "I do not like this. Perhaps it is a trap."

"What's the matter, brother? Are you afraid?" Cloud Bird scoffed. "We wait until they sleep. We crawl to the four-leggeds, cut the tether lines . . . be away before the sleepers awaken."

Red Calf started to protest, instead remained silent. His brother was right. One way or another, they had to return with these horses. If they did not Buffalo Horn would be furious. He would never forgive them.

#

The night was so warm and pleasant Joe, Michael and Hawk Beak sat up late talking, enjoying their companionship and full stomachs. It was the first square meal the two trappers had eaten in a long while. Belatedly, they rolled out their blankets in front of the tipi, preparing to sleep under the brilliant canopy of stars. As was their custom, Hawk Beak and Joe placed loaded rifles within easy reach. Almost immediately, Hawk Beak began to snore. Soon Joe also began to breathe heavily. Only Michael remained awake, taking delight in having his precious Magpie back. For a long while he watched and listened to the horses crop and chew. The black mare was almost invisible in the darkness but the white patches of his pony glistened like the white breasted magpie for which it was named.

Michael leaned back and closed his eyes. The champing of Magpie was music to his ears. How had he been able to get along without his four-legged friend? The first thing in the morning they would go for a long ride, perhaps all the way to the upper Umatilla to let Stickus know Magpie had returned. Suddenly, his keen ears caught strange sounds. Michael rose to his knees. Something was out there. The horses raised their heads, their ears pointing toward the hill. Then Michael saw the intruders crawling stealthily through the grass. Immediately, he knew who they were and why they had come. He reached under the tipi skirt and felt for his slingshot and bag of rocks. He armed the sling and waited, watching the two men crawl nearer and nearer their intended prey. Just as Cloud Bird raised up to cut the tether line, Michael whirled the sling and let a sharp rock fly. It caught Cloud Bird in the side. For a moment the stunned Cayuse raider could not breathe. A second rock whistled by his ear. He turned and fell, stumbling over Red Calf. Another rock whizzed overhead. The two brothers scrambled to their feet and ran as fast as they could. A final hurl of the sling sent a missile so near Red Calf's head, it cut a groove in his ear.

Tiloukaikt's guards, who had trailed the brothers, were as stunned as were Buffalo Horn's sons. What had happened? The raid seemed near success when the brothers ran as if a war party was on their heels. The guards hurried back to the village and reported to Tiloukaikt. The two riders from the lower Umatilla did not have the courage to carry out the raid, they said. Just when the mission boy's horses were in their grasp, without a shot fired, they took to their heels, skittering away like frightened mud hens.

Cloud Bird and Red Calf breathlessly arrived to give their account. "Hornets big as horned owls attacked us," Cloud Bird reported. Red Calf pointed to his bloodied ear as proof of the viciousness of the mysterious attackers. Tiloukaikt's guards hooted and howled with laughter. Infuriated, the brothers mounted up and galloped down the trail toward Buffalo Horn's camp on the Umatilla.

Feathercap, who listened to the stories of the watchers and then of the brothers, did not find the incident amusing. This was a deadly serious affair. Red Calf's ear had not been stung, it had been slashed by a mysterious weapon, silent and deadly. Buffalo Horn's sons were not timid or easily frightened. They would not run away from an ordinary enemy. Besides, they had to return to the lower Umatilla and face a furious father who did not accept failure from anyone, especially his sons.

The next morning Joe and Michael inspected the ground where the intruders had been routed. In the grass lay Cloud Bird's knife. When they brought it into camp Hawk Beak shook his head. "Yuh should've awakened me. I'dve blasted 'em with my Hawken. Those varmints weren't funnin'. If Michael hadn't been on the alert they'd hev taken our scalps."

Hawk Beak did not let the incident drop. He worried over it all day and into the evening. The following morning he packed his belongings and saddled his horse. He was off to visit his old friend, Red Craig, in Lapwai, he said. "Yuh kin stay an' git mixed up with these bloody Cayuses if yuh want," he told Joe. "I'm leavin' while the leavin's good. Follow when yuh git ready. Maybeso, the ol' redhead kin put us onto some beaver trappin'. We sure need to do somethin' thet'll give us a grubstake. Let's go, Blaze," he said to his horse and cantered away.

Feathercap's assessment of Cloud Bird's and Red Calf's predicament was accurate. When they arrived on the lower Umatilla Buffalo Horn greeted his sons with a scowl. He listened to the story of the failed mission, his fury mounting. "Your excuse is as weak as your spines -- hornets as big as owls with a sting like the bite of rattlesnakes. What do you take me for, fools like yourselves?" He turned his back on them. They were to set off for the cattle buying trip in California in the morning. After this debacle they could remain at home. It would be better to take old women and unweaned children, Buffalo Horn stormed.

The chastened brothers left the presence of their father, angry and disappointed. They had counted heavily on making the long, exciting trip to the land called California. To remain at home with the women and children was a disgrace they did not deserve. How could they be expected to fight against something they could neither see nor hear? What kind of magic did these people possess? They were sorely distressed. Until they discovered what mysterious weapon these people had they never would know peace again.

In the end Buffalo Horn relented. For all of his fierceness he loved his sons and felt lost when they were not near. He brusquely told Cloud Bird and Red Calf they could go but were not to ride out front. They had to stay in the rear and keep the herd bunched. One lost animal and they would be sent back. If they could have foreseen the future the entire troupe surely would have chosen to stay at home. The cattle buying venture turned into a tragedy, the consequences of which affected the people of the Columbia Plateau for years to come.

#

Already depressed by Tildy's letter, Hawk Beak's hurried departure lowered Joe Jennings' spirits even further. He missed the scarecrow trapper more than he liked to admit. He wondered why. Hawk Beak was always getting on his nerves. Perhaps it was because Hawk was a link with the past, a time when his father, Little Ned, was alive. However, Joe knew deep within himself Hawk Beak's absence was not the only reason for the hopeless feeling that gripped him. He was unhappy with himself. Tildy's letter pointed up what a failure he had become. She cried for help and he had none to give. He had no money and could not face returning home empty-handed. While he pondered what to do, he worked the fields with Michael. At least he could make a little contribution while he made up his mind what to do.

In spite of his gloomy thoughts, the Waiilatpu visit was pleasant. Joe enjoyed Michael's company. He also took pleasure in Narcissa Whitman's family of half-blood children. Every morning and afternoon young David Malin came to bring drinking water and once in a great while, a fresh baked pastry from the kitchen. After completing their household chores Helen Mar Meek and Mary Ann Bridger usually appeared to pull weeds or hoe. Farm tasks made impetuous Helen Mar fretful. After a few moments of work she would dash up and down crop rows with a bevy of Cayuse village dogs in pursuit, raising clouds of dust, undoing all the good work she had done. Mary Ann, more placid, stayed on the job, scolding her half-blood helpmate.

Evenings were especially pleasant. At the dinner table Michael, David Malin and Joe sat facing Marcus while the girls clustered near Narcissa. Frequently, two or more guests crowded into the room. When travelers fresh from the trail were present, more often than not, talk centered around the political situation. The dispute between the governments of Britain and the United States on where to draw the boundary separating Canada from Oregon Territory was always a major topic.

"At present Oregon is a land without a country," Marcus said one evening. "Neither the British nor the Americans have sufficient strength in numbers to lay claim to the land."

"What can we do about it?" asked Watson, who, with his family, had come across in the wagon train recruited by Whitman. Near the end of the journey his wife had fallen ill. The family had stayed on at the Waiilatpu mission until she regained her health.

"We can do a great deal. It is people like you who will bring this matter to a head," Whitman replied. "If sufficient American homesteaders lay claim to Oregon land, Washington will take notice. Sooner or later they will have to send soldiers to protect the citizens. That will be the next step in binding Oregon Territory to the United States."

"Soldiers! Troops stationed on the Columbia Plateau?" Watson exclaimed. "The British won't like that at all."

"No they won't," Whitman agreed. "What the British think doesn't bother me. They are reasonable people. We can negotiate with them. It's the Indians I worry about. They are not ready to live side by side with white settlers. Sooner or later one side or the other will offend. What may happen then is what worries me."

"Are you suggesting these Cayuses might go on the warpath?"

"Could be. Let us pray they do not."

"Hmm!" Watson tapped his fingers on the table top. "The missus is well enough to travel," he announced. "I'm thinkin' we should move on whilst the weather is good. If you'll excuse me, I'll go prepare the missus." He left so abruptly he cracked his elbow getting out the door.

Narcissa giggled. "That's the quickest move he's made since he arrived. Heavens be blessed! I thought he'd never get up the gumption to leave."

As the end of summer neared, Joe's depression returned. Increasingly, his thoughts dwelled on Tildy and Granddad Jennings. He should go home and help out, even if only to do the chores around the farm. Yet, the thought did not make sense. If Tildy and Granddad were so desperate for money they certainly would have sold out by now. If this had happened they would have no use for him. He would just be another mouth to feed and cost them all the more. That was what he told himself time and time again.

Michael silently watched his Boston brother suffer. Joe's thoughts were as easy to read as the printed word on talking paper. Joe was disgusted with himself. He thought he should return to his Boston home. He did not go because he was ashamed. He did not have anything to bring as gifts.

Michael wished he could help, but what did a Nez Perce half-blood have that would give comfort to either his brother or sister? He did have two horses. The hairy faces coveted Nez Perce bred ponies they called "Appaloochy." Perhaps they would be acceptable gifts. The black and white patched pony was certain to bring a good price. The day was warm but a cold sweat broke out on Michael's forehead. He could never part with his four-legged friend. Yet, he could not stand by and do nothing. When a relative was in need everyone in the family helped out, that was the way he been taught every since he could remember.

"Take my pony and mare and go east," Michael said, his heart in his mouth. Yet, he also felt a sense of relief. The difficult words were spoken. He could not take them back. "You must go to our grandfather and sister. They are in need."

Joe glanced at his half brother. His expression was guileless; the words came from his heart.

"Our people are in trouble. Should we not do what we can? The pony will bring many pieces of money."

Joe turned away. He had forgotten the generous nature of the red man. They gave even when it hurt. Michael's offer was like a slap in the face; his Nez Perce brother was a better and more godly man than he. He would sacrifice his most precious possessions for a family he had never seen and who would surely look on him with disdain.

XV

You must remember that, although we are red and you white, there is One above to whom we all have to give an account . . .
                                        Buffalo, Ojibway

In fall, 1844 more creaky, dusty, canvas covered wagons carrying exhausted travelers, trickled out of Blue Mountain passes. This year's band of emigrants was not as large as the one that arrived the previous fall. There was no Marcus Whitman extolling the merits of Oregon and not sufficient time had passed for news of the successful 1843 migration to filter east.

Weather was also a factor. Late spring rains in the Mississippi Valley delayed departure of wagon trains. Some families who would have ventured forth remained behind. Many who did set out, left too late and were caught by early Blue Mountain snows.

Shortly after the fall harvests were completed the tattered wagons began to pull up to the mission. As usual the travelers were greeted with enthusiasm and kindness by Marcus and Narcissa Whitman. The mission buildings and grounds began to fill with emigrant families. The noise, confusion and demanding manner of the newcomers shocked Joe Jennings. These people treated the missionary couple as though they were caretakers of a public house. They parked their wagons wherever it took their fancy, herded livestock onto the first accessible field, allowed children to run wildly through the garden patch, rooting up carrots, turnips, plucking tomatoes, ground cherries, berries -- anything they could stuff into mouths or carry away. Mission workers who attempted to stem the onslaught were ignored. Narcissa looked on placidly. "It's been such a long time since the poor things have seen a decent garden," she said.

Joe watched the destruction in disgust. A plague of locusts would have been less voracious and devastating. He had an uncontrollable urge to chase every one of the unruly varmints down and spank their bottoms good and hard. In the space of minutes they

ruined a summer's hard work. He abruptly left Narcissa and strode
purposefully toward the corral. It was time he saddled up and left.
He did not have the patience to deal with this unruly mob. Besides, if
he didn't move on he would miss out on the trapping expedition Hawk
Beak hoped to arrange with his Lapwai friends.

It was an unsatisfactory leave taking. When packed and ready
to go, Joe stopped at the mission house to say farewell. Narcissa, her
half-blood brood and several emigrant women and their children
crowded the breakfast table. Nevertheless, Narcissa insisted he join
them. She wanted him to wait to bid Marcus good-bye. Early that
morning the missionary had been called away to tend a sick child in
Tiloukaikt's village. The doctor's absence and Joe's presence left
everyone subdued. Except for a few petulant exchanges between
Helen Mar and Mary Ann, and quiet comments and shuffling among
the newcomers, the meal was eaten in silence.

Joe absently picked at the food on his plate well aware of the
bold eyes of the emigrant folks. Dressed in weathered buckskin, his
hair shoulder length and a stern, unyielding expression must make him
appear wild, sinister and uncouth. Even tiny David Mallin gave him an
apprehensive look. "Why had he stopped?" he wondered. He should
have ridden straight away. He had hoped to ask Narcissa to keep a
special eye on his half brother. From the detached manner in which
she treated Michael he wondered if she knew Michael and he were
kin. She couldn't be faulted. She had so many demands on her it was
a wonder she was able to remain on her feet. The new crop of arrivals, many physically unwell and terribly homesick, clamoring for attention, kept her running from daylight until far into the night. She had
to be exhausted. How she managed to keep her wits about her was
a miracle. Joe shoved his plate away and reached for his hat. He
should not take up Narcissa's time or energy. He would have to
forego saying farewell to her husband. Sometimes sick calls at
Tiloukaikt's village kept the doctor away all day, sometimes all night.
Joe got to his feet and thanked Narcissa for the meal.

"We should be thanking you, Joe," she said. "I don't know
how we could have managed without your help. We'll miss you very,

very much." She followed Joe outside. For a moment they stood looking into the distance where clouds hung over the purple hills. A chilling breeze gusted up the valley. It carried a smell of snow. Narcissa hugged herself with one arm placed over the other.

"I have a fear of this season and what it foretells," she said. "Autumn brings the chill of winter which kills the plants and makes the leaves fall. It's a time of death and decay . . . ." She shook her head. "Please forgive me. I shouldn't speak with such gloom on parting." She smiled brightly and quickly went back inside the whitewashed mission house. Before closing the door she gave Joe a wave of her hand.

Joe had the urge to go after her, to remain at the mission house until the doctor returned. He had the uncanny feeling some catastrophe was waiting to occur. While he hesitated, Michael rode up on his black and white pony. It was agreed they would ride together to the place where the trail split, where one track continued on and the other branched off to the upper Umatilla.

Narcissa Whitman had the strangest feeling of apprehension. She never should have voiced the terrible sense of doom which clouded her mind and forced her into these fits of depression. She pulled back the curtain to watch the brothers ride away. They were such young lads with all their lives ahead. She remained at the window until they disappeared from view. Joe was wrong about her. She knew all about the boys' relationship. The thought that they were brothers increased her depression. There was trouble enough in the world without creating more complications. Two families of different cultures brought together . . . ? She shook her head. It was beyond her ken to understand the difficulties they would face in the days to come.

Narcissa said good-bye to the emigrant guests, graciously accepted their thanks, brushed a few crumbs from the table and began to clear the dishes. Her thoughts remained on the brothers. They made her feel guilty. She could have done more. When Michael first arrived at the mission she had thought of adopting him as she had the three other half-bloods in her care. She had talked it over with Marcus. He thought she should but she kept putting it off. This lad who had fled his Nez Perce home made her uneasy. Each time she saw him she was reminded of the violent manner in which his father and step-father had died: the father found dead on the bank of a beaver stream with a Blackfeet arrow in his back -- the stepfather stabbed in the chest with his own skinning knife. It was a heritage that should befall no one, least of all an innocent young lad.

For a long while the brothers rode in silence. Joe, whose thoughts remained on Narcissa, was oblivious to the surrounding coun-tryside. Drab rolling brown hills stretched to the horizon. Only occa-sional clumps of cottonwoods, poplars and pockets of cattails gave the eye relief. The cool breeze freshened. Like live things, dry weeds began to bounce across the trail. Up slopes they bounded to disap-pear over crests of the brown hills. Their silent, ghostlike passage reminded Joe of Narcissa Whitman's dislike for fall and what the sea-son foretold: death and decay.

He had never thought of autumn as a period of melancholy. On the New England farm he always looked forward to fall with plea-sure. The season brought relief from hard work; it brought the enjoy-ment of school, the camaraderie of friends and the excitement of snow games and ice skating parties. Autumn produced the magnificent spec-tacle of maple leaves turning color. Crisp sparkling days made every-thing so indelibly bright. It was as if Mother Nature wanted to expose her many beauties before covering everything for the long winter's nights.

At the trail intersection the brothers stopped, intending to say their farewells. Instead, they hastily reined off the track. From the direction of the Stickus camp a horseman thundered down the trail. He spotted them, waved his arm and began to shout. Joe attempted to follow what was said but barely understood a word. Still talking, the rider lashed his mount and galloped on toward Waiilatpu.

"What is that all about?" Joe asked.

"He rides for Buffalo Horn. He says the people who went to California are back. There was a fight. Yellow Serpent's son was killed. The Californians kept the horses and refused to give them cattle in return. Buffalo Horn sends messengers to all Cayuse camps.

This man has been to see Stickus and now goes to Tiloukaikt. Yellow Serpent wants revenge. If Indian Agent White does not bring these California people to justice, Yellow Serpent and Buffalo Horn claim they will raise a war party and go after the killer themselves."

"Hmm!" Joe grunted thoughtfully. The news was disturbing. Yellow Serpent's son was well respected and the apple of his father's eye. He had attended Jason Lee's Methodist school in the Willamette Valley where he acquired the Christian name, Elijah Hedding, the name of a famous Methodist Bishop. Perhaps Jason Lee had taught the youthful Walla Walla too well. He began to think as a white man. He was outspoken in his beliefs. That was what probably brought him to grief in California. If a white man killed him it could have far reaching consequences. Yellow Serpent was not only leader of the Walla Walla tribe, he was also related by marriage to important Cayuse and Nez Perce families. If all three tribes went to war no white man on the Columbia Plateau would be safe.

"Perhaps we should ride back to the mission," Joe suggested. He feared for Narcissa. Overburdened with emigrant demands and in her depressed state, the threat of an Indian war might be more than she could manage.

Michael raised his eyebrows. "Is it wise to act upon what one man says? Let us go to the camp of Stickus. The people in the villages are the ones who will say if there is to be war."

Joe nodded. His brother's unselfishness and uncanny perception constantly amazed him. Michael's generous offer to give up his two ponies had opened Joe's eyes. He had refused but shame remained. The Nez Perce lad, who had never met Tildy or Granddad Jennings, stood ready to make a sacrifice far beyond what he, himself, was willing to do. Now, Michael sensibly advised caution while he would have undoubtedly spread alarm.

The camp of Stickus displayed no preparation for war. The Cayuse leader greeted them in his usual reserved but pleasant manner. He invited them into his lodge for a smoke. This time he went against the wishes of Marcus Whitman and filled and tamped the long stemmed pipe.

After each man had taken the traditional puffs of smoke, Stickus spoke. "You come about trouble with Walla Wallas," he said in his native tongue, then for Joe's benefit interjected English words when he could. "This trouble is of greed. Yellow Serpent and Buffalo Horn go to California with small herd. On trail they think big. They say to themselves they do not have enough horses to make good trade. They make raid on enemies, steal many horses. A mule is among stolen animals. California people seek horses, not mules. Elijah Hedding say they must take mule with horses. California people say no. Elijah Hedding quarrels with California man. California man say shut up. Elijah does not shut up. California man shoots. Elijah Hedding falls dead. Now Yellow Serpent and Buffalo Horn want war. War no good. Our people have Indian Agent White's laws. Are not they made for bad things like this?" He shook his head. "Our people unwise, make big mistake." Stickus fell silent. He cleaned and put away the pipe and sat staring into the lodge fire flames.

As soon as they could politely do so, the brothers rode away from the upper Umatilla camp. The visit with Stickus left Joe more depressed than before. The future for these people looked bleak. It would be a long, hard struggle before natives and newcomers lived in peace. They were just unable to understand each other. An incident like Elijah Hedding's killing could blow the country apart. White's set of laws was a mockery. The Indian agent was out of the country and Five Crows was weak. The most troubling part of the affair was that the man guilty of killing Elijah Hedding was in California, a six day ride from Cayuse country. At the trail junction the brothers stopped, Joe prepared to go to Lapwai and Michael back to Waiilatpu.

"What do you believe will happen?" Joe asked.

"Only the Great Spirit and God of white man knows."

"Hmm!" Joe grunted. The stoic countenance told him his brother had said as much as his Indian conscience would allow.

Michael lifted his hand in a farewell gesture and urged Magpie into a lope. At the top of a ridge he reined up to give a final wave. Joe waved back, wondering why parting with the little fellow always left a lump in his throat.

On the second day after leaving Michael, Joe pulled up in front of the cabin Hawk Beak's friend, Red Craig, had raised.

Red Craig was out front. "Slide down and let your saddle cool," he greeted. "Your partner, Hawk Beak, isn't quite up to snuff."

"What's the matter with him?" Joe had fully expected to find Hawk Beak raring to start on some sure get-rich expedition.

"He got liquored up and bet he could ride any horse in Lapwai. One of the locals took him to a corral of critters fresh out of the hills. Before I could put a stop to it, he saddled up an old roan, meaner than a billy goat. He barely swung aboard when the nag took to bucking. Hawk sailed off like a migrating bird and ended up smack dab against the top railing. Must've broke a couple of ribs. He can barely breathe. Come see for yourself."

On a cot lay Hawk Beak, his face the color and texture of bread dough. "I'm messed up worsen a hen scratchin' in fresh cow dung," he groaned. "If I was a critter Red'd shot me two days ago."

"He's somewhat better," Red observed. "Hasn't carried on like this since it happened."

Joe attempted to hide his concern. Even when Hawk Beak had been laid low with a bullet wound, he had not looked this bad. "I'd better go for Doctor Whitman," he said.

"That isn't necessary," Red assured. "Thunder Eyes, the medicine man, is taking the case personal; he swears he'll pull the old hoss through. Don't look down your nose. You'd be surprised what these native healers can do. Anyhow, by the time you get to Waiilatpu and back this old hoss will be on the road to recovery or six feet under, that's for certain."

Hawk Beak got better and was finally able to get to his feet and shuffle around the narrow cabin room. The two trappers kept an apprehensive eye on the weather. The cool breezes of September turned to cold winds of October. Dark scudding clouds swept in to dump rain on the valleys and snow in the high country. A messenger from Waiilatpu brought news that many emigrants were trapped in the Blue Mountains. Joe and Hawk Beak knew if they did not leave soon they would never make it through the passes until spring.

Weather was not the only threat. Elijah Hedding's murder kept the upland tribes in turmoil. From his home in Kamiah, Ellis, Chief of the Nez Perce, rode through Lapwai on the way to the Willamette Valley. He went to demand Elijah's killer be hanged in accordance with Indian Agent White's code of laws. Rumors were rampant. Travelers arriving from the Columbia River Plateau reported the Walla Walla and Cayuse were gathering a war party to march on the Willamette Valley. White had turned his back on Ellis, said the killing had taken place in California, out of his jurisdiction. Another reporter claimed Yellow Serpent and Buffalo Horn had marked members of Whitman's missionary party for reprisal. "Did not the Great Spirit Book say, 'Eye for eye, tooth for tooth, hand for hand, foot for foot?' If California man was not bound by Indian agent laws, mission people must pay," Yellow Serpent had declared.

The rider who delivered this news was Feathercap, the trouble-maker from Tiloukaikt's camp. He spent several days in Lapwai talking to anyone who would listen. He passed by Red Craig's plot of ground, sending the dogs barking. Hawk Beak, who had ventured outside the cabin, recognized him.

"What's that ugly galoot doin' here?" he asked Joe. "Yuh suppose he's one of the thieves thet tried to take our horses at Whitman's mission an' has come to try his luck in Lapwai?"

"I don't think so," Joe said but he, too, wondered what devilment the crafty Cayuse had on his mind. He was not a person that would ride all the way from Waiilatpu for no reason.

"I'm fit enuff fer travel," Hawk Beak said one day. "Let's take off in the mornin'. I don't like the feel of this place, don't know how the ol' redhead kin hole up here year after year."

The next morning a foot of snow covered the ground and continued to fall. Hawk Beak glanced out the window and swore. Red Craig plowed through the drifts and knocked on the door.

"'Peers you'll have to put off your buffalo hunt. The pass to buffalo country is hip deep to a tall giraffe."

"Buffalo hunt! Since when did we become buffalo hunters?" Joe exclaimed.

"Yeah, well it kinda came on me sudden like," Hawk Beak said. "I was layin' here with nuthin' to do but size up our situation. We gotta face up to it. Beaver trappin's no good. Prospectin's worse. What else kin a couple of galoots like us do? I struck on buffalo huntin'."

"You could do honest work, like farming," Red said. "I can tell you for certain, buffalo hunters aren't fancied by the Crow, Blackfeet and Sioux. They're mighty annoyed with people who kill their buffalo just for tongues and hides, leaving the carcasses to feed the buzzards and wolves."

It did not matter what Hawk Beak had decided. Snow continued to fall. The two mountain men were marooned in Lapwai. They had all winter to argue over what they should do.

XVI

The Indians are solicitous about so many coming into their country . . . the Indian will not like either to respect the interests of the whites nor the whites to forbear with the Indians.

Dr. Marcus Whitman, 1844

The early snows of 1844 had a devastating effect on wagon trains passing through the Blue Mountains. Dreadful accounts of suffering reached the Waiilatpu mission. Some five hundred emigrants were trapped by early snows. Terrified families saw their wagons sink into snow drifts, the animals that pulled them dropping exhausted beside the trail. Destitute of provisions and without adequate clothing, many travelers fell ill. Others nearly froze to death or starved.

The travelers who safely passed through the mountains were little better off. They arrived in Waiilatpu famished, dead on their feet. The oxen, horses, mules and cattle, all skin and bones, could barely hobble. The condition of the newcomers appalled the Whitmans. They did what they could to house and feed them but the numbers were too great. The mission buildings and grounds were filled to the bursting point. Those who had the stamina and wherewithal were urged to continue on to the Willamette Valley. As it was, Narcissa and Marcus worked like never before. "I am so thronged and employed that I feel sometimes like being crazy, and my poor husband, if he had a hundred strings tied to him pulling in every direction could not be worse off," Narcissa wrote in a letter to her parents.

Narcissa had good reason to feel overwhelmed. Among the arrivals were seven orphaned children from the Sager family, the youngest a baby born on the trail. The parents had died along the way. The good-hearted Whitmans took them in to rear as their own, bringing their adopted family members to eleven. "I don't know how we'll manage," Narcissa said, "but if the Lord casts them upon us, He will give us grace and strength to do our duty by them."

It was a courageous decision. Already in trouble with the

Mission Board for spending time and funds to aid passing emigrants, the seven Sager orphans put a severe strain on meager finances. More and more the mission was becoming an aid station for travelers rather than a center for civilizing and saving the souls of the Cayuse. No one saw this more clearly than Michael Two Feathers. Often twenty-five or more people crowded the mission house kitchen table at meal time. The emigrants were voracious. They wolfed down food as if they would never eat again. If the table cloth had been edible Michael was certain they would have consumed it when the serving dishes emptied. For a while the school was closed. There was a flood of applicants but no one to teach. Finally a man named Hinman offered his services. The first day of classes Michael counted twenty-six students, including himself. Most of them came from emigrant families. Not a single member of the Cayuse camp was admitted.

The specter of running out of foodstuffs soon haunted the Whitmans. After the initial wave of emigrants arrived, Marcus made an inventory of the mission provisions. The storehouses held a hundred bushel of wheat, several hundred bushels of corn and in corrals and pens were numerous beef, sheep and hogs. At the time he thought these supplies would see the mission safely through the winter. But many of the people the Whitmans thought would move on, remained in Waiilatpu. They found the missionaries' hospitality too pleasant to leave. Early in the spring Whitman had to call on Missionary Spalding in Lapwai for provisions and spend precious mission funds at Hudson's Bay to feed the voracious horde. "Goodness!" Narcissa said one evening after counting the thin sheaf of notes kept in a biscuit tin. "Soon we'll have to ask Mr. McKinlay for credit. It will be months before harvests replenish the mission larder. Imagine the scolding we'll get from the Mission Board."

Although Tiloukaikt and his band profited by selling foodstuffs to the emigrants, by springtime the storehouses of the Cayuse also ran dry. The people became so desperate they scrounged with rodents and birds in the fields for harvest leavings of wheat, corn and potatoes. While the emigrants feasted on the bounty borrowed from Spalding's Lapwai mission and purchased from Hudson's Bay, people in Indian villages were on the verge of starvation.

The half-breed Iroquois, Tom Hill, who had married a Nez Perce and taken up residence in Lapwai, took this time to visit Waiilatpu and again harangue Tiloukaikt's band of Cayuse. He reminded the villagers of his previous warnings. The white man was coming in bunches. They were as numerous as hairs on a camp dog. Soon they would push the Cayuse off their homeland.

"Look at them," he said, pointing toward the mission compound. "People over there feast on wheat, corn, beef, hogs and lambs. Where did this bounty come from? It came from you. The grain sprouted and grew in Cayuse soil. The animals were raised and fattened on Cayuse pasture. I tell you again, the hairy faced ones are cunning. Like Trickster Coyote, they wait until their prey is puny and weak, then rush in and take what they want. Soon you will neither have food nor land . . . ."

Hill's words fell on fertile ground. Feeling against the hairy faced invaders increased. Waiilatpu villagers began to wander into the mission compound seeking items to steal. Here and there a bag of grain disappeared. A slice of bread, a piece of bacon, a jar of jam and other small edibles mysteriously vanished. Emigrant wagons and mission outbuildings were broken into and pilfered: horse collars, harnesses and other leather products were taken. Boiling the tough leather items with gleanings from the harvest fields and gristmill, Cayuse women made ill-tasting gruels. The emigrants soon became aware of the thievery and complained to Whitman. The overworked missionary had no time for detective work. He told the complainers they would have to guard their possessions the best they could.

Michael who kept constant watch on the comings and goings from the Indian village, caught culprits in the act. One evening near nightfall he ran into Feathercap and his son leading a cow from the mission pasture, the source of much needed milk for several sick youngsters. The elder Cayuse with the face Narcissa could not stand, snarled at Michael like a trapped animal. "You have full belly. We empty bellies," he said and continued to pull the stolen heifer toward the Indian village.

Michael remained silent. This was wrong and could not go on but what was he to do? He was already in trouble with the Cayuse. He was the mission boy who did Whitman's bidding. He was Indian but not one they could trust. If he exposed Feathercap and his son there would be reprisals, not only on the mission but also on himself. The next morning an angry mother reported the cow missing. Marcus Whitman went to investigate. Tracks of the stolen animal were quite plain. They led directly toward the Indian village. Whitman strode back to the mission house shaking his head. Already exhausted and not well, he was at the end of his tether. He ran into Michael.

"What can we do about this thieving?" the missionary asked. "If we don't stop it the villagers will be stealing everything we have."

Michael agreed. Something had to be done. If the stealing was allowed to continue, people like Feathercap would become bolder and bolder. It was also an explosive situation. The emigrants were getting upset, threatening to shoot any prowler on sight. If that happened it could spark a riot that could not be quelled.

"Perhaps it would be good to give the villagers a feast and talk to them," Michael finally answered. "Food always pleases."

Whitman pulled thoughtfully on his side whiskers. "Yes, for sure the villagers are desperately hungry. We're mighty short on foodstuffs but we should share what we have. These people like nothing better than a big barbecue. Take Milligan's lame ox . . . I've had my eye on it for our mission flock but perhaps the poor thing would serve us better by sacrificing it to the villagers."

The barbecue feast was given. Instead of creating the good will Marcus Whitman and Michael had foreseen, it produced bitterness. Before Whitman could talk about the stealing, Tom Hill, who had remained in the Cayuse village, jumped to his feet. For two hours he harangued the people on the evils of the mission. He waved a hand at the skeleton of the barbecued ox. "Now you see how these people live. They enjoy good things like this while you people starve to death."

#

Henry Spalding's Lapwai mission also suffered from the barbed words of the half-breed Iroquois, Hill. During the mission's early days revival meetings attracted congregations of a thousand or more. In the spring of 1845 two hundred or fewer souls attended. Attendance at the weekly Sunday service almost came to a complete stop.

In other ways the damaging effect of Hill's bombast emerged. Increasingly, Lapwai villagers lost respect for the missionary establishment. Several nights running, rocks were hurled at the walls of Spaldings' home. A band of unruly youth stood outside and threatened to horsewhip him and his wife. Classroom sessions were upset. Eliza Spalding, who the Nez Perce had formerly taken to their hearts, was insulted daily. Tools were broken. Mission livestock were driven away and mutilated. The life of Spalding was even threatened.

Joe Jennings, who had wintered in Lapwai waiting for the mountain passes to clear of snow, observed the rising tide of sentiment against the missionaries with alarm. He liked Eliza Spalding, often helped her bring order to the classroom at the end of the school day. He felt sorry for her. She was pregnant with her second child. Not a strong person to begin with, as the unborn grew in size she seemed to shrink until Joe feared she might not survive childbirth.

Late one afternoon, when warm chinook winds peeled away the snow, Joe returned from a ride in the hills to find Hawk Beak arguing with an Indian woman. As he opened the door they turned on him. "Am I interrupting anything?" he politely asked.

"Yuh ain't interruptin' a damn thing," Hawk Beak snapped. "We been waitin' fer yuh, leastwise this woman has, name's Raven Wing, yer old man's widder. She thinks we stole her son from her, says we poisoned his mind again' his mother . . . talks lots of claptrap. Maybeso, yuh kin reason with her."

Unable to hide his astonishment, Joe boldly examined the Indian woman. Through the winter months he had often had the urge to meet her but decided, except to satisfy his curiosity, no good would come of it. Now that she was present in person he could not keep from staring. This was the one his father had fallen in love with and taken for a wife. This was Michael's mother and his stepmother! Her flashing dark eyes and upsweep of black hair reminded him of the Cheyenne lass he once fancied. Although her features now were marred by emotion, her true beauty was impossible to hide. No wonder his father fell for her. He wished he could have see them together when they first married. What a handsome couple they must have made. How cruel life treated them. Francois, that evil man, had split them apart, destroying their happiness.

"Thief! You take First Son. Keep in land of Cayuse." The woman came so near Joe could see little gray flecks in her otherwise nearly black eyes. Her English was broken but clearly spoken. At one time she probably had been fluent. Again his thoughts flashed back to his father, Little Ned, who must have patiently taught her the language. He could almost picture the two of them sitting by lodge fires speaking, explaining, loving -- the image was so clear in his mind he felt like weeping. Before things fell apart what romantic times they must have enjoyed.

"Why do you not speak?" Raven Wing's voice was shrill. She, too, was thinking back to the days when she had a man and a family -- to the time when things were good. She could not bring her mate, Little Ned, back from the other side but she could force this man to return her son.

"How cruel life is," Joe thought, "if they only could have met under better circumstances." He suddenly wanted to visit with her, talk about the days when she first met his father. What made them fall in love? What exactly made their marriage fail? Perhaps she would dispel the terrible rumor that she had conspired to murder his father. There were so many things he wanted to ask but she had a dangerous glint in her eyes that made him hesitate and edge away. Hawk Beak, who remained in the background, was not nearly as tongue-tied.

"What're yuh stallin' fer? Reckon with the woman. Yuh ain't got nuthin' to hide. Talk ta the womin. Thet's what she came fer, ta ask 'bout her boy. She ain't gonna bite. It's all in the family ain't it, yuh bein' her stepson? Why don'tcha tell her yer kin."

"Shut up!" The command came from the woman's lips. Raven Wing remembered Hawk Beak from yesteryears -- her first married winter in buffalo country. The memory increased her bitterness. He and her Boston mate, Little Ned, had been trapping partners. She had wanted to take her new mate home to Lapwai but Little Ned refused to go. He insisted on spending the winter trapping in the mountains. She had gone with him. Through the months her unborn child grew large until she thought he would burst through her skin. All winter long the trappers watched her belly swell, Hawk Beak's eyes the sharpest of all. He examined her like she was a mare about to foal, speculating on what gender of colt she was ready to drop. Now he was giving her the same look. She had a notion to carve out his eyes, but her quarrel was this youth who it was said claimed to be her son's brother. Although he did look much like her dead Boston mate, she knew it was a trick. The hairy faces intended to make her son one of their own and would do it anyway they could.

"I say again. You thief. You keep my son prisoner. You give him back. I want my son. He belongs in my lodge." Raven Wing's voice became increasingly shrill. She took another step toward the young man. She noticed his eyes -- blue like Michael's. Was he really Little Ned's son? Were Michael and he truly brothers? It could not be true. It was not fair. He had her son -- she had nothing but a terrible gnawing pain in her heart. An irresistible urge to carve out those searching blue eyes gripped her. One hand went to the fold of her skirt. The shiny blade of a knife flashed in the dim light. Like a cat, she leaped. Frantically, Joe twisted away, falling backwards over a bench. A hot flow of blood blinded him. The struggling outcries of Hawk Beak and the knife-wielding woman came from a great distance; finally, they faded into nothing.

Joe awakened to the sound of hushed voices. "Will he lose sight in the injured eye?" a familiar voice asked.

"It's too early to tell," another familiar voice answered.

The shadowy figures of Marcus Whitman, Red Craig and Hawk Beak gradually took shape. Joe's head throbbed unmercifully. His eyes would not focus. He put a hand up to find a thick bandage covered one eye and much of his forehead.

"Welcome back to the living," Marcus Whitman said in his cheerful beside manner.

"What happened?" Joe managed to croak.

"You had bit of an accident."

Memory of the encounter returned. It was like a horrible nightmare. Of course, the woman had been out of her mind. In a way he had to admire her. She wanted her son so badly she would commit murder. Not many mothers had a love as strong as that.

"What happened to the woman?" he asked.

"Thunder Eyes banished her," Hawk Beak answered. "Yer safe. All yuh gotta do is git on yer feet. We've plans ta discuss."

"There's plenty of time for that," Marcus Whitman interrupted. "Right now the patient needs rest." The doctor shoved Red Craig and Hawk Beak out the door. He fussed around checking Joe's pulse and examining the good eye.

"You had a narrow escape," he said. "You nearly lost an eye. If the knife thrust had gone deeper you wouldn't be here. I patched you up the best I can. Only time will tell how well. For a while you're apt to suffer dizzy spells."

The doctor's diagnosis was right. After he left, Joe got up to relieve himself and nearly fell flat on the floor. Hawk Beak heard him stumble and came to muscle him back into bed.

"Yuh'd best mind doc," Hawk Beak scolded. "Thet cut made yuh fuzzy headed. Git up fast an' sure as shootin' yuh'll pass out like a drunkin' sot. Even so, yer lucky as a mule in a patch of clover. Doc Whitman was in Lapwai watchin' over the missionary womin whilst she birthed a new Spaldin' sprout."

Before returning to Waiilatpu, Marcus Whitman came to inspect the wound and change the bandage. He took a small mirror from his bag and held it up for Joe. Above the left eye, crisscrossed with stitches, a patch of puffy, swollen flesh met Joe's gaze.

"Thet Injun womin sure put her mark on yuh nice an' permanent," Hawk Beak observed. "Yuh gonna hev a scar like a lopsided horseshoe."

"Probably more like a new moon," Red Craig contradicted. "The natives'll likely nickname him New Moon Joe."

"That's a lot better than One-Eyed Joe," Marcus Whitman dryly remarked.

XVII

Friendship can only exist where men harmonize in their views of things human and divine.

Cicero

The winter of 1844-45 also was a hard one for Joe's twin sister, Tildy. While on a church ice skating outing a weak spot in the ice gave way and Tildy fell in the freezing water. If Sandy Sanders had not acted quickly she would have drowned. As it was she caught a cold which turned into pneumonia. Gradually, as the layers of snow turned to blotchy slush, she regained sufficient strength to work around the house.

Tildy's illness had strange effects on those around her. Granddad Jennings gained new life. He cared for her as solicitously and with as much expertise as a trained nurse. Some nights he hardly left her bedside, yet never seemed to tire.

Sandy Sanders, the other man in Tildy's life, became almost too attentive and protective. Daily he brought gifts of hard to get fresh fruit or flowers. He often ordered Granddad to bed and would sit for hours telling Tildy stories or merely sat silently by her bedside. His tenderness and thoughtfulness were pleasing to Tildy, at the same time troubling. She was becoming obligated. The day would come when he would expect her to repay this kindheartedness.

In early spring, after Tildy regained her health, the Abernathys, who for so long had been next door neighbors to the Jennings, came to visit and say their good-byes. Saul, Bithiah and their parents were off to make their home in Oregon Territory.

"It's Brother Whitman's doing," Dad Abernathy explained. "Him wanting God fearing folks in Oregon is what made up our minds. If he can tame the heathen Indian, we can surely help tame the land."

Before the Abernathys took their leave, Sandy made his evening call carrying a bouquet of flowers. Avid eyes of the Abernathy clan watched him replace the old flowers in the vase with the new. He went about the task as if he had done it many times. Afterward he took a chair to sit beside Tildy. Dad Abernathy, who had fallen silent, noisily cleared his throat.

"I say, why don't you folks get hitched and join us? Think of the times we would have in crossing the plains. We could take farms together in Oregon and be neighbors like we were here in New England."

Sandy's face glowed; Tildy's face grew red. Granddad chuckled. "You're not trying to rush these folks, are you?"

Everyone laughed and turned the conversation to the latest happenings at the church. Tildy got up to make fresh coffee and set out a plate of cookies she had baked that morning with the last of the eggs and milk. Again, she faced the bugaboo of how to make ends meet. How she envied the Abernathys. They were free to travel to Oregon and start life there with a clean slate.

The Abernathys left early but Sandy Sanders lingered on. Granddad excused himself. He was suddenly so sleepy he could not keep his eyes open, he loudly declared. Hardly did the door close behind Granddad before Tildy found herself wrapped in Sandy's arms. His warm breath, smelling of cookies and coffee, came in panting gasps.

"Why don't we do as Mr. Abernathy suggests and get married. We don't have to go to Oregon unless, of course, you wish. You know how badly I love you. I have told you often enough."

Sandy pulled her closer. She could feel his heart pounding against hers. Like a cornered rabbit, Tildy found herself trembling. She attempted to break away but Sandy clung to her, holding her even more tightly. Gradually she relaxed. It was a comforting feeling to be enclosed in strong protective arms, and somewhat exciting. Maybe this is what she wanted after all. But she did not want to be a schoolmaster's wife in this gossipy village. Perhaps Oregon was the answer. Ever since talking to Missionary Whitman she had wondered about this magical place with its colorful Indians, evergreen forests, wild mountains and rushing rivers. Joe was there. They could be a family again. But what about Granddad? Building a home in the wilds would be hard on him, but if there was a home to move into . . . That was the answer.

"Yes, I would like to go to Oregon," Tildy said finally. "But we can't marry until you go there and prepare a home for Granddad and me. The trip will be hard on Granddad. He should have a proper home to move into when we arrive."

#

It was late spring before Joe and Hawk Beak left Lapwai. The mountain passes to the east were still packed with snow so they went south. "We'll head for Fort Boise," the skinny trapper declared. "We kin supply ourselves thar an' ketch up on the news an' decide what next ta do."

The country the trappers passed through was beautiful and unmarked. They encountered ravines and valleys carpeted with thick grass and populated with wild game that fled when they approached, disappearing into folds of green forested hills. In the distance loomed majestic peaks blanketed with snow so white and bright it hurt the eyes. Water, clear, cold and fresh from melting snows, trickled musically into the gullies feeding noisy, rock-bedded streams.

They crossed plains resplendent with blue-violet flowers. These were the camas fields that in late summer Nez Perce tribesmen invaded to dig for bulbs that they baked in earthen rock-lined pits. Joe paid these pleasant open spaces particular attention. Michael said camas harvests were the most enjoyable times of his life. Bands from all over the tribal lands set up camp to visit, play games, race horses, dance and feast on baked camas bulbs and the roasted meat of wild game.

After the camas fields the trappers climbed into the high country. Every day Mother Earth continued to display new splendors. Every day also brought pain. Joe's head ached. He experienced frequent dizzy spells. One morning while swinging up on the horse, he completely blacked out. He regained his senses to find Hawk Beak observing him with an expression of pity and disgust. The two trappers had their first serious quarrel.

"Yuh should've had better sense an' yuh wouldn't be in this

mess," Hawk scolded.

"What are you talking about?"

"Why thet cussed, knife wieldin' woman took yuh off guard an' drove yuh into the ground like a tent stake. I told yuh she was on the warpath."

"You didn't help much. You could have warned me she had a knife."

"Warned yuh. Yuh was moonin' at her like a sick calf. One gander at the woman an' yuh should'a knowed she was meaner'n a new sheared sheep."

"You let me walk into a trap," Joe insisted.

"How was I to know yuh didn't have the sense God gave a goose? I thought yuh'd been around long enough to tell she-devils from house cats."

The remainder of the trip to Fort Boise was made under an uneasy truce. By the end of the trip Joe hated the sight of his companion. His long curved nose, thin lips and hair roached up in a rooster's tail, more and more gave the tall trapper the appearance of a carrion bird. Even his voice took on the unpleasant hoarse caw of the crow. From the way he acted Hawk Beak could not stand the sight of him either, Joe thought. As soon as they arrived at Fort Boise Hawk Beak went directly to the trading counter, bartered a mule for supplies and packed up to take the trail to buffalo country.

"Pardner," he said, "It's time we split. We ain't perzactly hittin' it off. Sooner or later we might come ta blows. I don't fancy thet an' don't think yuh do either. Anyways, I cain't waste time dillydallyin'. If I don't get on ta somethin' soon, I'll be a candidate fer the poorhouse."

Sadly, Joe watched his trapping partner disappear into the sagebrush that lined the trail east. Hawk Beak was one of the members of the trapping brigade that had launched him on his life out west. He shouted for Hawk to wait. The wind carried the words back into his face. The trail had swallowed Hawk. For the first time in years Joe was alone -- partnerless. Despondently, he returned to the fort where he also bartered a mule for supplies. A short distance from the fort he set up camp. His head ached and he was sick at heart.

"Look at yourself," he scolded. "What a mess you've made of your life. You don't even have a friend to your name." No one heard him but his horse and mule.

After a few days Joe's headaches and dizzy spells lessened as did the feeling of loneliness. For the first time since the encounter with the Nez Perce woman he felt fit. The only fly in the ointment was lack of resources. Provisions were low. He had to do something to earn money or trade away his last mule. But he was so pleased to feel well again he did nothing but enjoy his new lease on life. He did not want anything to disturb this sense of well-being. Every morning he took a leisurely stroll to a hilltop where he had an open view of the approaches to the fort. An occasional band of horsemen emerged out of the sagebrush to pass from view behind the fort walls. Most of the arrivals were small groups of Indian people. They usually remained overnight, setting up camp in the grassy bottom land that lay between the fort and the Snake River.

One afternoon, out of the shimmering haze, floated the white crest of a covered wagon pulled by several span of mules. As the wagon grew in size Joe could tell it was no settler's outfit. The wagon was too long and wide and pulled by too many teams. The manner in which the mules stepped out, the crack of the bullwhip and the teamster's rolling gait seemed familiar. That evening as Joe staked out his horse and mule the fort factor stopped to visit.

"Yuh'd best get yer pasturin' while yuh can," he said by the way of greeting. "I'm told three thousand emigrants'll soon pass this way. Their stock'll cut this grass down like a mechanical mowin' machine."

He paused to spit and scratch. "A freighter's been askin' after yuh. Says yuh'n his boy was in the same trappin' outfit. Says yuh near got yer eye carved out by an Injun woman. He sure ain't tongue-tied. If the sample I got's any sign, he kin talk the hide off those mules of his'ns an' keep right on goin'. Reckon yuh know the galoot. Man like that's hard to forget."

"Yeah, I know him," Joe said, wincing at the report. "Where

did the garrulous teamster get all his news? Between Hawk Beak and him the story of his stabbing by Raven Wing would soon be known all over the west. "Name's Beamer."

"That's him. Says he ain't seen yuh since his boy got hisself killed in Blackfeet country."

"That's true." The inquisitive fort factor waited expectantly for Joe to continue but Joe remained silent. Memories of the awful day came flooding back. A raiding party appeared out of nowhere. Young Clay Beamer ran to save the livestock. Before the rest of the trappers got there to help, the war party had run him down. After the battle Clay and Buck Stone, leader of the brigade, lay dead. "Ah!" Joe groaned inwardly. Ever since that dreadful day nothing seemed to go right.

"You must have run into Hawk Beak," Joe said, after greeting the teamster at his camp that evening. The bean pole trapper was the only one who could have told of his encounter with the Nez Perce woman.

"Yep! The ol' hoss says you folks fell on hard times after Buck and Clay passed on." Beamer paused to cough and spit. "I've kicked meself a thousand times for lettin' Clay jine Buck's brigade. He was tearin' mad to become a mountain man. Buck Stone warned me. No one to blame 'cept meself. Sure don't help none. Since Clay's been gone my ol' woman hardly lets me in the house, let alone her bed. He was a good boy; he never gave me no back word or did nobody no harm."

"He was a good man -- a true friend," Joe agreed. "Clay could not have acted more bravely. He spotted the war party first. Straightway, he ran to save the livestock. He didn't have a chance. Redskins were everywhere."

"It's mighty satisfyin' to know he done his job good . . . ." Beamer's voice failed him. For a long while they sat quietly gazing into the campfire.

"On the way to the Willamette Valley, are you?" Joe finally asked.

Beamer shook his head. "No, this is the end of the line. Me

wagon's too large to cross the Blues. Besides, I sold the last of me freight. In the mornin' I'll be headin' back to St. Louie."

"You plan to make the trip again?" Joe asked, wondering if there was an opportunity for him in the freighting business.

"Yep, can't keep up. They's nearly three thousand folks 'tween here an' the Sweetwater. They'll all need vittles, powder, lead, soap -- things like thet. Ol' Steph Meek, maybeso you know him, Joe Meek's brother, is pilotin' a train. The ol' fox has the idea of a short-cut through the Oregon desert. Seems Hudson's Bay trappers go thet way to the Willamette Valley. Meek claims it saves two hundred miles. He makes a good argument. The Blues are hell to cross an' it seems Injuns on the ol' route are plenty fussed. Meek says best to avoid 'em. You been in thet territory. What's it like?"

Joe ran a finger tip over the tender scar above his eye. "Yes, you could say the Indians are fussed."

"Maybeso, you should touch Meek up fer a job. He'll need help pathfinderin' the new route. Hawk Beak an' I gabbed 'bout it. Seems you fellows know the desert 'bout as well as anybody."

"What else did Hawk tell you?" Joe asked testily. "Seems he can't keep anything to himself."

"He does chin wag a bit. I hardly couldn't get a word in edgewise."

The thought of Hawk Beak outtalking Beamer made Joe laugh. The big teamster gave him an odd glance, then chuckled, his big belly moving up and down like a butter churn. "Thet's right. The skinny loco bird out-winded me. Thet's goin' some, ain't it?"

"Could you use a good hand in your freighting business?" Joe suddenly asked.

Beamer gave Joe a long, studied look. "I could use a good man but if you're askin' for yourself, the answer is no."

Joe gave the teamster a surprised glance. "What's the matter with me?"

"Nuthin'. It ain't thet yuh're not a good hand. Its just thet every time I'd look at you I'd see my boy, Clay. Then my missus wouldn't cotton to you a bit. She thinks Buck Stone's trappers didn't take proper care of her only son. You know how bullheaded women can get? You can reason better with a runaway shoat."

Beamer stopped to hawk and spit. "Anyways," he continued, "you're too good a man for the freightin' business. It's donkey work for sure. You eat dust all day an' then can't sleep at night for worryin' about thievin' Injuns or bein' held up by desperadoes. They's a lot of trashy folks about, too mean to work an' worthless as a bucket of buffalo chips."

The teamster rattled on until Joe was glad Beamer had turned him down. No wonder his wife kept him out of her bed. To get any rest she would have to get off by herself. Joe escaped with the excuse of writing a letter to send with Beamer on the freighter's return journey to St. Louis. He borrowed pen and paper at the fort. He hadn't written home since learning of Granny's death. After pondering half an hour, he finally managed a few words of regret. He did not know what to say about selling the farm, so said nothing. He ended with the hope he could soon send money, perhaps enough to bring them to Oregon where they could all be together again.

Joe put the pen down and read what he had written. He started to scratch through the sentence about sending money. How would he get the wherewithal to bring anyone to Oregon? He didn't have enough cash in his pocket to buy a postage stamp. However, he let the sentence stay. Scratching it would make the letter too messy to send.

XVIII

Your old men shall dream dreams,
your young men shall see visions.
Bible: Joel, II, 28

On a hot, bright August day the first wagons of the 1845 migration struggled into Fort Boise. The oxen and mule teams plodded wearily down the trail, past the fort and into the bottom land where several hundred Indians had stayed the night. While womenfolk and children made camp the men unharnessed the teams and took them to pasture. Stray stock was driven in, bawling and running to feast on green grass that grew near the bank of the Snake. Joe, watching from his hilltop camp, saw that Hawk Beak was one of the herders. His question mark figure with the long black feather curled above his hat, set him apart from the others. Near evening he loped up to Joe's camp. He swung down and helped himself to a cup of coffee as though they had never quarreled or parted.

"I thought you were off buffalo hunting," Joe said, miffed at the casual way Hawk Beak made himself at home.

"Ran into ol' Steph Meek," Hawk lamely explained. "He told me collectin' buffalo hides was a occupation only fit fer Injuns. Huntin' an' killin' ain't no problem. Fleshin', saltin', an' stretchin' green hides is somethin' else. I don't know how Sublette an' Vasquez do it . . . must keep a bunch of slaves."

Hawk helped himself to more coffee. "Ol' Meek's takin' a wagon train 'cross the desert where we went prospectin'. He's chargin' five dollars a wagon to see the folks to The Dalles. Since we scouted the country an' know it 'bout as well as anyone, he wants our help mappin' the route. He'll split the pickin's with us if we see him through."

"Hmm!" Joe grunted. "I'll think on it."

"Yuh need work, don'tcha? What's ther to think on? Yuh better grab this job while yuh can. I had to sell yuh real hard. Ol'

Meek's suspicious'a anyone under thirty."

"If I remember correctly, we were glad to see the last of the desert. I'm not sure there's a route that will see these wagons through -- pasture and water for the livestock, at least not at this time of year. You know as well as I do water and grass are mighty sparse at best."

"Yuh cain't compare our piddlin' around with this bunch. These people're serious travelers. Look at 'em, they've already crossed two-thirds of the continent. They'll take to the desert like wolf hounds after a fox."

Joe shook his head. "I don't know much about wagon trains but for certain they can't travel as fast and easy as pack mules. That's what we took across the desert and ran into places where wished we hadn't gone. Think about it. No other wagons have attempted to cross the desert. If it's such an easy, quick route why haven't they tried it? I'll tell you why, they didn't want to die of thirst out there amongst rattlesnakes and scorpions."

Hawk Beak gave Joe a furious look. "Thet stabbin' hasn't caused yuh to loose yer nerve, has it?"

Joe stood up so fast he almost blacked out. "No! I haven't lost my nerve. I need a job but don't need it bad enough to lead a wagon train of greenhorns into a desert where there isn't enough water and grass to keep jack rabbits."

The next day more wagons came creaking down the trail. Joe watched the weary travelers make camp. When the loose livestock appeared, riders drove the herd onto pasture land at the bottom of the hill. The fort factor was right, Joe thought. After the wagon train passed, little grass would be left.

That evening Joe walked through the emigrant camp. The fading twilight gave the campfires an inviting glow. An aroma of meals cooking and willow wood smoke hung heavy above the cluster of canvas covered wagon beds. Near the river came the haunting whisper of a flute. A mother scolded her offspring. A young woman with corn colored hair thrust her head out of a covered wagon opening. She gave him a strange look, almost a rude stare. Joe doffed his hat and murmured a greeting. To his surprise she came at him with her arms outstretched.

"Joe! Joe Jennings! Remember me? I'm the neighbor girl next door, Bithiah Abernathy!"

It was Joe's turn to stare. The last time he saw Bithiah she was eleven or twelve, a skinny, wide-eyed kid who was always getting in the way. Facing him now was a tantalizing, fully developed female with mischievous eyes and captivating smile.

Before Joe regained his composure, Dad Abernathy appeared. "Well, I declare! Maw! Joe Jennings is here!"

Mrs. Abernathy came around the wagon, wiping her hands on her apron. Behind her loomed Saul. He had been just a little tike. Now he hulked over his mother and supported a wispy beard. For a moment Joe almost expected Granny and Granddad and Tildy to arrive for tea. They would sit at the kitchen table and discuss Parson Barclay's last sermon or the summer crops. The Abernathys did not serve tea but offered fresh baked bread and coffee. Bithiah sat on the wagon tongue and openly stared. Joe avoided her eyes, suddenly conscious of his worn, weathered clothes and long, shaggy, unkempt hair. He must appear little better off than a tramp.

"What's the matter with your manners?" Mrs. Abernathy scolded her daughter. "He ain't exactly a stranger. He's just Joe Jennings, our former Middlesex County neighbor."

"Yes, but hasn't he grown into the nicest looking man?" Bithiah said, her eyes sparkling. "Ooh! That scar! Gives me goose bumps, makes him look so worldly and mysterious."

"Hmm!" Dad Abernathy leaned forward to inspect it. "Appears dangerously near the eye and a might fresh. How'd it happen?"

"During an Indian fracas," Joe said, hoping Hawk Beak wouldn't arrive and spill the beans.

"Ooh! How thrilling!" Bithiah squealed.

"Tell me about Granddad and Tildy," Joe quickly asked. "I had a letter telling of Granny's death."

"Yes, brave soul," Mrs. Abernathy answered. "She was poorly for the longest time, then one night she didn't wake up. It was so sudden it took all of us by surprise. Tildy went to a church social with her fellow. When she came home Granny was gone."

"Your grandfather took it hard," Dad Abernathy added. "He sold the farm and moved to town. The big news is that Tildy's fixing to marry a fellow who's traveling with the train. Sandy Sanders is his name. Plans to throw up a cabin and bring Tildy and Granddad out as soon as he can."

"We tried to talk them into getting married before we left," Mrs. Abernathy broke in. "Tildy wouldn't hear of it. She sent Sandy ahead to prepare a home first. Saul! Go fetch Sandy. Joe should get acquainted with his future brother-in-law.

"Sandy's a nice lad," Mrs. Abernathy continued. "He'll do right by Tildy. Are you by chance married?"

"Not many women where I've been." Joe avoided looking at Bithiah who hung on his every word.

"I'm told frontiersmen find Indian women agreeable to setting up house, least for a spell." Dad Abernathy eyed him critically.

"Some do and some don't," Joe said, uncomfortable with the turn of conversation.

"What are you doing now?" Dad Abernathy continued.

"Kind of in-between jobs. Perhaps, I'll scout. Meek plans to take a train across the Oregon desert."

"That's our train. Saves time, avoids the Blue Mountains and fractious Indians. I'm sorry we won't be seeing the Whitmans but got to put the family first. They say the Indians up that way are warlike. Be nice to have you along -- someone who knows this country. Meek says he's been over the trail before but one can't have too many experienced hands around. I can tell you, we've had some real scrapes, most of them the fault of our leaders."

Bithiah clapped her hands. "Did you hear, Mamma? Joe is going to travel with us. Isn't that wonderful?"

"I haven't decided for certain," Joe quickly said, appalled by the way he had trapped himself.

"You must come! Our own Joe Jennings guiding us across the Oregon desert. Isn't that romantic, Mommie?"

Mrs. Abernathy nodded. "Yep, mighty satisfying. Your

grandma would be proud. She had such big plans for you. She thought you and Melody would make a good team."

"Really?" Joe exclaimed as though the thought had never once entered his mind. "Is Melody with you?"

"No, stayed behind, married a local lad. She'll be disappointed she didn't wait and come west with us. But all's well that ends well," Mrs. Abernathy mused. She eyed her younger daughter speculatively. "Yep, who would have thought Joe Jennings, our neighbor boy, would lead us to our new Oregon home."

"It's like a fairy tale," Bithiah said breathlessly. She clutched at Joe's arm sending a tingling sensation coursing through his veins. "You'll travel with us, won't you?"

"How can I refuse?" At that moment Joe felt so giddy he would have walked barefoot across the Oregon desert.

#

The summer of 1845 was again a period of hurried activity at Whitman's mission. The month of August was especially busy preparing for the emigrants that would soon trundle down the Blue Mountain slopes. The bustle and hurry to get provisions and quarters ready for the onslaught kept mission workers running from dawn until well after dark. Michael Two Feathers, caught up in the frenzied activity, had little time to give much thought to anything but his work.

The Cayuse village was also wrapped up in making preparations for the wagon train invasion. In spite of half-breed Hill's exhortations to rebel against the mission establishment, Tiloukaikt and other village elders directed the energies of their people into replenishing the village granaries, creating surplus supplies to be sold to Oregon Trail travelers who would soon arrive in their land canoes. Although still smoldering over the disastrous cattle buying trip to California, Buffalo Horn on the lower Umatilla and Yellow Serpent of the Walla Walla were busy with their herds and crops. For the present an uneasy peace existed on the Columbia River Plateau.

Late in the fall the mission school opened for emigrant students and members of the Whitman family. Except for Michael, no Indians attended. Michael found himself seated between Francis and John Sager and behind the Sager sisters, Catherine and Elizabeth. They eyed him with suspicion but he did not mind. He was back in the classroom amongst the books he loved. However, school was not the pleasant experience Michael anticipated. The teacher, Alanson Hinman, new to the west, did not have the time nor temperament to deal with people. Hinman ruled the classroom like a dictator. He intimidated the younger students with scowls and raps with a ruler. For even the slightest of classroom infractions, older boys were whipped and younger boys received stiff raps on the wrists with the sharp edge of a ruler. The harsh treatment made several students rebel, including Francis Sager who ran away, begging a ride from a family leaving Waiilatpu for The Dalles.

Coupled with nervousness in the classroom was anxiety on the outside. Michael's uncle, Vision Seeker, came for a brief visit. The tall man rode in at twilight. He swung down from his horse and, upon seeing his nephew in good health and for his safe journey, said a silent prayer of thankfulness to the Great Mysterious. Michael helped his uncle rub down the horse. Together they led it to water and staked it out to graze. Afterward, Vision Seeker sat near the fire and warmed his hands. Only then did he speak. "Our people at Lapwai are well," he said and then fell silent. Remembering his duties as host, Michael quickly prepared a light meal and set it before his guest. Neither uncle nor nephew ate much. Vision Seeker was accustomed to frequent fasting. Michael was too excited. He could not wait to hear what brought his uncle to Waiilatpu.

Vision Seeker brushed a gnat from his hair and finally spoke. "You wonder why I ride to Waiilatpu. It is to awaken you, my nephew. There is a wind on the plateau that stirs the grass and makes the trees whisper. It is the Great Mysterious speaking but no one pays attention. Anyone who watches and listens can see and hear there is trouble hiding behind these hills. Like lightening, no one knows when or where it will strike, but the dark clouds are forming. It is time to take cover." Vision Seeker fell quiet. He backed away from the fire and wrapped himself in a robe. "Now I think I sleep." He laid down and almost immediately began to breathe heavily.

For a long while Michael sat immobile, almost as if Vision Seeker's words had turned him into stone. In spite of his years of mission schooling, when his uncle spoke he had the feeling his studies had not covered the important things of life. Vision Seeker heard the Great Mysterious speak through the grass and trees where he never heard a word. Was this like the Christians who talked about being saved? Did some spirit come down from the clouds, speak to them and miraculously turn them into saints? He sighed and turned away from the fire and reached for his sleeping robe.

Vision Seeker brought other disturbing news. Michael's mother, Raven Wing, had stabbed his half brother, Joe, and was banned from Lapwai. She had gone to live with relatives in the land of the White Bird band. "You are now free and welcome to come home and live with your grandparents," Vision Seeker said. "You would be a great comfort to Lone Wolf and Quiet Woman. Lapwai is more safe than Waiilatpu . . . ."

Michael hesitated. His mother knifing Joe, shocked him. What an unfortunate life she had led. Her impetuous actions always got her into trouble. For the sake of his grandparents the proper thing to do was go home, but he was now accustomed to the people at Waiilatpu. In spite of Hinman's harsh manner, he did not want to drop out of school. He was attached to the Sager orphans, the adopted half-blood children and especially the Whitmans. They depended upon him. To leave would be an act of desertion. Then there was Joe. He would expect him to remain in Waiilatpu.

"I think it best I stay," Michael said finally.

Vision Seeker stared thoughtfully at the mission buildings. His gaze took in the mission house where the Whitmans lived, the rectangular edifice set aside for visitors, now filled with emigrants, and the smaller blacksmith shop. Tendrils of smoke rose from the two main buildings. The odor of food cooking drifted to the foot of the hill where they sat in front of Michael's tipi lodge.

"Today's odor of cooking may be tomorrow's smell of death." Vision Seeker said almost to himself. "Remember my nephew, even lodges made of wood and stone are temporary and so are people."

XIX

We had entered upon this new and untrodden route at a time
when our oxen were already worn down and footsore . . .
we were all tired and several of the company sick . . .

W. A. *Goulder,* REMINISCENCES OF A PIONEER

At Fort Boise Joe Jennings also received unpleasant tidings. When he told Hawk Beak he would take the scouting job, the lanky trapper shook his head. "Meek ain't gettin' the money he planned. 'Tisn't sufficient to share with a third."

"For God's sake!" Joe blurted. The Abernathys, Bithiah especially, expected him to accompany the wagon train. Also, he had offered to give Sandy Sanders, Tildy's intended, a helping hand with his livestock. It was the least he could do for Tildy. Joe returned to his camp near the hilltop. Furiously, he collected his gear. If he'd had Hawk's neck in reach he would have wrung it like that of a chicken's. He had no intention of going back on his word. At the fort he bartered his trapping outfit for provisions but kept the last mule and his horse. The mule looked so forlorn he named it Lonesome.

Before leaving Fort Boise Stephen Meek persuaded two hundred families to make the desert crossing. William Barlow, who could not stomach Meek's pomposity, cautioned the shortcut through the desert was a gamble not to his liking. He recommended taking the proven route to the Willamette Valley. Others, unimpressed by Meek's assurances the cutoff was safer and shorter, also kept to the old trail. A number could not decide. Either way they faced formidable hazards. As Barlow warned, Meek's cutoff took the homesteaders completely into the unknown. Yet, on the old trail they had the Blue Mountains to cross and had to travel through the lands of the unpredictable Bannock, Walla Walla and Cayuse. The Indian threat was especially ominous. Riders brought word the Walla Walla recently killed two Frenchmen who had camped on their homeland. This sobering news gave Meek's cutoff additional appeal.

Joe did not fear either crossing, probably because he had nothing to lose and was happy. For the first time in nearly six years he had a solid link with home, the Abernathys and Sandy Sanders. When he was with them his spirits knew no bounds, but it was mostly Bithiah who provided such heavenly bliss. Early one evening after they made camp on the banks of the Malheur (French meaning unfortunate) River, a banjo and fiddle began to play. Joe seized Bithiah and, much to her delight, began to swing her around. The quick movement made him dizzy. He clutched at Bithiah to keep from falling, then dropped awkwardly to his knees. He had temporarily forgotten the ruptured blood vessels hidden beneath the forehead scar.

As the dizziness faded away, he noticed Dad Abernathy's frozen expression. At first Joe thought Bithiah's father was worried about his health. Instead, he disapproved of dancing. "He that loveth pleasure shall be a poor man," Abernathy sternly quoted from the Scriptures.

For Joe the evening's gaiety dissolved. It was almost with relief he greeted Hawk Beak as he rode in and dismounted. After he introduced the trapper, Hawk Beak hunkered down beside the campfire, his sharp, carnivorous profile intensified by the flickering flames. Fascinated, the Abernathy family stared unabashedly.

"Hawk and I traveled together off and on for the past six years," Joe explained.

"Yep! Knowed him as a pup," Hawk Beak expounded. "Green as grass when we first met. Even so the youngster had grit. Right off he turned Rocky Mountain Saloon in St. Louie upside down -- outfoxed the biggest roughneck in town, a galoot named One-Eye Link. I kin tell yuh Link was a tough. He lost his eye wrestlin' a grizzly but he weren't no match fer young Joe, no siree!"

"Gosh!" Saul exclaimed. Bithiah clapped a hand to her mouth. Mrs. Abernathy looked apprehensive. Her husband scowled.

"Hawk! These folks aren't interested in falderal like that," Joe protested. What were the Abernathy elders to think -- that he spent his off hours carousing in saloons?

"But we are interested, aren't we, Bithiah?" Saul exclaimed.

"Who'd thought our Joe Jennings would do such heroic deeds!"

Encouraged, Hawk Beak continued. "Yep, this lad's as smart as a tree full'a owls. Not only did he best One-Eye Link once but twice. In a duel at the Green River rendezvous . . ."

"Hawk! Save some breath for breathing," Joe scolded. "What did you come to see me about, anyhow?"

"Meek was wonderin' if we could borrow yer pocket compass? Might come in handy should we run outta landmarks."

In this casual way Stephen Meek and Hawk Beak prepared themselves to lead two hundred wagons on the hazardous trek across the Oregon desert. On the banks of the Malhuer River the wagon train divided: 200 wagons followed Meek -- the others continued on the old trail through the Blue Mountains. For many the parting was a sorrowful experience. Who was to know when and if friends and relatives separated here would ever meet again. To make the departure even more unsettling, before breaking camp herders reported nine oxen missing. A party of Indians had slipped by guards and whisked the oxen away during the night. Consternation over the missing animals caused both trains to get off to a late start. When the difficulties were sorted out it was nearly midday. At eleven o'clock the first desert wagons finally wended away on a southwesterly course.

The desert crossing did not begin with promise. The rocky, hilly and dusty track made progress slow. At times wagon wheels sank into powdery soil that was ankle deep. Billows of dust rose up to choke man and beast. There was little talk. An open mouth collected grit like a fly trap. The fine dust penetrated everything: ears, nostrils, nose and clothes. Before the day was out undergarments turned as rough as sandpaper. To a person, members of the train yearned for a good bath.

Joe quickly discovered a wagon train was far more difficult to manage than a string of pack mules. Even when laden with full pack, mules ambled along at four or five miles an hour. The oxen lumbered along at less than half that pace. Where sure-footed, agile mules easily moved around brush, boulders and trees, wagons had to keep to more level and uncluttered terrain. The slow pace, the merciless sun and smothering dust, gave Joe new respect for the emigrants. They endured this day after day in their quest to make new homes out west.

The first evening on Meek's cutoff the travelers stopped to camp in a stream bed. There was sufficient water but skimpy pasture. The brown, withered grass offered animals little nourishment. The hillsides were barren of vegetation; on all sides they rose up rocky and steep. At this uninviting campsite Joe had the first opportunity to get well-acquainted with Tildy's fiancee. Sandy Sanders was far from handsome. His face had the color and speckles of a turkey egg. His hair was unruly, his teeth spaced too wide apart and his nose was a bit crooked. The moment he spoke his appearance was forgotten. His gentle easy manner left Joe feeling happy for his twin sister. Tildy had indeed chosen a good and faithful man. When he asked after Tildy, Sandy Sanders leaned back and gave him a slow smile.

"When I think of Tildy I'm a new person," Sandy said. "Some people take to drink to ease a day's worries. I think of Tildy. I am indeed a lucky fellow."

After finishing the evening meal, Joe and Sandy strolled among the wagons. Sandy introduced him to the Martins, Tetherows, Herrens, Hancocks, Fraziers, Packwoods, Sam Parker and others too numerous to remember. They were friendly folk but travel weary and concerned about the track ahead.

Later Meek walked around camp announcing the next good water and grass were eighteen miles to the west. He spoke with such assurance everyone was cheered. Hawk Beak, who trailed Meek, gave Joe a sheepish look; it was the expression he had when caught in a boldfaced fib. "Agh!" Joe uttered -- the scoundrels were guessing.

The next morning the wagon train made an early start. There was less dust but travel was just as hard as before. Fields of rocks, stunted brush and channels eroded by infrequent but violent rains, caused the teamsters' oxen no end of trouble. The burning sky, the dry wind, the creak and moan of wagons and harnesses that signaled strain on worn and fragile equipment, rubbed frayed nerves to the breaking point. The bleak horizon, seen through wavy heat lines, did little to reassure the emigrants they were headed for the rich homestead lands of the Willamette Valley. For a short while a mountain to the north took the weary travelers' minds off their troubles. John Herren, who kept a journal, measured with his eye and recorded it as three miles in height. The sight did not encourage Joe. In prospecting the desert he could not remember encountering a mountain of this size. Surely they were not already off course?

It was well after dark before Meek called a halt. The people were stunned. The campsite with good water and good pasture was a myth. There was barely sufficient water to fill the barrels and the ground was nearly bare of grass. The livestock suffered again. When the draft animals were hobbled, Joe walked past the Abernathy wagon. Abernathy, who sat hunched over a low fire, called out to him.

"What's the matter with these friends of yours?" he demanded. "They blow more wind than truth. What'll tomorrow bring? That's what I want to know. If it's more of the same, we don't need it. It's not too late to turn back and take the trail across the Blue Mountains."

Bithiah stepped out of the wagon. Although the other members of the family were in a blue funk, she radiated the exuberance of youth and good health that was impossible to squelch. She greeted Joe with a smile. "Don't carry on so, Pa. Joe'll see us through, won't you?"

"Of course. We're in a bad patch now but should hit good grass and water soon." Joe walked quickly away. He was getting to be as fluent a liar as Meek and Hawk Beak.

The following day Hawk Beak and Meek started the wagons on a course to the northeast. After half an hour's travel the guides galloped back to order the lead wagons to turn on a track almost due north. The wagon teams made a long pull uphill before turning northwest for an hour's drive. From here the route went due west along a ridge to face another uphill climb. From the summit a belt of green appeared in the distance, a certain sign of water. Before the lead wagons covered another mile the oxen began to low. The loose stock picked up their heads and sniffed the air. The plodding pace of the oxen turned into an awkward lope. Down the long slope the wagons lumbered, jolting over rocks and plunging through tangles of brush. The water famished animals paid little heed to their loads or obstacles in their path. Shouting teamsters were pulled along, forced into a run to keep up as the animals made the mad dash to slake their thirst.

The good campsite brought cheer to the emigrants but did not give Joe comfort. They had traveled nine miles, most of them in the wrong direction. At this rate it would take two months to reach The Dalles, he calculated. After tending to the livestock he strode grimly up to where Hawk Beak had made camp.

"What are you and Meek up to, anyway? You traipsed around today like blind bears in a bramble patch."

"Keep yer shirt on. We found water'n grass, didn't we?" Hawk Beak retorted.

"Look! You and Meek had better stop dawdling and take this guide business seriously. This isn't some prospecting trip. You have a wagon train of folks counting on you to see them through."

Hawk Beak stood up so quickly he tipped over the coffee pot. "We don't need yer advice. Since thet stabbin' yer as fearful as a worm in a hill of red ants. If yer crossin' this here desert with us, git ahold of yerself. We don't need yer weak-kneed complaints."

The trail continued rocky and hilly. Broken wagon tongues, worn out axles, collapsed single trees, cracked reaches, loose spokes and tires, slowed passage. Hot weather and dry wind dehydrated man, animals and equipment. Irate teamsters did not hide their frustrations. They cursed Meek and themselves for making the decision to take the trail into this bleak, unknown wilderness.

A week after leaving their friends on the Malheur, the wagon train broke out of the foothills onto a grassy plain. Travel was easier but Joe remained concerned. They continued in a southwesterly direction, not to the west or northwest toward The Dalles. On September eighth Packwood's baby died. Red-eyed from dust, grit, lack of sleep and grief, the mourners laid the tiny body to rest in a field of sagebrush. Afterward the train captain harshly ordered teamsters to drive over the grave. Local Indians were said to dig up bodies and mutilate them. Meek and Joe said the precaution was not necessary but the distraught travelers turned a deaf ear. They placed little faith in the words of mountain men.

The train plodded a mere six miles before making camp. The recent death, the short distance traveled and the fact provisions were low, had people worried and frightened. Their concern increased when Meek reported the next water was twenty-five miles away on the slopes of a flat-topped mountain that crouched like an animal against the distant, hazy horizon.

The column now consisted of one hundred fifty wagons and some two thousand livestock. Nearly fifty wagons had fallen behind. Broken harnesses and wagon parts and the search for lost livestock held them back. Five wagons had been totally discarded, their contents left beside the trail or placed aboard wagons of friends.

The train arrived at the mountain campsite near midnight. The exhausted travelers gathered in a low place to stare at a spring which barely trickled with water. In disgust someone named the place Lost Hollow, another called it Stinking Hollow. The water was not only in meager supply but brackish with alkali. An unpleasant smell hung over the campsite like a poisonous cloud.

"Meek should be strung up, leadin' us inta this intolerable mess," a vexed teamster growled. An angry murmur of agreement followed.

"Git a rope," someone hollered.

"There'll be no hangin'," a man named McNeese raised a rifle. "These guides are the only ones who know this country. Without them we're like a ship without a sail."

"If we had water we wouldn't need ship nor sail," someone peevishly jested.

Train Captain James McNary rode up and dismounted. "This is no time to quarrel! Be sensible. Think of your families. They're the ones who will suffer. I have spoken with Meek. He says we had better camp here until we locate the next water. Tomorrow we will send out search parties."

Haranguing and grumbling continued but lost its savagery.

Everyone knew McNesse and McNary were right. Killing off their guides would not extract the travelers from the fix into which they had fallen. When it was his turn at the spring Joe dipped up a bucket of brackish water and returned to where Sandy and he had camped. Instead of preparing for the night, Sandy leaned unsteadily against a wagon wheel. The freckles on his pale face stood out like warts.

"What's the matter?" Joe asked, startled by the sudden change in his companion. A feeling of dread engulfed him. Ever since leaving the Packwood baby's burial place high fever and debilitating weakness had struck people down. Some said the sickness came from drinking alkali water; others claimed sagebrush ticks infected the victims. Meek called the malady mountain fever. No matter what caused the fever, Sandy Sanders had it. He looked like death itself.

XX

We camped at a spring which we gave the name of the 'Lost Hollow' because there was very little water there.

Betsy Bayley, letter to sister Lucy, 1849

While Sandy Sanders lay feverishly tossing and turning in stinking Lost Hollow, Tildy Jennings, for the first time in years, enjoyed herself. The pressures of money and courtship were lifted. The local school had enlisted Granddad as a tutor. For several weeks two students appeared daily for lessons. Parents and school authorities were so pleased with the students' progress five more signed up when school reopened in the fall. The income was small but kept food on the table and bill collectors away from the door. The intellectual work gave Granddad a reason to live. He felt needed and worthwhile.

The absence of Sandy Sanders also provided Tildy with a feeling of relief. She didn't have to fortify herself every day to deal with amorous advances in order to keep Sandy as a friend. She did not think ahead to the impending marriage or the move to Oregon. She calculated it would take Sandy a year, maybe two, to get a home prepared and return for her. Surely, by that time she would adjust to the demands of matrimony.

With Granddad happy and money problems behind her, Tildy found time to visit with Melody Abernathy, now Mrs. John Stillings. An ambitious man, Stillings channeled most of his energies into making a success of the poultry business. After the first bloom of wedded bliss, Melody found herself treated more and more as a hired hand. In addition to the long barn-like structures that housed chickens, Stillings constructed another set of buildings for turkeys. Because of the danger of transmitting disease from one species of poultry to the other, Stillings kept them separated. The old Abernathy place was the turkey farm; the Jennings place was the chicken farm.

At first Tildy enjoyed visits with Melody. In a way she was envious of the luxuries Melody enjoyed. One of Stillings' first projects was to remodel the old Abernathy home. He brought running water into the kitchen and installed a downstairs bath. From Europe he imported a special water closet guaranteed to sanitarily flush away human waste, the first of its kind in Middlesex County.

The modern improvements impressed Tildy but she noticed Melody had little time to enjoy them. All day long Melody was either in the chicken houses or turkey shelters. In addition to keeping an immaculate home, John Stillings expected his wife to share the toil of raising several thousand chicks and baby turkeys into marketable birds. What surprised Tildy was how much care little chicks and turks required. According to Melody a house full of children would be far less demanding.

Gradually, Tildy spaced her visits farther and farther apart. Even then, she almost always found Melody putting out feed or cleaning poultry houses. The sight of Melody, with hair and clothes coated with feathers and poultry yard dust, depressed Tildy. From a cheerful, fun loving person, Melody had become an uncommunicative poultry house drudge. The luxurious home she took such pride in only infrequently was occupied. "Would her own marriage turn out like this?" Tildy wondered. She thought not, but one never could tell. A worm of worry began to drill away. She caught herself wondering how to break the marriage pact she had made with Sandy. For a long while she remained away from the Stillings' farm. Only at church did she see Melody and then merely nodded and said hello. They both knew they had nothing in common any more.

#

In Lost Hollow the exhausted travelers sensed disaster. Each campsite seemed worse than the last; stinky Lost Hollow was the most worrisome of all. Meek and his fellow guide appeared to be lost. They had no plan for the morrow. When asked about the next water and pasture they had no answer. "It's out there. We jest gotta find it," Meek vaguely replied.

"This will not do at all," train captain McNary said. "We cannot wait around. Fall is upon us. If we do not get a move on we'll be spending the winter in the desert. If you aren't sure of the next water, all of us had better join in the search." The next morning teams of horsemen were organized and sent riding to the north and west. If water was discovered one rider was to remain by it; the other would ride back and report the find. At daybreak one team of riders after another saddled their mounts and rode away from Lost Hollow. The women, some with whimpering babies in their arms, walked to the edge of camp to see them off. A small, half-dressed boy ran along-side his father's horse. "Daddy! Let me go with you. I want to see water." The pitiful plea rose above the clatter of horses' hooves.

Joe did not volunteer to join in the search. Sandy had been out of his head most of the night. He was back in Middlesex County elementary school, taking roll, giving lessons, disciplining students, keeping house and courting Tildy. The first light of day was beginning to appear before he finally fell into deep slumber. By that time Joe was dead on his feet.

All day those left in camp repaired equipment, took stock of their miserable supplies or merely waited for the searchers to return. The sun beat down unmercifully. A dry wind came up, whipping dust devils through the already dust covered camp. Tired, red-rimmed, sleepless eyes kept staring into the haze-filled horizon. Late in the day discouraged riders began to return from the search, horses staggering from exhaustion and thirst. No water had been found.

"This place ain't called a desert fer nothin'," a discouraged rider declared.

"We can't give up. There has to be water out there. I don't want to die in miserable stinking Lost Hollow," his wife cried.

Thirty families made preparations to leave. They reasoned that to wait for searchers to find water was a waste of precious traveling time that they ill could afford. They gathered around the stinky spring gathering what water they could to fill barrels, beef hide containers, wash tubs, butter churns -- any container that would hold the brackish liquid. The people quickly said their good-byes and drove away to the north. Those who remained behind anxiously watched. Should they follow or should they stay? They argued and bickered among themselves and still could not make up their minds.

Their indecision did not matter. The departing wagons traveled a mere five miles before making camp. The following day they traveled another few miles when they met up with Meek. The guide told them there was no water in that direction. If they treasured their lives they would return to Lost Hollow. Sheepishly the teamsters returned to join the rest of the wagon train. Hardly did the dust of their wagons settle before another group of wagons arrived from the east. The stragglers who had fallen behind had caught up. Although glad to be reunited with their friends, the reunion brought neither group much cheer. The wagon train's situation had worsened. The trickle of brackish water had to stretch farther than ever.

Among the wagons from the east was that of the Olafsons who made camp with the Abernathys. The two families had started the trail together but were separated before reaching Fort Boise. Mrs. Olafson bulged with pregnancy. She already had two girls, the youngest barely able to toddle. Joe became aware of the Olafsons when Bithiah came to look in on Sandy. She carried the toddler. From the way she cuddled the youngster it was obvious she loved babies. Joe found the attention she lavished on the Olafson youngster distasteful. It suddenly dawned on him he was jealous. He did not want to share Bithiah's delightful company with anyone, not even a baby.

The swollen population of Lost Hollow also placed greater strain on sparse pasture. Livestock had clipped the area bare of vegetation. Farther and farther the animals strayed into the thick fields of brush, their probing muzzles searching out dry, unappetizing cheat grass. All the while the famished creatures uttered anguished bellows. People also were desperate. To supplement scanty provisions, families attempted to cook and eat salty, sharp-edged grass the animals disdained. Others slaughtered cattle that they had hoped would be the beginnings of vast Willamette Valley herds. Fear of illness had mothers and wives terror-stricken. Every person in camp was a potential victim of the mysterious sickness that had laid Sandy Sanders low. Many voiced the belief if they did not soon receive relief, no one in the train would escape from stinking Lost Hollow.

Among the fifty or more riders who set out in the frantic search for water was Saul Abernathy. He badgered his father until he received permission. Before Saul rode away he stopped to ask Joe if he had any idea where he should search. Joe's first thought was to saddle up and ride with Saul. After taking a second look at his feverish patient, he decided he should remain behind. He was of more use in camp nursing Sandy and looking after the livestock. Yet, that very morning while riding after a heifer that had strayed, he saw a landmark that stirred his memory, a rocky butte that Hawk Beak and Hare Lip Bruce had sworn was a guide post that would lead them to a creek bed where there was certain to be gold. From its summit they made out a patch of green to the north and rode toward it. On the way they happened onto a band of antelope. They forgot about the rich creek bed and gave chase. At that moment food was more important than gold. It took them all afternoon to run down and slaughter two antelope. After they had butchered their kills they could not wait to build a fire and roast a haunch. It was nightfall before they thought of their destination, the gold filled creek bed. The next day they were so turned around they could not decide which direction to take up the trail. Instead of making a search for the creek, Hare Lip Bruce came up with another brilliant idea where he was certain they would find their pot of gold.

Joe walked with Saul to the edge of the encampment and pointed at the tip of the rocky butte that peaked over the horizon. "Yonder is a high mound of rocks that looks like an overturned stew kettle. There's an old Indian trail to the top where Indians send signals and scout for game. Follow this trail to the summit and look north. If my hunch is correct you should see a thin green line between two rocky ridges. It's a creek that eventually flows into Crooked River. Here! Take my watch." Joe handed Saul the turnip-sized time piece he inherited from a trapping partner killed in a Blackfeet raid. "Buck Stone, the man who owned this taught me a trick. He found water holes and beaver streams where no one else could."

Saul looked doubtful. "I ain't much fer lucky pieces, rabbit foot and sech. Pa says they're an abomination to the Lord."

"I'm not giving it to you for luck. It may help lead us to water.

If you see a green slash like I explained, stick your knife blade in the ground so it stands straight up. Place the watch so the shadow of the knife blade starts its fall across the watch face at six o'clock. Once you have done that, use the knife blade as you would a rear rifle sight, look north and sight across the watch toward the line of green. Make a note of where your line of sight falls across the watch and mark down the time of your sighting. Here, so you won't forget, take this piece of charcoal and scrap of buckskin. Place the buckskin beneath the watch so you can mark everything down just as you see it, then ride back here as fast as you can."

Saul looked doubtful. "What if I don't see nothin'?"

"You will," Joe said with confidence he did not feel. It had been a year or more since Hawk Beak, Hare Lip Bruce and he had passed this way, and they actually had not seen the creek. Perhaps his fellow prospectors and he had witnessed a mirage. Heat waves played funny tricks on one's eyes. They could have seen nothing more than an illusion of an oasis in this furnace of a desert.

Late in the afternoon, after making Sandy as comfortable as possible, Joe strolled over to the Abernathy wagon. Bithiah, her parents and Olafsons sat in the shade, their postures stiff with tension. Mrs. Olafson looked extremely unwell. Her husband stood up briefly when Abernathy introduced him as his friend, Luke. Afterward they sat in silence, listening to the buzz of wasps and the sounds of camp.

"What kind of goose chase did you send Saul on, anyway?" Abernathy finally asked. "I shouldn't have listened to him but he was all-fired anxious to take part in the search. If he doesn't get back . . ." He tightened his lips, keeping his tortured thoughts to himself.

"He'll do all right," Joe assured. " I pointed out a helpful landmark."

"Is that so? Well, if you're so cocksure of this landmark why didn't you point it out to that blasted Meek and your scarecrow friend, Hawk Beak? Curse the day we ran into them. We shouldn't have listened to either one. Here we are, stuck in this miserable hollow. Water's making everyone sick. The cattle's starving and most folks' provisions are depleted. Why we ever let ourselves in for this is beyond me."

Joe glanced hopefully at Bithiah. She did not come to his defense. She gave him a tired smile and continued to rock the Olafson toddler.

"Somehow I feel Saul will return with good news," Joe said cheerfully. "You shouldn't worry. We'll be out of Lost Hollow before we know it."

"What makes you so blamed confident? You're not coming down with the fever, are you? Scores of riders have been out these four days without finding water and here you suddenly say some rocky butte will guide us to it." Abernathy gave Joe a look of disgust.

Mrs. Abernathy attempted to turn her husband's ire by asking after Sandy. Dad Abernathy glared at her. Joe could see there was nothing to be gained by staying on. He excused himself and gave Bithiah an appealing glance. Her attention was fixed on the Olafson child.

Back at Sandy's wagon Joe was momentarily cheered. Sandy had awakened. He weakly asked how long he had been ill. Even this effort tired him. After taking a few sips of water he lay back and again fell into troubled sleep.

At twilight teams of dispirited riders began to appear. None of them reported success. Discouraged women began the tiresome task of scraping together something to eat. Along with the herdsmen, Joe went out to round up the gaunt, starving livestock. Dusk turned into night and no sign of either Saul or the two guides, Hawk Beak and Stephen Meek. Train Captain McNary ordered beacon bonfires lighted to guide the missing riders back to camp.

Joe sat in the dark listening to disgruntled talk. Tension within him mounted until he thought he would burst. He should have asked Saul to stay with Sandy while he went in search of the butte and the green line that marked the Crooked River Creek. If Saul did not return Abernathy would blame him. He would be as much of an outcast as Hawk Beak and Meek.

Through the night Joe waited in lonely vigil, dreading the time when daylight would come and he had to face the Abernathys. Near nine o'clock the next morning the sound of thundering hoofbeats aroused the camp. Riders galloped toward them from the north. A hush fell over Lost Hollow. Livestock stopped snuffling to prick up ears. Into camp rode Saul Abernathy and Stephen Meek. "Water to the north!" Meek shouted. "Get the stock in! Pack up! Hitch up! Roll 'em! Water an' grass ahead!"

For the first time in days there was no grousing. Men strode with purpose to round up the oxen. Women scuttled to collect pots, pans, bedding and other paraphernalia. Children ran through camp shouting at the tops of their voices. The excitement aroused Sandy. He sat up and rubbed his eyes. Bithiah came running up. She threw her arms around Joe and kissed him full on the lips.

"You deserve more than that," she said with a blush. "Saul says your directions were perfect. On the way back he ran into Meek. The ornery man is taking full credit for finding water."

"Doesn't matter who takes credit," Joe said, stunned by the suddenness and passion of Bithiah's attack. "The important things is that Saul is safe and we've found water."

Bithiah impetuously kissed him again. "That's for Dad acting so mean," she said before darting away.

"Just exactly what have you been up to while I was ill?" Sandy asked, smiling. "Do I see a spark of romance? Perhaps it's more than a spark. From the looks of your face it's more like a flaming torch."

XXI

God created this Indian country and it was like He spread
out a blanket. He put the Indian on it . . . .

Meninock, Yakama

Families that continued on the established route through the
Blue Mountains encountered difficulties of a different kind. For a few
days after bidding good-bye to their desert crossing friends on the
Malheur River, travel was easy. The road was well marked, water
and pasture adequate and, with only eighty-seven wagons to manage,
the column was able to make good time. On the third day they encountered a party of horsemen heading east. The leader announced
he was Elijah White, Indian Agent for the Northwest Tribes. The
travelers were glad to meet someone familiar with the trail ahead.
Though it was still early in the day, they made camp to hear the news.
What Elijah White told them was not to their liking.

"The situation is not good," White warned. "The Indians are
rebellious. I gave them a code of laws to govern their actions and all
they do is break it -- lie, rob, fornicate, murder . . . There is not a
single Commandment they do not abuse. You have to watch them
every minute. They're not to be trusted."

"Yer the Indian agent. Why ain't yuh done somethin' 'bout
this lawlessness?" a bushy bearded man with red eyes and peeling
nose asked.

"My good man, that's the very reason I travel east. I am
going to Washington and demand protection for you folks. We need
soldiers. We should have armed forts all along the Oregon Trail, from
Fort Laramie to the Willamette Valley. These Indians have to be taught
law and order or we'll never have peace."

"What about the missions and Hudson's Bay? Ain't they
doin' anythin' ta keep these Injuns peaceful?" a querulous voice asked.

"You can't count on either one. Hudson's Bay people are as
much your enemies as the Indians. They want Oregon for Great Brit-

ain. The mission people are not much better. They're so busy looking out for themselves they have no time to pacify the Indian."

"Why, we heard tell Marcus Whitman was the man who opened up the Oregon Trail for us folk an' was beggin' fer homesteaders to follow in his footsteps."

"Of course, he did. Right now he is waiting to sell you all your supplies at twice the price you can get them from anybody else. If I were you I'd bypass Whitman's mission and Fort Walla Walla. After you get through the Blue Mountains, cross the Umatilla River and head straight for The Dalles. It will save you time and money. The Methodist mission at Wascopum will supply all your needs at half the cost."

"What about the Injuns?" the bushy bearded man with the peeling nose persisted. "How're we ta deal with 'em?"

"Keep your powder dry and eyes peeled, hope for the best and hurry through the land of the Walla Walla and Cayuse as fast as possible."

"Hmm!" Bushy Beard was not satisfied, neither were many other members of the party. Perhaps they had chosen the wrong trail. By crossing the desert they would have avoided these hordes of "murderous redskin savages." Nevertheless, early the following morning they hitched the oxen to the wagons and turned to face the Blue Mountains.

"Good Luck! God bless!" Elijah White waved his hat as the wagons rolled past.

"I think thet fella has a burr in his britches," Bushy Beard muttered to his wife. "Funny, him talkin' the way he did against Brother Whitman. I guess not all is harmony amongst our Oregon brethren."

A few days later the travelers began to descend into the Powder River Valley. Again they had reason to question their choice of trails. Outriders galloped wildly toward the lead wagons waving their arms and shouting. "Hostiles! Hostiles!" The dreadful word cut through the dust-laden air. "Cayuse!" someone yelled. This was the name of the most feared people of all Northwest tribes. These were cold-blooded savages who murdered, mutilated, plundered . . . like a virulent fever, fear swept through the column, turning stomachs weak and tempers short. Children were hustled into wagons, men reached for their weapons and the God-fearing said their prayers. Horsemen driving the loose stock rode back and forth swinging their quirts, shouting "Hi-ya! Hi-ya! Git yer dirty behinds movin'." The animals, sensing the frantic mood of their masters, skittered hither and thither, shying at their own shadows.

"Circle! Turn the wagons. Hey! Get those wheels rollin'. Not so sharp. What're yuh tryin' to do, turn the damned thing over? That's right. Pull in there. Stop and unhitch. Don't stand there. Get those blasted oxen under cover."

A dust covered woman wearing a sunbonnet, cried out as a wagon careened near her child. The child screamed. She'd lost her toy, crushed beneath an iron-tired wheel. A teamster snapped at the heels of a team of balky mules. A dog, scampering to get out of the way, caught the blow. Tucking its tail between its legs, it leaped into a wagon, nearly smothering a colicky baby. The loose stock was driven in and barricades of mattresses, boxes and barrels were erected. Then, for a moment the chaos subsided. The woman who had cried out, attempted to repair her child's crushed toy. The child looked on, sucking her thumb. The teamster whose whip struck the dog, coaxed the pooch out of the wagon and tried to make amends. The dog came out of hiding, wagging its tail and began to sniff at the mattresses, boxes and barrels. The colicky child howled.

"There they are! Here they come!" the shout came from a lookout. Every eye turned to look in the direction he pointed.

"Shucks! It's a white man ridin' a mule and a youth on an Apaloochy -- rider looks Injun," the teamster with the whip reported. "'Peers they been ridin' hard. The animals're plenty lathered. Maybeso, they're runnin' from the hostiles."

A group of men led by Train Captain McDonald walked forward. "Howdy, mister," the train captain greeted the man astride the mule. "You took us by surprise. Our outriders said they sighted a war party. That's why we're laying up instead of traveling."

"Name's Whitman, Dr. Marcus Whitman. My companion is

Michael. Your outriders are to be commended. There is a party of Indians waiting for you to pass -- Cayuse and Walla Walla. They're in a foul mood. We rode all the way from Waiilatpu to warn you."

"Golly, it's thet mission fella the Injun agent was tellin' us about," Bushy Beard exclaimed. "Don't suppose he's so hard up fer business he rode all this way on thet flop-eared mule ta make a sale?"

"Shush!" his wife ordered. "You should be ashamed of yourself. He's come to save us. He's a good man, a man of the cloth."

Marcus Whitman dismounted and made the rounds of the crowd, shaking hands, introducing himself, asking after everyone's health. Michael Two Feathers remained in the background and silently watched. He was conscious of the many staring eyes. He had not forgotten his first experience with the wagon train Missionary Whitman had guided across the plains. These people seemed much the same. An Indian was an object of curiosity. As with a snake, they were attracted to him, at the same time repelled.

The evening was spent discussing the trail ahead and the Indian threat. Whitman suggested the column move along as scheduled. He and his companion, Michael, would ride out front. They knew the Cayuse and Walla Walla leaders. When the war party appeared they would greet them, talk to them, warn them of the revenge that they could expect if they did not allow the wagon train to pass peacefully through their lands. The emigrants' hearts sank. Neither the missionary nor the Indian lad impressed them. What could these two do to stop the horde of "savages" who lay in wait? Whitman attempted to ease their fears.

"When you encounter Indians you must be bold. Indian people are no fools. They know your thoughts almost before you know them yourselves. They detest cowards and admire bravery," the missionary instructed. "Do not make threatening moves unless you intend to carry them through. Remember, these people have feelings like anybody else. For ages this has been their homeland. We are the interlopers. Mother Earth is very precious to them. Treat the land as you would treat the land of your neighbor. We want these people to understand you want to be friends; you do not want their land but only are passing through on the way to the Willamette Valley."

The meeting finally broke up. The emigrants drifted away. They had heard a lot of words but none that inspired confidence. Missionary Whitman had done little more than lecture them like first grade children. No matter how brave a front they presented, few were convinced he and his Indian companion had any chance of blunting the expected onslaught of the "uncivilized heathen Cayuse."

"Thet mission fella has more faith than common sense," Bushy Beard said to his wife. "The only weapon those two rescuers have 'tween 'em is a slingshot an' a small bag of rocks the boy carries on his saddle horn. Kin yuh 'magine thet? An them hevin' the gall ta tell us'ns they'll turn the wrath of these murderin' Cayuse away with a little scoldin'. I'm wonderin' if living' out here in all this fresh mountain air makes a man lose his sense of reason."

The horizon was beginning to brighten when the bugle sounded wake-up. Soon sunlight painted long shadows across the campsite. Still befuddled with sleep, the travelers stumbled around, preparing themselves for the day ahead. The livestock, having been kept bunched together inside the circle of wagons, stomped and lowed. They were thirsty and hungry. Herders and teamsters drove the animals to water but allowed them little time to eat. The Grande Ronde Valley lie ahead. It was important the travelers cross it quickly. It was believed the war party preferred open country to mount an attack.

With a crack of whips and giddi-ups, the column of creaking wagons rolled away from camp. Sitting astride the bony, gray mule, its long ears flapping back and forth, Marcus Whitman led the vanguard. He had been in such a rush to get away on the errand of mercy he took the first animal handy. But he liked mules. They might balk now and then but otherwise were dependable. In accompanying the 1843 immigration across the continent, he had ridden one from the banks of the Mississippi to those of the Walla Walla. Nevertheless, with his soiled cap pulled down over his ears, his pointed beard thrust out and slapping the mule with his free hand, he cut such a ridiculous figure Bushy Beard laughed. "I swear, we're bein' led against the

Philistines by a man on an ass an' a lad armed with a slingshot. If thet ain't out of the Bible I'll eat my hat."

Bushy Beard's musings were cut short. Loping straight at the lead wagons came a band of whooping, painted warriors. Whitman reined his mule crossway in the trail and calmly waited for the ferocious looking vanguard to approach. The wagon train ground to an abrupt halt. Men looked to their weapons. Women folk and children scurried inside the wagons. The approaching warriors pulled their steeds to a stop. A cloud of dust billowed up to hide them from view. The travelers waited in trepidation. The dust cleared. Four warriors had broken away from the war party and surrounded Whitman on his gray mule and the boy on the black and white pony.

"Nothing can save us now." The scary comment came from the Walden woman in the lead wagon. Then all was quiet. They could not hear what Whitman said but the threatening gestures of the enemy were plain enough. Whitman was losing the battle of diplomacy. The missionary suddenly turned to wave a hand toward the forested trail side and spoke to the Indian youth. To the watchers' astonishment, the young man took his slingshot and whirled it around his head. The missile he loosed struck an old dead snag. Out of a hole in the trunk of the dead snag flapped a huge owl. It swooped close to the band of warriors, barely skimming over their heads. The warriors who had been arguing and gesturing, hauled on the reins of their mounts, making them rear back, away from the missionary and the Indian lad. The missionary raised his arm and pointed at the dead snag from which the owl had fled. "An owl seen flying in the daytime brings the news of death," his voice rose to a thunderous shout. "If you touch a hair on the head of these people that will be your fate. The Great Father of the Bostons will send ship loads of soldiers and guns as big as tree trunks to kill all of you who do harm to these people."

The leaders reined their war painted mounts away but again Whitman raised his arm. He pointed to a leader riding a dappled gray. In a commanding voice, he ordered him to stay. Whitman took the leader's rifle and motioned curtly for him to remain by his side.

"All right! Let's roll. Everything is under control," Whitman called back to the wagon train captain. With a snap of whips and a chorus of giddi-ups, the wagons began to move. Across the valley and into the hills beyond, the train rolled before breaking camp for the night. All the way the man on the floppy-eared mule, the Indian youth on his black and white pony and the enemy war chief on the prancing dappled gray, rode side by side, not uttering a word.

The camp that night also was unearthly quiet. Like shadowy ghosts, the women glided about cooking the evening meal. Just as ghostlike, the children and men folk glided in to eat. Prayers of blessing and thanksgiving were said but few other words uttered. Near the lead wagon, Whitman, the Indian youth and Cayuse hostage sat. Food was brought but the Indian leader disdainfully brushed the plate aside, his dark eyes flashing hate. First he glowered at the missionary and then at the Indian youth. As far as anyone could tell, all night the threesome sat warily watching each other without a wink of sleep.

The wake up call came earlier than usual. Breakfast was eaten cold. The first rays of sun were just lighting the treetops when the wagons began to pull onto the Blue Mountain Trail. Again it was a quiet journey with Whitman, his companion and their Cayuse hostage leading the way. Shortly before midday another group of Indians appeared. Again, with their hearts in their mouths, the travelers pulled their wagons to a grinding halt. This time Whitman and his youthful Indian companion rode toward the newcomers with words of welcome. The people were astonished to see the Indian youth clasp the leader by the hand. Whitman waved the column forward.

"Friends!" he called out. He turned to his Cayuse hostage and handed him back his rifle. The prisoner took the weapon and shook it in Whitman's face. With a wild yell, he kicked the spirited dappled gray in the ribs and galloped over the next rise.

"I'll be dad-burned if this doesn't beat all," Bushy Beard exclaimed. "One minute hostile redskins have us travelin' scared. The next thing yuh know we have a redskin bodyguard. I swear this man Whitman has more tricks up his sleeve than Merlin the Magician."

"What about thet Injun lad on the spotted pony? He ain't no

slouch neither. Thet trick with the slingshot beat anything I ever saw," Bushy Beard's son said.

"Yeah, there's something spooky about the whole business. Thet owl comin' out of the old dead snag like thet, how do yuh suppose they managed thet? Took all the fight outta these Cayuses, like they'd seen a ghost. And what about these friendly Injuns? How did the missionary and the Injun boy conjure them up?"

The evening camp was full of cheer and good will. Whitman introduced the Indian rescuers as Nez Perce. They had been on a hunt and brought with them two carcasses of elk. They presented them to Train Captain McDonald. He immediately ordered them barbecued for a feast to celebrate their wagon train's deliverance. Before sitting down to eat, the leader of the Nez Perce, a man with a broad intelligent face, dark hair that fell to his shoulders and a single feather thrust into a head band, held up his hand. Stunned, the audience grew quiet to watch. For a long moment he stood silent. He was communing with the Great Mystery. Then in perfect English he repeated the Lord's Prayer. After the meal, he stood waiting until the crowd grew quiet. He again said a silent prayer, his arms thrust out to include the entire universe, at the end of which he said a few words the audience understood. "I am Timothy of the Nimpau, a Christian and member of the Presbyterian Church. I hold my hand out in Christian fellowship. We all are one in the sight of God. May you proceed in peace and in the grace of our Lord, Jesus Christ."

XXII

*We had a clear, full moon to light us on our toilsome way . . .
and after traveling about 20 miles we reached the
long-sought spot at daybreak.*

Journal of James Field, 1845

The discovery of water threw the inhabitants of Lost Hollow into a furor. People who had been lethargic suddenly became bundles of energy. "Hurry! Hurry!" Parents shouted at children and each other, then ran hither and yon, performing little chores that did little to help them get underway. Husbands ran for the teams forgetting to take their halters. Wives madly threw things together mindless of where they landed. Children scurried back and forth getting in the way of their elders, piling in and out of wagons screaming with excitement. Needed repairs were suddenly discovered. Husbands blamed wives for overlooking them and wives blamed their husbands.

During the height of the turmoil, Olafson's toddler wandered off. Her mother, Bithiah and neighbor women ran screaming, searching through the low growing brush until she was found. Stubborn, slow-moving oxen would not be hurried, they stumbled over wagon tongues and stood on hitching chains. Livestock dodged into the brush and had to be flushed out. Water containers were dry and had to be filled. Tramping feet churned the spring murky until late comers scooped up syrupy mud that was hardly fit for human or beast. It was late afternoon before Meek led the first wagons out of smelly, distressful Lost Hollow.

The afternoon waned. Darkness fell but a bright moon came out to flood the desert plain with light. All kinds of wildlife appeared along the track. A coyote slunk out of the shadows and just as quickly disappeared, kangaroo rats emerged from their burrows in search of food, making great leaps from one withered bunch of vegetation to another. A pair of snakes slithered around a rock, their eyes glowing in the bright moonlight like green emeralds. Lizards scurried this way and that. A jack rabbit bolted from a bush and raced to safety.

Joe, walking alongside the wagon, saw all these things as if in a dream. His head ached, his body felt feverish -- he barely could feel his legs move. Was it the dreaded fever or lack of sleep? He attempted to decide but it was too much trouble to think. He plodded on, the tug of the reins kept him on the track and awake. Several times he stumbled only to quickly regain his feet. He had to keep up. No one wanted to be guilty of slowing the wagon train.

Guided by the Big Dipper and North Star, the wagon train plodded northward all night. To make certain stragglers did not go astray, bonfires of dry sagebrush were lighted to blaze the trail. People began to grumble. "Where is this water?" Abernathy's voice could be heard above the creak of wagons and clump of hooves. "Is this another one of Meek's will-o'-the-wisps? He says there's water and all it amounts to is stinking stuff one wouldn't wash his socks in."

In the late hours the rough going began to take its toll. Teamsters snapped at their teams, cursing the day they set off for Oregon. Children fussed. The ride was too jolting and noisy for them to sleep. In order to lighten the loads every able being walked, stumbling over brush and stones and staggering in and out of gullies that crossed the path like battlefield entrapments. Sandy Sanders, who had been riding, got out to plod along with the rest.

"You are not ready for this," Joe scolded, but Sandy would not return to the wagon. Then, at daybreak the tired oxen lifted their heads. Their pace quickened. They sniffed the air and began to low.

"Water! They smell water!" a teamster shouted.

There it was, the first green they had seen for days. A ravine, thick with willow trees, patches of grass and clumps of bulrushes lay ahead. A swarm of water birds flew up to sweep away, following the line of green to the north and west. The oxen began to trot, then run, the burdens they pulled forgotten. Bawling and kicking up their heels, the loose livestock loped to the front. This spurred the oxen on.

"Cut loose the teams! They'll pitch the wagons over the cliff!" Meek bellowed the frenzied order.

Unencumbered, the teams raced toward the inviting line of

green. The banks of the ravine dropped off so precipitously it was hard to see how the animals could make it down to the stream. When it seemed the livestock would pitch over the cliff, a steep path that for centuries led wild animals to drink, opened up. Snorting, bellowing and jostling for space, the mules, horses, cattle and finally the oxen slid, scrambled and rumbled down the incline to thrust their muzzles into clear water soon roiled and darkened by the churn of hooves.

For a while everyone reveled in the change of fortunes. Youngsters skipped and splashed in shallow pools. Their elders strolled the creek banks as though on holiday. Joe found himself in a group with Tetherow, Herren, Martin and a man named Terwilliger. Herren, who carried a blue enamel bucket, filled it with camp water. In scooping the pail full, water sloshed on the ground washing away a covering of fine sand to expose oddly shaped pebbles. Herren scraped several out of the sand. They were heavy and had a dull metallic gleam.

"Looks like brass," Terwilliger observed.

While the men examined the pebbles, Hawk Beak strode up. "Meek says we'd best make camp by the water. Tomorra we'll foller the creek bottom to the north and west."

Herren put the pebbles in his pocket and studied the steep bank. "Won't be easy to bring loaded wagons down that slope. Unless I miss my guess a drag'll be needed to keep them from running up the oxen's backs."

"Could mount a pulley up there. Tie a rope to each wagon and brake them down," McNary suggested.

"Where do you fasten a pulley?" Tetherow irritably asked. "There's nothing up there to anchor on but flimsy sagebrush."

"A team and braked wagon could hold against the downhill wagon," a tired voice offered.

"I don't like it," Abernathy criticized. "Once you're in the canyon how do you get out? A good rain could soften these cliffs and bring them down on top of our heads. Anyways, after the mess we been in I ain't sure I want to do as Meek says. Why my boy, Saul, was the one who found this water. Meek took all the credit so we wouldn't do him harm."

The angry feeling of discontent and distrust experienced in Lost Hollow returned. Some insisted on following the creek bed north as Meek ordered. Others argued for staying on the bench land and taking the direct route across the sagebrush and low growing juniper covered plain. Whichever trail they chose, it was imperative they hurry. It was mid-September. By this time on the old route they would have been through the Blue Mountains.

In spite of their exhausted condition from the overnight trip, the people were so agitated hardly anyone got a wink of sleep. Arguments raged from one campfire to the next. After Meek made the rounds of the camp, trying to keep peace among the travelers, he and Hawk Beak withdrew to stay the night on the creek bank. Neither Joe nor Sandy entered into the debate. From his prospecting journey Joe knew either route would be hard going but no one asked his opinion. Besides, he still felt feverish. During the night more members of the party had fallen ill. The night journey had drained Sandy. Joe feared he could have a relapse. If both of them were incapacitated who would take over their wagon and livestock? That was the worry on Joe's mind as he fell into troubled sleep.

The travelers who did sleep, awakened to find the argument unsettled. People were so vehement on the subject that family members refused to speak to each other. Finally, to settle the debate and keep the wagons on the move, it was decided to split the train into two parts. One train, guided by Hawk Beak and captained by Riggs and McNary, would follow the creek. The remainder of the wagon train, guided by Meek, would travel directly west. This group included the Tetherows, Herrens and Abernathys. For some travelers the choice was difficult. They mistrusted Meek but believed they would make better time by taking the high trail. Sandy decided it was best for his gaunt livestock to follow the creek. This presented Joe with a dilemma. He wanted to travel with Bithiah but duty demanded he remain with Sandy. He started to argue with Sandy and immediately decided against it. It was Sandy's wagon and livestock. He had the right to do with them what he wished. Besides, since the Olafsons had rejoined the wagon train, he'd barely had a minute alone with

Bithiah.

The creek route wagons began the descent to the creek bed. Most of the teamsters used the drag method McNary suggested. First they locked the wagon wheels by chaining them to the wagon boxes, then attached a drag rope to the rear axle that was then fastened around the axle of a stationary wagon that was braked and blocked. As the descending wagon made its way down the slope the drag rope was slowly played out, making it impossible for the vehicle on the incline to run away. By the time it was Sandy's turn to take his wagon on the downhill trip, the crumbly soil had been churned to powder. A stiff breeze sent dust devils swirling in angry funnels. Joe reined the team around until the wagon was poised above the steep track which led into the ravine.

"Can you manage?" Sandy anxiously asked. The freckles on his face stood out like splotches of red paint.

"Of course I can manage," Joe answered. He was still tired and feverish and his head ached unmercifully but, like everyone else, finding water had given him a new lease on life. He gripped the reins and eyed the downhill grade. It was a bit steeper than he had previously realized.

Abernathy, with Saul and Bithiah by his side, walked up to watch. Abernathy glanced down the steep incline and shook his head. "To be on the safe side why don't you use the drag?" he said to Sandy. "Your wagon is higher than most, making it somewhat top-heavy. If it gets off balance and starts to tip, this wind could send it lickety-split over the side."

"It's up to Joe," Sandy said.

"I don't need a drag," Joe insisted, annoyed with Abernathy. Not once had he given him credit for his help in finding water.

Joe gee-hawed the oxen around until the wagon wheels were squarely in the deeply furrowed tracks made by previous wagons. He stepped back to make certain the braking chains had locked the rear wheels fast. The deep furrows would hold the wagon on course -- channel the wagon wheels down the slope like water flowing down a stream bed, he thought. He tightened his grip on the reins and clucked at the oxen. Suddenly, a particularly vicious gust of wind struck. Screeching like a banshee, it whipped and tore at the wagon cover, making the entire wagon shudder and the oxen lunge ahead. Joe pulled the reins taut.

"Steady! Steady!" he shouted, holding the team back. To be on the safe side maybe he should have a drag. He glanced at Abernathy's unctuous visage and changed his mind. The locked wheels and deep, silt-filled tracks were certainly sufficient to keep the wagon from running out of control. "Giddi-up," he ordered, slapping the reins on the oxens' backs.

The oxen leaned against the wooden yoke, slowly the wheels began to inch down the sharp descent. The hooves and wagon wheels stirred up a dust that seemed to funnel straight into Joe's face. Trying to avoid it, he leaped up on the shoulder of the cut. Suddenly he felt faint. A wave of dizziness engulfed him. He reached for the side of the wagon bed. The reins fell from his hands. He stumbled and fell, sprawling into the dust filled track. Bithiah screamed. She and her father jumped into the track to pull him clear of the wheels. Spooked by the commotion, the oxen lunged forward. The canvas canopy billowed out like a sail. The wagon tipped precariously sideways. The snapping canvas spooked the oxen even more. They lurched toward the abyss. Then, with unbelievable suddenness, oxen and wagon pitched over the edge. A flock of magpies, disturbed by the thunderous crash, took flight. The last Joe remembered was birds fluttering above him like chattering black and white kites.

XXIII

His laws never gave us a blade, nor a tree, nor a duck, nor a grouse, nor a trout . . . he comes as long as he lives, and takes more and more, and dirties what he leaves . . . .

Charlot, Flathead

Buffalo Horn was furious with himself and everyone around him. He had organized the attack on the wagon train only to be thwarted by the meddlesome missionary and his Nez Perce half-blood. To make his humiliation complete, he had been taken prisoner and held hostage and not a one of his war party had lifted a hand to come to his rescue. The ancient superstition that an owl seen flying in the daytime was a sign of death, made the warriors as useless and witless as toothless beaver.

Buffalo Horn was beside himself. Would he ever be able to hold his head up again? He took his quirt and strode outside and shouted for his sons. When they sheepishly appeared he looked them up and down and scowled. If anyone should have come to his aid it should have been his sons. First born Cloud Bird, for whom he had such high hopes, was not too strong in the head. Red Calf had more brains but let his brother guide him. Perhaps it was his own fault. He always had given the orders, telling his sons what they should and should not do, but that was the way his own father had trained him. What had gone wrong? It had to be the times they lived in. The young people of today saw their country going to ruin. Their home-land was overrun by hairy faces. These invaders from beyond the River of Many Canoes had no respect for Mother Earth. The wheels of their wagons left tracks in the land like iron bellied snakes. They felled trees that got in their way. They ran off horses, stealing some and scattering the rest. They needlessly slaughtered game leaving good meat to rot. They left camps dirty with debris. They did all these bad things and then had the audacity to dictate laws, telling the Cayuse what they should and should not do, subjecting them to punishment unbelievably cruel.

"Father, was it so bad?" Red Calf finally interrupted Buffalo Horn's bleak thoughts.

Buffalo Horn gave his son a scathing glance. "It's something I don't wish to talk about. What has happened has happened. Our plan failed. We must think of something else." He furiously walked back and forth snapping the quirt against his leggings. What evil will these hairy faced ones do next? Since the coming of the missionaries one bad thing after another had occurred and from the looks of it they would never stop. Like the spring winds, these people in their rolling lodges kept coming and coming, getting stronger and stronger until one day they would blow the Cayuse away. They were intent on passing through Cayuse lands and nothing would stop them. Perhaps the owl flapping out of the woods truly was a messenger of death, foretelling the demise of the Cayuse.

Buffalo Horn's face hardened. The Cayuse might not stop the intruders but they could do much to annoy these hairy faces, pick away at them like hungry blue jays -- dash in and snatch a possession here and there. That was the kind of campaign to wage. It would keep his warriors happy and give the people pride in knowing they did not grovel before these hairy faced invaders. He knew just the place to start this campaign. He beckoned to his two sons.

"You saw the black and white pony taken from our pasture and the magic weapon that stung you like hornets as big as owls. . . ."

\#

The villagers of Waiilatpu also were dismayed at the way Missionary Whitman and the half-blood boy had turned the table on the Cayuse/Walla Walla war party. Still smarting from the defeat, Tiloukaikt's two sons, assigned to watch the trails, spotted the missionary and his half-blood companion riding side by side on the return journey to Waiilatpu. "They come alone. Why not ambush them? They tricked us -- kept from us good plunder. They deserve to die," Tiloukaikt's impetuous eldest son, Edward said.

"Should we not first speak to Father?" his less daring brother, Clark, asked.

The brothers watched the approaching riders in silence. They feared their father but were at the stage of life when making coups and taking revenge was important. Like Buffalo Horn, they had been shamed. Until that shame was removed they would not be at peace with themselves.

The Tiloukaikt brothers were handsome young men, especially Edward. He held himself proudly. He was next in line to be head of the Waiilatpu band. Although his father frequently chastised him, he knew he was the favorite son. He was able to get away with escapades that would bring Tiloukaikt's wrath down on the head of Clark. "Ah!" he uttered scornfully. "You have the courage of a rabbit. I will ride up and strike these mission people down."

"You do this alone," Clark reined away.

Edward urged his horse forward, then stopped. A coup like this with no witness did not make sense. Besides, his father would be furious. Tiloukaikt was distressed by the failed ambush and mission's presence on Cayuse land, but had respect for Missionary Whitman.

"Brother, for once you are wise. Let us report to Father the return of these meddlers. He will say what we should do."

Tiloukaikt listened to his sons' report in silence. He, too, wanted to lash out, do something hurtful to the mission meddlers but making a raid in the Blue Mountains was one thing; to outright kill people near his home village was something else. "It is not good," he said. "We wait for better time." He saw the disappointment in the eyes of his sons. They thought him too old to fight battles -- that he let the mission rule everything he did. He studied handsome First Son who he hoped would one day take his place. What kind of leader would he make? All he seemed to desire was to make coups, plunder -- spill blood. Perhaps he should take a mate. A family might settle him down. There was the maiden, Little Fox -- young but they grew up fast. Tiloukaikt would have been horrified to know one day First Son would defy him by taking an emigrant woman for a wife.

\#

Missionary Whitman and Michael Two Feathers returned to the mission without fanfare. Thwarting the Blue Mountain ambush planned by the Cayuse and Walla Walla was taken in stride -- just another chore that had to be done to keep the settlement of Oregon Territory on schedule. That was the attitude of Marcus Whitman. Immediately upon his return to Waiilatpu he began to prepare for the influx of wagons that would soon roll in. Corn and wheat had to be ground and sacked. Cattle, pigs and sheep had to be culled out of the herds for slaughter. Potatoes, squash, turnips and the like had to be harvested, cleaned and readied for sale. Quarters had to be prepared for the sick and elderly. Space had to be cleared for people to park their wagons and set up camp. Firewood had to be collected and latrines dug and shielded. The list of chores was endless.

More and more the Whitman family included Michael in their activities. This gave him the opportunity to learn the ways of New Englanders. In the back of his mind lingered the hopeful thought that some day he would journey with his brother Joe to the homeland of their Boston relatives. When that time came he wanted to be able to conduct himself well. His big fear was the eastern relatives would find his manners embarrassing. Every mission house visit he closely watched the mannerisms of the Whitmans and the special things they did in the daily conduct of their lives. His quick mind noted their habit of precise speech and conduct, even down to the way Missionary Whitman picked his teeth on the sly after a meal.

Like a squirrel gathering food for the winter, Michael collected these bits of information and stored them away in his head for the future. The manner the parents reared their children particularly interested him. It was so different than the Indian way where children were allowed the freedom to do much as they pleased without fear of punishment. The Whitmans, especially Narcissa, liked a well disciplined household. She established rules, assigned duties and saw to it the rules were abided by and duties fulfilled. She did not scold but severely pointed a finger at a miscreant or at a chore left undone.

Household tasks were the lot of older girls while older boys, John and Francis Sager, worked the fields, helped in the gristmill and saw to it the livestock had sufficient pasture and water. In spring and summer all old enough to lend a hand took part in cultivating and harvesting the crops. Even five year old Matilda Jane Sager walked up and down crop rows ringing a bell to frighten away the birds.

Michael took a special interest in the Sager brothers who were near his own age. They were so different in temperament. John, was much like himself, a quiet reserved person, said little but went about his work with determination and never left a task uncompleted. Francis rejected discipline. He did not care if he worked or not. He would start a task, find it tiresome and leave it for someone else to finish. The harsh treatment meted out by Alan Hinman, the teacher, infuriated Francis. "All the man knows is whip, larrup, beat," he complained to Michael. Francis also resisted the demanding religious side of mission life. "I've had it with Scripture talk," he announced after a tedious prayer meeting and Bible study conducted by visiting Henry Spalding. "Christ and the Disciples must have done things besides perform good deeds and think pious thoughts?"

Michael sympathized with Francis. When it came to religious matters the Whitmans seldom deviated from a strict schedule. Every day began and ended with prayer. Every youngster old enough to comprehend was charged with learning a daily verse of Scripture which was recited en masse during Sunday services. Saturday nights were reserved for Bible study. On the first Monday of every month prayers for the missions were held. During the winter season a weekly prayer meeting was observed every Thursday. On Sabbath mornings all those who could read were assigned religious readings. Those who could not read were given religious pictures to contemplate. After a lengthy prayer, a hurried breakfast was eaten, then it was off to Sunday school where the verses learned during the week were recited. A sermon and discussions of morning readings followed. In the evening more readings were assigned. The Ten Commandments were discussed, along with proverbs and parables. It was easy to tell when evening study ended. Francis Sager ran from the mission house to circle the corral three times, yipping like a demented coyote.

When Francis Sager announced he was leaving for the Willamette Valley, it did not surprise Michael. Francis did not fit into the strict mission life the Whitmans imposed. Nor was Michael surprised when the Whitmans left on an overnight trip to see the children who were left behind run wild. They reminded him of trapped animals suddenly set free. The younger ones dashed in and out of the mission house with abandoned glee. It was all staid John Sager and dependable Catherine Sager could do to get them to settle down for the evening meal.

As the month of September passed and the first weeks of October slid by, a feeling of gloom settled over the mission compound. In spite of his heroic efforts in thwarting the wagon train ambush, Marcus Whitman discovered the people he befriended had no intention of returning the favor. Whitman had made it a point to personally invite every emigrant family to Waiilatpu where grain and other foodstuffs awaited. Only a few families accepted the invitation. Most who did appear had sick members who required medical attention or were too weary to journey on. The majority of emigrants took Elijah White's advice. From the Blue Mountain passes they went directly to the Umatilla Crossing and straight on to The Dalles. The produce that the people in Waiilatpu had so tirelessly cultivated, harvested and prepared for sale was left to mold and gather dust. In hopes of making some sales, Whitman loaded a wagon with flour and other foodstuffs and, accompanied by Narcissa, drove to where the emigrants crossed the Umatilla. They were met with rebuffs.

"We hev sufficient provisions ta git us'ns ta The Dalles," a teamster with holes in the knees of his trousers explained. "We gotta save every penny we'uns kin," was typical of the responses the missionary couple received.

Apprehensively, Michael watched the Whitmans leave for the Umatilla. Not only was he worried about their fate but also about his own. For several days he had seen Cloud Bird and Red Calf loitering around Tiloukaikt's village. He knew exactly why they were there -- they had come for Magpie. Every night and day he kept watch over his four-legged friend. When he was invited to the mission house he tethered the pony close to the door. The Sager brothers joked about his attachment to Magpie, saying he would take the black and white pony to bed with him if it were not so large.

Michael kept his fears to himself. He knew full well the humiliation Buffalo Horn had suffered. He was a proud, arrogant man. To endure the indignity of being disarmed and held at gun point was a degrading experience -- one he would never live down. The fact that Magpie, a horse spirited away from his herd, was involved in the shameful affair was something he would not forget. It was only natural for Buffalo Horn to send his sons to do the job they had bungled once before. While the Whitmans were away was exactly the time they would choose to strike. If they came for his ponies they might take it into their minds to run off the other livestock or worse. Michael did not want that to happen. He knew the best thing he could do was to remove the temptation Magpie and the black mare created -- take the ponies out of Buffalo Horn's reach.

Immediately after the Whitmans disappeared from sight, Michael rolled up his belongings in a sleeping robe, tied the bundle to the back of his saddle and brought in the black mare from the pasture. He stopped at the mission house to tell Catherine and John Sager he was leaving. The youngsters put up a fuss and John argued, walking with him to where Magpie and the black mare waited.

"Mother Whitman will not like this a bit," John said. "At least you'll come back to see us again, won't you?"

"Of course, I will return," Michael said gruffly, touched by his friend's concern. He quickly swung upon Magpie's back and pulled on the black mare's halter line. At the gate he turned to raise his hand in a last farewell. He reined Magpie on the trail north and east. Vision Seeker had urged him to return to Lapwai. That was where he would go. He and his ponies surely would be safe there.

#

Michael's arrival in Lapwai was as emotional as was his leave taking in Waiilatpu. When the high bluffs on the north bank of the Clearwater River came into view, dogs spied him and began to bark. As he approached the village, children scampered out to squeal and shout. He hardly came to a stop in front of his grandfather's long lodge, when Lone Wolf appeared, his usually solemn face wreathed in a broad smile. Quiet Woman rushed up to give him a smothering hug, then stepped back to clap her hands with joy. Vision Seeker and Running Turtle appeared to add their greetings. Michael's heart pounded as if it would burst. He hadn't realized how much he missed his family. Villagers came to say hello and wish him welcome. The evening meal was a feast. It began with Lone Wolf saying a silent prayer, thanking Mother Earth for the food and their grandson's return. He pointed to the sky, to the ground and to the four directions east, south, west and north, then bobbed his head three times. They were ready to eat. How different from the long, loud blessing and prayer sessions at mission house meals. Michael wished Francis Sager were present to witness the difference.

However, as the days passed, Michael discovered all was not well in Lapwai. If anything, the Nez Perce were in greater turmoil than the Cayuse. The campaign of Thunder Eyes, the shaman, to oust outsiders from the valley was in full sway. Groups of rowdy youth went from one lodge to another, harassing families from other bands who had settled in Lapwai to be near the mission. Missionary Spalding's edicts were openly flaunted as was the code of laws imposed by Indian Agent White. One evening a group of young men collected in a field near the mission house to gamble, lighting the area with fires fueled by rails taken from the fence that enclosed the mission grounds. Michael and Vision Seeker, awakened by the commotion, came to see what was happening. Dressed in a great buffalo coat, Spalding stepped from the mission house and raised his hand for attention.

"Listen to me," he shouted. "Gambling is forbidden. It is a sinful practice that must cease . . . ." The revelers seized the missionary and threw him to the ground, then rolled him into the fire. Michael was aghast. This was a man of God. Surely a bolt of lightening would strike to send the attackers to their deaths. Instead, the voice of Vision Seeker thundered across the open space. "Stop! You shame our forefathers who taught us to be proud and brave. Go to your lodges. Leave this man be."

Spalding was released. Vision Seeker and the huge buffalo coat had saved him from getting badly burned. The missionary quickly retreated into his home. The revelers drifted away but the discord was renewed the following day. The mill dam was demolished. Fences around the mission grounds were pulled down. A delegation went to Spalding's home and ordered him to leave. When the missionary refused, the windows of the mission house were broken and dirt and rubbish thrown in. Michael and others who had attended the mission school, were insulted and taunted as missionary lackeys and slaves.

The happiness Michael experienced the day of his arrival turned to dismay. What had happened to his people? Even Lone Wolf and Quiet Woman appeared befuddled. Running Turtle did not seem to know which side he was on. He scuttled from one end of the valley to the other returning with rumors that kept Lone Wolf and Quiet Woman in a dither. Only Vision Seeker remained the same. Every day he went to the hillside to meditate and watch over the herd. That was where Michael found him the day he decided to leave.

"I wish to borrow a horse and leave Magpie and the black mare in your care. They are not safe in Waiilatpu."

"Ah, you return to Whitman's mission?" Vision Seeker asked.

"Yes, coming home was a mistake," Michael explained. "I no longer take pleasure here. People have changed. I do not understand them. Perhaps Cayuse are no better but I know why they do what they do."

Vision Seeker studied the lad who had suddenly turned from boy into man. His father would have been proud of him, he thought. He had suffered every possible adversity yet had risen above them with his dignity and common sense intact. He was the product of two cultures and seemed to have come up with the best qualities of both.

"My honored nephew, trouble is everywhere. Remember what I told you . . ." Vision Seeker fell silent. It did not matter what he had said. The young man had to find his own way. That was the way things were meant to be.

XXIV

. . . the crazed brutes were halted, but not before two lay quiet with bullets through their skulls.

Catherine C. DeMoss, *BLUE BUCKET NUGGETS*

The suddenness of the tragedy took everybody by surprise. With backs to the gusty wind to keep the penetrating, blinding dust from their eyes, the stunned crowd stood on the bluff and stared in disbelief at the wreckage. Steph Meek strode back and forth muttering to himself as if by saying the proper words the disaster would go away. Sandy's crushed wagon looked like a discarded, broken toy. At the edge of the stream bed four wheels were thrust upright like legs of an overturned bug. Underneath the crushed remains of the wagon box the canvas canopy lay spread out on either side of the wreckage like a gray shroud. An ox lay nearby, its side pierced by the splintered wagon tongue. Another ox futilely struggled to free itself from its yoke and harness straps. Each struggle was followed by a painful bellow. One or more of its legs were broken. The other two oxen lay at the bottom of the hillside, silent and unmoving, apparently dead. Tildy's bridal chest had burst. New linens, a blanket, dish towels and other items Granny Jennings had carefully stored away for the big event were scattered along the stream bank.

Two of McNary's men, already on the creek bottom and with rifles in hand, ran to shoot the wounded, struggling oxen. The painful, moaning sounds ceased. The emigrants turned their attention to the body of Joe Jennings. What in the world could have happened to him? The young man had keeled over as if poleaxed.

Gradually the dark fog of unconsciousness turned to harsh sunlight, so bright it hurt Joe's eyes. For a long moment he lay still, attempting to reconstruct what had happened. Critical voices helped him sort things out.

"Thet wagon jest picked itself up an' sailed off like a four mast schooner. In all me born days I ain't seed nothin' like it."

"Yep, those high canopy wagons're known fer catchin' the wind but it was the drivin' thet did it."

"Thet it was. I don't know how mountain men gain sech fame. They kin trap an' skin varmints but other than thet, what're they good fer? Look't thet wagon. Ain't nothin' left but a bunch of kindlin'."

Hawk Beak was the only one who put in a halfhearted word in Joe's defense. "Some months back he got a powerful bad stabbin'. He ain't been quite right in the noggin since."

"Something was wrong with his thinking, all right. Should've known better than take that rig down with no drag. I tried to reason with him but he's as contrary as a sow with a batch of sucklin' pigs." That was Abernathy's voice.

Joe listened with a growing sense of shame. He opened his eyes to see Sandy's homely freckled face hovering anxiously above him. Joe inwardly groaned. After this debacle how could Sandy even speak to him?

"You must have caught my fever," Sandy said. "It turns one weak as dishwater." He helped Joe to his feet. The crowd fell silent and stepped back. Joe abstractly brushed at his dusty clothes. He stopped. What was the matter with him? Everyone and everything was coated with dust. He stepped to the far side of the trail and glanced at the wreckage he had caused. It was worse than he had imagined. Everything Sandy owned was in ruins. Instead of helping Sandy and Tildy get off to a good start in their marriage, he had destroyed them.

"I'll make it up to you," Joe said in a voice that trembled. Then abruptly fell silent. What a ridiculous statement. How was he going to get the wherewithal to help anybody?

"Don't worry yourself," Sandy consoled. "No one was hurt. Material things can always be replaced, except for the oxen and they aren't a total loss. Short as we are on rations, their carcasses will provide much needed meat. Quit fretting. We'll slaughter the oxen and have a feast."

Sandy's lack of concern made Joe feel even worse. How

could any man be so compassionate? He had gotten out of a sick bed and here he was consoling him as though he was the sick one and had suffered the losses. "You're not well!" he scolded "You shouldn't be up and around like this! Maybe we can dig a mattress out of that mess so you can lie down."

Bithiah, who had stood silently to one side, looked at Joe with piteous concern. "Don't take on so. Things are not as bad as they look. Pa says we can make a two-wheel cart from the wreckage and resurrect a lot of the household goods."

"Yep," Abernathy agreed. "To put you fellows right, I'll loan Sandy our spare team. Now, let's get after those dead oxen. This bunch of travelers could sure use a good feed."

For almost the first time since leaving Fort Boise there was a cheerful camp. Plentiful water, pasture and the feast of oxen meat made the future look brighter. In a boisterous mood, Luke Olafson who, as usual with his family, took dinner with the Abernathys, christened the campsite Dead Ox Creek.

The next morning the two trains departed; one followed the creek bed, the other turned west to cross the sagebrush and stunted juniper plain. With Abernathy's help, Sandy and Joe resurrected the workable parts of the smashed wagon. Laboriously, they sawed the wagon bed in two. Saul and Dad Abernathy harnessed a team and hauled the back half up the slope where they constructed a vehicle that had the appearance of a giant rickshaw. When they finished Abernathy eyed it critically. "Me thinks this contraption would make better passage crossing the plain. That creek trail appears mighty rough. Since these are my oxen, I'd like to have you follow along with us."

Sandy agreeably nodded. "We'll go wherever you say. Right now, all I want is to reach the Willamette Valley with a whole skin."

The following day the last of the wagons of the cross-country column departed. Sandy and Joe remained behind to sort through Sandy's belongings. As they pawed through the wreckage Joe recognized familiar objects: a feather bed, two patchwork quilts, butter churn, spinning wheel, Dutch oven, a set of cast iron skillets, even a chamber pot. Joe readily could see Tildy's fine hand behind Sandy's inventory of possessions. Many came from the Jennings' old family home.

It took a long time for Sandy to decide what to take and what to leave. Everything had to be hand carried or loaded on the back of Lonesome Mule and packed up the steep canyon trail. Joe did not trust himself enough to drive the two-wheel cart into the creek bottom. He had the uneasy feeling if he brought it down he never would be able to get it out. The first item Sandy chose to take was Tildy's broken, but now patched, bridal chest.

"I wouldn't leave that behind for anything," he said.

The fresh cool desert twilight was beginning to fall when the awkward, two-wheeled conveyance rolled away from Dead Ox Creek. Neither Sandy nor Joe looked back. Joe didn't want to be reminded of the humiliating experience suffered there. Sandy could not stand to see his precious possessions left behind.

Late on the third day they caught up with the wagon train. Before they had time to unhitch, Bithiah and Saul descended. "We were worried," Bithiah announced. "Pa was thinking to send Saul back to find you."

"Wish you had," Sandy joked. "We needed a cook. Joe's grub tastes like he mixed in his dirty socks."

"Don't joke about food around camp," Bithiah warned. "Folks are in such sorry shape they're eating berries and dried grasshoppers they get from the Indians."

"Tetherow sent a half dozen riders ahead with pack animals for help," Saul added. "They set off on an Injun trail. They're hopin' it'll take them to The Dalles in two days."

"Hmm," Joe uttered. "I wonder if Hawk and I didn't travel that trail once. If so, it's longer than you'd think -- uphill, downhill. Water -- it can't be found with a divining stick."

"You'd best tell Tetherow. He's more or less in charge. An Injun took Meek and Tetherow to a mountain top to show them the lay of the land. There's Crooked River to the north and Deschutes River to the west. Both run through terrible canyons. Tetherow figures folks'll be starvin' afore we cross either one. To make matters worse, mountain fever is strikin' down people right and left. Mrs. Olafson has it bad. Her baby arrived -- born dead."

The sickness was even more catastrophic than Saul reported. Almost every wagon contained one or more people too sick to walk. Six in one family lay prostrate in their wagon bed. Their groans and constricted breathing could be heard all over camp. Still the wagon train traveled on. Fear drove the travelers. Food was running short. The chill of autumn was in the air. In the west snow-clad mountains warned winter was dangerously near.

September 23rd was a day every train member would re-member with dread. During the night four members of the party died, one of them Mrs. Olafson. Luke Olafson and his two girls watched tearfully as the Abernathys and other neighbors laid their wife and mother to rest. The heartsick family lingered at the side of the lonely sagebrush shaded grave until Bithiah picked up the toddler and car-ried her away.

On September 24th the train traveled all day and all that night before finding water, only to see it frustratingly out of reach. They had come upon Crooked River Canyon, a cut more than three hundred feet deep in solid rock. Smelling water, the livestock came alive. They began to trot, then broke into a run. Teamsters cursed and sawed on lines to no avail. Herders shouted and pressed against the loose stock. Two thirst-crazed cows bolted free. Meek, inspecting the canyon depths, wheeled around and threw up his rifle. "Shoot! Shoot!" he yelled. The two lead animals fell in their tracks, shot through the head. This did not deter the thirst-crazed teams. "Cut the harness straps! Turn the critters loose," came a frantic shout.

A volley of shots and hard riding by herders turned the live-stock to send the animals thundering through the underbrush along the canyon rim. The freed teams, still harnessed and yoked together, wheeled about to follow. Frantic teamsters ran along the canyon rim, snapping whips and cursing, expecting any second to see their pre-cious oxen pitch into the precipitous abyss. For miles the livestock thrashed through the brushy terrain until a break in the canyon wall allowed passage to the river.

"We'd best make camp here," Tetherow announced needlessly. Without teams the wagons could not move and the travelers were too exhausted to round up the runaway animals. The men gathered at the edge of the canyon to inspect the stream that rushed through the gorge hundreds of feet below.

"Look at it. Might as well be on the moon," someone declared, his voice filled with despair.

Joe had to agree. The water that rushed pell-mell over the rocky stream bed was so far away it looked more like a silvery ribbon than a river. On either side walls of rock rose like parapets of ancient battlements. There was no scaling them.

"We could go down those extra miles to the break in the canyon wall and get our water there," someone suggested.

"Who has the will or energy to do that?" a voice retorted.

"Perhaps with sufficient rope we might lower a bucket and pull up enough water to get through the night," Abernathy said.

"There ain't enuff rope in the whole blinkin' wagon train ta reach," a teamster said in a weary voice."

However, ropes were collected, knotted together and a bucket fastened to the end and lowered. The wind caught the flimsy container and gave the rope a wrench, nearly pulling it from Dad Abernathy's grasp. "Aaah!" he groaned. "The Good Lord wants us to suffer more. The precious water is there but He placed it out of our reach. From this distance a rope and bucket will never make it."

"If we had a steady hand who'd let hisself be lowered to yonder ledge, I reckon he could guide the bucket down," a gray bearded spectator suggested.

"What're talkin' 'bout? There ain't nuff room thar fer a mountain goat," his beardless companion scoffed.

Joe studied the ledge, a mere rock that jutted from the shear canyon wall. The thought of being lowered onto it gave him the shivers. "If Sandy and Saul holds me fast, I'll try it," he blurted.

Bithiah gasped. "Dad! Don't you dare let Joe go. I'll drink with the cattle first."

Ignoring his daughter's threat, Abernathy knotted lengths of rope together, tying one end around Joe's chest. Joe glanced into the canyon depths. Usually heights were no bother but the deep, narrow gorge, the bottom of which looked so far away, made him suck in his breath. Near the water a swarm of swallows swept back and forth, so small in the distance they resembled gnats. He grasped the rope so tightly, the rough strands cut into his hands. He inched toward the cliff edge. A rock gave way. His feet fell from under him. Watchers screamed. From Joe's lips came a choking cry. The rope around his chest snapped taut. A cloud of black dots blinded him. He could not breathe. A twist in the rope spun him around. His vision cleared. He glanced down. The rock he had displaced floated through the air like a kite. His blood turned to ice. Desperately, he clawed for the rocky wall. There was nothing he could grasp. He dangled hundreds of feet above the canyon floor. In a frantic second, his life flashed before his eyes. This was how it was to die. Suddenly, with a bone-breaking jar, he bounced against the rocks and fell upon the narrow ledge. "Thank God!" he said with the fervor of one who had just escaped death.

"All right, send down the bucket," he finally managed to yell. A cheer went up. Down came the bucket, but as it did when lowered from the canyon rim, the wind sent it sailing away. Then, for a second, the wind slackened. The bucket plummeted to hang tantalizing above the sheeny surface of the fast moving water.

"Quick! Another length of rope," Joe shouted. "This won't reach." Another rope and then another were added before the bucket dipped beneath the water's surface. The weight of the rope and the pull of the wind on rope and swaying bucket were almost too much for the men on the canyon rim to manage. Slowly, with Joe guiding the rope, the bucket reached the top. Dad Abernathy swore. Barely a few cupfuls of water remained.

"Once more," Abernathy ordered. But the next try was just as fruitless, then the wind strengthened. The bucket sailed away with such force the men holding the rope hardly could pull it in. Joe, exposed on cliff wall, was buffeted unmercifully. "Pull me up!" he screamed. Safely on the canyon rim, Bithiah threw her arms around him. "Oh, Joe! I was so afraid!" she cried. "Don't ever do anything like that again."

For a short moment Joe walked arm in arm with Bithiah. For this kind of reward he would go down on the ledge and stand on his head. Yet, the feeling of bliss was short-lived. The Olafson girl came running up, crying. "There is a death in the neighbor's wagon," she blurted. "Oh! No," Bithiah uttered, dropping Joe's arm. "I must go. The poor family'll be distraught."

That night six members of the party died and were summarily buried. The dispirited, travelers barely could look at each other. Which one of them would the Grim Reaper's scythe cut down next?

The following day, when the teams were rounded up, harnessed and hitched, the wagon train reversed itself to travel east to the break in the canyon wall where the livestock had descended to drink. Here, between two rocky outcroppings, the river widened and the banks on either side dropped away to provide a reasonably safe crossing. The wagons forded the river to pass through a coulee forested with pungent juniper. For a while travel was easy. The mood of the travelers improved. Perhaps they would make it to The Dalles after all. Spirits soared even higher when Saul, who rode ahead, hallooed and galloped wildly back. "Wagons're comin'!" he yelled.

"Hurrah!" a teamster shouted. "We're saved. It's the relief party from The Dalles." Those astride horses raced ahead, then pulled up. Hawk Beak's lanky frame, topped by the crow feathered hat, came over the crest of a hill. "It's thet damned scarecrow stooge of Meek's," a voice said in disgust. "Must be the McNary train thet followed the creek."

McNary, Parker and Riggs and the others who had followed Dead Ox Creek came into view. The meeting of separated friends did bring some cheer. For a few moments warm greetings were exchanged. A discussion of which trail was best ensued. Both trails had taken a heavy toll. Both parties had traveled the same time and arrived at the same place; no advantage was declared.

As the evening wore on the joy of reunion turned to bitterness. At their present rate of travel The Dalles still lay a week to ten days away. Most families had exhausted their provisions. In some wagons the sick were too far gone to survive. Outright terror hung over the column. "It's a death train," someone morbidly claimed.

That evening, while Joe and Sandy attempted to make supper out of what remained of their meager rations, Hawk Beak appeared. He squatted down to help himself to a cup of what passed for coffee. Irritated, Joe started to lash out. Hawk's harried expression made him hold his tongue.

"'Peers the people're gettin' a bit nervous," the skinny guide finally spoke.

"Are you just finding that out?" Joe retorted angrily. "They are not nervous, they're downright scared to death. In the last few days we've buried a dozen people. Many more are on their last legs. They're saying you and Meek murdered them as sure as if you had shot them down with a gun."

"Thet's not right thinkin'. It's the will of God thet some're dead an' others livin'.'"

"I wouldn't try that argument on Best, whose wife and two young ones are at death's door, or Harry Noble who lost two sons. If I were you I'd be mighty careful. These people are half out of their minds with grief and worry."

The train moved on to stop at a camp with ample water and good grass; Sagebrush Springs, someone named the place. The wagon masters decided the exhausted livestock needed a day of rest. Ahead loomed the massive bulk of a mountain. Scouts returned to report canyons and ravines on either side were too boulder strewn to allow wagons to pass. There was no alternative but to make the steep ascent up the mountain. After that, only one major obstacle blocked the way to The Dalles -- the treacherous Deschutes River.

The day at Sagebrush Springs provided the travelers with little rest. The men tightened wagon wheels, greased axles, spliced wagon tongues, reinforced singletrees, mended harnesses and did other chores required to put equipment and gear in workable condition. The womenfolk beat the dust from blankets and quilts, washed clothes, tended the sick and tidied up wagon interiors.

In going over their cart, Sandy and Joe discovered a linchpin had worn thin. If it broke on the long pull up the mountain the double tree might break free. If that happened they could either be stalled on the steep incline, or worse yet the two-wheel cart might roll back into the path of the next wagon in the column.

"Perhaps Herren has a spare," Sandy said. "He carries all sorts of junk in his tool box."

Herren and two helpers were busy greasing axles. With a pole Herren pried up a corner of the wagon. When the wheel cleared the ground the helpers pulled it, exposing the axle which they then coated with a mixture dipped from a grease bucket.

"Maybeso, there's something you can use in the tool chest," Herren said when Sandy explained his need. Herren opened a wooden box stuffed with tools, scraps of iron, tin and an assortment of bolts, screws and nails. Laying in a tray were the strange pebbles Herren discovered on the bank of Dead Ox Creek.

Sandy, who had not seen them before, picked one up and studied it. "What is this?" he asked.

"Something I found along the trail. Someone said they looked metalic." Herren took a pebble and laid it against the iron tire of the wagon wheel. He gave it a rap with the head of a hammer. The pebble didn't break, instead it flattened into an oval disk. Sandy grabbed the object from Herren. Excitedly, he scratched on the surface with a nail. "I'll say it's metal. It's precious metal. Unless I miss my guess, it's gold. This is a gold nugget!"

XXV

*Sept. 29. all day gitting up hill laid without water
beried 3 heare . . .*

Diary of S. Parker, 1845

"Gold! Gold!" the cry was repeated all over the emigrant camp. Herren was swamped with requests to view the precious pebbles picked up on the banks of Dead Ox Creek. Hawk Beak came up to Sandy demanding to know if the nuggets were really gold. "Hmm!" he grunted sourly when Sandy told him they were indeed genuine. "We probably overlooked a fortune when we prospected thet region; we were so dumb we didn't know jack rabbit droppings from wild honey. I'd better take a gander. If I take a notion to go prospectin' again I want to recognize the stuff."

The wave of gold fever died as quickly as it emerged. Gold would not fill empty bellies or make the sick well. The wagons pulled away from Sagebrush Springs toward the massive mountain which blocked the travelers' path. On a creek bank near the base of the mountain the people made camp to spend an unrestful night. The mountain hovered above them, blocking out the stars like a blanket. All the next day the mountainside rang with the snap of bull whips and cursing shouts. If wagon wheels stopped turning it took Herculean efforts to get them rolling. Some wagons barely made it to the top. Others stalled. A few slid back, only stopping when teamsters frantically locked the brakes and threw boulders behind the wheels. Drivers doubled up their teams; sometimes triple teams were needed to move the heavier and bulkier wagons.

The exhausted travelers made camp on the barren mountain top. It was a desolate, heartbreaking place. That evening three graves were dug and three bodies laid to rest on the lonely wind swept summit. After the burials outrage replaced grief. Wild threats and curses rent the air. Meek and Hawk Beak were singled out and damned and re-damned to eternal hell.

"You'd best warn your friend," Sandy advised Joe. "The mood this crowd is in there's no telling what they might do. Lay low yourself. From the way the people talk any mountain man they decide to string up will be good riddance."

As was their custom, the guides camped a short distance from the circle of wagons. Joe arrived to find the campsite empty; Meek and Hawk Beak had taken flight. The only evidence they left behind was the smoke of a smoldering fire. A low roar of sound, turning into the terrible cry of a malicious mob, swept across the mountain summit. A red-faced farmer from Missouri led the pack. In a big fist he carried a coil of rope. To find their quarry had fled, created an even greater cry for vengeance. They turned on Joe. Frenzied hands grabbed his clothes, nearly jerking him off his feet.

"Yuh warned 'em! Yuh helped the dirty curs get away!" the red-faced leader bellowed.

Joe pulled free to have other hands wrench him to the ground. The rope encircled his neck. Its rough surface cut into his skin. For the first time ever, Joe experienced stark fear. These people had gone mad. They thirsted for blood and would not stop until satisfied. The noose tightened. He was yanked to his feet. A dozen hands pulled on the rope. Like a balky mule, he was dragged toward the nearest pine tree. The rope cut deeper into the tender flesh. His Adam's apple felt crushed. His breath came in short gasps. He sounded like a wind-broken horse. Joe stumbled. Again he was jerked upright. Everything started to turn black. Then a piercing shot brought the painful ordeal to a stop.

Sandy burst into the crowd waving Joe's double-barreled scatter gun. He shoved the muzzle in the Missouri farmer's face. "Turn him loose or I'll let you have both barrels." He pulled the twin hammers back to full cock. The mob hushed, stunned as much by Sandy's ferocity as by the lethal weapon.

Reluctantly the Missouri farmer dropped the rope. Joe struggled to free himself from the noose and took a tortured breath. "All right!" the Missouri farmer growled. "Yuh made yer point. But thet Meek an' Hawk Beak had better not show up. We won't bother ta hang 'em. We'll shoot 'em down like sheep killin' dogs, jest like they deserve." One by one and then in small groups the crowd drifted away to disappear among the wagons and tents of the cold, wind-swept encampment.

"What a very brave thing you did, Sandy," Bithiah exclaimed.

"I'll say it was," Joe agreed. He felt so weak and shaky he leaned against the rough bark of the pine tree that was to have been the gallows. He put a hand up to his rope burned throat and shud-dered. If it hadn't been for Sandy's quick action he would be swing-ing lifeless from a tree limb. The attack of the mob seemed more frightening and deadly than that of the Blackfeet war party which felled Buck Stone and Clay Beamer.

#

The temper of the camp cooled, as did the weather. On the unprotected mountain top, snow-chilled breezes swept down from the north and west. For those sleeping in the open, and for the live-stock herders, it was a long and bitter night. The next morning the weary campers loaded up to pull away as silently and dispiritedly as if setting out on a wake.

All day the wagon train traveled a rocky track through rolling hills. The bleak, barren landscape offered little relief. Everything looked the same: rocks, a scattering of stunted trees and field after field of low-growing brush. Finally, after nightfall, the train arrived at much needed water. All through the night slower wagons pulled in, some with family members too exhausted to set up camp. Again it was a place of death. Five more bodies were laid to rest. Burials had become so commonplace they merely were one more camp task.

On October 2nd the train came to the east bank of the turbu-lent Deschutes. At first glance it appeared a crossing would not be too difficult. Outriders discovered a break in the river bank. Loose cattle and horses were driven there and forced into the water. The current caught the struggling animals, hurtling them downstream. Just as it appeared the herd was lost, the current flung the livestock against the far shore where the animals frantically clawed their way up the steep slope.

"I'm not chancing my wagon in that stream," Abernathy declared. "If the current doesn't sweep us away, we'll still never make the pull up the far bank."

The weary travelers paced the river's edge in despair. The Dalles was a mere thirty miles away. It might as well be three hundred. Like an impregnable barricade, the Deschutes' icy swift waters and steep banks, blocked the way. Train captains gathered in a group to discuss what to do. They decided on a crossing where the banks were less abrupt, then changed their minds. The current was especially swift and was certain to sweep the wagons away. They had come too far to lose everything here.

The wagon train's misery deepened. Mrs. Butts, who for days lay ill, died. Her husband vowed not to bury her body until they crossed to the far side of the river. No one attempted to dissuade him. Two boys who had gone exploring, saw a fish jump in the stream. They announced their find and began to cut and rig fishing poles. For a short while the thought of fresh fish absorbed everyone's attention. What to use for bait was the big question. No one had anything that would tempt the wily mountain trout.

Evening fell. The rushing waters mocked them as the travelers prepared to spend the night. "There has to be a way across," Abernathy said. "Perhaps we can float the wagon beds over. Yes, that's the thing to do. We'll construct a makeshift rope ferry like some I've seen in the east. You stretch a cable from one bank to the other . . . ." He hurried away to lay his plan before the captains. The captains agreed it was a good idea but how did one get a cable secured on the far river bank?

"There's only one way. Somebody'll have to swim it across," Abernathy said, "but I don't know who that will be, half of us can't swim and the other half are too weak."

"Yep, whoever 'tis will have to be fit or he'll drown," Parker observed. He was frantic to reach medical help in The Dalles. That day his two sons and daughter had fallen ill with the fever.

There was no pressure on him to volunteer, but Joe did. He was a strong swimmer and believed he could make it across. After the near lynching he did not owe the people a thing, yet it seemed important to do something that would offset the ill-feeling against mountain men. Too, he was indebted to Sandy for saving his life, and in the back of his mind, he saw it as an opportunity to impress Bithiah. She was spending entirely too much time with Luke Olafson and his kids.

Abernathy bustled around to help Joe prepare for the crucial swim. He tied a light rope around Joe's bare chest which, if the crossing was successful, would be fastened to a heavier rope cable that would be pulled across the river and secured to a rock or tree. The cable rope was the key to the operation. When anchored to the far side a pulley would be hooked on to it. Another rope, running through the pulley wheels and with one end fastened to a wagon box, would make it possible to pull the wagon box and its contents from one bank to the other. "There," Abernathy said after knotting the rope that encircled Joe, "you have nothing to fear. If you get into trouble we'll pull you ashore like a hooked fish."

"Yeah!" Joe uttered. Only a fool would risk his neck like this. The water looked even more turbulent than he thought. He threw a piece of pine bark into the stream. The current caught it up, hurled it against the near bank and then sent it swirling into the center of the stream where it swiftly bobbed out of sight. The demonstration was far from reassuring. Joe could just see his battered body bouncing from one rocky bank to the other, finally coming to rest lifeless on some far off sand bar.

He walked upstream to a rocky point that hung over the river. He reasoned a running jump would take him over the main current. He hit the water with a splash. "Oo-ee!" he howled so loudly a mule began to hee-haw. It was like being immersed in a bucket of ice. But he had no time to think. The current picked him up as easily as it had the piece of bark, hurtling him downstream. An undertow pulled his body beneath the surface and slammed him into a rocky outcropping. He gulped for air. Icy water poured up his nose -- into his throat. He gasped again -- again there was no air. Flashes of light darted before his eyes. His tortured torso scraped the gravel strewn channel floor. Desperately, he planted his feet and lunged. His head emerged in watery foam at the base of a promontory on the far bank. He clawed at a rock. Fingernails broke as the water picked him up and tore him away. He felt a wall of gravely earth. Again he clawed, digging his torn fingers into gravel and soil. The water released its grip. He was safely ashore. He could not believe his luck. He was alive!

Weak and numb from the cold swim, Joe attempted to pull the ferry rope across. Swift current caught it, nearly pulling him back into the river. Finally, he wrapped it around a pine and tied it fast. "Hurrah! We're half way ta The Dalles," someone across river yelled.

The crossing did go quickly forward. Wagons were disassembled, the wagon beds caulked and made water tight. Like flat bottomed boats, guided by pulleys and a pull rope, they were floated to the far bank. First wheels and wagon parts were sent across in the makeshift rafts, followed by wagon contents. The wagons were reassembled, reloaded and pulled away to make room for the next in line.

Sandy's cart, made of the back half of a wagon bed, presented special problems. To keep the cart from shipping water, Sandy and Joe boxed in the front end. There were no extra boards or planks so they substituted the canvas top. They stretched it over the open end and tacked it in place. Abernathy ferried the wheels and parts over in his wagon bed. All Sandy had to do was get the cart and its contents safely across.

The cart barely left shore before the current swirled it around. The weather worn canvas ripped. Water poured into the cart bed. The food box, Tildy's bridal chest and one of Granny's prize patchwork quilts were sluiced out to go bobbing downstream. For the first time Sandy's composure broke. "Oh! God!" he cried out, "What will happen next?"

It was a difficult crossing for many. Six in Parker's family lay ill, several so weak they barely could move. The Butts family ferried the body of wife and mother across to dig a grave and lay her to rest. The west bank of the river also was the final resting place for three other souls who departed this earth on the banks of the Deschutes.

When the outlook was at its darkest, a relief column appeared. Black Moses Harris, the legendary mountain man known for his tall tales, led a small party that brought flour, beef on the hoof and other foodstuffs. Sandy and Joe discovered his presence while camped in a cottonwood grove. The dark-faced mountain man rode up with a small train of mules. Joe couldn't believe his eyes. The last time he had seen Black Moses was at the Green River rendezvous in 1840, before Buck Stone and Clay Beamer were killed.

"'Peers, like most of these folks, yuh lads're at the end of yer tether," Black Moses said, examining the strange cart and its pitiful load. He hunkered by the fire to spit a stream of tobacco juice into the flames. "If yuh hev a pot, I've a bit of coffee, an' eatin' vittles if yuh hev a mind ta fix 'em."

The evening passed pleasantly. Black Moses, never one to say one word when he could use two, told stories interspersed with news. "They say three thousand folks crossed the plains this season," he began. "People here're gittin' thick as needles on a porcupine's butt, ones as different as hawks an' pigeons. They was a company of fifty or so wagons from New England so churchified they wouldn't turn a hand on the Sabbath. Made tolerable good time at thet. Joe, yuh come from thet part of the world, any of yer people in thet bunch?"

"No, Sandy is the nearest to any relative I have making the crossing. He's pledged to my twin sister."

"I'll be dogged! Thet proves what I'm sayin'. Fer the life of yuh, yuh cain't tell what kind of folks these newcomers be. I'd wagered this young fella was as shy as an old maid skinnin' a pole cat, an' here he's fixin' ta tie the knot. What about yuh, Joe? Deacon Walton said a Cheyenne lass had set her cap fer yuh."

"Deacon talks too much," Joe said, furious at his former trapping partner. What was Sandy to think, he was a squaw man like so many mountain men? "That was years ago when I started with Buck Stone. Never saw her again. She probably has two or three kids by now."

"Probably has," Black Moses agreed. "Cain't believe it's better'n' four years since ol' Buck bit the dust. 'Member him when he first hit the west. Great un fer book larnin'. Somebody told me went ta Harvard College. Maybeso, he did. He always was larnin' somethin'. Giv'im a' hour with any kinda Injun an' he'd be talkin' ther tongue better'n they did. He'd go powwowin' in ther lodges, sometimes all night. When he came back he'd set what he larned in a book.

"Anyways, I got me best whoppers listenin' ta Buck. Fer instance, thar were a Cheyenne tale he telled 'bout an Injun lass hevin a love affair with a snake. 'Magine lovin' a snake! Another Injun story was 'bout a' Injun who hung his eyes on a tree. A white man sees the Injun do it an' tries ta do the same. He got his eyes out but couldn't put 'em back. The galoot was fit ta be tied. A buffalo comes by. The man asks ta borra his eyes but they don't fit -- half stuck out an' half stuck in. Ever' time I see a pop-eyed gink I want ta ask if he left his regular eyes hangin' on a tree.

"Yep, Buck had tales of huntin', warrin', 'bout coyotes, owls, skunks, fish, deer ... An ol' Sioux tol' him 'bout a' Injun woman who, while carryin' her unborn papoose, was skeered by a beaver. Dad blast it if she didn't birth a kid who swam like a fish, gnawed down trees an' built dams of mud an' sticks. He growed hands like claws, had buck teeth an' was covered with hair." Moses shook his head. "Yep, Buck had more yarns than a dog has fleas."

For the first time in days, Sandy and Joe went to sleep well fed and in good humor. But the following morning they again faced the grim task of hitching up and traveling on toward The Dalles. Black Moses was even somber and untalkative. Only after a second cup of coffee did he speak.

"I'd best push off an' locate more stragglers," he said. "I ain't got much ta offer an' even 'em supplies're slim. The folk at Wascopum Methodist mission don't go fer charity givin'. Reverend Waller's hard-shelled an' feisty as a snappin' turtle. So tight-fisted he wouldn't give a crust of bread ta a starvin' man on the Sabbath. Course, cain't much blame him. More people're comin' through The Dalles than yuh kin shake a stick at. Folks're bypassin' Waiilatpu -- rollin' all the way from Fort Boise without replenishin' provisions expectin' ta git 'em at The Dalles. Yuh kin 'magine, supplies're gittin' thin."

"Wonder what happened," Joe said. "Last fall the Whitmans

planned to expand their production so they would have ample provisions available for this fall's arrivals. I hope the Whitmans and the mission are all right."

"Far's I know everythin' up country's fine. Thar were a bit of a' Injun fuss but they say it were squashed. Course anythin' kin happen when Injuns're involved. Whosomever thought ol' Little Ned's widda womin would go at yuh with a knife."

"Who told you that?"

"Why yer friend, Hawk. Him, Meek an' me had a few snorts. Yuh know, Hawk don't need much persuasion when it comes ta pullin' the cork. Course, Hawk an' Meek didn't need a' excuse ta hoist a few. A fella with blood in his eye were hot on thar heels, mad nuff ta kick his own mule. Said he'd lost two sons crossin' the desert. Swore he wouldn't rest 'til Meek an' Hawk was six feet under. Quoted the Good Book: 'Eye fer eye, tooth fer tooth,' somethin' like thet."

"What happened? Was there trouble? " Sandy asked.

"No. I headed the guy off 'til Meek an' Hawk could git thar nags an' vamoose. Meek took off down river. Hawk went the other way, said somethin' 'bout prospectin'."

"Prospecting!" Joe uttered half to himself. Hawk Beak planned to make his fortune at Dead Ox Creek! Why hadn't he thought of that? With a pocket full of gold nuggets he could make it up to Sandy. If he managed to get enough of them he could afford to take Michael east, bring Tildy and Granddad west -- ask for Bithiah's hand . . . . The chilly morning air and the blaring hee-haw of Lonesome Mule brought him back to earth. Without a grubstake he would never make it beyond The Dalles.

XXVI

*. . . an Indian named Tamahas came to the mill and wanted
corn ground. Not getting it done as soon as he thought he
ought, and being a fractious fellow, he became enraged.*
Catherine Sager, THE WHITMAN MASSACRE OF 1847

Michael returned to Waiilatpu to find it an anthill of activity.
During his absence Whitman had recruited three mechanics from the
fall wagon train. One was a blacksmith, another a woodworker who
turned out chairs, stools, bedposts and the like and the third was a
millwright. The latter repaired the gristmill and soon had it operating
smooth as silk. The Whitmans warmly welcomed Michael. Hardly
before he knew what was happening they had him back at work tending
to the gristmill, grinding grain for the mission family, emigrants and
Waiilatpu Cayuse villagers. On busy days the mill worked from early
morning until late at night. Those who wished to have grain ground
came and waited their turn. Everything appeared tranquil, but Michael
was not fooled. Underlying the peaceful surface there was a swelling
undercurrent of hatred and mistrust.

On a particularly busy day at the gristmill it came forcefully to
Michael's attention. Tomahas, a Cayuse villager who was a known
troublemaker, got tired of waiting in line. To vent his impatience, he
threw sticks into the gristmill hopper. The mission family was in the
midst of eating the evening meal when terrible clacking sounds began
to reverberate through the house. "What in the world is that?" Narcissa
Whitman asked.

Catherine Sager pulled the curtain back and looked out the
window. "Something's wrong at the gristmill," she reported. "Oh, my
God!" the millwright uttered. He leaped up and ran for the gristmill
followed by Marcus Whitman and little David Malin running as fast as
his short legs could travel. As the millwright passed the line of villagers waiting in line, Tomahas, a person of short temper, stepped out
and knocked the millwright off his feet. Tomahas then made for the

missionary, ranting about the length of time he had to wait. Before he could touch Whitman, another villager seized Tomahas, attempting to calm him. Tomahas jerked free and ran up to Whitman, shouting.

"You grind mission corn. You make Cayuse wait. You take Cayuse land. You do not pay. You make Cayuse sick. You give medicine. It make Cayuse die. You do bad things. You leave this land . . ." His harangue was cut off. This time by Tiloukaikt, head man of the Waiilatpu band of Cayuse. Only after making Tomahas promise he would leave, did Tiloukaikt set him free. Still ranting threats, Tomahas jumped on his horse and galloped away.

Michael, who witnessed the confrontation, was stunned by the viciousness of the troublemaker's attack. "The millwright and Missionary Whitman were fortunate this time but next time watch out," Michael thought. Tomahas was a dangerous man. He had a long memory and would not forget the humbling incident.

In spite of short tempers and high feeling among the Cayuse, the late fall of 1845 proved a pleasant time for Michael. The mission school was in session and he was asked to attend. Another pleasant surprise was to see Francis Sager in the classroom. Marcus Whitman, now legal guardian of the Sager orphans by order of J. W. Nesmith, Probate Judge of Oregon Territory, agreed to help both John and Francis get off on their own. He promised to provide the boys with educations and start herds of livestock that would be ready for them when they reached adulthood. Whitman discussed the plan with John and sent a messenger to the Willamette Valley to inform Francis of what he had done, pleading with the runaway to return to Waiilatpu.

Francis, who had not enjoyed his stay in the Willamette Valley and badly missed his brothers and sisters, welcomed the invitation. Besides, his nemesis, schoolteacher Alanson Hinman, had moved on. In his place the Whitmans employed a youthful man named Andrew Rodgers, no relation to Cornelius Rodgers who drowned at the falls of the Willamette. Andrew had stopped at Waiilatpu in hopes Marcus Whitman could heal a friend ill with tuberculosis. The Whitmans took the sick man in and asked Rodgers if he would remain and take charge of the mission school. A man with hair the color of ripened corn,

Rodgers was almost the opposite of dark, glowering Alan Hinman. His soft way of speaking and gentle demeanor quickly won the hearts of the students.

The presence of Andrew Rodgers was also noticed by the Cayuse. Tiloukaikt's watchers reported a new member of the mission had arrived. Because of his corn colored hair they named him, "Man with Yellow Hair." Rodgers laughed when told his Indian name. Michael did not think it humorous. There was nothing wrong with the name. It was the manner in which members of Tiloukaikt's village said it that bothered him. Andrew Rodgers was a marked man. He would have two years to live.

Michael gleaned a great deal of information by listening to the people who came to have their grain ground. The death of Yellow Serpent's son and the fact no attempt was made to bring the killer to justice, continued to weigh heavily on the minds of the natives. It was well known among the Cayuse and Walla Walla that Indian Agent White had left for the east. This, they regarded as a cowardly act. Why should they continue to obey the code of laws? When trouble arose, the man who had imposed the laws on the upland tribes had run away like a frightened goose. Again, there was talk that the life of a missionary should be forfeited as the proper way to avenge Yellow Serpent's son's death.

Michael secretly believed the Tomahas affair at the gristmill was the first of many incidents. As happened at Lapwai, they would get worse and worse, eventually leading to bloodshed. A few days later he was certain the chain of events had started when Young Chief, accompanied by Buffalo Horn's son, Red Calf, came thundering into the mission compound.

Young Chief's people lived on the west bank of the middle Umatilla. His land adjoined that of Five Crows and Buffalo Horn. He was a person of considerable wealth and was related to many important plateau families. His brother was Five Crows, now chief of the tribe. His half brother was Tuekakas, head of the Wallowa Nez Perce. His nephew, Halket, had gained fame by attending school in Canada where Anglican Black Robes taught him how to plant, tend crops and speak and write the English language.

"Mission boy! Take my horse," Young Chief sullenly ordered, spying Michael standing beside the corral. He handed the reins of his sorrel to Michael and turned to stride toward the mission house. Red Calf glanced at Michael with disdain. Instead of handing him the reins of his mount, he dropped them, letting them trail on the ground. The way the two riders grimly eyed the mission house and inspected the grounds made goose bumps pop out on Michael's skin.

Michael quickly tethered Young Chief's horse and ran to his tipi. Hurriedly, he picked up his slingshot and bag of rocks. He went along the fence bordering the mission compound, stopping where he had an open view of the mission house front stoop. Missionary Whitman had come out. He and Young Chief faced each other. Red Calf stood to one side, watchful, his arms akimbo. Michael flopped on the ground and wriggled forward until he could hear Young Chief's hoarse voice. As he expected, Young Chief was reiterating a long list of complaints. Every point he made was accompanied by the wave of a clenched fist or wag of a finger. Frequently, he dropped his hand menacingly to the head of the tomahawk that hung from his belt. Michael placed a stone in his slingshot. But the distance was too great to be accurate. He crawled nearer until he could hear the words of Young Chief more clearly.

"These people who come from beyond the River of Many Canoes bring with them death. They bring a sickness that makes the Cayuse die. Your medicine is worthless water. It make white people well. It make Cayuse die. Do you believe we have no brains; we do not see these things? The death of one of our people is like the prick of a knife. It is like losing a drop of blood. It drains away our strength. More deaths, more blood. Our people get weak. Soon they are no more. Can we let this happen. No! These people that come in land canoes must leave, if they no go -- big trouble." He did not give the missionary a chance to reply. He walked to the corral where his horse was tethered and swung into the saddle. Red Calf was already mounted. On the way out the riders passed Michael who leaned against the rail fence. Red Calf noticed the slingshot. He reined up his horse. "Your weapon no magic. Your spotted pony no safe."

Michael watched them go, his heart beating fast. Did Buffalo Horn and his sons know he had left Magpie in Lapwai? Did that prying Feathercap find out and tell them? He groaned. It was getting so no one or no thing was safe anywhere on the plateau.

There was no let up in the sequence of disturbing events. Not long after the encounter with Young Chief and Red Calf, the thump of drums and the chilling chant of mourning drifted across the grassy open space that separated the mission compound from the Cayuse village. All night it went on. The next day a party of warriors left the village heading north. Marcus Whitman and the new man, Rodgers, came out of the mission house. The missionary saw Michael and called him over. "What is this all about?" he asked.

"It is a war party. Where they go, I do not know."

Two days later the war party returned. Michael could tell they had fought a battle but there was no victory celebration. Bodies were draped over two horses and several riders barely could hold themselves in the saddle. Before the afternoon was over Feathercap came to the mission house and asked for Medicine Man Whitman.

"Man bad sick," he said.

As he often did, when Dr. Whitman tended to the ill in the Cayuse village, Michael went along, carrying the doctor's bag. Near the edge of the village Feathercap waited to guide them. As they entered the Cayuse village the bloodcurdling cry of death rang out. A woman tearing at her hair and clothes stumbled from a tipi. She fell on the ground, writhing in agony. Three women and a young girl ran to her, dragging her away, all shrieking at the tops of their voices. Feathercap went ahead to open a tipi flap. On a bloodied sleeping pallet lay the body of a young warrior. One hand was severed and his face slashed. Lying beside him was a war shield and a lance.

"Too late! Come!" Feathercap pulled the doctor into the next lodge where another warrior lay; two women and a child hovered over him. Blood oozed from a wound on his neck and arm, but he was alive. Dr. Whitman dropped to his knees. "Fetch clean strips of buckskin and make hot water," he ordered. The women quickly complied.

While the doctor worked on the wounded, people gathered to watch. Gradually, Michael pieced together the story of what had happened. A party of buffalo hunters crossed into the land of the Snakes. A Cayuse hunter went to scout for game and did not return. Searchers found his mutilated body. A nearby camp of Snakes was blamed. The Cayuse would not rest until they extracted revenge. A war party was formed and attacked the camp of Snakes. The defenders were prepared. Several Cayuse warriors were killed, and others badly wounded. Among them were the dead warrior in the tipi next door and the man whose life Whitman was attempting to save.

Doctor Whitman finally stood up and rolled down his sleeves. "I have done all I can. It is all up to God whether he lives or dies." He picked up his bag and nodded to the two women who had assisted him. On the way back Whitman sighed. "I wonder how long it will take to civilize these people," he said more to himself than to Michael.

When they arrived at the mission house Narcissa Whitman came to meet them, her usually pleasant blue eyes troubled. "A messenger arrived with awful news. The people who crossed the desert with Meek suffered terribly. Many died and others are too ill to leave The Dalles. Oh yes! A rider from the east brought a letter for Joe," she said to Michael. "You must keep it," she instructed. "I can't be trusted. As the good Lord warned, 'Watch and pray, that ye enter not into temptation.' I have been praying but every time I see a letter from home I can't wait to open it and find what news it brings."

Michael took the letter and carefully placed it in a buckskin pouch his grandmother, Quiet Woman, had given him. Unlike Narcissa, he was not tempted to find out what it said. He recognized the sprawling curlicues as the handwriting of the Boston sister, Tildy. Her last letter brought news of the death of his Boston grandmother. Did this letter contain a similar message, the death of his Boston grandfather? Did these Boston people, like the owl, only send messages of death? He shivered. Perhaps that was why the missionary woman did not want the letter in the house.

XXVII

. . . for rank selfishness, heartlessness, avarice, and desire to take advantage of the immigrants . . . the Mission of The Dalles exceeded any institution on the Northwest Coast.

Elisha Packwood, family record, 1845

"The Dalles! Hurrah! We've arrived at The Dalles!" The news drifted from wagon to wagon. The sight of the Columbia River pleased some; others were too sick and exhausted to care.

"Hurrah -- hell!"a teamster muttered. Like so many who crossed the Oregon desert, he had lost almost everything he possessed. There was no joy in his heart. His wife and baby lay in the swaying wagon near death. The Grim Reaper, who had kept so busy during the crossing, continued his ghoulish work. More and more victims fell to his scythe. The wife and two children of Samuel Parker died. His four other children were sick, his oldest so ill Parker doubted she would live to see her Willamette Valley home. Mrs. Terwilliger and Mrs. Wilson died. In all, twenty who survived Meek's shortcut found a final resting place at The Dalles.

As Black Moses had reported, the Wascopum mission station at The Dalles was ill-prepared to provision an influx of newcomers. Reverend Waller, in charge of the Methodist mission, received a torrent of criticism. Elisha Packwood, whose baby lay in a lonely trail side grave, denounced Waller and his mission helpers as treating the arrivals with "rank selfishness, heartlessness and avarice." Foodstuffs were scarce and costly. Whitman charged five dollars per hundred weight for flour at Waiilatpu. The emigrants paid eight and ten dollars for the same amount at The Dalles. Those who traveled the Blue Mountain route and took Indian Agent Elijah White's advice to by-pass Waiilatpu, swore they would tar and feather the Indian agent should they meet again.

To add to the desert crossing survivors' woes, they still faced formidable obstacles. To continue on to their final goal, the Willamette

Valley, they either had to take rafts and canoes or travel along the narrow, boulder-strewn river bank, a trail that even pack trains had difficulty negotiating. Those who chose to float down the river confronted treacherous Cascade Falls where travelers were forced to transport themselves and their belongings over a three mile portage.

On a dismal rocky patch near the river's edge, Sandy and Joe made camp. The mid-October wind whistled through the Columbia River Gorge, chilling them to the bone. The Abernathy wagon was nearby. Bithiah and Luke Olafson sat on camp stools peeling potatoes. The domestic scene, their conversation and an occasional hoot of laughter carried on the gusty breeze, made Joe scowl. Since Olafson joined the train he barely had been able to see Bithiah alone. If Luke Olafson was not present, his children were, clinging to Bithiah's skirts like chicks to a brood hen.

"If we look pitiful maybe they'll invite us to supper," Sandy said hopefully.

"I doubt it. That hanger-on, Olafson, has the place staked out." Joe's scowl darkened. He was furious with Bithiah and with himself. He had stood around like a ninny and let that oaf Olafson steal his girl right out from under his nose.

"Yeah! He and Bithiah are a bit chummy," Sandy callously observed. "Appears you had better put your brand on that gal, and do it soon. You have been acting the bashful schoolboy too long. It doesn't get you anywhere with that ripe and ready Abernathy maiden. Now, when I was courting Tildy . . ."

"Ah, be quiet. What makes you think I should take a wife? Look at me. I don't have a cent to my name and not a prospect in sight."

Later, after they had consumed a tolerable meal made from Black Moses' leftovers, Abernathy strolled over from his wagon accompanied by Saul. "Howdy!" Abernathy greeted. He squatted by the fire and gave it a poke with a stick. "The missus and I've been wondering what your plans be?" he asked Joe.

"Hadn't thought about it much," Joe lied. Lately, the subject occupied most of his sleepless hours.

"Perhaps we can help. Some of us have the idea of taking the loose stock over the mountains. Mission folk say the route's satisfactory for livestock but won't take wagons."

"That's probably a wise move. What does it have to do with me?"

"Saul and Luke Olafson volunteered to manage the herd. Howsoever, we'd feel more comfortable if a third rider went along, someone like yourself who knows the mountains. We'd make it right with you."

"I see." The thought of herding a bunch of wild stock over the mountains with Luke Olafson was the last thing he wanted to do. "Luke's girls, surely he doesn't plan to take them across the mountains?"

"Bithiah and Mrs. Abernathy'll see to the kids. We'll be rafting Luke's goods down river with ours."

"Hmm!" Joe grunted. Luke Olafson and his kids had virtually become members of the Abernathy family.

"It's a great idea," Sandy exclaimed. "I'd like to send what remains of my livestock over the mountains."

"I'll think on it," Joe said. He surely needed to acquire a stake but there had to be a better way to do it. Besides, if Luke took off over the mountains Bithiah would be free, at least out of sight of that obnoxious Norwegian. But what good would that do him? He didn't have a bean in his pockets. He had no right to speak to anyone about getting hitched. Maybe he should trail after Hawk Beak, look for the gold in the desert. With money he could replace everything Sandy had lost and could get married to boot. Then there was Michael in Waiilatpu. He had promised Michael he would return and together they would travel east to see Tildy and Granddad. Promises! Promises! -- so easy to say and so hard to keep. He threw himself on his bedroll and stared at the stars, only near dawn did he sleep.

The next day a rider passed the emigrant camp announcing he was on his way to join the Whitman mission at Waiilatpu, did anyone have messages to send? Joe debated, should he send Michael a message? What he should do was go to Waiilatpu himself. No, he was not prepared to go there yet. However, it would do no harm to write his brother a letter, tell him they might have to put off the planned trip back east. Perhaps they could make it in the spring. Michael would be disappointed but what else could he say? He printed the few words on a sheet of paper with pen and ink borrowed from Mrs. Abernathy, sealing the missive with candle wax. On returning the pen and ink, he nearly stumbled over Bithiah. She was feeding the Olafson toddler her morning gruel. He said hello and attempted a smile which he feared turned into little more than a grimace.

"I'll take the job," Joe told Abernathy. "Let's get the critters moving. We don't want to get caught in the winter snow." He said it loud enough for Bithiah to overhear. If his decision made any impression on her it didn't show. On the way by she gave him a tired grin. Both Olafson children occupied her, the older girl clung to her skirt, solemnly sucking her thumb and Bithiah held the other in her arms.

#

The motley collection of cattle, horses and mules did not take easily to mountain travel. The way was choked with huckleberry vines, poisonous mountain laurel, thickets of aspen and sharp-needled evergreens. Cantankerous cows hurtled into underbrush so thick it swallowed them like bogs of quick sand. Horses did everything they could to avoid going in after them. They snorted, shied, bucked and when finally forced in, did so with such viciousness riders were scraped from their saddles. Unaccustomed to such riding hazards, Saul and Luke Olafson soon lost their hats and their composure. Blood streaked from cuts on their hands, arms and faces. Their voices turned hoarse from swearing and cursing.

Joe, who knew the country, was better prepared. He pulled his hat down over his ears, bowed his head, ready for anything the trail demanded. Savagely, he chased strays around boulders, trees and through the impenetrable brush. He kept asking himself, "Why have I taken this thankless task," getting increasingly furious as time went by. He had wanted to get Bithiah's attention. It was as childish as that. He deserved every bit of punishment he got. He was a creature without sense and without anything else. He had not a penny, no ambition, no luck with women . . . The hardest part to take was that he had no one to blame but himself. The lovely Cheyenne maiden fancied him but he foolishly didn't even ask her name. Before her there was Melody Abernathy. She would have teamed up with him at the drop of a hat. He had been afraid of her and had run away. Now, it was Bithiah. It was obvious she liked him but what did he do but let that Olafson family claim her for their own. He gave the horse a vicious swipe with the reins. He would not give her up -- not to that Olafson bunch -- never!

Although there was the constant fear the livestock would arouse a cranky bear or a hungry mountain cat would attack, methodically the herders pushed the herd up the long mountain slope without loss. When they broke into the clear at timberline, they stopped to rest and admire the view. To the north rose the glistening slopes of Mount Hood. To the south, as far as the eye could see, snow-clad mountains lay in a zigzag row. To the west miles and miles of evergreen forest stretched to end in a haze-filled horizon.

"My stars!" Luke Olafson exclaimed. "It's an ocean of evergreens!"

Grimly, Joe nodded. The hard part of the crossing was behind them. Soon he would be free. When the job was finished he would leave these people. He hoped never to see the sallow face of Luke Olafson again. Yet, for the first time on the mountain trip his anger subsided. That night he went right to sleep without giving himself a long harangue. It was fall in New England. The maple leaves had turned brilliant red and orange. He was milking the cows when they stopped chewing their cud and began to stir. Granddad opened the barn door. "Watch out!" he shouted. "The stock is breaking loose!" Joe jerked awake. He looked wildly about. It was no dream. The cows lowed and horses snorted; mules uttered frightening heehaws. Saul, who was standing guard, came running. "I cain't get them to settle down. Somethin' has them spooked!"

Luke Olafson, his hair standing on end, rolled out of his blankets with a rifle clutched in both hands. "Injuns!"

"Easy does it," Joe cautioned. "If it were Indians we would

already be dead and scalped. It's a bear or mountain lion. Let's circle the stock."

Hardly did he utter the words when he saw it, a tawny colored object creeping out of the shadows. Automatically, Joe threw his rifle up. He was too late. The tawny marauder was not to be denied. The big cat lunged for the nearest animal. Belatedly, Joe caught the animal in his sights and fired. The big cat turned its head to snarl, the wicked teeth dripping blood, then melted into the shadows. Joe could not tell if he had wounded it or not. But the big mountain cat had accomplished its cruel mission. A Jersey heifer lay in a bloody, crumpled heap. Joe groaned. It was Bessie, the cornerstone of Sandy Sanders' potential herd. Now he was in deeper debt to Sandy than ever.

"Damnit!" Joe uttered so savagely, his companions edged away. His anger returned in all its fury. Why hadn't he done the right thing, made peace with Hawk Beak and gone buffalo hunting? Everything he had done since joining the wagon train had been one disaster after another.

XXVIII

*Like a morning dream, life becomes more and more
bright, the longer we live.*

Jean Paul Richter

Without warning, Lonesome Mule began to bray. An answering hee-haw echoed out of the forest. Luke jerked a rifle from its scabbard. "Injuns!" he declared, jumping down from his horse and taking cover.

The hee-haw of the mule did not alarm Joe. In fact it gave him a feeling of elation. Finally they were nearing civilization. He could soon ride away and do something worthwhile. "Might as well mount up," he said to Luke. "Probably some settler is rounding up a lost cow. No respectable Indian would ride a mule."

Luke sheepishly remounted. The three horsemen rode to an open spot on a ridge from where they had a view of the trail to the west. In a short while a quartet of bearded horsemen, the last one leading a mule, broke out of the trees.

"I'll be dogged," Luke exclaimed. "It's me brothers."

Luke's brothers had refused to travel across the desert with Meek. Instead, they had taken the Blue Mountain route. The train enjoyed such good weather they arrived in the Willamette Valley a month earlier than expected. However, the last hundred miles between The Dalles and the mouth of the Willamette River took a heavy toll.

"Yep," Manny, the eldest Olafson brother said while the men sat around the evening campfire. "We made what I'd say was a good journey but it wasn't without its adversities . . . two drownings that I heard of an' a whole raft an' other stuff lost. Most of these people never rafted afore. Didn't know sic'em about polin', packin', loadin', off-loadin' or even gettin' theirselves ashore. It got some of us thinkin' there's a better way to get these pilgrims from The Dalles to the valley. Sam Barlow, especially, believes we can make a road across these mountains. We're scouting to see if he's right."

"Yeah, thet's what we're thinkin'." For the first time, the fourth member of the party spoke, a hard-eyed man with a scarred cheek, not related to the Olafsons. He gave Joe the impression of a hawk in a flock of pigeons. Hard-Eyes filled his scarred cheek with tobacco and spit. "Ain't yuh a friend of thet lanky fella thet teamed up with Steph Meek guidin' the wagons 'cross the desert?" he asked Joe.

"I know him." Joe avoided looking at the man, a real tough. What was he doing with the Olafsons? And why should his relationship with Hawk Beak interest him?

"Yer friend an' thet Meek fella're pretty clever fellas -- chargin' five cart wheels a wagon ta cross thet stinkin' desert. Thet was like leadin' Christians inta the Colosseum. Ain't sayin' I blame 'em. They was makin' a good thing outta nuthin'. In fact, I admire 'em. Clear a pathway through these mountains, an' we kin do the same. Five smackers an' save yer hide from goin' inta the river. I'd say a cheap price ta pay."

Joe stared into the fire. The comment did not require an answer and he did not give one. There was something cold-blooded --chilling about this guy. Even with all the Olafsons and Saul Abernathy present, he felt uneasy. Hard-Eyes was paying him entirely too much attention. Perhpas his imagination was running away with him. He had to stop being so nervy. He got up, made certain his animals were all right, and bade the group around the fire good night.

"You'll not be needing me," Joe told Saul the next morning. "From here on you can follow the trail blazed by your friends."

The Olafson brothers were agreeable. They could handle the stock fine. They said their good-byes and turned their attention to breaking camp. Hard-Eyes gave him a curt nod. "Perhaps we'll see each other on the trail," he said. Only Saul appeared distressed at his leave-taking. For a short distance he accompanied Joe.

"It troubles me to see you go. I thought sure you'd be takin' a homestead in the valley," Saul said as they parted. "What am I to tell Bithiah? She'll be put out, probably skin me alive when she hears I let you go. Besides, you haven't received your pay."

"Tell your dad and Bithiah I'll be back and we'll settle up. Right now I have things I must do." Joe reined his mount up the trail, pulling reluctant Lonesome Mule behind. He did not blame the mule for balking. The way ahead did not look inviting. Clouds, dark with rain, that in the higher elevations would turn to snow, hung threateningly overhead. By mid-afternoon snow did fall. Tree tops became hidden by low scudding clouds. The wind picked up to funnel wet snowflakes into Joe's face.

All day Joe pressed forward, sometimes riding, sometimes leading the weary horse and Lonesome Mule, finally stopping at dusk in sight of the Deschutes. The next morning he topped the summit where Sandy had thwarted the lynching. At nightfall he made camp near Crooked River Crossing. On the third day, just as he sighted the familiar butte that marked Dead Ox Creek, it started to rain. To keep out of the storm he made early camp in a protected draw. He did not sleep. The penetrating cold and excitement kept him awake. If all went well on the morrow he would be picking up pebbles of gold.

Before morning the rain turned to snow. Big wet flakes tumbled down to build a blanket of white. By daylight it lay six inches deep. Wet and chilled, Joe aroused himself. He chewed a piece of dried beef and saddled his horse. For an hour or more he rode in a snow-filled cloud, guided only by ruts left in the soft soil by the hundreds of iron-rimmed wheels that had passed on the torturous trek to The Dalles. When it seemed they, too, would disappear, the snow abruptly stopped. The clouds parted to reveal the sun. A soft, almost spring-like wind blew in from the west. The snow cover began to melt. The wagon tracks, filled with loose soil, turned into channels of slippery mud. In the distance a spiral of smoke drifted skyward. Soon came the raucous hee-haw of mules. Hawk Beak's big bay and two pack animals stood in a draw, packed, ready for the trail. Except for the noisy greeting of the mules, the ravine was eerily quiet. Joe dismounted and took the rifle from the scabbard. He tethered the horse and Lonesome Mule to a bush and walked carefully toward the draw. Ahead was the incline on which he had wrecked Sandy's wagon. In the creek bed below a dying campfire smoldered, sending up lazy tendrils of smoke. Some of the items Sandy left behind were nearby.

"Hawk! Where are you, Hawk? It's me, Joe Jennings." Mockingly, the words echoed back from the far side of the ravine.

"I know who 'tis." Hawk, who was on the far bank of the creek, stepped into the open, a rifle loosely held in his claw-like hands. "I been watchin' yuh slip up like a slinkin' coyote."

"What's the matter, Hawk! I thought we were friends."

"No more we ain't. Yuh an' thet gang of yers wanted to hang me and Meek ta the nearest tree."

"But - but . . ." Joe could not believe his eyes. His former friend's rifle barrel pointed directly at his head, a claw-like finger taut against the trigger. Joe started to protest. The look on the man's face made him think better of it. He dropped to the ground just as Hawk Beak fired. The bullet shattered a sagebrush branch inches away. A flying splinter cut Joe's cheek. Joe rolled behind a cluster of sagebrush and cocked his Hawken. Hawk Beak leaped behind a boulder to reload. Joe shivered. The damp ground and Hawk's deadly greeting had turned his body cold as ice. He tried to get a grip on his thoughts -- make sense out of what was happening. Had his former trapping partner gone crazy? Over the years they frequently got on each other's nerves, but a shootout? Never! What was he to do? Reason with him? "Hawk! Let's lay aside our guns and talk things over."

There was no answer. Carefully, Joe raised his head to look into the ravine below. Suddenly the ground beneath him began to shake and tremble. He threw himself flat, clutching his Hawken. A low rumble like that of distant thunder grew in intensity. It became a roar, ending in an ear-splitting crash. A rush of air hurtled up the slope. For a moment the sun disappeared. Mud, sticks -- debris of every kind showered down like a thick blanket of hail. A deafening silence followed, a hush like the calm after a storm. Only the startled hee-haw of Hawk Beak's mules and the caw-caw of a distant crow could be heard. The sun came out brighter than ever before.

Joe cautiously raised his head, then got to his feet and stared. Dazed, he strode toward the creek. It was no longer there. The escarpment on the far side of the creek had disappeared. Gradually it dawned on Joe what had happened. The rifle shot had triggered a landslide. The snow laden, water sodden cliff had collapsed. Hawk Beak lay buried beneath tons of earth and rock! Stunned by the thought, Joe dropped his rifle and ran forward. His first thought was to rescue his friend. He got to the edge of the great heap of jumbled dirt and rocks and stopped. The harsh enormity of the tragedy struck him. Nothing in the creek bed below survived. Right before his eyes a stream had vanished and a man had been buried alive.

The raucous hee-haw of a mule brought Joe out of his daze. Hawk Beak's hobbled horse, Blaze, and three mules had their heads turned his way, their ears erect as if to say they, too, could not believe their eyes. Joe half slid and half tumbled down the slope onto litter that covered the creek bed. He unhobbled the animals and led them away from the creek that was no longer there. He tethered them a safe distance from the slide area and returned to stand over the former creek bed. He shivered. What if he had been in the creek along with Hawk? He, too, would have been smothered by this great pile of rubble. What a terrible death. The thought made goose bumps rise all over his body. Poor Hawk! He came seeking his fortune, instead he found his final resting place at the bottom of Dead Ox Creek.

A sudden urge to flee the area came over Joe. Hurriedly, he put a lead rope around Blaze's neck and extended it to each of the mules, letting Lonesome Mule bring up the rear, but what was he to do now? The dream he had of filling his pockets with gold nuggets had ended in tragedy. How he wished for the old days when he first appeared on the frontier. What a great thrill it had been to join Buck Stone's trapping brigade. Then one by one the trappers faded away, everyone meeting violent death. First it was his father, felled by a Blackfeet arrow; then Buck Stone lost his life while trying to save Clay Beamer from losing his scalp. Next the Canuck, Francois, died by his own skinning knife. Now, Hawk Beak entered the next world in the most bizarre manner yet. Of the old brigade only Deacon Walton and he were left. It was incredible. The life of a mountain man was short indeed. How long would it be before the man with the scythe came to collect Deacon Walton and Joe Jennings, the last members of

Buck Stone's trapping brigade? A great desire to see Deacon gripped Joe. He needed someone he could talk to about the tragedy he had witnessed. He reined his mount east.

The remainder of the day Joe threaded his way along an old hunting trail. Only at dusk did he stop. He hobbled the animals and built a small campfire. He sorted through his meager food sack. He would not get far on what was left. Perhaps a search of Hawk Beak's packs would turn up something edible. He took a pack from the nearest mule. It was so heavy it slipped out of his hands and fell to the ground. The covering split; out fell a canvas pouch. Joe untied the thongs that sealed the pouch. It held no foodstuffs. Joe started to tie up the thongs, then stopped. The pouch was full of strange pebbles, the kind Herren discovered on the edge of the creek! He dug into the next pack -- more canvas pouches! Excitedly, Joe opened the packs of the next mule. They also were filled with pouches of gold! Joe sat back, stunned. The riches of Midas lay before him.

#

It was near dusk when the tall rider rode into the mission compound to pull his weary mount to a halt at the corral. He dismounted, took off his hat and swatted his trouser legs. Dust spurted from the cloth like puffs of smoke. "Hi-ya, young fella," he said to Michael Two Feathers, who pitched hay to the corralled animals -- two mules and a gaggle of nondescript horses. "I'd be obliged if'n yuh'd find room fer this critter. He's 'bout done in. It's a long hike from here to The Dalles." He tossed the bridle reins to Michael as though he were a stable hand. "Whereabouts're the Whitmans? I bring messages from the valley."

Michael motioned toward the whitewashed mission house. The newcomer's arrogance made his blood boil but he took care of the sweaty animal as carefully as if it were his own. He removed the bridle gently. The bit had cut the horse's mouth until it bled. He smoothed a dab of salve on the wound, talking quietly to the nervous animal as he did. He had a sudden urge to go after the man, shove him into the dirt and ram the bloodied bit into his mouth, let him see how it felt.

That evening Michael sat at the dinner table with the man from The Dalles who reported on down-river news, especially dwelling on the disastrous wagon train journey across the Oregon desert.

"Yep! I kin tell yuh fer certain those people suffered the tortures of the damned. I hope their sufferin' wasn't in vain. Homesteadin' out here ain't what it was claimed. On the way up river I was followed by Injuns all the way. They trailed me like coyotes thet'd caught the scent of quail. I kin tell yuh there's trouble ahead. If I were yuh, I'd be thinkin' 'bout cuttin' out. Who knows when these plateau Injuns'll bust loose. When they do the chances of this mission weatherin' the storm're 'bout even with a Christmas goose."

"There'll not be any cutting out for us. We've put too much of our lives in this place to give up now," Marcus Whitman said. He gave his wife a kindly glance. She smiled and nodded in response.

Michael stood up. He neither liked the rider from The Dalles nor the blunt manner in which he spoke to the Whitmans. Perhaps it was the way he said "Injuns," as if they were wild, bloodthirsty creatures on the same level as wolves. Yet, the feeling of revulsion Michael felt was tinged with fear. He remembered well Vision Seeker's visit, the expression on his face as he stared across the mission grounds and the words he had said, "today's odor of cooking may be tomorrow's smell of death." Perhaps the rider was right, maybe the mission was soon to fall. Michael gave each Whitman a slight bow and politely excused himself, something he had learned from observing better mannered mission house guests. The rider from The Dalles held up his hand for him to stop.

"I haven't delivered the mail," he said, thrusting a hand in a bulging pocket of his weathered canvas coat. From a corn husk pouch he took out a handful of letters, two to Narcissa, four for her husband and one addressed to Michael Two Feathers. Michael was stunned. It was the first such message he ever had received. He gingerly took the letter, handling it as if it were a hot coal. Receiving messages on talking paper was not the way of his people. They wanted to receive words face to face, watch the messenger, make certain he spoke with a straight tongue. But here he was, faced with a talking paper. Was it a message of death like the letter his brother Joe had received? He stumbled out the door and started for his tipi lodge.

Although eager to open her own letters, Narcissa Whitman let them lay. Somehow, the letter Michael received troubled her more than the rider's dire prediction for the mission. She pulled aside the kitchen window curtain to watch the Indian youth make his way across the yard and down the path. The shadowy figure faded into the gloom until just the patch of white clutched in his hand could be seen.

"Ah!" Narcissa muttered to herself. There was only one person who would have written Michael, his brother, Joe Jennings. What message did he send and why did he send it? He was supposed to return to Waiilatpu and take his Nez Perce brother east. She inwardly groaned. Joe had sent word he was not returning this fall. For the second straight year, he was breaking his promise to take Michael to visit their father's relatives. That was the pity of mountain men marrying natives. They never thought of the difficulties their children would have in facing life with two cultures tugging at their heart strings. What did life hold for this boy? For that matter what did life hold for her own adopted half-bloods -- her whole family?

The darkness outside suddenly seemed terribly threatening. A cold clammy chill gripped Narcissa, making her shiver. The words of Young Chief had come to mind -- "The people from beyond the River of Many Canoes bring with them death . . . a sickness that makes our people die. We cannot let this happen . . . ."

Was the Cayuse man warning them the mission people were responsible and would pay the price -- an eye for an eye as the Old Testament taught. . . or would they turn the other cheek . . . .? Ha! These proud independent people turning the other cheek . . .!

Hastily Narcissa drew the curtains together, shutting out the night. "It doesn't do any good to worry about tomorrow," she uttered to herself. "We all are in the hands of God."

Ye know not what shall be on the morrow.

James 4:14

After Word

The background and historical events of CAYUSE COUN-TRY were reviewed in pre-publication by several eminent authorities. Lydia French Johnson to whom the book is dedicated, is a descendant of William "Red" Craig, mountain man, Indian agent and first white homesteader in what became the state of Idaho. Craig married Isabelle, the Nez Perce daughter of Hin-mah-tute-ke-kaikt (Thunder Eyes) who Missionary Spalding baptized "James." (Both Craig and Thunder Eyes play important roles in the Lone Wolf Clan Book series.) During the years offspring of this union intermarried with the Cayuse. Lydia's grandmother, Cistine Williams Cowapoo, was the last member of the Cayuse tribe who spoke the "whole language."

Lydia French Johnson has spent a lifetime living and working with her people. She and her husband, Isadore, were active in reviving native arts and crafts and were instrumental in forming the Speelyi-mi Indian Arts and Crafts Club. According to legend Speelyi (Coyote) taught "the people" how to make nets, baskets and other crafts. We are indeed honored to have her contributions in preparing CAY-USE COUNTRY for publication.

#

Keith Clark, coauthor TERRIBLE TRAIL: THE MEEK CUTOFF, 1845 - Caxton Printers Caldwell, Idaho 1966, and his wife, Donna, graciously reviewed the events surrounding the Oregon desert crossing, one of the more disastrous events in Oregon History. Keith has had a distinguished career as educator and historian. Among his many awards are the Eloise Buck Memorial Prize for literary achievement from Oregon College of Education and, along with co-author Lowell Tiller, the Heritage Award for research and contributions to Oregon history. In 1964 Keith was awarded a Coe Foundation Fellowship in American Studies at the College of Idaho.

Donna Clark made a valuable contribution to the historical facts of CAYUSE COUNTRY with recently discovered excerpts from John Herren's Diary. Herren picked up the gold nuggets on the bank of the stream given the fictitious name, Two Ox Creek.

A SPECIAL NOTE FROM THE AUTHORS

We encourage readers to visit many of the historic places herein described. At Lapwai, Idaho one finds a lovely shaded area where Missionary Henry Spalding is buried and his mission stood. One hundred twenty miles to the west, at Waiilatpu, WA, is the site of Whitman's mission. Guarding it from a hilltop is the white swordlike obelisk mentioned in the Foreword. The vantage point overlooks the old mission grounds, the wagon trail from the slopes of the Blue Mountains and the mass grave of the Whitman massacre victims.

The site of old Fort Walla Walla is under water but driving west on Highway 730, on the left escarpment you will see two stone pillars, the fisherwomen Coyote turned into stone. North, across the Columbia River, are Horse Heaven Hills. It is said Cayuse people retired their horses here, setting them free to live out their declining years. You may see wild horses coming down the hillside to drink.

At Biggs Junction, turn left on highway 97. Beyond the city of Madras, Oregon you will pass over Crooked River Canyon. At the south end of the bridge (a new one presently under construction), turn right at Ogden Scenic Wayside which borders the canyon. Imagine you are dying of thirst while looking down at the surging waters below, so tantalizing close but so far out of reach. We urge you to continue south. Turn left at the sign that points to Smith Rock State Park. Here the sheer cliffs of Crooked River drop away. This opening allowed the emigrants' livestock to water and made it possible for the wagon train to ford the river and continue on its way.

To get an even greater appreciation for the terrain the 1845 wagon train encountered, drive south on secondary roads to the foot of Wagontire Mountain where the emigrants were marooned at Lost "Stinking" Hollow. From here look north and attempt to locate the creek bed where Herren picked up the gold nuggets. Over the years the site of these fabulous riches became known as the Lost Blue Bucket Mine. Many have searched for these riches but to this day they have not been discovered, perhaps they have been protected by Hawk Beak's ghost.

ABOUT THE AUTHORS

Bonnie Jo Hunt (*Wicahpi Win* - Star Woman) is Lakota (Standing Rock Sioux) and the great-great granddaughter of both Chief Francis Mad Bear, prominent Teton Lakota leader, and Major James McLaughlin, Indian agent and Chief Inspector for the Bureau of Indian Affairs. Early in life Bonnie Jo set her heart on helping others. In 1980 she founded Artists of Indian America, Inc. (AIA), a nonprofit organization established to stimulate cultural and social improvement among American Indian youth. To record and preserve her native heritage, in 1997 Bonnie Jo launched Mad Bear Press that publishes American history dealing with life on the western frontier. These publications include the Lone Wolf Clan series: THE LONE WOLF CLAN, RAVEN WING, THE LAST RENDEZVOUS, CAYUSE COUNTRY and forthcoming LAND WITHOUT A COUNTRY.

#

Dr. Lawrence J. Hunt, a former university professor, works actively with Artists of Indian America, Inc. In addition to coauthoring THE LONE WOLF CLAN, RAVEN WING, THE LAST RENDEZVOUS, CAYUSE COUNTRY and forthcoming LAND WITHOUT A COUNTRY, he has coauthored an international textbook (Harrap: London) and published four mystery novels (Funk and Wagnalls), one of which, SECRET OF THE HAUNTED CRAGS, received the Edgar Allan Poe Award from Mystery Writers of America.